The
SECOND CHANCE CINEMA

THEA WEISS

ATRIA BOOKS
NEW YORK   AMSTERDAM/ANTWERP   LONDON
TORONTO   SYDNEY/MELBOURNE   NEW DELHI

An Imprint of Simon & Schuster, LLC
1230 Avenue of the Americas
New York, NY 10020

For more than 100 years, Simon & Schuster has championed authors and the stories they create. By respecting the copyright of an author's intellectual property, you enable Simon & Schuster and the author to continue publishing exceptional books for years to come. We thank you for supporting the author's copyright by purchasing an authorized edition of this book.

No amount of this book may be reproduced or stored in any format, nor may it be uploaded to any website, database, language-learning model, or other repository, retrieval, or artificial intelligence system without express permission. All rights reserved. Inquiries may be directed to Simon & Schuster, 1230 Avenue of the Americas, New York, NY 10020 or permissions@simonandschuster.com.

This book is a work of fiction. Any references to historical events, real people, or real places are used fictitiously. Other names, characters, places, and events are products of the author's imagination, and any resemblance to actual events or places or persons, living or dead, is entirely coincidental.

Copyright © 2025 by Written by Thea, LLC

All rights reserved, including the right to reproduce this book or portions thereof in any form whatsoever. For information, address Atria Books Subsidiary Rights Department, 1230 Avenue of the Americas, New York, NY 10020.

First Atria Books hardcover edition October 2025

ATRIA BOOKS and colophon are trademarks of Simon & Schuster, LLC

Simon & Schuster strongly believes in freedom of expression and stands against censorship in all its forms. For more information, visit BooksBelong.com.

For information about special discounts for bulk purchases, please contact Simon & Schuster Special Sales at 1-866-506-1949 or business@simonandschuster.com.

The Simon & Schuster Speakers Bureau can bring authors to your live event. For more information or to book an event, contact the Simon & Schuster Speakers Bureau at 1-866-248-3049 or visit our website at www.simonspeakers.com.

Manufactured in the United States of America

1 3 5 7 9 10 8 6 4 2

Library of Congress Control Number: 2025001599

ISBN 978-1-6680-8040-5
ISBN 978-1-6682-1371-1 (int exp)
ISBN 978-1-6680-8042-9 (ebook)

*For Chris, who inspired me to write a book,
and Maeve, who inspired me to send it out*

OPENING CREDITS

It was on Lucas's birthday, when he was least expecting it, that his first love made an appearance inside the home he now shared with his girlfriend, Stephanie.

"Well, open it!" Stephanie said, handing him a gift. Under the wrapping paper was a hardcover coral book with the title spelled out in bright yellow script: *The Compendium of Forgotten Things*. Lucas thumbed it open. The pages held a collection of places that had almost faded away. One story featured a pinball bar in a lost desert town; the next, a miniature museum devoted to antique postcards. The style of the writing was familiar. "What is this?" Lucas asked.

"It's by a new author," Stephanie said. "Ellie Marshall?"

Needles pricked Lucas's palms as his hands flew to the back flap. Ellie grinned at him above her author bio, wearing gold earrings shaped like tiny castles. God, she was beaming. The havoc she'd caused in his life had served her well.

"Like it?"

"Yeah." He tried to sound casual. "Yes. Yeah. Yes." He needed to ground himself. No good would come from revisiting the way Ellie had broken up with him—or the way she hadn't, rather. One moment, he'd rented a roller rink to throw her an 1980s-themed birthday party. The next morning, she slipped away. All of her was gone so easily—the citrus and herb smell of her sheets, her unbelievable writing that she read to him with her stomach pressed against her chair, and the scattering of matchboxes she never used because she liked candles conceptually but didn't trust herself around them. As he skimmed the pages, one of the lines stopped him in his tracks.

"A first love is about finding yourself," it read. "A second love is about sharing the self you found with someone new." His frustrated sigh came out too loud.

"Are you okay?" Stephanie asked. A rainbow stretched across her cheek from the early-afternoon light.

"I'm great," Lucas lied. The book was heavy in his lap, a frozen steel anchor. He wrapped his arm around Stephanie. She was the one who had helped him find himself, not Ellie. *Ellie.* Lucas had tried to forget Ellie. He'd done his best, at least.

Until today.

How was it that Ellie still got to him so many years later? And then, there was that irritating part about the first and second loves. Ellie was writing about Lucas without knowing it. She'd played such a big part in his story. Would he even take up a page of hers?

1

The first thing Ellie noticed about the bar was the friendly, cursive logo that invited a singsong voice: *Finn's!* The second thing Ellie noticed was the unfortunate piece of paper tacked beneath that logo: a FOR SALE sign. She forced her shoulders not to sink. The image of the heartbroken owner and all the cast-off patrons had to be set aside. She had made it here in time. She could still do something.

"Special place, isn't it?" the bartender asked once she'd settled in. A brass spoon swirled through her bourbon, and then he slid the glass over. The first sip of the old-fashioned sizzled on her tongue. "It's been in the family a long time."

Special wasn't a good enough word. Finn's was extraordinary. The shoebox-shaped lounge held forty people, tops. It had been lovingly crafted from wood slats that were painted a forest green. Warm light was decanted inside frosted globe pendants, and a vinyl player spun jazz records from another era. Behind her, candles on small marble tables illuminated the only art on the walls: watercolor paintings of sailors who looked like they'd just gotten lucky. It was a place someone would have to hear about, mid-whisper, to find. Already, Ellie could feel her heart beating faster. Her body melted into the worn leather stool, ready to stake its claim.

"You don't have to worry," Ellie told him. "Finn's isn't going anywhere."

"What's the plan?" the bartender wanted to know. His long, lean frame pressed toward her. He adjusted suspenders that weren't part of a uniform.

"The plan is . . . magic," she said, with a sarcastic finger twinkle.

Ellie's work wasn't magic, though. She simply wrote about forgotten places that were set to close down, which usually kept that exact thing from happening. Many had lauded her "the bar whisperer" or "the restaurant heroine," but these flatteries gave her too much credit. The stories wrote themselves if she listened. So, she let her eyes flutter closed and dropped into the patchwork of conversation around her. Muffled rain fell outside the glass, adding a soft layer to Billie Holiday getting gutsy. Right as she took out her notebook to jot down the word *belonging*, a new voice was in her ear.

"Hey," it said.

A man had taken the stool to her right. He was a couple years younger than she was, or maybe just more optimistic. Dark, curly hair framed rosy, round cheeks—was he blushing? He looked midwestern sweet, like the sort of person who would laugh at a joke even if it weren't funny to avoid hurting the other person's feelings. While Ellie had to admit he was good-looking, he wasn't her usual type. She went for wildcards. Recently, there had been Jonathan, the tattoo-artist-slash-bass-player, and Clay, who led daredevil rock-climbing trips in Sedona. This man, whoever he was, had the tame air of a school crossing guard. And yet, she felt herself lean in his direction.

"I'm Drake," he offered, with a wave.

"Ellie."

"Ellie. I didn't mean to interrupt." He pointed at her open notebook. She closed the cover.

"Not interrupting."

"You're writing"—Drake scratched the stubble on his chin—"let me guess, a steamy vampire thing." His dimples were hard at work.

"It's not vampires." Ellie bit her maraschino garnish off its stem. She could almost hear one of her mother's compliment-insults about her being a bold woman. Italics on the *bold*.

"Oh. Uh. Zombies, then?" Drake fidgeted with his hands. He wasn't shy, but a little nervous, maybe. Definitely nervous. Not the type to approach women at bars. Fiercely loyal. An unspoiled only child. Ellie was assuming things based on his body language and a faded denim jacket that most people would've discarded by now. She was also avoiding answering questions about her work. After becoming successful, it was alienating to tell people what she did.

"Life's more interesting with an element of mystery," she said. "Isn't it?"

Drake shook his head no. "Yeah, I would not call myself a mystery lover. I'm a creature of habit. I want to know what I'm getting into," he admitted. "That's why I eat at the same three restaurants and get drinks right here."

Ellie pushed back on her stool. "The same three places? What's that all about?"

Drake scooted toward her, and their arms grazed. Both glanced at where they touched, but neither of them pulled back. "Well, when you've found a good thing," he said, so close to her face, "why not stick with it?"

Ellie's laugh caught in her throat. It wasn't funny, but surprising, as he was essentially arguing against the very principle that inspired her work. She needed a sip of her drink. "Because," Ellie said, letting herself get animated, "somewhere out there could be a great thing. The best thing. And by going to all the same places again and again, you're missing out."

Drake tapped the dividing line between their arms. "And if you're always looking for something else, you might not score a birthday party invite from your waiter at Taste of Hong Kong."

There was a weird streak to him Ellie hadn't seen coming. She liked it. "Your waiter invited you to his birthday party?"

"Yeah. Yeah. But I didn't go." Drake grabbed his drink and played with his too-long hair. Ellie also liked that he needed a haircut, she decided. She liked his goofy shirt, too, which she noticed when he draped his jean jacket on the back of his stool. On it, a dinosaur and its prehistoric friends squatted, midsong, by a raging bonfire. "I didn't go for long, I mean," Drake said. "Just played some shuffleboard." Their knees brushed under the bar. "Now, please let me off the hook, and tell me what you're writing."

Ellie gave in and explained that she was basically life support for hidden gems. "A career nostalgic, if you will." She discovered incredible offbeat locations—from restaurants to dance halls—that were in danger of closing. Then, she helped revive them by writing their stories. The whole time she spoke, Drake's eyes stayed glued on her. Ellie admitted she had written a book but downplayed it by saying it was a "coffee-table book," and when she mentioned her television show, she referred to it as a documentary.

"So, you write about these places and make them all cool again?"

"No," Ellie said. "It's not like that. The places I write about were always cool. I capture the feeling of being there. I paint the whole picture, but I try not to embellish it. I love every part of my subjects, flaws and all." This was the most she'd talked about work in a long time. "Anyway, people want to find these places. They just need to be pointed in the right direction."

"Aha." He chuckled. "So, I was right about the zombies." He sat up a little, proud of himself. "Because you make old things undead." Drake's hand knocked on the wooden bar. Ellie was drawn to his lifelines. She wondered how fast those hands could tear fabric and undo buttons.

When Drake got up to go to the bathroom, the voice of doubt in Ellie's head wondered if he would come back. She wanted him to come back. That was new. Last week, she'd crawled down her date's fire escape to avoid a conversation about breakfast. Drake was different. Behind his ice-blue eyes and devotion to three restaurants, Ellie sensed a vibrant inner world. What if he slipped away without getting her number? She willed him to return, and he did, smelling like a pine forest, which made her suspect he'd put on cologne for her.

"Maybe not *all* mysteries are bad," he decided as he slid back onto the stool next to her. "I mean, there is Nancy Drew."

"The books?"

"The dog." Drake took another sip of beer. "Mine, my dog."

"You named your dog after a fictional teenage spy?"

"Not exactly. She had the name when I adopted her."

"Does it suit her? Nancy Drew?"

Drake shrugged. "Sort of," he said. "She's a golden, on the older side, with a habit of eating things that aren't really food," he explained. "She also seems to be aging in reverse."

As they nursed another drink, Ellie learned that Drake loved building homes and wanted to start his own construction business. He was drawn to the way a family would move into a space and share so many important moments within its walls. Maybe that was the result of a happy childhood, he admitted. "But that wasn't what you asked." He tsked and cracked his knuckles. "You asked what I do *now*, which is project manage identical new-build homes that most families will live in for about two to three years before moving somewhere better. Homes without a legacy, I call them. I kind of hate it. That was too honest, wasn't it?"

"You know, you sound fairly nostalgic yourself," Ellie gleaned.

"Me?" he asked. "No. It's the opposite. I'm a dreamer, and I'm always looking forward. I see a blank wall and think about how a dad is going to measure their kid getting taller there. In the future."

Ellie was trying to pinpoint what she liked so much about Drake when the bartender came back. "Have you saved this place yet?" he asked, setting their checks down. Finn's was closing for the night. Drake swooped up both checks before Ellie could make a move.

"Still working on it," she said.

He walked away without acknowledging the comment.

"I think Sam's jealous," Drake noticed.

"Why?"

"Because I got to have drinks with you." His grin was so genuine. God, he was cute; she was doomed.

"That's such a line."

"Nah. It can't be a line if it's true," he told her. "A squiggle, maybe." Drake signed for the checks and asked if he could walk her home. Ellie glanced out the window. The overcast sky looked like it had a personal vendetta against them. "I've got an umbrella," he said, reading her mind. Ellie's apartment was more of a train ride away, but she agreed to a long walk.

It was brisk for a late-spring night. Without words, Drake pulled his jean jacket off and slid it over her shoulders. Outside, he expanded his trusty umbrella and held it above them. "Hey, thanks for letting me walk with you. I'm enjoying trying to solve The Case of the Girl at the Bar."

Ellie nudged him as they started down the sidewalk, letting some of the rain into their bubble. "Sounds like you've read some Nancy Drew."

"Of course I have. Who hasn't?" Drake wrapped his arm around her and drew her in close. All the lights in her body turned on, brightening rooms Ellie hadn't known existed.

What Ellie liked about Drake, she decided, was this. He was a beer guy without being a sports guy, a denim guy without being a horse guy. A definitive Pisces. He'd felt guilty for a second when he mentioned outmaneuvering the bartender, his level of empathy unwavering even when he was the victor. His voice went up an octave when he mentioned Nancy Drew. Drake had been invested in her work without being threatened by it, or worse, wanting to use it as some small ladder for himself.

Mostly, she could picture sitting in comfortable silence for hours at a time in bed with him.

She was getting ahead of herself.

Ellie had slipped up that night, she knew. She needed to focus on the story, and she'd barely spoken to anyone else at the bar. But maybe Drake was the story. Maybe the hook about Finn's was what had happened naturally: it was the type of place where a woman could meet the last good single guy out there. It was cheesy, and Ellie was no romantic. This reminder made her do what she did best, the long-practiced art of self-sabotage.

"What's wrong with you, anyway?" Ellie asked.

"Come on." Drake's hand found her back. He was getting—slightly—bolder. "What kind of a question is that, 'what's wrong with me'?"

"You just seem kind of perfect," she said, gesturing for them to turn onto the street that eventually led to her apartment. Drake followed her lead.

"I was thinking the same thing. So, what's wrong with you—"

"Seriously, though. What's your baggage?" Ellie caught a glimpse of them reflected in the glass window of a wine store. They looked great together. It wasn't too much of a stretch to think that maybe this would be their wine store one day. She'd ask Drake to run out and buy a bottle while she stayed home and botched the dinner. "Wouldn't that be refreshing? If we just spilled all our secrets, right here, right now?"

"Yeah, I guess," Drake agreed. "But see . . ." His tongue clicked against the roof of his mouth. "I don't have any baggage."

Ellie rolled her eyes. "Everybody has baggage."

"Okay fine, maybe, mine is more like a carry-on," Drake said. "It's a nice travel backpack. Practical, compact."

They were only a few blocks from Ellie's apartment when she

started into the intersection. A walk signal hadn't lit up yet, but there were no cars on either side and no sound of wheels sloshing through the rain. The storm had turned the streets into a private city just for them.

"Aren't you going to—" Drake stood alone on the curb.

"I looked both ways." Ellie was already halfway across the street. The rain had slowed, but it was still coming down. "Why wait for the light when you can look for yourself?"

"Well, I've been told I play it safe," Drake said, following her footsteps with slight hesitation. "In fact . . ." The shelter of the umbrella found her again. "I even had to psych myself up to suggest a walk. I don't normally walk at night, especially in the rain. But, you know. Umbrella. And also, I wanted to keep talking to you."

Ellie grinned. "Well, thanks for not leaving me to drown, Mary Poppins."

The urge to invite Drake up to her apartment was strong, but whatever was happening here was meant to aerate. Besides, Ellie couldn't remember what kind of clothing Rorschach would be waiting for them on the floor.

"Thanks for the walk," Ellie said. A curtain of rain fell between them as she stepped back.

"Yeah," Drake told her. "Well, now I know where you live. Wow. That sounded creepy. I just meant I should probably get your number, too."

"*Probably* get my number?"

"Just playing it safe again."

"Oh, come on, Drake. I talked to you for three hours at a bar and walked with you for what would've been a three-minute ride home." Ellie held out her hand. Drake reached to grab it. "Your phone," she chuckled. "I was asking for your phone."

"Right." He pulled his cell phone out and handed it over, stepping closer to shield her from the storm again as she typed her number in and assigned it a playful name he read aloud. "The Girl at the Bar." He nodded.

Ellie kissed his cheek. "Good night, Drake."

She could feel him watching her as she splashed through a few rain puddles and greeted a neighbor who was always walking her dog at an inopportune time. Ellie pretended to look for new mail, even though she already had earlier that day, to feel him there a second longer, his eyes on her.

The next morning, Ellie sat on her balcony with a half-finished crossword. A sound jolted her out of her thoughts as she struggled to figure out six down, "a powerful attraction." The sound was a text.

Guess I'll see you soon, jacket thief, it read. Drake's jacket was sitting inside the sliding glass door. It dangled from the back of her dining chair as if it had always existed there, waiting to be worn again.

Magnet, Ellie scribbled into the crossword squares before responding, *How do you feel about Mexican food?*

I feel good about it if it's tonight, Drake replied.

Then: *Sorry. That was forward.* Ellie could almost hear his throat clearing between the messages. She tossed her legs up on the chair opposite her and waited for another response. A cardinal flitted down onto the balcony, splashing its feathers in a puddle.

Then: *Let me rephrase. Are you and my jacket free for dinner?*

Ellie hesitated. Drake liked the version of her he had seen last night. This was the best version of Ellie—the version that had been practiced and refined over the years to create a certain impression. This Ellie was fun and carefree and kept the dark parts tucked away—the parts of herself that, if revealed, might send Drake running.

Ellie tried to set those parts aside a little longer. Despite the conversation she'd started about baggage the night before, he didn't need to find out her whole story yet.

Yes, she typed, looking over at his jacket as if it might weigh in on everything that would follow. *We're free tonight.*

2

2.5 YEARS LATER

"It's not that your new stuff is bad," Nolan told her, trimming the leaves of the *Pothos* plants that lined his black onyx desk. "I don't want you to think I'm saying that. Lately, though, your writing . . ." Ellie willed him to set the pruning scissors down, but he continued to twirl them in the style of an old-west gunslinger. "Lately, it's just been okay."

Okay.

Nolan had played the statement off casually, but Ellie knew it was the reason for their chat. Months ago, they had met at a matcha bar, and he asked to hear about her new projects. After reading those projects, he'd suggested a catchup at his office to share "a few thoughts." Now, his smile attempted to ease the blow of her newfound okay-ness.

The smile almost worked. Nolan was the distinguished caliber of handsome she would never go for; he smelled like a high-end casino and dressed in traditional British menswear despite a growing collection of modern office furniture. In the five years Nolan had been her agent, his black hair had been overtaken with gray, he'd become a father to a feisty toddler, and he'd gotten annoying about wine. All differences aside, Ellie trusted Nolan's opinions on her career. He was the only person who was honest about her television show being a flop before it launched.

"Look," Nolan said, "you're going to break through this funk." He tossed the scissors down and they clattered onto the Noguchi coffee table. "You just need to knock on some new doors and hunt down your voice."

He made finding her voice sound violent.

Nolan sank into an oddly shaped Scandinavian chair and crossed his hands over his knee. He reminded her of an actor playing a therapist. "It's all too comfortable right now," he said. "It's your passion that's missing." Ellie let her mind wander off to the weather, her dinner plans, and hypothetical desserts she would never bake, before she asked the inevitable.

"When was the last time the stories worked?"

Nolan looked at the floor. So rarely did he lose his je ne sais quoi, but he truly hated direct confrontation, Ellie knew. "The piece about Finn's Bar," he finally admitted. "That was the last really good one."

So, two years ago. Two and a half, actually.

Ellie's recent pieces should've been electric. A music shop that once sold a keyboard to Carole King and an ice cream store with flavors named after the owner's family history both had potential. The fact that those places ended up closing was on her. She felt the weight of their failure, the suffocating responsibility of not being able to do something for the five, soon to be six, businesses that shuttered since she'd written about them. Soon, their legacy would be left behind, traded for pour-over coffee shops or food halls with generic, chipper names: The Hello Factory. Shindig Food Community. So much for her magic gift of sparking revivals. Ellie had a streak of bad luck she couldn't seem to shake.

Nolan seemed to pick up on her defeat. "Just find something you're obsessed with," he suggested. "Unhealthy obsession's a good look on you."

....

Ellie, the text she received in the parking lot said. *I hope you're well.* She unlocked the car and tossed her purse onto the passenger seat. The message had the cadence of a stranger, but it was from her father. *Naomi said we should send an engagement gift*—and he added the gift emoji there—*but we're not sure what you're like.*

What you're like, Ellie read again. The typo was an understatement. Since her engagement months earlier, her best friend, Jen, had thrown a lively karaoke celebration for their friends, and her mom had offered to plan a more formal engagement party. This text, however, was only the second wedding-related peep she had heard from her dad.

Ellie didn't want a gift from him or the stepmom she'd met a handful of times. An occasional check-in about the wedding would've been nice, though. She had shared the news over email, since her dad couldn't be reached by phone, which removed all the warmth and excitement from the announcement and turned it hollow. He'd replied with a simple "Congratulations." As usual, there weren't any follow-up questions. There was no offer to help.

Even small interactions with her family reminded Ellie that her special day could never be normal. Recently, she had woken up from a nightmare that every chair on her side of the aisle would be empty. Because just as the text had accidentally given away, these days, they barely knew her at all.

As she pulled out of the parking garage and crunched over the remnants of fall leaves, she decided to go to the only place that would put her at ease and cast her family drama from her mind. All Novel Things was the perfect little bookstore, with shelves that were huddled too close together, a free tea station, and nooks that invited the reader to stay a while. Finding her own book there and imagining the other shelves and mantels it lived on in readers' homes was a sacred experience for Ellie. She had started this ritual when all those first reviews came out for her TV show, calling it "pretentious and removed."

Today, though, her book wasn't in its usual spot.

"Hi," she said to the bookseller at the front desk. She'd never seen him there before. "Can you help me find a book? It's *The Compendium of Forgotten Things*."

"We used to have that one," he told her. "I don't think we stock it anymore."

"Since when?" Ellie asked. She'd missed the memo on this news. There had been several copies of her book when she last visited a few weeks earlier.

The bookseller shrugged. "We're a curated shop. We don't really carry a lot of coffee-table books anymore." He said it like she was asking for a BeDazzler, not a book.

"It's not exactly a coffee-table—"

The bookseller repeated that it was a "curated" store. Ellie started to hate the word she'd used so often herself. "Coffee-table sales must really be down, huh?" she asked.

"Not really," he said without looking at her.

"Well then," Ellie lamented, watching him check the price on a kid's embroidery kit. She must've looked silly to him. What did he think of her vintage, 1970s ocean-blue sweater with bell sleeves? He was wearing silver hoop earrings and a stylish cropped vest. He had a mullet. She needed to relearn what was trendy. The word *trendy* wasn't it. "People need something to set on their coffee table, right?" she asked.

He shrugged. "Minimalism is in. You know, less clutter."

Clutter.

The places she loved most were now considered clutter. What if she had to watch them—slowly and excruciatingly—turn off their lights one by one? What if she'd given them a little bit of hope only to have it taken away? Ellie feared what it meant for them, and her, to become irrelevant.

· · · · · · · · · ·

Ellie tried not to show Drake how heartbroken she was when she came home that evening. She adored their new, old home. Their blue-gray house was snugger than most Queen Anne styles and was "completely falling apart," as Drake put it. Despite his assessment, she could tell he secretly loved all the home improvement projects it required, the storied architecture, and the wraparound front porch where she often found him sitting in the mornings before work. When they first toured the house, he insisted it would be difficult to find modern hardware to go with a structure built in the early 1900s. Still, he surprised her by suggesting they place an offer on it a few days later. Ellie thought the house looked like a castle, the curved windows in her office, the high tower with a spired roof.

Drake waved at Ellie when she walked inside. The phone was curled under his neck as he unpacked a box of glassware. Three months into the unpacking, they still had random boxes waiting to be opened. Ellie enjoyed the intentional process of holding each item to discover where it wanted to live. Drake was eager to put everything in its place as quickly as possible.

"No, Mom." He chuckled. "It's not called *haunting*. It's *ghosting*." He looked at Ellie and pretended to take a sip out of a pint glass before setting it on the floor. "Because they're two separate things. Haunt is what a ghost does. Ghost is when a living person stops responding." These simple moments Ellie sometimes caught between Drake and his parents on the phone—snippets of him explaining modern pop culture or engaging in nonsensical debates—underlined what she was missing in her own family. "Anyway, I've got to go, Mom," he said. "Ellie is home."

Drake turned the television off as Ellie set her things down. He'd been watching a home improvement show in the background. Ellie liked to tease him about his habit of working off the clock. It was research, he said. He felt like the hosts, with their magnetic personalities and chemistry, were his old friends. "Are you okay?" he asked, seeming to detect her bad mood.

"According to Nolan I am," she said, flinging herself into the Ellie-shaped spot on the couch. Nancy hopped up and set a wet nose on her denim miniskirt. Ellie rubbed her stomach to accentuate the point she was about to make. "I'm super hungry." Then, "Can we go out?"

"Sure, yeah." Drake got up and refilled Nancy's water bowl in anticipation of leaving. "How about The Garlic Bread Place?"

Ellie wanted to go somewhere different today, somewhere special. She debated telling him about her bad meeting, how her favorite bookstore no longer sold her work, and how the result of these things meant more places she loved might close for good. The facts, when strung together, sounded like the start of a bad stand-up routine. She decided against sharing them. There was no reason to ruin a perfectly good date night with Drake.

"We always go to The Garlic Bread Place," Ellie said. "Let's try something different tonight."

3

Ellie and Drake did not try something different that night; they went to The Garlic Bread Place. By the time they started looking up new restaurants, they were too hungry to choose another option. Ellie ordered the same Eggplant Parmigiana at their usual four-top with a white plastic tablecloth. What had happened to her? She was supposed to be in the field of rare discovery. This repeat eggplant business had to be part of the problem.

"Bring wine, too," she begged the young, pretty waitress. "You can bring a bottle out. Your pick."

The waitress glanced up from her square yellow pad and moved closer. "Don't I know you?"

Drake brightened. He was eager to brag. "She has a book," he gushed. "And a show! *The Compendium of Forgotten Things*—"

"It's not a big deal. You probably just know me because we come here a lot," Ellie deflected.

Recognition spread across the waitress's face. Slight recognition. It was minuscule. "Right!" she said. "Oh, wow. I loved your show."

The same Dean Martin playlist Ellie had memorized refreshed another loop. "There's no way you loved my show," Ellie said. When Drake gave her a look, she realized she had been rude. "I just meant, you've probably not seen it," she added, which certainly made things worse. "It's hard to find the show on streaming. There's actually a rip-off of *The Goonies* that appears when you type it in." A warning flashed in Drake's eyes as he started to stress eat the bread that came before the garlic bread.

"I'm going to put the order in," the waitress said, backing away from the table. She attempted a smile that came out twisted.

Drake gave Ellie a second to pull herself together. Then, he leaned over the table and said the right thing. "People can love you and your work. You know?" His hands reached out for hers. "You're pretty damn lovable. Even though figuring you out takes a little sleuthing."

The timing of this line landed perfectly with the gift he handed her next. Ellie tore open the newspaper-covered package to find a hardcover Nancy Drew book. The title had been crossed out and replaced with *The Case of the Girl at the Bar*, which was the same title as her story about Finn's that he'd framed and hung on the wall of their living room.

"Thank you," Ellie said. "Thanks. I'm pretty lucky I get to marry you." She brushed Drake's hair out of his face. The waitress dropped off their wine and the garlic bread Drake had ordered, then scurried away before she could be pulled back into their conversation.

"Yeah, about that," Drake said, tearing off a piece of the hot bread and popping it in his mouth. "Are you sure you want to marry me?" It was a joke, of course. "I mean, a renowned writer like yourself, a television-show host, *and* a goddamn detective." He pulled his hands away and slammed them on the table for emphasis. The condiments jumped.

"Yes," Ellie told him. She opened the book. Inside its cover, Drake had occasionally crossed out the name *Nancy* and replaced it with *Ellie* in his youthful scrawl. Her engagement ring sparkled on her finger as she navigated the pages. Drake had managed to find the exact ring she would've chosen for herself. It was an oval, teal sapphire that reminded Ellie of a doorknob to a beautiful place—feminine, but not flashy, with tiny diamonds set on each side of the stone. Drake's gifts showed he was listening. Even a few dates in, he'd given her a vintage music box with a spinning dancer inside that reminded her of one she had growing up.

"Of course, I want to marry you," Ellie added.

If she was being honest with herself, that was the only thing she was sure about.

"Well, that's a relief. That wedding photographer I just hired is going to be expensive. I was channeling Milburn Pennybags when I sent the check."

"Milburn—"

"Mr. Monopoly. Get with it."

Ellie laughed. She noted the relief on Drake's face. He'd managed to alleviate her frustration or at least put a bandage on it. He kept the conversation silly while they ate their food, performing a classic tarantella dance on the table with his fingers. The eggplant was perfect, and every bite made Ellie's mouth water more. Sometimes, familiar and comfortable things were nice, she had learned when they moved in together. Familiarity could look like a movie night routine or a bedtime ritual of reading in shared silence. She didn't blame Drake for the way she'd fallen into patterns. It was her role to shake things up and drag them to new places. Now, she sensed, it was time for her to do it again.

"How about a walk?" Ellie suggested after the check came, along with a complimentary tiramisu. Ellie wondered if the free dessert was on account of her being recognized, the weird energy, or something else entirely.

"Where were you thinking?" Drake asked. He split the dessert in half and took a bite. "I can disappear this dessert and we can get another one. We could go to The Gelato Fairy? Or that French bakery around the corner. What's it called?"

Ellie reached her fork out for her portion of the tiramisu. "Let's just get a little lost," she said.

His eyes narrowed. "You know how I feel about being lost."

"Not *lost* lost." She knew by now that *lost* was a frightening word to Drake. "What I meant was," she said, "let's just see where this night takes us."

Ellie felt the tension of the evening melt away as she and Drake traced the neck of the city. They paused to admire the neon signs that bloomed in the window of a palm-reader shop. Drake didn't smoke but mused that, if he did, he'd want to look like the hipster with pompadour hair they passed nursing a cigar. Ellie held her hand out to spin Drake when she heard a saxophone pouring from the window of a high loft. This night was giving her the adventure she'd craved.

"What was all that about, at the restaurant?" Drake finally ventured to ask. "With the waitress?"

Ellie pulled her jacket tighter. "I'm sorry. It sounded rude as soon as it came out. But I'm fine."

"Okay. Well, you didn't seem fine," he said.

Here was the picking apart Ellie loathed. She had allowed Drake into her thoughts and life more than she'd thought was possible. She'd told him everything that happened with her parents, and most of what happened with her brother, Ben. She'd even mentioned that she had struggled to commit in past relationships. But right now, she didn't want to open the scary vault of the day and take stock of her mental cobwebs. If she pried herself open, her pain might all tumble out and refuse to disappear. Drake was everything to her, but sometimes she wondered if she'd be able to give him enough of herself—the intimacy and vulnerability he deserved.

Drake paused to get his bearings. Ellie swore she could hear his thoughts. They didn't walk without aim anymore, and they'd never walked this far from the car. "I'm thinking we should head back," he suggested. "It's getting kind of late."

"No." Ellie urged them forward. "I want to keep going."

"All right. Well, while we walk, you can tell me what you're feeling. You don't have to bottle it all up, you know." He squeezed her into him, maybe to coerce a confession.

Ellie led them through the main square of Chinatown, around a few corners, and onto a new street filled with a row of boutiques. Windows housed oven mitts midwave, needle-felted snowmen, and boxes wrapped in quirky patterned paper. It was only the last weekend of October, but Big Christmas was on a mission to start the holidays earlier every year. Luckily, Ellie still had a few weeks before her mom's five-course dinner happened—and her dad's grain-free cookies arrived by mail.

"It was just a bad day," Ellie said, finally filling the silence. "Can we talk about something else?"

"Sure. Okay. Like what?"

"I don't know. Why don't you tell me about work?"

"Work?" Drake sighed. "Work is . . . boring."

He was always saying: "Work is boring." For someone who pushed her to open up, Drake also stored parts of himself she couldn't access. He was sentimental and romantic, unafraid to cry when moved. His disappointments, though, were kept to himself.

"Pretty street, isn't it?" Drake asked. He was nodding to the trees and shops spread out in front of them. A cold gust made the branches shiver. It *was* a pretty street, but Ellie noticed something unusual ahead of them. A small gap was set between two of the stores, outlined by a brick archway. Ellie moved toward the opening.

"Ellie?" Drake asked, following behind her.

The doorway led to an alley. The opening in the brick marked the beginning of an adorable little alley that would've been so easy to walk right by. A fog hovered above the steps. Pastel-hued storefronts on each side of the cobblestones were lit by the glow of lampposts fit for casual strolls and Gene Kelly spins. The alley felt much more like a film set than a real place in a big city. Ellie expected someone to leap out and call "Cut!" but the quaint detour remained silent.

A static fluttered around her, the knowingness of a place drawing her closer. This was how it always happened when she was on the brink of discovery. A building, or a bar, or a haunted taqueria would summon her and become an entry in *The Compendium of Forgotten Things*. Finally—yes, finally—it was about to happen again.

Beyond a sprinkling of cafés and bakeries, a sleepy Irish pub, and an ice cream shop, with a rose-colored awning, called Mae's Famous Scoops, the storefronts were empty. Their footsteps echoed up the walkway. The streetlamps flickered out one by one until Ellie and Drake were left standing in the near dark.

"Well? You ready to head back?" Drake asked.

Ellie wasn't ready. Drake had missed something up ahead, but to be fair, she almost missed it herself. Faint light glazed the cobblestones at the very top of the alley. Drake threw his hand above his eyes and squinted. "What is that?"

The light grew brighter as they moved toward it and came upon the thing Ellie would've most wanted to be in this place. They were standing at the entrance of a glamorous vintage movie palace. A circular gold ticket booth adorned with Greek gods and goddesses, her old friends Poseidon and Artemis and Ares, made the first impression, and a marquee lined with flickering, Broadway-style bulbs spelled out the title of a film she'd never heard of before. Ellie turned her hands into binoculars against the cold glass doors of the cinema.

She gasped at what was inside. Luxurious red carpet led the way to twin stairwells that curled up both sides of the lobby like ribbons on a gift. Clinging to the rounded ceiling was an enormous chandelier. It was as elegant as an opera house—one of those fantastic cinemas that were nearly obsolete.

"*The Story of You*," Drake read off the marquee. "Must be an art house thing."

A voice cracked from inside the ticket booth. "Will it be two for the midnight movie?" Ellie hadn't realized a person was in there. A galaxy of red acne dotted the teenage ticket boy's cheeks. He was too tall for the confined space, a giant manning a tollbooth for dolls.

Ellie grabbed Drake's wrist and looked at his watch. The seconds hand crept closer toward *11:55*, as if they'd planned it that way.

"Hey, no thanks," Drake said. "We're good."

"No, we're not," Ellie insisted. She forced a casual tone. "I mean, yes. Yeah. We would like two tickets, please."

Drake pulled her away for a sidebar. "It's late," he reminded her. "These theaters play experimental stuff at midnight. *The Story of You* sounds like a movie where somebody cries too long in their shower."

Ellie felt herself huff. "Who cares what the movie is? I've got to see the inside of this cinema."

Drake yawned to make his point. "It's just, by the time we get back—"

"I need this!" Ellie unintentionally stomped her foot.

Drake took a step closer and lowered his voice. "Ellie?"

"I haven't seen a movie in forever."

"We do Monster Movie Thursday every Thursday night."

"I mean, in the theater. In a theater like this. Drake, this is an architectural wonder. You love this stuff."

The ticket boy stared at them, either waiting for a decision or wishing for them to leave.

"You're right." Drake ran his hands through his hair. "Yeah. Okay. Let's do it."

Delighted, Ellie asked for two tickets again.

"So, this will be one ticket each, of your . . ." The ticket boy ran his finger down a white piece of paper in front of him. "Your ten total tickets," he said. He grabbed two metal boxes from the back of the desk and set a small spool of the pink paper tickets, like the ones Ellie had been given at raffles or carnivals, inside each lid. "We limit admission to the Saturday midnight movie," he said. "And each of you will get a spool of only ten tickets."

"Why?" Drake asked. "Seems like a weird policy."

"Very weird. Very specific," Ellie agreed.

"How do you even stay in business here?" Drake interrogated. "I mean, isn't that the point? To get people to come back?" He was right, Ellie thought. The cinema didn't even have a name on its marquee. Forget a social media presence—this place barely had the chance to build word-of-mouth business.

"I just do the tickets," the ticket boy said. He shuffled around for something on his desk and located two blank name-tag stickers and a marker, which he passed over through the slot. "Write your name on those." Drake wrote on his sticker first, then handed the marker to Ellie. They passed the marker and stickers back through the small slot, which the ticket boy slapped onto each of the metal boxes.

"Five dollars each," he said. "Ten total. Cash only."

Drake pulled some cash out of his pocket, and they traded the money for their tickets.

Participating in something spontaneous felt so satisfying. Everything else Ellie had done in recent months was predictable. Even the shoes she was wearing were sensible. She tried to recall the last time she'd worn a clever pair of heels and made the least sensible choice possible.

It didn't matter. Because, right then, she could feel a forgotten part of herself coming back.

4

The lobby lived up to its promise. Everywhere they wandered smelled of rose and bergamot, as if from a starlet's elegant wrist. At Ellie's feet, the carpet pooled out in a red floral lake, and above her head, the palatial chandelier reflected onto champagne-colored walls, creating a carousel of light. She could almost hear the ghosts of Bette Davis and Olivia de Havilland whispering halfway down the stairs, taking stock of the crowd as they waited for the picture to start. "Imagine all the fancy ladies who have stood right here," Ellie marveled.

"You're a fancy lady," Drake said. Their eyes shot up toward the ceiling; the sound of their voices had fluttered at least twenty feet above them. No one else was around, which meant the tiniest noises broke through the quiet. Ellie's footfalls reverberated on the carpet. In the bathroom, water thudded into the polished porcelain basins. They were also the only people inside the dazzling domed auditorium with tiered, red-velvet rows.

"Whoa," Drake said when they stepped inside.

"Incredible," Ellie agreed. They tiptoed forward, swallowed by empty seats.

"I don't know if I've ever seen an actual movie palace," he shared. "It's even more incredible in person. I mean, look at how extravagant everything is. The way all the styles come together." Drake's eyes widened as he looked around the room. Ellie sensed he was about to geek out. His love of physical spaces transcended construction—he was in awe of the blueprint and beginnings, too. On many occasions, she'd walked into the house to find him huddled over a stack of architecture magazines while buzzing about a thoughtful use of windows.

"I'd say the brass proscenium arch around the screen is inspired by the Beaux Arts movement," Drake told her. "And check out the attention to detail on the foliage there"—he pointed to the tiny vines and leaves along the arch—"that's pulling from the Greeks. I'm pretty sure the gold mask sconces on the walls are, too. But then, the lobby staircases and chandelier are a different vibe, French Baroque, maybe. These old movie palaces mashed up lavish styles, which made average guys like me feel like kings for the night. And I've gotta say, it works." He kissed Ellie's cheek. "I'm really glad we came in here," he said. "It's amazing. Thank you."

Somewhere above them, a projector turned on. Ellie chose a row near the middle of the house as two gold-tassel curtains parted to reveal a screen, which was soon overtaken with a hot, round spotlight. They settled in. The lights faded from the eyes of the brass theater mask sconces that Drake had pointed out. Each one held a different expression—from a stiff grimace to a cheeky grin. Drake's arm found its place around the back of her chair as a preshow cartoon played. Four cartoon hot dog friends danced out to the sound of a tinkling piano. "Tonight's feature," crooned an announcer, "is *The Story of You*." The hot dogs showed off their best Charleston, and the announcer laid out a series of instructions.

Don't record what you see here tonight, or the picture will stop.

"Hey, about the conversation earlier . . ." Drake started. "I just meant that you can tell me anything. There's nothing that's going to scare me off. You know that, right?" He wasn't paying attention, not even as a hot dog dug its fists into a bag overflowing with popcorn. What would it be like to eat a hot dog stuffed with popcorn? Ellie wondered. She wanted to focus and memorize every detail about this place. It grated on her that Drake had chosen this moment as his first time to talk over a voice of authority.

If you need to stretch your legs, exit to the lobby, and the picture will pause.

"I feel like sometimes you store problems away instead of looking at them," he said. "And I'm here to help you sort through anything. All of it."

The Story of You *is only for you.*

"What did he mean by that?" Ellie tapped Drake's shoulder and pointed to the screen. "*The Story of You* is only for you?"

"Ellie. Did you hear me?"

The cartoon finished with a hard call-to-action to buy popcorn at the snack bar.

Then, the screen turned a vibrant, magnetic black, and a title flashed against it.

TICKET ONE: *BABIES*

Shortly after the title disappeared, an impossible thing happened, followed by the sound of a belly laugh Ellie didn't know she had in her. Could this be real? Could it possibly?

"What is this, Ellie?" Drake's voice, next to her.

The film's setting was familiar: A condo in the suburbs.

The film's era was: Well, it must have been the early 1990s.

"Is this a prank?" Drake asked.

The film's star was, somehow, unbelievably: Drake. Baby Drake. Yes, it had to be Baby Drake, wailing inside his crib, balling up his fists—and his mom, Beth, lifting him up into the air, swinging him into the kitchen, and Drake's dad, Robert, holding a modest square cake lit by a candle in the shape of the number one.

"Seriously," Drake said. He launched out of his seat. "What . . . *Is this?*"

All Ellie knew was that they weren't watching a regular movie. By some magic, they were watching his life.

Yes, they really were, she processed. They were *watching* his *life*.

Everything Ellie should've wondered about—the logistics, why they were seeing these things, how the hell a theater could project their own memories—escaped her. When faced with the surreal and intangible, Ellie dove in headfirst. She physically leaned as close to the screen as possible. Electricity hummed under her skin, her breath fast and thrilled.

Drake was saying something in the seat next to her, but his voice fell away with the rest of the questions, and she gave herself permission to be mesmerized.

After Baby Drake's parents helped him blow his candle out, the scene moved to a new location. In a mall, Baby Drake was passed to the Easter Bunny, whose ears sagged and fur was pilling. "Smile," Beth said. Baby Drake wallowed in angst, his face flushed a deep red. A woman with shopping bags in both hands stopped to see what the fuss was about. Beth showed no sign of embarrassment. "It's fine," she told the nosy woman. "He's a baby." As in, *move along*, but nicer. A flash went off, capturing Drake midscream with the scary bunny.

The same photo was then hung on a kitchen wall. Drake's legs thrashed in his high chair as he shouted out a string of babble. Beth bent down to kiss the top of his head.

The memories from Drake's young life sped forward.

Drake learned to walk on the gray shag carpet of his parents' bedroom.

Drake belched over Thanksgiving dinner during a long-winded, but well-meaning, speech about gratitude at his grandmother's tchotchke-lined dining table.

Drake was carried on the hip around a buzzing, small-town hair parlor by his mom.

Then, something fluttered in front of Ellie's face.

Drake—the adult Drake—was waving his hand to get her attention. Ellie finally glanced up. She had noticed the blur of his shape darting around the aisle as she watched the screen but hadn't bothered to see what he was doing. Why would she? They were being given the chance to watch his childhood. She didn't want to miss a single moment.

"So, the movie screen is just, like, a normal screen," Drake concluded. "There's a storage area behind it, too, but there's mostly old junk back there." He had performed a full audit of the space. How long had they been there? Ellie had lost all concept of time. She was too captivated by the movie.

Then, something happened that caused her to audibly shush Drake as he tried to make sense of it all. The image on the screen was overtaken with fuzzy dots, turning the picture blurry—as if a film strip was being pulled from a projector.

And then, Ellie's own memories began to play.

Baby Ellie was pushed around a park in her bassinet. Her father was behind it—*Dad*. A little boy walked at their side. Ellie heard herself gasp. She could feel herself being physically pulled toward the screen, her heart warm in her chest. *Ben*. He was so young. He looked delighted to trot alongside them, stopping every now and then to grab a stick off the ground or kick at a rock. He was only two years Ellie's senior—a toddler who was just old enough to say "love you" to her bassinet, then teeter down a woodchip path toward a shiny yellow slide.

"Ellie?" Drake asked as he continued to investigate the theater like a drug-sniffing dog. He moved his search to the floor. "Talk to me. What is this movie? What is going on?"

"*Quiet,*" Ellie insisted, floating above her chair on a private, cozy hovercraft of happiness. She wasn't about to let reason bring her back to earth.

Ellie and Ben sat next to each other at a never-ending, candlelit table in matching plaid sweaters.

Ben covered Ellie's eyes and showed her a cartoon portrait he'd drawn of her.

Their mom, in casual pants—*slacks*—held hands with their father—*held hands*—inside a toy store while Ben and Ellie tumbled through the aisles, and—

Ellie's body was being moved for real this time.

Drake pulled her out of her chair, down the aisle, and through the double doors that swung into the lobby. And just like that, her beautiful, complicated past had evaporated.

5

"Everywhere." Drake sighed. "I've looked everywhere." He was on their couch, searching for internet proof that the cinema existed. "A few people mentioned a historic movie theater being in that spot, but I can't even tell if it's open anymore. There's also no mention of what it shows. Or showed."

"That makes sense," Ellie called from the kitchen as she let Nancy out. When she trotted back inside moments later, her fur was covered in a layer of dead leaves. "If there was an old-timey cinema in our city, I would know about it. Also, *this theater played our memories* isn't the kind of thing you normally find on review sites."

It was morning, and they still hadn't slept. Out the window, faint pink light brushed the rooftops of the other Queen Annes and Craftsman homes. A lone runner glided down the sidewalk that opened up to the city skyline in silhouette. Ellie sat on the couch, curled the toes of her wool socks over the coffee table, and began to pick the leaves off Nancy's coat. How many times had they missed out on this view by calling it a night too early?

"It feels like there should be a record of something so . . ." A tiny earthquake rocked his hand. "Unbelievable."

Drake's nerves reminded Ellie that there were two types of people: those who dove into the crevices of invisible things and those who confined themselves to the stories that fit the logic of daily life. Ellie fell into the first camp. Drake was in the latter.

Getting along was so effortless for the two of them that she often forgot what set them apart.

But earlier that night, she'd been reminded of those differences.

"What the . . . What the hell was that?" Drake had stammered after he dragged her into the lobby to make sense of what they'd seen.

Ellie hesitated. She wasn't sure how to proceed—the fastest path to witnessing herself, and her brother, on-screen again. "Maybe," she suggested, searching for a form of logic that would appease him, "it's playing home videos somehow?"

Drake shook his head at the suggestion. While his mom had snapped endless photographs throughout the years, she was paranoid about video cameras because of something related to Nixon. Drake's early memories weren't on film.

"Well, I think we should go back in there," Ellie said softly. "Maybe we made it all up. Right?" But when they swung open the auditorium doors again, the movie continued exactly where it left off. Tiny Ellie and Ben were sprawled out on a red play mat in the middle of a giggle fit. Ellie saw a bright light coming from Drake's chair. Before she could stop him, his phone was held up to the screen.

"What are you doing?" she snapped.

"I'm getting proof." He waved his hand around in the air. "Of whatever this is."

"No," she said. "That won't work." She was right. Sure enough, the movie stopped playing the moment Drake pressed Record. The auditorium screen turned black. None of the unbelievable parts had been captured on his phone.

"Because of the dancing hot dogs," Ellie explained. "They spelled out the rules for this place. You can't record the movie, or it will stop playing. And, like the announcer said, the movie pauses when you step out to the lobby. That also happened just now."

Drake tucked his phone away. Luckily, the movie picked up right where it left off—but as soon as it did, Ellie felt Drake's arm tugging her back toward the lobby. The ticket boy, who was busy wiping down a shiny slushy machine, was his target. "The movie," Drake barked at the snack counter. "Why is . . . it our lives?"

Ellie stepped forward to interject. "Can you tell us more about the movie?" she asked, trying to emanate composure.

"The midnight screening is *The Story of You*," the ticket boy said. He spun away from them and yanked the microwave door open, removing a bowl of silky butter sauce that he walked over to the popcorn machine. "Is there a problem with the picture quality?"

"No, that's not the issue," Drake nearly shouted. "The issue is that it's our story. We're the story!" When the ticket boy finally glanced up, he asked Drake if he wanted a sample of the popcorn. It wasn't very good, he noted. It would be free, though.

"Can we talk to the manager?" Ellie asked, attempting to make "manager" sound cotton soft.

The ticket boy reached for a large white binder. He flipped through the pages, scanning each one with the tip of his finger. "Natalie's on vacation this week," he said. "She's doing nothing at the beach."

Ellie hesitated. "Maybe . . . we could give her a call?"

The ticket boy crouched behind the counter and moved on to sorting candy that was already organized in neat rows. "That wouldn't be doing nothing at the beach," he replied. His eyes were shrouded behind a row of Junior Mints and Milk Duds. "Would it?"

. . . .

Now, back in the quiet of their living room, Drake was about to smash into the coffee table. He paced around it in a circle, double-checking that the front door was locked on every second or third lap. "I don't get how you're . . . *relaxed* about this," he said. Ellie burrowed her shoulders into the couch and tuned out his voice. She wanted to stay in the moment, to stay bathing in that rare pink morning light. When she tuned back in, he was asking if they could've been drugged. "At the restaurant, maybe? That waitress had the right haircut for that."

"She had a haircut for drugging?" Ellie asked, with a laugh. It was a ridiculous suggestion. She reached for his arm as he closed out a lap and pulled him closer. "Sit, Drake."

"Why?" he asked. His pulse was beating on the side of his neck.

"Because you look like you're going to have a heart attack," she said. "And because, something incredible just happened, and I want to enjoy it."

Drake stopped for a moment and hinged forward at the waist. He was studying her; he prided himself in being an expert in all things Ellie. Finally, he sat and took her hands. "Look," he said. "I understand why this meant something to you. It must have felt great to see yourself as a kid. Your dad. Ben. But I'm just . . . freaked-out by this whole thing, to be honest."

"I understand," Ellie said, because she did. She was so quick to shut out his doubt that she hadn't noted it was a reasonable reaction. "I can see how it would be spooky. It's unknown. But it's also amazing, right? The cinema is this ode to nostalgia. It's everything I love in one setting. Movies. Old things. Memories. It's a place that helps us remember what we've forgotten, and that's basically my life's work, Drake. We have to go back."

Everything she'd told him was technically true.

But there was something else drawing her there. Something she wasn't ready to say just yet.

"I hear you," Drake said. "But, Ellie . . ." His words were calm, but his posture stayed tense. "Something is telling me that we should forget this ever happened."

The statement sounded an alarm in her.

Ellie pulled herself together and spoke Drake's language. "Beach vacations don't last forever."

Drake shrugged. "Yeah, so?"

"Why don't we go there next Saturday night when the manager is back?" Ellie pressed on, trying to navigate his doubt. "Then, we'll get answers." If they did that, they would know they hadn't hallucinated, she explained. They would learn how it worked. "Come on," she prodded, her fingers creeping up his arm. "Don't you want to figure this out? Just a little bit?" Yes, this would work. Seated next to her was the man who loathed unsolved mysteries.

Much to her relief, Drake reluctantly agreed. "Okay. Just to ask a few questions. That's it, though." The sun was more energetic now, spilling light onto the neat green lawns outside. "But, Ellie," he warned, "promise me something." He turned her chin in his direction. "Don't go back there without me. It's . . . it could be dangerous."

"I won't do that," Ellie said. She didn't think the cinema was dangerous, but she agreed that she probably shouldn't return without backup. "Next week, then." She nodded. "It's a date."

When Drake finally went to bed that morning, Ellie stayed up and watched a movie. She was too energized by what had happened to sleep. *Heathers* was iconic, but it paled compared to the magic of watching their real lives projected on the screen. The comparison wasn't fair. Ellie's focus on Winona and friends drifted as she recalled seeing herself so young and innocent. But those early experiences were only the tip of the iceberg. Under the surface of the memory was something more complicated.

When they went back, the cinema would play everything she'd been hiding from Drake.

And from herself.

Ellie pulled the blanket up around her. Even if she wanted to, she couldn't have described what happened that night in college to Drake; she only knew the bare bones. Her memory had blocked out the sequence of things and even *how* the horrific event began. The how part—not being able to remember those details—had haunted her for fifteen years.

Ellie had done her best to leave that night in her past. First, she threw herself into other people's stories. She rebelled against what was expected of her. She ran from people before they could get close enough to discover an awful truth about her that she couldn't pinpoint herself. She tried to make friends with the forgetting, to convince herself it was better that way. But none of those strategies removed the guilt that hovered above her head.

So, lately, Ellie had done something different: she tried to remember her past instead. If she could only recall exactly what happened, maybe she could absolve herself. Time had turned her into an amateur sleuth, chasing down details that were slippery at best. How fitting, she thought, that Drake once compared her to a teen detective. Still, she'd come up with nothing. And in lieu of the truth, she assumed the worst. A voice would forever whisper in her ear, a mean little lark: *You did this. Everything that went wrong, so very wrong, was your fault.*

Earlier that night, Ellie was presented with an opportunity to piece the story together. To finally confront her past. She would need to watch the worst moments of her own life all over again—with Drake at her side.

A chance to know the truth was irresistible. She wouldn't let it go. But if what she suspected was true, could he ever see her the same way again?

6

Ellie had been trying to forget about their engagement party for weeks. On her last visit to her mom's house, they silently languished over dinner like two women in a dreary oil painting. Their conflict had a long lineage; Ellie could never quite squeeze into whatever box her mother tried to place her in. She was never going to be a *modest* dresser who *networked* and married someone *well-off*. But maybe the party was a peace offering. After all, Sandra Marshall best expressed herself by way of expensive catering.

"Your mom's place is beautiful," Drake said. He'd visited the giant white house only twice; first for one of the aforementioned dinners, and again for a cookie exchange where her mom's friends had tried to pass the work of gourmet bakeries off as their own.

"It is beautiful," she agreed. While Ellie's personal style was more whimsical than her mother's, she had to admit that Drake was right. Sandra Marshall was an expert at tacking on cheer for the outside world. Today, the home's exterior was embellished with fall decorations. Tasteful autumn wreaths dotted each window, gourds in a restrained fall palate huddled together on the porch, and two hunky designer scarecrows flanked the black front door.

Ellie checked the time as they exited the car. It was five exactly. She had wanted to arrive fashionably late so they didn't have to stand there awkwardly and wait while her mom fussed around the foyer, but Drake felt that would be inconsiderate of them.

He set a timer to make sure they left with enough wiggle room to pick up flowers from the grocery store. Ellie warned him this gesture wasn't necessary. It was, after all, their party.

What she was thinking, though, was that her mom already had a florist on staff.

As they rang the doorbell, Ellie began an invisible countdown in her mind: two hours. Her mom was making a rare effort. Ellie wanted to meet her halfway. Weddings brought people together sometimes. She doubted it would work for her own family, but it was worth a try. She could do anything for two hours.

The door swung open. Much like the house itself, her mom looked perfect without showing the exhaustive effort that went into that perfection. The lines of her silver linen top and navy silk skirt complemented her lean frame, especially when met with the posture of a politician's wife. "You're here!" she said. Then, "Finally."

Ellie wasn't sure what the *finally* was supposed to mean. They were right on time. It was the handful of guests who had already arrived—early—who were the rude ones. Ellie's confidence dwindled as she surveyed the formal scene her mom had arranged. Maybe an hour and a half was enough time for their visit.

"Hi, Mom," Ellie said.

"It's great to see you, Sandra." Drake handed over the grocery store bouquet. Sandra's button nose, which Ellie knew was her least favorite feature, scrunched up for a second before she reached out to accept it. Drake shot Ellie a hesitant look as it changed hands; he must have spotted the posh floral display worthy of a five-star hotel in the entrance. "My folks send their regrets."

Drake was being polite about his parents' absence. Ellie's mom had planned this party without checking to see if the date worked for them, and Beth and Robert were already booked for a nonrefundable vacation. Beth had gone back and forth for weeks on whether to skip it, but Drake insisted they go. The Nielsons rarely broke their routine or left town. The fact that their "trip of a lifetime" was a lodge three hours from home with "a really decent dinner buffet" was proof of this.

"Thank you, Drake," Sandra cooed. "Come in. Make yourselves at home."

Ellie imagined that other adult children bounded up the stairs to their old bedrooms or leaped onto worn-in sofas to indulge in their favorite comfort movies. Instead, she froze in the entrance like a stranger hypnotized by the smell of crisp apple. Two caterers in black uniforms stood at the heart of the cream-colored furniture in the formal living room, waiting for more guests to arrive and grab their crudités. A bar was stacked high with crystal glassware, and NEGRONI was written underneath the hand-painted sign announcing a signature drink.

"I didn't know you liked a Negroni," Drake said.

"I don't," Ellie told him. She turned to make sure her mom was out of earshot. Sandra was already greeting a few more guests at the door. As Ellie watched the room begin to fill up with vaguely familiar people, she wished she'd taken a more active role in planning this event. Jen, Marc, and their other close friends weren't anywhere to be found. She also felt the absence of her immediate family. Ben would have a lot to say about the decorative needle-felted gourds on the mantelpiece and the home's many shades of white. "Look at this, sis," she pictured him telling her. "Once again, we return to our former abode—the love child of a Nancy Meyers movie and a Restoration Hardware catalog."

Ben would've made this party fun. Even her dad's presence would've made it interesting.

But the only faces Ellie recognized were her uncle David, who liked to brag about stocks, a few casual childhood friends, and her cousins Martha and Jonathan—fraternal twins, both attorneys. Many of her mom's esteemed aquaintances from the country club chattered around the room about things like pickleball fundraisers. The party had almost nothing to do with the two of them. It was a pageant of sorts—a chance for her mom to paint the illusion of closeness with her daughter in front of a crowd.

A glass clinked at the top of the stairs. "Hello, all," Sandra said. She brushed her hair off her shoulders. It had been dyed blonde for so many years that Ellie didn't know its true shade. "Thank you for being here. And for helping me eat all the little meatballs and cheese circling around. It's an important job, you all have here today." Her mom's friends laughed at this humor attempt. Ellie was certain Sandra had avoided the meatballs and cheese entirely, nibbling at a few briny olives to fit in. "To those of you who don't know her, I wanted to introduce my daughter, Ellie." Sandra gestured to her from the top of the stairs. "Ellie is an esteemed writer. And a television host." Sandra cued the group to "ooo" and "ahh" with the appropriate wave of her hand; she could be such an entertainer in public.

"And next to Ellie is her fiancé, Drake," Sandra said. Drake nodded hello. "He works in construction." Ellie bit her lip hard. The way she had knighted them by their jobs set her on edge. Plus, the way Sandra said it didn't even make what he did clear; he was a project manager *for* construction sites. He also hated his current job and constantly spoke about the business he wanted to start. Ellie feared her mom's introduction would bring all that up, but Drake seemed unbothered.

"They met . . ." Sandra glanced down at Ellie, searching for clues. Did she even know the story of how they met? Ellie wasn't sure she had ever asked. "Well, I'll let you tell it."

"We met at a bar," Drake said. Everyone gathered in the formal living room and kitchen turned their attention from the stairwell to where Ellie and Drake stood in the foyer.

"We met at a lounge," Ellie clarified. For some reason, she felt the word *lounge* would help this group. It surprised her that she cared.

"We did," Drake agreed, giving her a funny look on this point. "I went there all the time because I liked how the bar... lounge... was always the same. It felt familiar. And then, Ellie walked in one night. There was this shift in me, I guess. We sat and talked for hours. I walked her home in the rain." He cleared his throat and held his hands up. "Just a walk, I swear."

The crowd laughed a little at what was implied. Ellie was impressed by the way Drake took the stage, especially since his group gatherings rarely extended beyond dinners with their friends or his parents.

"I don't like walking much," Ellie explained, "or the rain. But I agreed to a *long* walk in the *rain* after talking to Drake because I wanted to spend more time with him. I was worried at first. He seemed too perfect. You know? Like, what is this guy hiding?" This confession was met with a polite collective laugh. "But once I got to know him, I realized he's not perfect at all. He's a total goofball, this one. I love him a lot," she said. "And that's the way that we met."

Sandra blotted her eyes with a handkerchief; the story had affected her. Was she happy for her little girl or sad that her daughter hadn't ended up with someone in finance? "To Ellie and Drake," she said.

Glasses raised around the room. Ellie felt herself performing. She couldn't help it. The need to be on was in her blood. She didn't want any of this fanfare on her wedding day—the forced camaraderie, or the reminder that key members of her family wouldn't be there.

For about the thousandth time, Ellie daydreamed of eloping.

After an hour of talking to the guests they didn't know, Ellie took Drake's hand and led him upstairs for a moment of calm. Her bedroom had been untouched for years. Styles clashed in every corner. The base layer was feminine and frilly, but little touches of Ellie's taste shined through. Sandra had never understood her poster for a band with Death in its title or the collection of vintage paper moon portraits that hung across from the canopy bed.

Ellie sat down on the thick white rug as Drake surveyed the room. On this floor, Ben had cracked open a root beer, used the can to cool down her ears, and pierced them. On the mattress behind Ellie, her first boyfriend, Charlie, had furrowed his forehead while trying to do the homework she had finished in minutes. On her tall ceiling was the floral glass pendant that her dad had affixed. Ellie recalled a rare, good conversation between them as he moved up a tall ladder. She read him a story she wrote, and he laughed at all the right places. When William climbed back down, he looked at her with new eyes, signaling she'd graduated from a child to a peer.

"Nice space," Drake said. "It's very you. And also somehow . . . not at all you."

Ellie agreed. Being there brought back so many memories. But the memories were vague outlines, nothing like the real and vivid scenes she'd encountered at the cinema. They fell away quickly.

"Do you think we should get back downstairs?" Drake asked, thumbing through a stack of her old DVDs. "People are here for us, you know."

Ellie made no move to get up from the floor. "They're here for my mom," she said. "This is basically a big show-off for her. And what's with the Negronis, anyway?"

Drake shot Ellie a look of warning. He was so polite that it pained him when she began to tread into rude territory, especially when it involved her family. "Ellie—"

"It was nice of her to try," Ellie told him. "But this day is more proof she doesn't get us at all. What we like. Who we like. Everything Sandra Marshall does is about looking good to other people."

Someone cleared their throat in the doorway.

Ellie turned to find the subject of their conversation staring at her.

"Mom."

"I wanted to see if you two would join us for dessert," Sandra said, without acknowledging what she'd overheard.

"Sure." Ellie nodded. Then, "Sorry. I shouldn't have said that. I didn't mean—"

Sandra had already turned to go back downstairs. For the rest of her party, her mom seemed unfazed. Kind, even. She bragged about Ellie's achievements. She recounted stories Ellie had told her about Drake. The evening was more enjoyable than she'd anticipated. It felt good to be in her mom's warmth.

"Thanks for all this, Mom," Ellie said when things were wrapping up. "I liked the party. You've been really generous."

Drake went to gather their things, leaving the two of them alone. "Well, you know that I'm not one to make a scene," Sandra said.

There it was. Ellie was the *scene*. She was the one who stirred up the drama. It was Sandra's job to make the family more presentable. The giant photo hanging above them on the wall was proof of this. In it, her dad sported a rare smile, and Ben had a carefree arm tossed around Sandra. Ellie was in front, all her teenage whims set aside in lieu of temporary good behavior. She wore a pink—a carnation-pink—dress.

No one who entered the house Sandra now lived in alone would've guessed that the seemingly happy group had fallen apart. The photo gutted Ellie with a small knife. "Hard to believe that's us," she said. "Sometimes, I don't remember who I was back then."

"I remember, Ellie," her mom said. "You think you're so different. But you're just the same."

The tone had an accusation to it. For once, Ellie wished they could air things out and talk about everything her mom blamed her for. Everything that kept them apart. But before she could tread into those treacherous waters, Drake returned to her side.

"Ready to go?"

"Yeah." She gave her mom's shoulder a gentle touch. "I'll see you in a few weeks for our holiday dinner, Mom?" Ellie asked, even though she suspected that after today, they would push their next encounter out as far as possible. Sometimes, it was easier to pretend.

"Of course," Sandra told her. She didn't seem mad, exactly. She was more removed. Maybe that was worse. "I'll be in touch."

The door clicked shut. Drake walked Ellie through the leaves and back to the car. As they were driving away, Ellie got lost in her private world. Today had proven yet again that she excelled at making a mess of things. She feared this would become a repeat of the night with the waitress exchange and that Drake would try to peel back more layers and family secrets that she didn't know how to answer.

"Important thought," Drake started, and Ellie waited for his prying question.

"Maybe we should do a canopy bed in our room? Frilly. Fringe?"

Ellie cracked a smile. "Yeah. Of course, Nielson," she said. "I'm a hundred percent on board with you."

7

It was Saturday again, the night that the manager was due back from the beach. But instead of going to the cinema as planned, Drake dragged Ellie to their friends' house deep in the suburbs for Scrabble. Hours had passed since they'd first sat on the corduroy sectional set Jen found at a furniture warehouse. "It's affordable," she'd gushed, "and comfy, too." The knot forming in Ellie's back was proof that only the first part was true.

"*Vex*," Marc announced at the start of the game. He'd laid down his tiles almost instantly, but that was classic Marc—quick to show his cards or his feelings. He'd been that way in all the years Ellie had known him.

The last *ten years*. It was hard for Ellie to believe that Jen and Marc had been together that long. She could still remember the night they met at the tiki bar—layers of dark rum, frozen pineapple whirling inside blenders, and chatty mechanical parrots swinging overhead. Jen had bumped right into Marc while he carried a fishbowl drink to his friends. He'd spilled only a little, but she insisted on buying him a new one. Marc told her, within minutes, that he'd never met anyone like her. That brief encounter had led to this: Jen and Marc having a home together and a baby on the way. It always amazed Ellie how one tiny choice, one tiki drink, could change a life.

Jen tossed a cozy wrap over her maternity yoga set and kicked her platform indoor slippers up onto the matching ottoman. The slippers were one of the many free samples she was given as the marketing director of an eco-friendly footwear line. They were silly-looking, she admitted earlier that night, but it wouldn't be very eco-friendly to throw away a free sample.

Jen leaned closer to the board to inspect Marc's word. "*Vex?*" she asked. Her right eye twitched. It was always the sweet ones who treated board games like Olympic Qualifiers. "Seriously?"

Yes, vex, Ellie thought to herself. *To cause distress*. Vex, what Drake was doing to her now, putting up obstacles to avoid the thing Ellie needed most. She'd even scrawled the cinema visit on the calendar of cats floating through space that held his schedule. That morning, Ellie noticed Drake had made one of his own additions beneath a Ragdoll cat cartwheeling through the Big Dipper.

Game Night!

Ellie wanted to press the issue. But with Drake's resistance, she needed to be strategic. She had to wait for her moment.

"*Vex* is a real word," Ellie said, directly to Drake. He missed the barb.

"Well, *wine* is a word, too." Jen chimed in. She borrowed the first *e* from Ellie's *ephemeral* to spell out *w-i-n-e*, then pushed herself to stand, fighting against the wobbles of the third trimester. "Speaking of, let's pour some. I'm going to drink vicariously through all of you."

"I'd love a glass," Drake said, sinking deeper into the couch. He was so carefree here, in the land of layered rugs and a four-wick Harvest Apple candle. "I could use a little liquid inspiration for this next round."

"I'll come with you," Ellie told Jen. She could sense the conversation heading toward another question-and-answer session between Marc and Drake about plumbing or backsplash tile. Drake was an expert in the finishes of these types of homes, despite his total aversion to working for a planned community.

"I feel like I'm going to fly away," Jen said. She steadied herself on Ellie's arm. "Like a hot-air balloon." Jen swung the door to the kitchen open. Everything still had the new-house smell that clung to Drake's clothes after a day at work. Ellie missed when Jen and Marc lived a short drive away in a two-bedroom apartment with a rooftop pool and a neighbor who was always barbecuing something that shouldn't be barbecued in the common area. When Jen brought Ellie here for the first time and chauffeured her around the pristine suburban streets with a borrowed golf cart, it was hard to accept that this was her friend's new life.

"I can't believe I forgot *vex*," Jen confided behind the kitchen counter. "Of course, *vex*. Like, Marc vexed me by forgetting to pick up snacks. He drove past the grocery store without grabbing guac. I swear, things were getting Shakespearian before you came over."

The clock on the kitchen oven was screaming at Ellie. *10:50*, it bellowed. They could still make it to the cinema in time. Therein lay the beauty of a midnight movie.

"It's late," Ellie said as three wineglasses clicked onto the granite kitchen island. She offered an exaggerated yawn to drive home her point. "Are you sure you don't want us to go?" Ellie hoped that her best friend would kick her out of her house. *Her best friend*. These were her friends—Drake's friends now, too, of course—but Ellie had known them first. She was being petty. The house, the Scrabble, the vexing. She loved Jen and normally wouldn't want to be anywhere else. Tonight was the exception.

"Oh heck, no," Jen said. "I slept all day. I'm—well we're—ready to party."

Ellie nodded and tried to get comfortable on a leather farmhouse stool that kept chiropractors in business. There was that critical voice again. The cinema was making her desperate, moody.

Jen reached for a baguette and a butter dish engraved with two bears holding hands. "I guess we'll have bread. There aren't any snacks, so this is the next best thing. I'm the one who has to carry a baby. How hard is it to procure carbohydrates? It seems not that hard. Anyway, I'm blabbering, Ellie. I am blabbering because I have no updates." She was playing with her hair too much, a tell that she was working something out. "All people want to know about lately is if I'm having ginger chews."

"Ginger chews?" Ellie asked.

"They're supposed to help with all the stomach stuff in pregnancy."

"Do they?"

"Shit, no." Jen put her hand on her stomach. "Sorry," she whispered. The apology was for the baby. "Also, everybody asks *how are you* all the time. Just *how are you*, in text form. I've run out of things to share. I love talking about baby stuff. I do. I just miss having actual stories to tell."

Ellie fished around for a response. All the baby talk made her pour more wine in her glass before she was even a few sips in. Drake wanted kids; he always stopped to talk to babies at restaurants. He'd make an amazing dad, Ellie knew. She was worried about herself. Kids were a great idea for someday, but the longer she waited, that someday became imminent. Someday was a frightening knock on the door, a pest control person with a special onetime offer or one of those high school kids wrapped up in a magazine scam. Ellie was terrified to answer the knock. Was she capable, after everything that had happened, of being responsible? Of being someone's mom?

"Please tell me something good," Jen begged. "Tell me about dancing on bar tops."

"Which bar top?"

"Any of them, dude. We used to be wild."

"Used to," Ellie said. "Life's different now."

"Yeah." Jen sighed. "I miss it. Our antics. Your myriad of suitors. That's a good Scrabble word, isn't it? *Myriad.*"

"There weren't that many suitors."

"Oh please. You collected suitors like I collected Dooney & Bourke knockoffs."

Ellie glanced at the time. It was 10:55. They were thirty minutes away from the bottom of the alley, which meant Ellie needed to start wrapping things up and get Drake out the door. Because, if not tonight, when? Because who knew how long a magical theater would stand for? Because what if Ellie somehow missed the exact thing she was desperate to see? "Do you ever just . . ."

"What?" Jen leaned forward, ready to nosh on any gossip or secret served up.

"Do you ever wish you could relive your past? Not just talk about it, but actually go back in time and witness the person you were?"

Jen bit her lip. "You seem kind of serious tonight. Is something going on, Ellie?"

Ellie considered shading in the rest of her thoughts. She shared everything with Jen, but she knew she couldn't admit where her head was at that moment. *There's this magical theater*, she would begin. Even for someone whose bedroom bookshelf was lined with smoldering adult fairy tales, there was only so far that a person's imagination could carry them. Jen would have to see the cinema to believe it.

Suddenly, an idea struck Ellie. What if Jen did see it?

Drake would be furious. But having their friends come along would give them even more backup. Marc and Drake could parse through facts together. Maybe the extra company would make Drake feel more secure. The four of them could connect over this for the rest of their lives, beyond Connect 4. Conversations would always cut deeper.

Ellie tore off a bite of the bread. She spent forever chewing, then grabbed her wine to wash it down, wine she could quickly feel coming back up her nose.

"What is so funny?" Jen asked.

"The bread . . . It's so hard." Ellie laughed. "I think I broke a tooth."

Jen grabbed a piece and crunched down. "This is terrible." She rubbed the side of her jaw. "We've got seriously stale bread. We've got bad games. I think I hate Scrabble."

"Me, too," Ellie agreed. "And I'm the target audience."

Jen spun the bear butter holder around. "Right now, I would give just about anything to do something different." She was begging for an adventure. There might be consequences, Ellie knew. Marc, practical as he was, might further convince Drake that the whole thing was dangerous. Jen might actually inflate and blow away out of pure shock. But the good that could come was bigger, she decided. Jen needed an adventure almost as much as Ellie needed the truth.

"Let's go out," she heard herself saying.

"Tonight?" Jen asked. She snapped her fingers and pointed them in Ellie's direction. "Hmmm . . . I don't know. I've got *Dateline* to catch up on."

"What happened to your need for a good story?"

Jen cracked a smile. She fanned her hands out under her face in mock mischief. "What did you have in mind, Miss Ellie?"

"Well, I know a place," Ellie told her. "A place that outdoes dancing on any bar top."

8

Ellie learned that night that Drake was a bad actor. When she paused their game to suggest taking their friends on an adventure, he bent over with a stomachache. She wrestled him into Marc's car as he rattled off excuses to head home instead: work, then a possible power outage in their area despite near-perfect weather. Drake brooded as they strapped themselves into the backseat and listened to Jen and Marc debate which color to paint the nursery.

"I'm thinking sage," Jen said. The car backed out of the driveway.

"Isn't sage a vegetable?" Marc asked. His eyes flicked over to the rearview mirror.

"It's an herb," she explained. "And a color."

Ellie had plugged the pin for the alley into Marc's phone. They rounded a corner and slid past a small park that looked like it had never seen a person. The subdivision was asleep, except for a couple in matching reflector jackets walking a fluffy white dog. Knowing that they were sneaking out and breaking their friends' curfew gave Ellie a tiny thrill, until she was interrupted by the chirp of her phone.

Seriously? Drake had texted. Ellie could feel the hostility from the other side of the car.

Three typing dots followed. Thinking, thinking.

You couldn't wait?

Ellie typed: *You wanted backup.*
This is a bad idea, Ellie.
Three more dots.
A BAD idea.
You agreed to talk to the manager tonight, she replied.
We could go a different night.
You said we would do this.

Ellie was sweating. Marc was a temperature deviant, she'd noticed. He kept the heat too high in the winter and the air too cool in the summer. She rolled her window down as they flew past a flurry of big-box stores, relieved by a burst of air.

"I'm really glad we're getting out," Jen said in the front seat.

See? Ellie might've typed if they were still texting, but she didn't want to start up a debate again, so she switched her phone to silent and tucked it inside her purse.

"Ice cream is a good idea," Drake said.

Jen wasn't good at hiding disappointment. "The mystery adventure is . . . ice cream?" she asked, twisting to face the backseat.

"No," Ellie insisted. "No. The adventure is not ice cream."

"I can always go for ice cream," Marc said. With his free hand, he took a bite of the stale bread he'd packed for the drive. "We're running low on good snacks."

Jen pouted.

"I just don't love Ellie's plan," Drake told them. From across the way, Ellie could see the warped skyline reflected in his eyes. Sometimes, at night, she watched herself there, two tiny, confused specks on fixed television screens. "I don't want to do Ellie's thing," he insisted.

Jen turned toward Marc. "The kids are fighting."

"Must be all that wedding planning," Marc added. "It gets to you, doesn't it? The spreadsheets, the phone calls, those glass jars—"

"Mason jars," Jen clarified. "They're called mason jars."

"We're not fighting," Drake and Ellie spat out at the same time.

Then, Drake alone, too scared to look at her, said, "I just think that Ellie's idea is dangerous."

"Dangerous!" Jen said. "Well, we like danger."

Marc grunted in the driver's seat.

"But it's like, a safe danger, I assume?" Jen clarified.

Drake sighed. "It's more, like, mind danger."

"It's safe," Ellie told them. "It's just hard to explain."

As they parked near the bottom of the alley and piled out, Ellie's sense of wonder took over. Drake left Ellie to open her own door. Jen mentioned how she'd been wanting to come to this part of town; she'd heard there was a shop that sold caramel apples with complicated flavors.

Ellie headed the pack. They started up the hill, passing the leftover café chairs and trekking beyond Mae's Famous Scoops, which was still lit up for late-night stragglers. Drake made attempts to veer their group off course, but Ellie had her eye on the target. When she neared the cinema, though, her throat hollowed out. She couldn't move.

Something had changed. Something was wrong.

Maybe, she told herself, the cinema was just closed for the night. Old theaters closed all the time for special events or screenings. But when she landed there, square in front of the building, it was much more closed than she'd anticipated. Nothing was as it had been a week earlier. Horror settled in.

The marquee that spelled out *The Story of You* was now empty. The ticket boy was nowhere in sight, his booth covered in weathered graffiti. Years of rain had pelted the plywood covering the entry doors. Through the slats, Ellie could see the lobby was a universe of decay. Thick industrial plastic coated the floors, and a big black ceiling opening where the chandelier used to be now housed a galaxy of dust. There was so much dust that looking at it made her sneeze.

The footfalls of the other three landed behind her.

"Wow," Marc said. "Cobweb central, huh?"

"It's like a prom for spiders in there," Jen joked.

Ellie turned to face them. She met Drake's eyes first, and his expression wasn't what she expected. Drake was placid as a lake. He must have been telling himself that none of it was real. To him, what they'd encountered was a bad dream.

"Uh, this isn't the actual stop," Drake said quickly. "We found this place the other night." Ellie joined the row of her friends and the four of them gazed upon the decayed marvel. An open wound. "Ice cream," Drake said. "Mae's Famous Scoops is the best." They had never been to Mae's, but the shop would be open quite late. Ellie remembered the lights had just turned off as they'd climbed up the alley the week before. "Their scoops are so good, you could almost call them dangerous," he quipped.

Inside the ice cream shop, coins rattled in the miniature jukebox at their bright pink booth. Like Jen's house, Mae's was the type of place Ellie would have loved on any other night. Jen and Marc ordered a banana split to share, and Drake went with his trusty mint chocolate chip. Ellie watched the door waiting for a sign—the ticket boy or someone who came in claiming to be the cinema's manager, but they were the last customers. The night had spun in Drake's favor. He was in the middle of telling a story she'd already heard about a plumber acquaintance who didn't know how to fix sinks. When his eyes caught hers across the table, Ellie swore they said, "I told you so."

"You were right, Drake," Jen said later as they climbed back into the car. "That wasn't just ice cream. That was amazing," which made Ellie feel impossibly sad. Her friend didn't know what could've been, what she'd missed, the life-altering experience they might have shared. They were all strapped in the car again with the headlights on, ready to pull off the curb, when Ellie was struck by a thought.

"I forgot something in Mae's," she said. "A scarf."

"You weren't wearing a scarf," Jen reminded her.

"It was minimal. You wouldn't have even noticed it. I'll be back in a second." She flung the door open and hopped out of the car without permission. Drake didn't follow, so Ellie opened his door and made a demand. "You're coming with me."

Once they were on their own, he repeated what Jen had said. Ellie hadn't worn a scarf.

"A car full of scarf police."

"What are we doing?" Drake's hands were in his pockets. She sensed his mind was already back in the suburbs. "We just proved that it wasn't real," he said. "The theater was never real, Ellie. We imagined it that night. Okay?"

Ellie ignored him. She was on a mission, moving past the café tables and beyond the now-locked doors at Mae's. Nearing the cinema, she discovered that the theory she'd pieced together was correct.

When they saw the resplendent building again, Ellie's world turned Technicolor. Everything was restored, all the glittering lights, the marquee, and even the chandelier inside, to exactly what it had been the week before. No plywood. No dust. "*The Story of You* is only for you," Ellie marveled, breathless and alive.

"What in the world—"

Ellie ran up to the ticket booth and knocked on the glass window. The ticket boy popped up like a doll inside a wooden crank box.

"I didn't think you were coming." He sighed.

Ellie stole a glance at Drake's watch. It was two minutes past midnight.

"This was just . . ." Drake stepped back and took in the restored theater. Ellie sensed a shift. His need for concrete answers about how a place could simply undo decades of wear in a matter of minutes had grown bigger, perhaps insurmountable. One unexplainable event was mind-blowing. But a second unexplainable event had tipped him over the edge. He would not, Ellie sensed, be able to let it go this time. "I thought," he gasped. "I thought we made this up. But this place was, like, shuttered," he said. "This can't be . . . What is happening?"

"*The Story of You* is only for you," the ticket boy told him.

"Why does everybody keep saying that?" Drake asked.

"It was in the cartoon the first night," Ellie reminded him with a hand on his shoulder. "Meaning, this place only opens for us." They had tested the other two instructions the first night. The third rule explained in the video was also true.

Drake darted up to the brass doors and started to touch them like a toddler, only believing things to be real if he could feel them. With Drake occupied, Ellie used the opportunity to sneak a question to the ticket boy in a low whisper.

"Hey, if we skip the movie tonight, do we lose a ticket?"

"No," he said, staring at her like she'd uttered the dumbest thing on earth.

Drake muttered the word *how* as he continued to sniff around the entrance. Then, he strode over in giant steps and pulled Ellie aside. "We're going to go in there," he swallowed. "I need to know what's happening right now."

"We'll come back next week," Ellie said casually.

"What . . . no. Why?"

Ellie waved goodbye to the ticket boy and began to pull Drake down the alley. "We need to get back to our friends. They've been waiting too long anyway."

"But—"

"We don't want to be the jerks keeping a pregnant person out past bedtime, do we?" Ellie asked, yanking his arm forward harder. "Also, Nancy needs us. She's been home alone a long time. And this theater isn't going anywhere."

On this note, Drake stopped to turn around. "I mean, it literally just did."

Ellie sighed. "Look, we know that it opens every week on Saturday night for us. So, we'll take the next few days, write down all our questions, and come up with a plan. You don't want to forget to ask the manager something important, do you?"

"No," Drake agreed. His shoulders relaxed in response to Ellie's rational suggestion. The way he was hypnotized by the new development worked in her favor. He didn't realize she was playing a card. If they spoke to the manager while Jen and Marc waited for them at the bottom of the alley, there wouldn't be time to watch the movie. If Drake got his answers, she would have no reason to bring him back there.

And after everything they'd just seen, Ellie realized, Drake needed answers more than ever.

9

Drake suggested tacos on the drive back from Jen and Marc's house. Ellie was hungry, too. Her defeat had kept her from ordering a scoop at Mae's, and the sight of a glowing taco sign made her stomach growl.

"Fantastic Taco," Ellie read as the car dove under a spinning hard shell and fell into line. Drake's fingers drummed on the wheel. "Clearly, it's not a *fantastic* taco. Although Questionable Taco doesn't have the same ring to it—"

"Ellie," Drake said, dragging her name out. "Focus. We just saw a place undo decades of damage within, like, minutes."

She had been there for it. She didn't need a reminder. What Ellie needed was a way to crawl inside Drake's brain and have a look around. She sensed that his thirst for answers about the cinema would be enough to get him back there, but she wanted one more tool in her arsenal: a way to convince him to stay and watch the movies. "Tell me what you're feeling, Drake," she said as the car inched forward. "What *really* makes you so nervous about of all this?"

He tsked. "Well, for one, this place seems to magically disappear and reappear." The cinema hadn't technically disappeared. Ellie wasn't going to point that out. "But, it's more than that." She gave him the space to carry out the thought without interrupting. "If I'm being honest, I'm also afraid that we'll see something bad in our past." Drake glanced her way. "I mean, what if I see you having sex?"

"You see that all the time—"

"With someone else, I mean."

Ellie feigned an aghast expression. "It's not that kind of a theater."

Drake's foot released its hold on the brake, and the truck rumbled forward. "Careful," Ellie snapped. They stopped inches from a minivan filled with teens late for their curfew.

"What if you loved one of those . . . sex people?"

"What if I loved a sex person?" Ellie crossed her arms over her chest. "Well, I didn't. You, Drake, are actually my first big love." Surprise took over his face, followed by something else. Pride. Then, only because the question had presented itself, Ellie asked, "What, did you have some running-through-a-field type love story before me that you never happened to mention?"

The fact that Ellie hadn't loved anyone before Drake was unusual at her age, she knew. The idea of romantic love had reminded her of two gorillas she'd seen at a zoo. After Ellie observed them for a while, the female and male gorilla had started a food fight of sorts. She thought those gorillas represented what she had heard about marriage. Resentment built up as people spent a lot of years stuck together. Eventually, they started to throw food at each other.

Now that she was engaged to someone she loved, Ellie was much more hopeful.

Drake still hadn't answered her question.

"So, you had some big love story before me, huh?" She crawled her hands up his back, deliberately playful. The topic of their past relationships was one Drake had avoided from the beginning. He wanted to focus on *them*, he told her on their third or fourth date. It seemed novel at the time. Now, she couldn't help but notice how quickly Drake changed the subject.

"It's just . . . What if I did something that would make you see me differently? Like, what if I went cow tipping?"

"You would remember cow tipping. The cows are fine." The car lunged forward again.

"I mean, the equivalent of cow tipping," Drake said. "What if I made fun of someone? Broke some girl's heart."

Ellie squinted to try to see the menu, searching for a palatable option. If anyone were tipping cows, it would've been her.

"You have to admit the cinema is amazing," Ellie told him, switching gears.

Drake sat with this a minute, then nodded in agreement. "Of course, it's amazing," he said finally. "I mean, I was a baby. I could see my mom again—young—and all the goofy expressions I made. So yeah, it's amazing."

Ellie was winning him over.

"But look, things are really good with us now. Right?" Drake asked. They were, but he didn't wait for her response. "I don't want to go hunting around our pasts to find something that messes with our future. What if we get into some big fight about what we see—something that doesn't even matter now?"

They pulled up to the window, and Drake handed his credit card over, then set two lukewarm tacos on Ellie's lap. He had a point, she knew. The cinema could change the way they saw each other. It could put a rift between them, bringing the past right home when they were supposed to be moving forward. But as terrified as she was for him to observe her life before they met, her need to know what she'd forgotten was stronger.

The taco verdict, Ellie decided after the first bite, was "less than fantastic." Tomatoes spilled out onto the wrapper as she ate. They kept the conversation light while driving home, but Ellie wasn't fully paying attention. In the driveway, Drake unbuckled his seat belt, opened Ellie's door, and gave her a look she didn't quite recognize.

"For the record, you are my only big love story, Ellie," he said. "That's why I want to protect this."

The outdoor lights were dead, which was an unusual oversight on Drake's part. Ellie lost track of his face in the dark. Their boots crunched over the stone path and up the front steps. Then, back inside the house, the same look she'd noticed before on Drake's face came into view again. She could see it now, for exactly what it was.

He'd just lied to her.

Ellie's insomnia was relentless that night. Drake was hiding something. She knew that anytime he concealed the truth, he was trying to avoid hurting her. But as Ellie had told him and displayed so many times, she wasn't a jealous person. Life didn't allow for a truly clean slate; people came with fascinating, complicated histories. People including herself. Whatever Drake was so nervous about her seeing, Ellie could handle.

How could she prove this to him?

Things would've been so much easier if there wasn't a wedding on the horizon. Labels and rituals meant something to Drake. If she were already his wife, already committed to him officially, she had the sense he'd be more willing to go to the cinema together. *If only*, she thought, for the hundredth time. *If only* they had just eloped in Vegas a few months earlier, Drake would have more confidence that no matter what Ellie saw, she wasn't going anywhere.

"I think we should elope," Ellie had suggested as they dragged their suitcases over tired carpet and past a row of slot machines blinking a rainbow of lights.

"You're serious?" They stepped onto the elevator. Drake rested his weight against a poster advertising a Salisbury steak special. The steak was gray and lined with wear. Ellie wished she hadn't let Drake choose a hotel with a gray steak special. He'd wanted to plan the trip himself in honor of their engagement. It was thoughtful, so she'd let him.

The elevator dinged. Ellie followed Drake to a room at the end of the hallway. She was serious, she insisted. The possibility of getting hitched without the hassle of other people was tempting, wasn't it? Drake considered the question as they unzipped their bags and swung the drapes open, revealing floor-to-ceiling views of the Strip under the relentless afternoon sun.

"Let's do it then," he said, looking out the window.

"Really?" she asked.

He pulled her close. "If it means I get to marry you sooner, I'm in."

The chapel they found was a retro white church illuminated by two halves of a neon heart that bounced together to form a whole. Ellie skipped to its pulse across the parking lot. A woman who had taken a smokey eye too far ushered them inside and situated them at the back of the room to witness drunk humans—potentially business colleagues—make a huge mistake.

Ellie's excitement shifted to doubt as she looked around. The stained glass windows were actually plastic. The Styrofoam columns near the fabric-floral archway had taken both too much and not enough inspiration from the Roman Colosseum. Then there was the soundtrack—were those organs playing? Elvis moved his way up the aisle and onto a small elevated stage where the happy couple stood awaiting their nuptial king.

"I know I suggested this," Ellie told Drake under her breath. The groom stumbled. The bride, who was confirmed to be his colleague, snickered in response.

"Yeah?" Drake asked.

Ellie flattened out the wrinkles on her thrifted wedding dress, which they'd picked up hours earlier. "I don't think this is right."

Drake's face fell a few stories. "You don't think . . . getting married is right?"

"Not in this venue," Ellie said. As if to prove her statement, the organ music stopped, and Elvis started to sing and sway.

"Who cares about the venue?" Drake insisted. "We're getting married." He kissed her cheek. "That's all that matters."

"Well, maybe I don't want to do it this way," Ellie said, firmer this time. In theory, Vegas was the perfect situation for a wedding—there was no one around to stir things up and nothing to go wrong. But Drake deserved more. She knew he dreamed of elaborate speeches and rehearsal dinners, of passed hors d'oeuvres. He'd once used the word *showstopping* in reference to their first dance. She wanted to give him all of that and more. Still, he looked startled by her words.

"Why not?" he asked.

"Because this place is terrible," Ellie pointed out. "And also, you're dressed like a walking mall kiosk." Being in Vegas brought out Drake's shopper alter ego she'd never met before. Since their arrival, he'd purchased two fake designer wristwatches, a gold muscle tank Ellie hoped he would quickly come to regret, and a blended cocktail attached to a cheap beaded necklace.

Drake's teeth clenched so tightly together that when he blew air out, it formed a whistle. "I want to marry you, Ellie. Please tell me you want to marry me."

She had never given Drake any reason to doubt she wanted to marry him. Ellie scooted to fully face him. "Of course I want to marry you. Look, I'll marry you wherever you want," she told him. "And you know I love the kitsch. But are you sure this is what *you* want?"

Elvis hit a piercing high note that made them push back in the pew. Ellie watched Drake's eyes move around the room, from the Styrofoam columns to the artwork that belonged inside a cheesy Italian restaurant. "Why are there artichokes on the wall?" he asked.

"Those are flowers, Drake." She took his hand. "But do you

really want to be playing the 'flower or artichoke' game at our wedding?"

His slow nod turned into a fast, decisive one. "Okay. It isn't right."

Before leaving the chapel, they claimed their complimentary photo shoot with Elvis. They had already paid for the wedding package, and they should at least have a way to commemorate it, Ellie insisted. Mostly, she wanted to lift Drake's mood and prove to him that the night wasn't a bust. So they joined Elvis at the staged photo area in front of a white limousine. Ellie set a rose in her mouth, Drake held her hand, and Elvis revealed a shiny gold flask in his pocket that gave away he was about to be off the clock.

"I'd never want to forget this," Ellie said. The photographer, who may have also been the chapel's owner, snapped away.

"Are you that drunk?" Drake asked.

"No!" Ellie said. "But you know what they say. What happens in Vegas—"

"Stays in Vegas," Drake finished as the final photo snapped.

Ellie jolted up in bed and flung the comforter off herself. *Vegas* was the answer to all their problems, wasn't it? Drake was worried about how she would react to his past, but the cinema could be their Vegas: whatever happened there could stay right there. They could simply watch the movies, and upon walking out, go about their lives as if none of it existed. And if they did this, Ellie could get the answers she so desperately needed, and it wouldn't have to impact their relationship.

Even better, they could experience each other's childhood memories. What went into a sly smile in a single photograph could be understood with deeper context. Ellie and Drake could hear the voice on the other side of the camera. They could see the foundation of the person they loved being built right before their eyes.

Photos. Photos would sell Drake on what she was thinking. He didn't stir when Ellie closed the bedroom door and tiptoed downstairs. It was five in the morning. She had plenty of time to dig around the garage before he'd wake up.

A cold gust flew across her shoulders as she opened the door and flicked on the light switch. The outdoor shelves were a mess of boxes; a downside to living in an old home was that it didn't come with much closet space. People in the past must have owned fewer things. That had been Ellie's philosophy for a while, too. *Throw it all away* was the mantra of her early twenties. If she could free herself from the heirlooms, photographs, and knickknacks that defined her back then, maybe she could move on from the pain.

But somewhere, more recently, regret had taken the place of her nonchalance. She began to mourn the physical objects she'd given away. Now their home brimmed with vintage items, other people's discards in need of safekeeping. A three-legged coffee table with a chipped top. Hundreds of matchbooks she never used. The white shag rug with a single missing square. Who had collected the scraps of Ellie's past? She hoped her things had found a good home as she stared up at the single cardboard box that housed all her childhood photos and videos.

MEMORIES, the lid read. She blew the dust off the top.

Within an hour, Ellie had tacked hundreds of old photos to their blank living room wall. Her hands moved over the glossy prints, mixing images from her own life chronologically with Drake's based on the pen-marked numbers lining the back of each one.

There was *Ellie's first day at school* when she wore a royal blue parka and a pair of silver clip-on earrings.

There was *Drake's eighth birthday* when he wore a robot suit made from cardboard boxes.

There was *Ellie's thirteenth birthday party* when Ellie sat in a sea of balloons wearing real earrings. By then, Ben had pierced her ears on her bedroom floor.

Next was *Nielson Family Christmas, 2002*. In a wide-framed shot, Drake sat next to a large red toy train that wound its way around a tall Christmas tree brushing up against the ceiling.

"What is all this?" Drake asked after he woke up and saw Ellie's wall. He'd walked right by her to make them coffee without noticing the new photo gallery in their living room and almost spilled his giant cup when he came back in to kiss her good morning.

"We were so focused on cow tipping that we missed the best parts," Ellie told him. "This, these kinds of moments, are the things we could see." Drake softened. He was getting closer to agreeing with her. She could feel it. "What if the theater is our Vegas?" she suggested.

"I don't get it." Drake bent down to look at a photo of Ellie on a skiing trip. She explained that they could experience the wonderful moments without the consequences of the bad ones. "You could have a second chance to see your first snow. Your first kiss. Your Forrest the Fox mascot costume. I mean, I could actually watch you as the school mascot—"

"You've chosen the worst possible memory to convince me with," Drake said, examining a row near the floor.

"We could agree to never talk about the cinema after we leave. Once the doors of the real world open back up, we can leave it all behind. Because what happens at the magic cinema stays at the magic cinema," she explained.

Drake considered the suggestion. He was staring at a photo of himself wearing ice skates. He pointed to it with a distinct fondness. "This was the year my dad built an ice rink by hand in the back of the condo," he told her. "My family didn't have a lot of money, but man. They knew how to make things special."

"Is that . . . a yes?" Ellie asked.

Finally, Drake gave a reluctant nod. "Yes, with a caveat."

"Of course," she agreed, nodding. Even though they weren't technically married yet, marriage was a compromise. Ellie knew she'd bent Drake in her direction, and she'd do anything she could to make him comfortable with going back.

"To do this right," Drake said, moving to the kitchen to track down pen and paper, "we're going to need some ground rules."

THE RULES

RULE ONE:
What happens at the cinema stays in the cinema, as discussed.

RULE TWO:
No one else can know about the cinema. They wouldn't believe it, anyway.

RULE THREE:
Yes, this means that Ellie cannot write about the cinema.

RULE FOUR:
Ellie and Drake will, no matter what, get married as planned. The wedding venue deposit has been paid, and that was expensive.

RULE FIVE:
Ellie and Drake will not go to the cinema alone. Movies should always be viewed with the other person there to eliminate secrets.

RULE SIX:
Ellie will not judge Drake for being a "total hopeless romantic" in the past.

RULE SEVEN:
Drake will not judge Ellie for her "interest in questionable men with even more questionable tattoos."

RULE EIGHT:
Ellie and Drake will return to the cinema every week until they use all ten tickets. This gives them plenty of time before the wedding to process what they've seen.

10

The next Saturday night, they found the cinema open again.
Round marquee bulbs hummed around the title—*The Story of You*—and cast a welcoming glow over the alley. Ellie peeked through the doors. The chandelier gleamed without a speck of dust in sight. Outside, the ticket boy was perched at the booth wearing his familiar white uniform and apathy. "That'll be ten dollars," he said, pulling the second movie ticket from each of their labeled boxes.

"Can we talk to the manager?" Drake asked as he gathered the bills from his wallet. "Before we watch."

The ticket boy fumbled around his desk for a pack of gum. He pulled one of the sticks out, set it between his teeth, and folded the silver wrapper into a sloppy 747. Eventually, he offered a heavy nod. "I'll have Natalie find you inside," he said, the echo of the speaker amplifying his annoyance.

Natalie wasn't who Ellie expected. She readied herself for another surly teenager or video store clerk who moonlit at a vintage theater. The person who surfaced behind the concession counter was a generation older than them and had the confident build of a stunt woman. She was ready to fight fires and villains in a billowing gold suit. The only thing interrupting all the gold was regal, wavy gray hair leading to a name tag that read *Natalie*, with a customizable section beneath the name where she'd written "Ask me about the beach."

"I heard you were looking for the manager?" Natalie asked. When she stepped out from behind the counter, Ellie's focus moved to her shoes. Natalie was wearing, along with the gold suit, a pair of white Chuck Taylors pulled fresh from the box.

They waited a beat too long to answer her question. Drake was stalling. Ellie was supposed to tee this discussion up, it seemed. Where could she possibly begin? "We were just curious about . . . you know," was where she landed.

"Yeah, I hear ya." Natalie sighed with her whole body, as if accepting her role in a fight sequence she'd ultimately leave unscathed. Another truck on fire, another damsel in distress, another day. "I know it's not great."

"What isn't great?" Drake asked.

"The popcorn." Natalie glanced over her shoulder to face the popcorn in question. The ticket boy had moved inside and was in the middle of preparing a fresh batch. He poured hot microwaved butter sauce over the kernels in a practiced zigzag. "It's an old machine and it comes with a lot of quirks. We think it might have belonged to a carnival in a past life." Ellie noticed some soft music emerging from the machine. It had the light tinkle of an ice cream truck.

"The popcorn is fine," Ellie said. "I mean, we haven't tried it, but I'm sure it's good." She could feel Drake's questions becoming more imminent.

"Phew. That's good to hear. I get riled up about the popcorn." Natalie propped her elbows on the counter behind her and leaned back, like she was still at the beach, with imaginary palm trees swaying above her toned arms and calves. Ellie guessed Natalie didn't worry about things like sweat, bugs, time-share presentations. "Well, what is it then? Is it the picture quality?"

Drake was about to burst. "We need to know why your movie theater is playing *our lives*. And why it only opens for us. And how it looks completely worn down one moment and then minutes later—"

"Okay. Wow." Natalie nodded. "Lots of questions." She tapped on her name tag. "You know what's great about the beach? Almost no questions. What was not great about the beach was the lobster. You'd think they'd do lobster well, being by the water, but it was fishy. *Fishy.*" Natalie curved back behind the counter to grab a nibble of the popcorn from the silver pail. "Uh-huh," she said, munching on a few kernels. Her face scrunched up, confirming her earlier assessment. "Speaking of fishy, you were too nice about this popcorn." She turned her attention to the ticket boy. "Not your fault, bud."

"The popcorn is fine!" Ellie and Drake insisted, in unison. Natalie drowned her sorrows with a shot of generic cola. After a sip, she smiled, wandered out from behind the counter and spread her hands like she was finally about to reveal something.

"Let's chat."

She waved for them to follow as she strode across the lobby and up the grand steps of the right-side stairwell, leading to a second level. They were climbing a towering, tiered cake. "By now, you've probably figured out that this movie theater isn't like other movie theaters you've visited," Natalie acknowledged. "We only open for one movie every Saturday at midnight, and that is *The Story of You.*"

"Yeah, we've noticed," Drake snapped. His need for information was insatiable.

"*The Story of You,*" Natalie said, "is a movie that combines the memories of its audience."

"Why are we the audience?" Drake asked.

Natalie paused halfway up the stairs and leaned forward to examine the subtext of their relationship, reading them less like an eye chart and more like a crystal ball. She didn't seem to find what she was looking for. "Well, maybe there's something you need to revisit. From your past. Something that's keeping you from moving forward?"

"No," Drake said, lightning fast.

Absolutely, Ellie thought. She swallowed and changed the subject to a less loaded one. "What about the tickets?" she asked. "Why are there only ten showings? I mean, watching someone's memories could be never-ending."

They were on the move again. At the top of the second level, Natalie peered over the banister. She seemed proud of the place, more the impassioned tour guide, less the employee. They were eye level with the chandelier. Each individual strand of soaring jewelry sparkled. Ellie joined her in appreciative silence, but Drake refused to settle down. He was a ball of chaos.

Natalie stepped back from the railing. "Have you ever seen *Miss Congeniality 2*?"

"*Armed and Fabulous*," Drake filled in.

"Right. Well, in *Miss Congeniality 2*, you don't see boring parts of Sandra Bullock's day, do you?"

"What?" Ellie and Drake asked, in unison, again.

"You see all the high stakes, right? But not once do you see Sandra reading the back of a cereal box to find out the iron content."

"Umm," Ellie started.

"When you go in there"—Natalie pointed to the auditorium—"you're only going to see cinematic parts of your lives. Things worthy of a big screen. For the two of you, that's ten tickets. For some people it's longer. Or shorter. Each movie is bound together by a theme, something like—"

"*Babies*," Ellie filled in. "That's the one we saw the other night."

"Exactly," Natalie replied, moving them to finish their ascent up the stairs.

With a little push, Natalie guided them inside the open doors of the balcony entrance. They had missed this second level of seating on their first visit. "This right here is the best spot in the house," she said. Ellie agreed. It felt more intimate than the rows down below. She liked being high up, slightly removed from the action. "Here's all you need to know," Natalie explained. "You want to watch the movie? You enter the auditorium where we are now. If you want to stop the movie and go to the bathroom, you exit to the lobby." Natalie pointed to the entrance line that separated the second-level lobby from the inside of the auditorium. "When you come back in, it'll pick up where you left off. Make sense?"

"Is it safe?" Drake needed to know.

"Movies are only dangerous when you overthink them," Natalie said.

"But back to my main question," Drake pushed. "How does any of this actually *work*?" He held his hand up to Natalie like he was about to touch her to see if she was an apparition.

"I'm just the manager." Natalie's tone was light. "Look, the magic of cinema is that it's supposed to leave you with questions," she said. "Go with it. Enjoy the show."

By the time Drake turned around to protest—and before either of them could ask her about the beach—Natalie was gone.

As soon as they found their seats, the cartoon hot dogs started to do the Charleston. Once they took a bow, a title appeared over the screen.

TICKET TWO: *SCHOOL*

Drake looked about ten now, and the little girl crying in the front row of the classroom had a hold on him. No one else bothered to check on her after the bell rang. Kids bumped through the rows of desks, their shoes squealing past cardboard dioramas and bad volcano projects. Then, Drake and the girl were alone.

"My mom cries sometimes, too," he said, pulling at the sleeves of his blue-striped shirt. "Usually about game shows. Seeing people bring home a new dishwasher makes her feel things." The girl sniffled and rubbed the tears off her porcelain cheeks. "Do you want to eat lunch together, Sarah?"

"Sure," Sarah said, gathering up an Everest of tissues.

At the cafeteria table farthest from the other kids, Sarah and Drake shared peanut butter sandwiches. Hers was messy, and Drake's came inside a brown paper bag decorated by hand-drawn balloons. He offered Sarah a bite of his off-brand chips, but she waved them away. "It's my clothes," she admitted, prying open the lid on a milk carton. The straw dove in through the open diamond. She took a tiny sip.

"What is?"

Sarah did a facepalm. "My clothes are why nobody got me a gift for Valentine's Day. They're all hand-me-downs." She gestured to her enormous overalls. A faded floral blouse was tucked into the sides of the denim. Most of the girls in their class had gotten gifts, she told him. There was something wrong with her.

"There's nothing wrong with you," Drake said. As quickly as he reached out to touch her shoulder, his hand jerked away. The gesture must have seemed too grown-up.

"Just look at Brittany Fields," Sarah lamented. They turned to study an energetic blonde girl in a short tartan skirt and strappy silver tank top.

"I like your clothes," Drake told her. Sarah took another swig of milk. "Boys are just dumb," he said.

"You're a boy," Sarah reminded him.

"Well, what's her name? The girl you need a gift for?" Drake's mom rolled down the driver's-side window and grabbed the cash canister from a long, clear bank tube. "Thank you," she shouted through the speaker, slurping down the remnants of an Arnold Palmer inside a Styrofoam cup.

"It's not for *a* girl," Drake clarified in the passenger seat. "I need to buy a gift for *all* the girls."

"All right," Beth told him with a wink. "As long as you can stick to the budget, kiddo."

One of the benefits of shopping late for the holiday was that the Valentine's gifts were already marked down at the store. Drake's budget was enough for every girl in his class to receive a single rose and a small box of chocolates. At home on his bedroom floor, he strapped a rose to each box with some leftover twine from his mom's crafting supplies.

The next day in class, he handed the boxes out. Crushes formed around the room as Drake moved through the rows. When he landed at Sarah's desk, she mouthed, "Thanks." A hand shot up at the back of the room.

"Yes, Billy?" the teacher asked.

"I just wanted to thank our class lover boy." Billy wielded a slow-clap, revealing sweat-stained pits. "Bravo, lover boy."

Lover boy. The word was flung like a boomerang around the classroom, into the halls, and became a chant. *Lover boy! Hey, lover boy. Move it, lover boy!* Drake ate his white-bread sandwich alone on the outskirts of the cafeteria. Sarah wouldn't even sit with him that day, perhaps fearing the social implications of attaching herself to the newest class outcast.

Snow fell onto the railroad tracks as Drake walked home after school. A train whistled in the distance. As he ventured onto Main Street, the yellow awning of his building, The Edison, stuck out in the frozen white world. Drake flung the door open and pounded up the carpeted brown stairs to his second-floor condo. His parents were playing dominoes at the old kitchen table where one of the legs was always breaking.

"What's wrong?" Beth asked when she noticed his defeat.

Drake tossed his backpack on one of the kitchen chairs. "Not talking about it."

"Sure," Robert said, tapping a domino and debating his next move. "We don't have to talk about it—"

"The Valentines were a huge mistake." Drake sulked over to the table and picked up one of his dad's dominoes, setting it back down on the wrong train. "The whole school is making fun of me."

"Bet they wish they thought of it first," his dad said, sliding the rogue domino back in its place.

Red and yellow LEGOs dotted the gray carpeting inside Drake's bedroom, and posters from Spielberg movies lined the walls. He launched onto his bed, tucked himself under the race car sheets, and ignored the knock on the half-open door.

"Inside-out," Beth whispered.

Drake rolled over in her direction. "What?"

She tiptoed in the room and sat on the edge of the bed. "That's what they called me in school. I put my gym uniform on the wrong way one time, and . . . well, that was that."

Drake scrunched his nose up. "That's dumb."

"It was." Beth nodded. "But it was still embarrassing. And then, it was over. That's the good thing about bad things."

"What is?"

"They pass. All of them, they just—whoosh." She pressed her thumb onto one of the cartoon race cars. "Zip on by." Beth gave her wisdom a second to land before getting up and moving back to the door. "Why don't you take a nap before dinner? Dad's heating up a frozen pizza—"

"What if I'm Sarah?" Drake asked.

Beth turned back to him. "Sarah?"

Drake smashed a pillow over his face. The cushion muffled his woe. "What if nobody ever wants a Valentine from me again?"

Beth pulled the face pillow off. "We all feel that way, at some point or another." She kissed Drake's forehead. He pretended to hate it. "But, hey. You're going to find someone who always wants to be your Valentine, and who you love more than anyone. And when you do, don't let her go."

"You have to say that," he groaned. "You're my mom."

"I'm saying that because it's true." She pulled his blanket to his chin. "You're a good egg, Drake."

"I don't like eggs."

"It's an expression, sweetie."

As Drake drifted off to sleep, the bedroom door clicked shut. A little snore landed in an instant, then the world around him got blurry. The colors in the image turned into moving spots. The elephant night-light distorted and became a faraway star, and then Drake's young dreams switched over to a new character in the movie.

Ellie.

The prep school, with its bleak white walls, was a good place to be bored. Ellie had lost track of the teacher's words. Her focus turned to a sprinkler ticking its way across the lawn out the open window. She wanted to be down there, stomping through the grass and ruining the lace dress her mom picked out that made her look like a pastry.

The wardrobe fit the occasion, at least. She was stuck in a baking class.

"Ellie!" her teacher snapped. Parents liked this teacher. She was a matriarch of summer school who enjoyed her authority over her students a little too much.

"Sorry," Ellie said. She set the pen down.

"All right, ladies." The teacher tightened an apron around her cream, A-line skirt. "Let's get baking!"

Sandra Marshall insisted that baking was one of the more useful life skills, despite rarely doing it herself. In her mother's mind, conflict could be resolved by a well-orchestrated floral display, an afternoon high tea, or a rhubarb pie. The teacher had just explained that rhubarb was a vegetable. Spending her birthday making a pie out of vegetables seemed like a tragedy to Ellie.

The knock at the door couldn't have come at a better time. Whispers darted across the room as five neat rows of girls turned to see who was responsible. When Ellie joined them, she spotted the daring green eyes she knew so well.

"My mom wants me to pick up my sister," Ben said with the charisma of a movie star trapped in a much younger body.

"I'm sorry, Mr.—"

"Marshall," Ben offered. "Ellie's brother."

The teacher surrendered the measuring cups to her wood cutting board. Flour puffed out around her face in a cloud. "We need a parent's note to dismiss summer students."

Ben gave her a slight nod. "I hear that. The thing is, Ellie won an award."

The teacher raised her neatly plucked eyebrows. "What is the award?"

"Little Miss . . . She's won the Little Miss Manners Contest." Ellie coughed to cover up her laugh. Using a believable excuse would've been too easy. Ben delighted in finding complicated ways out of family obligations—fake Cub Scout troops that needed a leader for the weekend or school projects turned into cutting-edge business ventures. "It's part beauty pageant, part manners contest," he elaborated. "Anyway, we have to hurry so Ellie can get into her dress."

Amazingly, the plan worked.

"Part beauty pageant, part manners contest?" Ellie recapped outside of the school. "Mom is going to ground us into the next century."

"Well, lucky for us, Mom is not going to find out. You're looking at a seasoned escape artist." Ben led her away from the school building. As they walked, the rules bent and lost their shape. Youth made lines more nebulous. Ellie followed him without asking where they were going. "Besides, nobody should rot in summer school on their tenth birthday."

"I guess so," Ellie agreed. "I think I was about to bake my own cake."

"Pie, Ellie. I saw the recipe on the blackboard. It was a pie." Ellie straggled behind him. The shoes she'd been forced to wear were to blame; they were a pair of white kitten heels all wrong for hijinks. Ben stopped and waited for her to catch up, with his hands on his waist. "Despite your current getup, you'd make a terrible housewife."

A short walk past the parking lot and a long stretch of Tudor homes led them to a small downtown area. Ben pushed open the doors of a shop that exploded with bold colors and patterns strung from circular racks. Their hands grazed an ocean of textures, and Ben called out the type of person who would wear each garment. "Motorcycle lady!" he shouted as he flung a leather jacket off the hanger and slid it over Ellie's arms. A slight spin in front of a long mirror revealed a pair of white angel wings and script font on the back.

"Property of Bobby," Ellie read. "How did you know about this place?"

"I found it last week." It was only the second week of summer school for them, which meant Ben hadn't made it through a single sitting of his beginner's Latin class. He set his hands on her shoulders. "You want the jacket?" Ellie shook her head no. What she did want was a pair of shorts, she said. Not expensive khaki shorts made for private boat charters like her mom picked out. She wanted the denim ones in her hand, which were embellished with highlighter-pink stitching along the pockets.

After Ben paid for the shorts, he bought her an ice cream, too. "I loved that place," Ellie told him, lowering herself onto the hot curb. She spooned a runny bite of Rocky Road into her mouth.

"Cool, huh?" Rainbow sprinkles dotted Ben's nose. "It's not like the new expensive stuff Mom buys," he said. "It's all old. Vintage."

Ellie had never heard that word before. *Vintage.*

"Did you use your allowance for the shorts?" Ellie asked. "I can pay you back."

Ben shrugged. "Don't worry about it." He broke into his Marlon Brando impression. "Happy birthday, Little Miss Manners."

"Thank you."

"You're welcome." Ben rubbed the top of Ellie's head, which messed up her hair. She left it that way.

By the time Ellie and Ben made it back to the school, Sandra's car was waiting by the parent pickup. Their mom was hard to read. She barely looked up from the women's magazine she had fanned over the front wheel, using the spare minutes to find her perfect summer lip shade. They gave each other a look as they buckled into the backseat. Had their mom seen them walking from the opposite direction from where their classes let out? Were they busted?

Maybe Sandra had missed the shopping bag in Ellie's hand. Or maybe, based on her little smirk that Ellie hadn't noticed back then, Sandra Marshall loosened the grip on her otherwise strict rules because it was Ellie's birthday. Maybe, just maybe, she had actually let their big escape slide.

11

As the movie ended and the tasseled curtain glided shut, Ellie wished she and Drake were at a diner. Under the light of a Googie-style sign, with a bottomless cup of black coffee in hand, they could talk about what they saw all night.

"That was incredible," Drake would tell her, smacking a sugar packet with his thumb before emptying it into his mug. "The vintage store . . . It sparked your love of everything old and forgotten, didn't it?" He'd stop his thought to question her grin. "What is it?"

"Nothing," she'd say, on the edge of her seat. "I was just thinking about how you are a lifetime romantic."

"And you, Ellie, have always been a rule breaker at heart."

"In my defense, that baking class was the worst. I'm pretty sure it's why I get dodgy around kitchen stores."

"Hey, speaking of pie—"

They'd debate splitting the strawberry rhubarb to stay on-theme, but eventually go with French silk instead.

"You were an adorable kid." Ellie would reach her fork out for the first bite when the dessert came. "I mean, that whole Valentine's Day fiasco took a boatload of confidence."

"I wanted to make Sarah feel better," Drake would admit, fighting off Ellie's fork in jest. "I wouldn't say I was confident. At all." He'd raise an eyebrow. "Is anybody confident in grade school?"

Ellie and Drake would stay at the diner until the coffee stopped flowing and the pie case slowed its pastel orbit. Drake would drive them home. They would sing in the car like happy people do, too loud, off-key, a blissful melody.

But Ellie knew her diner fantasy was just that. A fantasy.

The rules they had set prevented them from talking about what they saw. Instead of opening up, they stood in the lobby and stared at each other in silence, attempting to process what they'd experienced in the privacy of their own minds. Together.

"Are you okay?" Drake asked beneath the great chandelier. Ellie could feel him searching her. Maybe he was stacking up the similarities between child Ellie and adult Ellie—how her hair had darkened from strawberry to a fiery red or the wrinkles that had set in at the corners of her eyes.

The parts of Drake that Ellie loved most had developed so young, she knew now. While other kids—herself included—were busy gossiping or pulling fire alarms, Drake was concerned about the feelings of people around him. Everyone else in his class had ignored the crying girl. Drake stopped to offer comfort and friendship without judgment.

"Are you okay?" Drake asked for the second time because Ellie still hadn't responded.

"I'm great," she said. A bingo spinner of letters jumbled inside her mouth, forming combinations that demanded to be spoken. She tightened her lips to keep it from happening.

"Are you sure?"

Ellie gave Drake a kiss on the cheek and set her head on his shoulder. "Yeah. Of course. Let's head home," she said.

But they didn't head home right away. On the drive back, Drake took a wrong turn that let Ellie know they were on the same page. Even if the rules prevented them from talking about the memories, they could still celebrate what they'd seen. So they set out on a mission to track down more candy, cookies, and frozen pizzas than any reasonable adult would consume.

They had decided—without saying it outright—to stay kids for the night.

"Your carriage awaits," Drake announced as he rolled out a shopping cart and encouraged Ellie to take a seat inside it. Her jaw dropped a little; he joked a lot, but rarely instigated mischief. The wheels rattled as they wound through the aisles fast enough to make the cereal boxes shift on the shelves. When they slid back out into the cold night, arms loaded with bags, Ellie reached in her pockets for her gloves, only to find them empty.

"My gloves!"

"You're cold?"

"No. Yes." Ellie moved toward the car. "I must have left my Good Luck Gloves at the cinema. I guess I set them on the seat or something."

"We can go back," Drake offered. He grabbed the passenger door for her and threw the bags into the backseat. They were her favorite gloves—the ones she'd worn the night she had met Drake, embroidered with little rosebuds at the wrists, providing zero warmth. But Ellie longed to be back home, with their couch and their junk food.

"It's fine," she said. "We'll grab them next week. It's not like the other customers will steal them, right?"

Junk food overtook their kitchen table when they got home. Ellie opened the bags of candy that didn't go together, and Drake shuffled around for something in the hall closet. When he returned to the living room, his arms were loaded with knit blankets and a restorative sound machine Jen had gifted them, still unopened in its box.

"It plays owl sounds," Drake said. He pulled the machine out and set the switch to "forest mode." Fake owls hooted on the banks of a fake rippling stream. Nancy, who had been midnap, attempted to hoot back a response. "Now we just need a fort."

It took only two chairs and a few throws to build a blanket fort. They ate their pizza inside it; gooey cheese burned the roof of Ellie's mouth. While perched on their elbows at the entrance, Drake pointed to their ceiling and listed off names of indoor constellations he'd invented.

"Ceilingus Minor," he said, in reference to a small crack he'd already repaired three times.

"Breathtaking," Ellie admired. "Is this how you used to woo all the girls?"

"Oh yeah. I'm great with star stuff. Astronomy. That is what it's called." Then, "Hey."

"What?" Ellie asked, not yet ready for the moment to end.

"I realized there's something important I've never asked you," Drake said.

Ellie waited for some kind of wayward shoe—an ugly, out-of-season shoe—to drop.

"Are you ticklish?" Drake asked instead. And before she said yes, he was on top of her. Their giggles were out of control. It was the untamed laughter specific to childhood, laughter that felt like freedom.

12

Before the third pink tickets were off their spools, Ellie was asking about her gloves. "They're white," she described. "With beaded roses on the wrists." The ticket boy showed no sign of recognition. "You know, the decorative type of gloves that quiver in the face of cold weather. Did you find any gloves last week?"

He shrugged as he passed the tickets through the slot in the booth. "Not sure."

"What do you mean, you're not sure?" Ellie tried to curb her annoyance. The ticket boy could restock snacks for guests who never came and vacuum already clean carpets, but he couldn't give a second thought to her favorite, special gloves.

"Do you have a lost and found or something?" Drake asked.

Inside, Natalie confirmed that they did. The lost and found was near the entrance of the lobby. Individual items, each with their own descriptive plaque, rested on four tiers of dusted shelves, like a small gallery exhibit. Ellie's gloves were waiting in the top left corner of the bright glass case: *Ellie's Good Luck Gloves*.

Drake crouched for a better view. "What is all this stuff?"

"It's the lost and found," Natalie explained. She slid behind the case to face them. "Actually, not *the*. It's *your* lost and found. Things you've lost track of or left behind." A closer look revealed that Natalie was right. The lost and found consisted entirely of their forgotten items. Here, their memories seemed to take on a different, more physical form.

"This case isn't always here, is it?" Ellie asked. She hadn't noticed it on their first two visits.

"It's like any lost and found," Natalie told them. "You have to ask for it."

Ellie bent down next to Drake and peered inside the case.

On the top shelf, next to her gloves, was a preserved red rose left over from *Drake's Valentine's Day Fiasco*.

Ellie's mint-green spiral notebook was split open on the next shelf, which allowed a glimpse into her messy handwriting on *The First Draft of Ellie's Book*. She liked to write things by hand when she could, but her penmanship, which she called "drunk chicken," made it challenging to follow her own train of thought.

"I think I lost this thing on purpose," Drake said. He was in a staring contest with a plush fox head. Its knowing eyes were pushed up against the glass. *School Mascot*, the plaque read.

Ellie laughed. "This was your mascot costume? It's terrifying."

"Yeah, I'm aware," Drake said. "They gifted it to me because it was terrifying. The school replaced the costume after my stint." He ran his hands through his hair. "Parents were complaining."

Several more exhibits lined the bottom row. A *Do Not Disturb—Writing in Progress* sign from Ellie's childhood bedroom. A piece of silver hardware from the time Drake and his dad first fixed the kitchen sink together—*Drake's Early Inspiration*. A hand-drawn map of the abandoned mansion Ben brought Ellie to when they were teenagers—*Midnight Map*. Then, Ellie's focus moved to something more damning on the bottom shelf. The plaque caught her eye first, followed by a familiar object. If the lost and found indicated what they might see on film, this devastating tiny item had confirmed her suspicions. The reasons she had insisted they go to the cinema would present themselves.

Witness to Ellie's Accident.

Drake didn't notice when Ellie jerked away from the glass.

"How many things can we take?" she asked Natalie, eager to escape the situation.

"Just take what you need—"

"We need the gloves," Drake snapped with urgency. Had he noticed her unease? He must have been more tuned in than Ellie realized. Only when she met his eyes, the truth revealed itself. He was looking at the red carpeting and shifting his weight back and forth. Something inside the lost and found case had rattled Drake as much as it had her. Ellie tried to figure out what it was as Natalie passed the gloves over, but he was too quick to pull her toward the right-side stairwell.

With the gloves safely on her hands, Ellie and Drake returned to the balcony seats they chose on their last visit. "Looks like this movie is kind of a hot ticket tonight," he said.

He was kidding. They were the only customers, as always. The lights lowered and they settled in. Nerves swirled in Ellie's stomach while the Charleston played and the hot dogs danced. Eventually, the screen went black and a new title surfaced.

TICKET THREE: *TEENAGERS*

A school gym had been done up for a dance. The soaring disco ball made the nautical-themed decorations sparkle. Kids danced in groups, their arms anemone in a sea of heavy bass. An archway of blue and white balloons marked the portal to an evening of fun.

Teenage Drake was sitting on the hallway floor next to a cardboard welcome sign at the dance's back entrance: SHIP'S AHOY. He was so fixated on something above his head—was it the ceiling?—that he barely noticed when a trail of navy crepe paper slithered past his feet.

"Oh, shoot," the girl said. She bent and peeled the fallen decor off her delicate black sling heel, then nodded to the spot next to him. "Is anyone sitting there?"

The *wow* in Drake's head was almost audible. The girl was impossibly tall with dark hair pulled into an elegant updo. Fallen wisps framed her heart-shaped face and expressive brown eyes. She had a natural self-confidence, Ellie could tell—a person oblivious to the usual pitfalls of being a teenager. "I could use a break from all the Top Forty," she admitted, pulling at the tulle on her peach cocktail dress. "It's a lot of vocal runs and lofty commitments."

Drake nodded to indicate the spot was open. The girl slid her back against the wall and got comfortable beneath a framed photo of a high school basketball hero who went by Mike the Machine. She was inches from Drake, which made him squirm inside his coffee-brown suit, fit for a wedding singer.

"I'm Melinda," she said. "I'm a senior."

"I know." Drake struggled with where to put his hands and settled on his lap. "I'm Drake. Sophomore."

"Drake Sophomore." Melinda's legs tumbled out in front of her. She seemed not to fear the ugly tile. "So, what, Drake? You don't like cookies?"

"Huh?" He was putting in great effort not to stare at her.

Melinda nodded toward the gym. "They've got cookies in there."

"I like cookies," Drake said. "I don't like dancing."

Her hand searched for something inside of her small black purse and located a napkin-wrapped cookie. She split it into two halves and handed one of them to Drake, squishing her gum into the empty napkin. "Why hang out at a dance if you don't like dancing?"

Drake took a bite of the cookie. "It wasn't my idea." She motioned for him to fill in the gaps. "My mom," he said. "My mom thought this would be good for me. She used the phrase 'rite of passage' a lot on the drive over."

"Right." Melinda ate her cookie half in one bite. "Well, if it makes you feel better, I'm a bad dancer."

"You look good," Drake blurted. "At dancing, I meant. You look like you know how to dance." It seemed his strategy for avoiding eye contact was making mental notes of the surroundings. *Doorway. Science Lab. Cork board thing.*

"I've got no rhythm," Melinda admitted. She shot the napkin into a nearby trash can with surprisingly good aim. "Plus, I have two left feet." Suddenly, one of her hands found his. "But maybe together we've got a pair?" Without waiting for his answer, Melinda helped pull Drake to a stand. "Come on," she said. "It'll be fun."

He followed her into the gym. As they swam through the lights to the sound of Dido's "White Flag," royal and baby-blue streamers tangled in their hair. Melinda set her wrists over Drake's shoulders. All around them, the auditorium brimmed with summer longings. Yearbooks split open and ink on nervous hands would soon be replaced by frozen soft serve and kisses on picnic blankets.

"What were you doing in the hallway? Before I sat down?" Melinda asked.

"Oh, uh. I fixed this leak in the ceiling," Drake admitted. "Just a small one. It's temporary, but it'll hold for a while."

Melinda's eyes narrowed. "You fixed a leak?"

"I keep tools in my locker," he said. "My dad says you should always carry tools." Drake shrugged, growing a little more comfortable. "I guess I can't help fixing things."

"Well, as my mom would say, it sounds like you're a good egg," Melinda told him. "I'm not actually too sure what that means." Before he could commiserate about the saying, a sky-high, teen heartthrob butted in to dance with her. This was her boyfriend, it appeared. Of course she had a boyfriend. But Melinda held off on switching partners until the song played its final note.

"Come on, Melinda," the large square-shaped boy called. "Let's get out of here."

Melinda gave Drake a kiss on the cheek. "Nice to see you, Drake Nielson."

He'd never mentioned his last name.

When Drake's parents picked him up, he thanked his mom for making him go to the dance. Back in his bedroom, the memory caved in on itself. The images turned into a fuzzy soup as they had with the first two movies, which meant Ellie and Drake were about to switch places.

Yellow headlights slashed a dark mountain road. Inside the car, Ben spun the volume knob. Classical music poured from the speakers; violins and creeping keys were trying to spook each other. The steep ascent pressed Ben, Ellie, and their dates against their seats, holding their breath for a fast drop that never came.

"What is this place, anyway?" Charlie asked from the backseat. *Charlie*, Ellie's first boyfriend. He looked the same as she remembered, like a golden retriever of a quarterback. Hearing his voice brought back the sweat smell of him under her sheets. Despite having almost nothing in common, their attraction had been undeniable.

"It's a house," Ben said. "Of the haunted variety," he added, with the appropriate amount of theatrics.

Charlie's buy-in was instant. "*Whoa.*"

"I have this old friend who is a paranormal expert. He says this place gets more activity than anywhere in town." Ellie nodded along in solidarity. She loved Ben's stories, even if they strayed from the truth. Hours earlier, the two of them had heard about an abandoned "eyesore" from their dad's friend on the board of the historical society. Now, they were driving out to the—probably not haunted—eyesore to explore it. "You want to hear the whole story?"

Ben's girlfriend tensed in the backseat. Her French manicured fingers clung to the edges of her cardigan. Ellie could remember so much about this girl. She wore small daisy clips in her hair and intentionally pronounced certain words with an English accent because her family had summered in London. What Ellie couldn't remember was her name.

"You're going to love this one, Marnie," Ben said. He drummed his hands on the steering wheel.

Marnie. His girlfriend's name had been Marnie, and she wasn't his type. Ben had a thing for theater girls, weird girls, and girls deeply invested in fringe causes outside of their control, like nearly extinct bugs or rare types of household mold. Ben had broken up with Marnie a few weeks after this. Ellie had dumped Charlie around the same time, before his homecoming game. She really didn't want to attend a homecoming game. "Sorry, Charlie," she said. Ellie wondered, in the aftermath, how many women would say that to him throughout his life.

Wind rattled against the sides of the car. As the road veered to the right, the startled black eyes of a deer gleamed out from a thicket of trees. Ben took a deep breath to signal he was about to start his made-up story. "A long time ago, this woman moved into a mansion," he said, rolling the window down. Chilly air settled on Ellie's shoulders. "You know, a widow with buckets of money, that kind of woman. This widow was known for two things." He extended two fingers above his head for emphasis. "She wore black for a year straight, *and* she spoke about her dead husband like he was still kicking."

A small green dinosaur on the rearview mirror bobbed along as an opera singer joined the frantic instruments. Ben had bought the dinosaur in a gas station after getting his license. Will-asaurus, he'd named him for an attendant who helped him fill his first tank. While their parents excelled at teaching manners and menu pronunciations, relaying real life skills was left to chance—or in this case, a stranger.

"Our widow, well . . . she starts inviting suitors up to the mansion." Ben glanced up at the mirror to make sure he still had a captive audience. "So, these dapper gents go up to the house to have a nightcap, and they start to disappear. Feathers were ruffled, but nobody found anything. Fifty years later, a nice couple moves in. They plant a garden."

An outline of a house etched itself at the top of the hill.

"The husband goes to dig out an old well that's getting in the way of his tomato plants and that's where he finds the bodies. *Six* bodies. The suitors were thrown right down there with the dead husband."

Charlie was suspended forward, his jaw dangling midair. Ellie could sense this was her chance to back up Ben's campfire story. "I think I've heard this one," she chimed in.

"You have?" Marnie shivered.

Ellie nodded. "The dead husband went into a rage over the other suitors." She forced a tremor in her voice. "Now he haunts this place. When you see his ghost, he pulls his heart right out of his chest." Marnie gasped as the car flew over a bump.

As they neared the house, it grew features. The Gothic hideout was built from forlorn brick, and a wide stone entryway formed a mouth caught in a scream. Ben's foot pressed on the brake, and the car halted to a stop after another bend in the road. "There!" he whispered. "Do you see it?"

"See what?" Charlie asked, his gullible face searching. Marnie's shoulders scrunched up to her ears.

"In the woods." Ben tapped his window. "Something moved out there." He threw the car in park and stepped into the night. In his studded leather jacket, smudged black eyeliner, and moody skinny jeans, this new look marked the entrance to his rocker phase. Ben didn't play instruments, but that didn't stop him from dressing like the bassist in a pop-punk band.

Wham! Something slapped the back of the car. Charlie gripped the headrest in front of him like a life jacket, and Marnie's crimped hair nearly hit the ceiling. Then, laughter sounded from outside. Ben ducked back into the front seat, and they started up the hill again. He held his palm in the air, awaiting Ellie's high five. "Easy crowd," he said.

The car glided into an elegant motor court where a valet or butler would've greeted guests. Two angels sprouted from the center of a stone fountain that had been turned off for years, and weeds blanketed a porch draped in cobwebs. Despite all that, the structure was impressive, more of a castle than a house. "Here we are, intrepid travelers," Ben announced, killing the engine.

The inside of the house called for flashlights. Luckily, Ben had planned ahead. One by one, they flicked their lights on and beamed them over the abandoned living room and up a stairwell that rose toward a second story.

"Why are we here?" Marnie pouted.

"Can't you picture it?" Ben tucked his flashlight under his chin. "An inferno in the fireplace right there." He galloped to the center of the living room. "Here, a table where they'd put a silver tea set. Up there"—he pointed to an empty wall—"a personal art gallery belonging to the dead husband." By the time Ben finished his tour, Marnie and Charlie had wandered off on their own. Ben kicked at some fallen wood on the ground. "Fine people we've picked, sis."

"I can see it," Ellie said, in awe. "I can see the potential here."

They passed their dates in the kitchen and moved toward a blue-tiled room where an indoor pool had been. The details of what once was took shape as Ben bounced the flashlight against the walls. There was a maid bringing drinks out, Ellie felt, an echo of happy squeals that traveled into the vaulted ceilings, the lapping of water from a little girl's arms.

"I think there's something else over here." Ben waved Ellie outside. "Come on." They stepped onto a sprawling outdoor veranda turned to shambles. "Sit," he insisted, hopping down onto some dilapidated stone and settling into a cross-legged stance. It was almost certainly a dangerous place to sit.

"You couldn't just let them think it was a regular old house," Ellie said.

"It's not a regular old house," he told her. "It's special. I just expanded the story to get their attention. Creative license."

"Well, everything's better with a few ghosts," Ellie replied.

"Not exactly." Ben tilted his head toward the sky. "You know, I'm probably more afraid of ghosts than our friend Marnie."

Ellie assumed he was kidding. Ben was fearless. He was also drawn to the macabre. Halloween was about watching every scary movie together. This ritual was a relief to their mom, since their costume choices would've alarmed the neighborhood. One year, they'd dressed as Drew Barrymore and Ghostface. The next, they reimagined the films of Tim Burton. Sandra startled when she entered the kitchen and found Ellie ripping open a bag of chips with scissors for hands and Ben's Lydia Deetz egging her on from the other side of the marble island.

"Seriously?" Ellie asked. "I'm supposed to believe *you*, Ben Marshall, are scared of ghosts?"

"I am," Ben admitted. He got quiet. "They're a reminder. No matter how big or small a life you live, eventually we're all just . . ." He swirled his hand through the wind. "Forgotten. Unless," he said, holding up his flashlight under his chin, "some weird kids come to visit and save you from that fate."

Before Ellie could respond, Charlie and Marnie found their way outside. It wasn't long after this night that the two of them started dating. Maybe the outing was the moment it began, their courtship blossoming thanks to the excitement of being in a forbidden place late at night.

Ben pulled a tape player from his pocket. He clicked the Play button and David Bowie joined them for a dance to "Oh! You

Pretty Things." Halfway through the song, Ben handed his Polaroid camera to Marnie and pulled Ellie aside for a photo. The stars in the night were crisp and bright; they asked, much like the house, to be remembered, too.

"You're quiet," Drake pointed out on the car ride home.

"I'm fine," Ellie said. She wasn't fine. She wished she could call Ben, for it to be that simple. Ben was the person who would immediately believe her about the cinema; he wouldn't need convincing that magical places could exist just for them.

Ellie feared Drake was going to pry, but in a saving grace, her phone dinged first. Ellie opened the email. The sender wasn't Ben, of course, but they were completely unexpected. "Umm."

"What?"

"It's an email from my dad." Ellie debated if she should share the contents with Drake as she scanned the short paragraph.

"What does it say?"

She sighed and surrendered. On any other night, she'd delete it, but seeing Ben opened up a longing for some taste of family. Even if the taste was bad, like the homemade almond milk her dad brought her on his last visit.

"He wants us to come out for Thanksgiving," Ellie told him. "With five days' notice."

"So? That could work."

"What about Nancy?"

"Ask if she can come with," Drake suggested. "I think your dad would like her. They're both free spirits."

"No," Ellie said. "No, no, no." Drake gave a look that implied they should say yes.

"No!"

13

Five days later, the two of them were headed to her dad's house with one free spirit whining in the backseat. Ellie's regret deepened as they got off the freeway. Why had she said yes to this plan when her dad didn't actually like Thanksgiving? He wasn't big on conversation, gratitude, or any of the elements a traditional holiday dinner would evoke. Ellie debated turning around for the entirety of the three-hour drive to his cabin in the woods, which was located at the intersection of Nowhere and Remote.

These days, Ellie and her dad were pen pals. The cabin had no cell service and bad Wi-Fi. William's wife, Naomi, was deeply granola and resistant to technology, so there wasn't a landline either. Selling his successful orthodontic practice to retire an hour from a grocery store was a choice. Ellie imagined that her dad drove to that grocery store to send his email invitation and the rare text messages she received from him.

"I'm getting the feeling like we're the high schoolers here," Ellie said. The road continued to dissolve as they pushed toward what she hoped was a driveway. The time was only a little after five, but the dusk had deepened several shades, making it hard to get their bearings.

"Which high schoolers?" A light flickered on in the distance, beyond a patch of overgrown trees.

"You know, the teenagers in the movie who wanted to party in a cabin, but there's a killer on the loose?"

Drake tossed his phone into the cup holder. "You've really never been out here?"

"Haven't had the pleasure." The wheels hit a branch that cracked so loud, Ellie thought a bone had snapped. Her car was built to handle the occasional puddle or a gentle patch of snow—not whatever undergrowth they were driving over. She regretted turning down Drake's offer to take his truck. It would handle better in the woods, he'd said, but Ellie resisted. She liked to be the conductor on drives, selecting the music and determining the gas stations and roadside attractions that were worth a stop. Still, the truck would've made more sense.

Ellie hadn't prepared for this outing, in so many ways.

Two figures appeared on the wet wooden porch as the car crawled closer. Warm light poured out from the front windows, illuminating her dad as he shifted down the front steps. His arms stretched in a big wave above his head; he was saying hello or fending off a bear. Either way, it was new to see him take up this much space. For years, William had curled himself into a tight, button-down-clad ball that cowered behind her mother. It was nice seeing him look comfortable in his casual flannel shirt and jeans.

Ellie threw the car in park.

"Well, we made it." Drake exhaled. She could hear the nervousness in his voice. He had met her dad and Naomi only once about six months ago; they took a road trip to have dinner at a halfway point on Drake's insistence. The neutral hotel restaurant Ellie picked had a fireplace that should've made a strong conversation starter. Unfortunately, the hostess seated them on the opposite side of the lounge, an eternity from the roaring fire. They covered crunchy topics Ellie and Drake knew nothing about over mediocre flatbreads. Hotel restaurants always served flatbreads.

"Kiddo," William called as Ellie exited the driver's seat and helped Nancy out of the back. Her dad went in for a hug. The smell of pine and earth latched onto his shirt and skin. Behind them, Drake teetered his weight between their two duffel bags. Duffel bags were smart. Duffel bags said, *We're only staying one night.* Naomi insisted on grabbing both of the bags as she motioned them inside. William slapped Drake on the shoulder, as manly men do. "Let's get in there," he said. "Dinner's on the stove."

Turkey and cranberry sauce would've been too obvious a choice. Her dad and Naomi's Thanksgiving involved a lawless soup: beans and mystery meat, tiny macaroni noodles, and what tasted like baking spices. An antler-shaped fixture loomed above their heads as they chewed. The fixture had come with the cabin, Ellie assumed. Surely, the man she'd grown up with, and had to at least still know a little, would not have chosen that fixture.

"So, Ellie," Naomi started, "how are your articles going?"

Ellie tried to hide her frustration. It wasn't that she didn't like Naomi. She was a nice person, even though she smelled of essential oils and looked like she cut her own hair over the sink. Naomi had worked for years as a nurse, but Ellie strained to picture her in scrubs. She only wished Naomi hadn't called her work *articles*. "I'm dabbling with a few ideas," Ellie said. Her spoon clinked against the bottom of the bowl. She was hungry, despite the collision of flavors.

"We need to catch up on our reading, Will," Naomi said. "He likes scary stories."

Ellie finished her soup. "You do, Dad?"

"Hmm? Oh, yeah." He nodded a little. "Yeah. Scary ones. Nothing too violent."

"Speaking of violence," Naomi started. She wasn't good at segues. "The other night, we found a dead rabbit on the porch. He was all torn up, poor little guy." Ellie must have been quick to show her disgust because Drake darted in to change the subject.

"Maybe we could all say what we're grateful for?" he suggested. While Ellie appreciated his attempt, her family tended to avoid discussing things like gratitude or feelings of any kind.

"I'll go first," William volunteered. Ellie braced herself on the table to keep from falling out of the chair in disbelief. Her dad picked up a napkin and wiped some soup off the corners of his mouth. "I'm grateful to have you here, Ellie. And spend some time with you, Drake. We've got"—he rubbed his chin and concentrated—"what, about six months until the big day?" Ellie was surprised that her dad was keeping track of their wedding. In fact, he hadn't brought up the wedding at all beyond his recent offer of a gift.

Ellie had never responded to that message, she realized.

Drake nodded. "Almost exactly," he said. "Everything is right on schedule. We're going cake tasting tomorrow afternoon. And once we've ordered the cake, she's not getting out of this." Ellie chuckled. William's features tightened, as if Drake's suggestion was meant to be taken seriously. He seemed to think Ellie might run out on her own wedding, and the cake would be the fence to prevent that from happening. Ellie wasn't going anywhere, which she tried to convey by linking her arm around Drake's. Her dad stared into his soup.

"Well then, I guess it's time we got to know each other better," William said. "I'm grateful you drove out here, too. I know it's a long one, and this place . . ." He studied the room with fresh eyes. "This place probably isn't your style," he said to Ellie. His voice was gentle.

"It's fine," Ellie told him because she wasn't sure what to say. She considered complimenting the watercolor bison painting on the wall that had been posed like a president. "Thank you for having us," she offered instead.

When William finished sharing his gratitude, Naomi was next in line. She was grateful for moths, she said. Ellie feared her soup might come up her nose. Most people took moths for granted or thought of them as pests, Naomi explained. But she liked the way they could move out of the dark toward the light. "They're hopeful creatures."

Drake was thankful for Ellie. Family. The food, which he lied and said was delicious.

Then, it was Ellie's turn to speak. "I guess that I'm grateful for . . ." She reached for a sip of her water, wanting to stop what she was about to say and struggling to find the pause button. The need to know was too strong. This need had a six-pack, Hulk arms. "Why did you invite us here, Dad?"

William pushed his bowl away. He paused and analyzed Ellie for a long moment. There was no unspoken language between Ellie and her father, just the lived-in confusion of neither of them knowing how to talk to the other and being afraid to admit that. Her question hovered in the air above their heads, an uncomfortable layer right beneath the light fixture. "I'll clear the plates," he said, which ended the conversation.

Ellie, Drake, and Nancy escaped to the guest room after dinner. It was a mutual escape. When the dishes were done, her dad said, "We'll be outside for a bit." There were only two chairs out there. It seemed his new routine involved reading Stephen King under the light of the moon. He had all the time in the world to devour *It* and *Children of the Corn*, although none, apparently, for reading his own daughter's book. She'd sent him a copy back when it came out. He'd never mentioned it.

"I like how quiet it is here," Drake said, next to her on the twin bed. Ellie was dizzy. None of the lamps in the house seemed to fully work, which made the bears on the wallpaper look like they were dancing. Ellie readjusted herself on the mattress. It was abominable, that mattress. They also had a dog in their bed.

Nancy usually slept on the floor, but tonight, all bets were off. Whenever she was somewhere new, that space became hers to conquer. Ellie had already caught Nancy lying on every piece of furniture her dad owned.

"I hate the quiet," Ellie said.

"Yeah, well, who knows?" Drake reached his arm out for her. "Maybe you'll change someday. Maybe you'll want us to get a cabin of our own. Seems like that kind of thing runs in your blood."

Ellie despised the phrase "runs in your blood" even more than the wallpaper. Those words made her choices seem inevitable, as if every moment or trait was already mapped out. What Drake said was an easy-breezy idiom for someone who got along with the people who raised him. The quilt nibbled at her arms. Drake was never in a rush to leave his parents' condo when they visited. Dinners dipped toward midnight, the four of them flipping through Beth's scrapbooks and half-watching television, Robert always sending them away with some little gift or trinket that he'd picked up in town.

How much of Ellie's dad, exactly, did run through her blood? If they were to have kids, would Ellie also be a source of continual disappointment?

"Whatcha thinking over there?" Drake asked.

"Nothing," Ellie said. She got up and retreated to the minuscule attached bathroom. The lights were dim when she turned them on. One of Naomi's moth pals head-banged the fixture. By the time Ellie finished brushing her teeth, Drake was falling asleep, and she was ready, sort of, to talk.

"I just still think," Ellie started. "I mean, it's weird, right? This visit. He hasn't extended us a serious invitation the whole time we've been together. He abandoned our family and ran off to the woods. And now, out of nowhere, he wants the company of his daughter?"

"Maybe your dad thinks you're judging him." Drake yawned. "For his place, his choices, Naomi. It's different from your old life. He knows that."

"Judge?" Ellie balked. "I don't judge people. I don't do that."

"Okay," Drake said, weighing his words. "Well, did something big ever happen between you two? Something that started all of this . . . weirdness?"

"There was one big thing, yeah," Ellie told him. "But there were also *a lot* of little things."

Drake kissed her forehead. The bed retaliated with a loud squeak when she scooted to the edge of it and sat back down. "I'm exhausted," he said. "You tired?"

Ellie wasn't tired. The idea of staying in the guest room became unbearable. Each time she tried to get comfortable, the springs of the mattress sank their claws deeper. So, she zipped up her puffy coat, collected some musty blankets, and retreated to the front porch.

It was cold outside; she couldn't see her own breath, but a chill tickled her back. On so many occasions, Ben had misled her about the nature of the woods. He made the trees and the stars seem like a lush, atmospheric adventure waiting to be peeled open. The air had been electric that night at the abandoned mansion; being outside felt safe because they were together.

But now, she was alone, and the shadows of the trees grew taller in the dark. Every rustle put Ellie on edge. She wouldn't be able to sleep anywhere here, which was confirmed when the rustling became louder. Ellie startled, stood, and moved to the edge of the porch. Normally, she ran from pending danger, but her curiosity got the best of her. Cocooned inside a blanket, she moved down the first step, onto the second, and then the animal behind the sound showed itself.

A rabbit with black eyes lit by a low moon sat at the edge of the porch. Its eyes seemed to widen at the sight of her, but the creature settled in place when Ellie paused her steps. She was never sure what she was supposed to do around animals other than dogs. "Hello," she said with a wave. "How is your night going, friend?"

The rabbit stayed still. She wondered if it was here on neutral terms or to search for its fallen companion. Her stance turned to a crouch out of curiosity, but as soon as she lowered herself, the rabbit was gone, darting back to whatever mysterious place it came from.

Ellie returned to the porch chair. Then, after a few minutes of rocking and yawning, sleep took over.

"Funny finding you here," Drake said the next morning, stretching his arms over his head. Nancy was at his side. "It's beautiful out." He was right, in a factual sense. The air was crisp, the sunrise had crested the backs of the rolling green mountains, and mist covered a walkway of leaves leading to the cabin. Drake wore a matching beanie and sweatsuit that somehow looked incredibly put together. He took a sip of his steaming coffee. "Can't believe you're up before me," he told her.

Ellie started to explain that she'd dozed off outside but paused. The admission wasn't worth all the questions that would follow.

"Who's ready for breakfast?" William asked, poking his head out the door. "Naomi's cooking."

"I'll go help," Drake offered. "I'm good with pancakes and stuff."

It was an excuse to leave them alone. He wasn't good with pancakes and stuff.

William took the seat next to Ellie and stared off into the trees. The surroundings were less menacing by day. Some of the branches even looked like they were holding hands. "About your question last night," he said. "Why I asked you here." Ellie turned to face him. Whatever this was, addressing the issue, was another unexpected change in her dad. "I invited you because I wanted to see you," he said. "There wasn't some ulterior motive. I want us to get together more often. Just, keep in touch."

"You're the one who left," Ellie said. Her rocking chair started to groan. "You left and you make it sound like . . . I should be making the effort. Dropping by for cookies without an invitation."

William rested his hands over his eyes to block out the rising sun. He looked older than he had last night. It was uncanny to see this version of him stacked up against the one who had made brief cameos in the movies. Actually, outside of the *Babies* ticket, Ellie hadn't seen her dad on-screen at all.

"I think about that fight sometimes," he said. "Back when we all visited Ben in your twenties. I shouldn't have chosen that moment to press on things." Before Ellie could respond, he stood up to check on the breakfast, shape-shifting from an empathetic, caring person back into his unfeeling self.

"Get a phone," Ellie insisted. "This whole pen pal thing isn't working for me."

Her dad turned back to her through the open door. "I thought you were a writer."

"Yeah, well, not all of us can be as prolific as Stephen King."

"Right." He nodded. "You know, I'd like to read his take on Finn's Bar."

Before Ellie could ask her dad what he meant, Drake called them into breakfast. Naomi didn't keep pancake supplies or real eggs, so they were served some kind of fake egg product with frozen blueberries from a friend's garden that now had freezer burn.

"We only have a few hours until cake tasting," Drake said after they ate. "We should hit the road. But thank you so much for hosting us. It's been great to hang out with you two." When he stood, Nancy jumped down from the couch. Ellie followed, even though a part of her wanted to stay. When she rose, she was eye to eye with something on the top of her father's bookshelves.

In a sea of horror books, crime novels, and a mismatched collection on medicinal plants, there was one book that was entirely out of place.

Her book.

She opened the pages while Drake gathered his things. They were dog-eared and underlined with notations throughout the text. *Brilliant*, one of them said, in the piece called "Yellow Dress." *Made me laugh*, said another, about halfway into the book.

Ellie was quick to point fingers at her dad for the disintegration of their relationship. Yet here he was, reading her book to the point of wear. He had never been good with words, but he was working on it. Meanwhile, Ellie herself had done little to reconnect with her family after everything that happened.

Everything that happened. She couldn't help but wonder if there were missing pieces to the Marshall estrangement. How many details had she overlooked about the people she loved from a distance—failed attempts they had made to connect with her?

Ellie had a feeling she'd find out soon enough.

14

That afternoon, while other people slept off their Thanksgiving dinners or waged wars in department stores over large appliances, Ellie and Drake loaded up on sugar. What Ellie hadn't told Drake was that their cake tasting also served another purpose. She wanted to find out how Flour and Flower was doing. The owners, Tad and Madelyn, had recently traded their humble red food truck for a refurbished firehouse, and Ellie was eager to see their new space. It was a risky move without a big following.

Ellie thought she might be able to help.

But when they arrived, the bakery and plant store was brimming with customers. What business needed to post deals and events online when customers could drum up a buzz on their own feeds? The slick silver pole at the center of the room was inoperable, but it offered a strategic photo opportunity. As if to prove this, a twentysomething couple handed their phone to a stranger, then dangled from each side like two mismatched wings. *Our love's on fire*, the caption would read. Or, *Fighting fires. Taking new names. #FlourandFlower.*

"Thanks for planning this," Drake said as he finished up a bite of rose-vanilla cake. The tasting area was set up like a low, stylish bar. "It really means a lot."

Tad slid a new cake plate in front of them. Ellie clapped with excitement.

"We love your work, man," Drake told him.

Tad shrugged. "I just decorate the cakes. And make the paintings." He pointed to a few original works of art on the walls featuring a regal-looking corgi. "Anyway, my wife, Madelyn, is the baker. She's the mathematical mind. Precise about everything. Has it all down to a science in the kitchen."

When Tad went back to work, Drake took a bite. The fork clattered as he tossed it down. "This one's just as good as the last one." He was wrong, though. The slice in front of them was the best of the bunch. A fragrant sourdough blackberry base with salted vanilla buttercream and a hint of cardamom formed an intoxicating alliance. Drake waved his hand to invite some kind of response. "Well, what do you think?"

Ellie and Drake weren't all that different from Madelyn and Tad; Drake handled the logistics in their relationship, and Ellie handled the creative flourishes. When it came to their wedding, though, she'd let Drake take on both of those responsibilities.

As a result, Drake had planned a few elements that she would never have chosen herself. Their wedding was to take place at a banquet hall, which he had reserved for May 12, the three-year anniversary of their meeting at Finn's. The decorations were to be in the style of a sweet-sixteen party. Drake also hired a DJ who focused on pop hits and slow jams circa the early 1990s. Everything, he felt, had to happen on the exact timeline he built. He'd spent a week charting every possible date and milestone, even adding some wiggle room for error or holdups. Sometimes, he couldn't help bringing his work brain home with him.

"The cake is really up to you," Ellie told him. "It's your day." She'd meant it to sound generous.

Drake scooted his chair back in response. "*My* day?" He recoiled from her, visibly hurt. "Where are you in this equation?"

"Come on," she said. "You know what I meant."

A few minutes later, Tad slid a new plate in front of them. The beautiful chocolate square was etched with gold flakes. "German chocolate," he said, fiddling with one of his many piercings. "But it's not actually all that German. We use a spicy dark cacao I picked up in Mexico City."

Ellie made the chef's kiss sign with her hand.

"She doesn't get any," Drake said. "It's my day, apparently." He pouted and pulled the plate in his direction as Tad walked away.

He was right to be offended. Of course, her involvement was important to him. "Look, I'm sorry," Ellie offered. "All this sugar is making me bonkers. I just meant, our wedding day is more for you," she clarified, reaching her fork over to grab a bite. It was a decadent bite with a velvet texture. Heat from the spicy chocolate made her eyes water. Drake wouldn't look at her. "What matters to me are the moments we share alone, not the moments that other people experience."

"Why, Ellie?" Drake asked. He took a huge bite of the cake and waved his hand in front of his mouth to diffuse the heat. "I mean, you are the queen of the thoughtful experience. I figured that's why you called off Vegas. So we could plan our perfect day together."

Ellie had wanted *him* to have a beautiful, perfect wedding, she thought. And Drake was incredibly intuitive. How, she wondered, could he not pick up on the reason why she wasn't excited about this? People would look at Ellie on that day and see all her problems. Big events called attention to families. She didn't want hundreds of eyes on her.

But she also didn't want her own fears to take away from Drake's enjoyment of their day. After all, a wedding wasn't only about her past. It was a celebration of their future, together. A fresh start. "The blackberry is my answer," Ellie told him with finality. "I'm choosing the blackberry."

Drake softened as he took in her suggestion. "The blackberry," he said. "I love it. Thanks for picking that."

"You're welcome." Ellie fought him for the last bites on the plate. "I could help with some other planning stuff, too."

"Yeah?"

"Yeah. I could shop for decorations. Maybe a record or two to play."

Drake gave her a playful nudge.

"What?" she asked.

"Nothing," he told her, holding his hands up. "It just sounds to me like you're looking for an excuse to go antiquing or something."

After they ordered the wedding cake, Ellie told him about a vintage shop she'd wanted to check out. The two of them spent the afternoon together, hopping between stores and hunting down treasures they could add to the table settings.

At their last stop, Ellie grabbed a brown corduroy suit off the rack that reminded her of what Drake wore to his high school dance. As she held it high in the light of the store window, another item joined its side. Drake lifted a black skater dress pierced by safety pins. It was exactly like the one she'd worn to the abandoned mansion.

"I think these two look good together," Drake said smiling, without referencing the cinema directly.

"Yeah. I do, too," Ellie agreed, even though she wondered what the two of them would've been like together in high school. She guessed her outward rebellion would've scared Drake off. She also wondered if her younger self would have been observant enough to look beyond the bad suit and young nerves and see that Drake was perfect for her.

But that didn't matter. Their teenage selves were fun to visit. They were also entirely different people. The person standing next to Ellie's adult self was right for her now. Drake set the dress down and turned to kiss her in the middle of the store. For a moment, everything slid away.

Going to the cinema was starting to feel like a weekly routine for Ellie and Drake. The following night, they walked through the fog, up the alley, to the booth for repartee with the ticket boy, across the lobby with a quick wave to Natalie, up the stairs to the balcony, and then settled into their seats for the evening. They waited for the lights to lower, consumed by a growing curiosity of whatever title might summarize the evening.

At least, Ellie was consumed by this.

Then, much to her relief, a title appeared that seemed innocent enough.

TICKET FOUR: SPARK

Snow blanched the world of its color. It fainted onto the trees, the brown brick school buildings, and the slick concrete steps where twentysomething Drake sat.

"We've got to stop meeting like this," a voice behind him said.

Drake turned toward the voice. It was Melinda, again. Cold flakes dotted her windblown hair. She looked more natural now. Her face was free of the liner and pink lipstick she wore to the dance. "Drake, right?"

"I . . . yeah." Drake's hands dove into his coat pockets. "Hey, Melinda."

Melinda sat next to him without asking this time. She took a puff of a professor's pipe and tried to pass it over. Drake shook his head no. "Are you here for the weekend?"

"I moved back after college," he said. "I'm kind of figuring things out. And working a lot while I do that. I pick up shifts at the hardware store. I work in construction. I'm also starting my own construction business."

"Wow." She nodded. "How's all that going?"

"Oh, I mean, I haven't done it yet," Drake clarified. "The business part. Eventually, though."

"Why construction?"

"I don't know . . . Umm . . . A house is, kind of, where life happens," Drake said, his eyes alight. He leaned forward onto his knees. "Couples fall in love. They learn to live with each other's quirks. They bring home kids from the hospital and watch as those kids grow bigger, learn to drive, and move out." He cleared his throat and looked over at her to make sure he still had a captive audience. He did. "Years later, everybody comes back together under that same roof for holidays and birthdays to reminisce." Drake was in a trance, picking up speed. "So many of their important moments stay in one space. I think the rooms where we spend our lives should be special."

"That's pretty profound," Melinda said. Her lips sent another plume of smoke into the air.

"No. I . . . I've just been watching my parents' struggle with their space. They kind of bump and collide through the rooms." Drake made a motion with his hands meant to signal chaos. "I'm going to change that for them someday."

Melinda offered the pipe again. "Live on the edge, Drake," she said. "It's not going to bite." Drake accepted this time. It was clear he had never smoked by the way he coughed, but Melinda didn't call him out on it.

The two of them peeled apart little bits of their lives like the skin of a fruit. Melinda had never left town. She admitted that staying in one place had helped her feel the most like herself. "Speaking of which," she said, "are you busy right now? I want to show you something."

The snow fell faster as they went for a brisk walk, each flake in a race with the others to find its landing. Melinda and Drake peeked inside the windows of a candy store, a produce shop, a soda counter. Eventually, she pointed to a purple sign above an antique store. MY MOTHER'S SHOP, it read.

"You worked here in high school." As soon as the words came out, Drake pretended not to know them as fact. "Right?"

A parade of dresses brightened the window. Melinda unlocked the door to the shop, removed a BE RIGHT BACK sign, pulled Drake inside, and went through the motions of making herself at home. She yanked the cord of an onyx floor lamp, tossed her coat on a wood hanger, then pressed the button on a hot-water kettle. Her knees found the top of the front counter as she shuffled for something on a high shelf. They were surrounded by antique wares.

"Hot chocolate," she said, snapping her fingers. She located some cocoa powder and emptied it into two chipped mugs. "Yes, to answer your question. I worked here in high school. And this is my store now." Melinda shimmied off the counter. Her feet plopped back on the ground. "It used to be my mom's. She named it for her mother's love of antiques, and well, the name still works."

"Where's your mom now?" Drake asked, looking around to see if they were alone.

A black cat crawled out from the corner of the room and gave a pathetic roar. Melinda bent to pet the top of its head. "She passed a few years ago. She was sick for a while. People always say the grief fades, but I find it just evolves. Changes its medium." She stood back up and tried to shake the sadness out of the room.

"I'm sorry," Drake said.

Melinda handed him a cocoa mug and moved closer. "Have you ever lost anyone?"

"My grandma. But not a parent or anything."

"That's a big loss," she acknowledged. "I've noticed this thing where, when someone dies, you start to lose who you were with them. Maybe that's why I stay in town. My mom built our whole life around this place, you know? Our family friend, Clara, from

Clara's gifts, actually paid the first month's rent here. The store started with nothing. Just a few pieces of furniture. And my mom turned it into a magical place I love." The cat got up and sulked back toward a hidden lair. "Anyway, that's Pasta."

"Pasta?"

"She came with the name when I adopted her. I think she's more of a Martha, though." Melinda darted back behind the counter and grabbed a flowy white shawl to wrap around herself. "It's freezing. Can you shove the door?"

"Huh?"

"It sticks. Shove it. Like it hurt your feelings."

Drake pushed on the door with a certain amount of strength, and they were sealed into the warmth. Melinda explained the stories behind some of the relics she'd picked up. In the center of the room, there was a vanity where a woman might sit and admire herself in a dress before bringing it home.

"I don't know anything about antiques," Drake said.

"That's not why I brought you here. I wanted you to see it and be proud."

"You did?"

"Isn't that what we all want from people we used to know? To see us and be proud of us?" Melinda took a sip of cocoa. "To say, ah, how great she ended up there! That fits." She made the motion of connecting dots with her fingers as she sat down on a blue Persian rug that lined the floor.

"I think it's really great you ended up here," Drake said, taking a seat opposite her.

"Thank you." She ran her finger around the edge of the mug. "I believe that people should be honest with each other about what they want. Life's short, and it's infinitely better when it's spent in truth."

The snow outside made it impossible to see anything.

"For example, I want to dance," Melinda said. Their eyes met.

She sprung up to put on some music. The notes were layered and hypnotizing. Drake stood, too. Her arms circled around his neck. The shapes of their bodies inched closer together in the vanity mirror. Eventually, Melinda's head rested on his chest, and his arms wrapped around her waist.

"I think that . . . I want to kiss you," Drake said when the record finished. "But only if that's okay. Only if—"

Melinda kissed him first. It lasted forever.

No one was coming out to shop in the storm, so she flipped the little window sign to CLOSED and put it back up. They stayed tucked away until the late afternoon turned over into night. While all the people they grew up with were sleeping nearby, they were dancing.

And then, the scene faded, blurred, and Ellie flinched as something far less romantic—and far more revealing—took over the screen.

15

Ellie and Drake should've left the cinema as soon as her next memory started to play. If there were ever a moment to call it a night early, this was it. But Ellie's logic flew out the window as she connected with this younger version of herself on-screen. She was confident, carefree, and so very in shape. It was hard to let this Ellie slip away. By the time Drake stood and tilted his head toward the exit, it was too late.

"Ellie?" Drake looped around her in circles by the snack bar. She was the nucleus of his panic. "I think we should talk about this."

For once, Ellie leaned on the rules. She held her hands up in protest underneath the behemoth chandelier. "But we can't."

Drake gnawed on the edge of his thumbnail. Ellie could sense him rummaging for an excuse. "I guess we can't talk about it," he considered, then snapped his fingers in the air with an *aha*. "Although, technically, we're still in the theater. Right?"

Ellie sighed. If they were going to have this discussion, they needed a private location without the ticket boy or Natalie as their audience. Then, she remembered the empty ladies' lounge and pulled him toward the small carpeted staircase leading to the basement. "I think I might throw up," Drake said as his hand planted a firm grip on the cold brass railing.

"Great," Ellie said. "That's exactly the reaction I was hoping for."

∙∙∙∙∙∙∙∙∙∙∙

The ladies' lounge defied the concept of a modern restroom. Rosebuds burst from light pink wallpaper that wrapped around a tufted mahogany chaise rising from the middle of the plush mauve carpet. Gold vines circled six vanity mirrors paired with round accent stools below, and a slip-shade chandelier kept watch over it all. In the attached room where the actual toilets were, each stall door was carved from marble.

"Way nicer than the men's room," Drake observed. Ellie guided him over to the chaise. The color had drained from his cheeks.

"Are you really going to throw up?" She rubbed his back.

"No," Drake said. "I . . . maybe."

It was just sex, Ellie thought. If his reaction was this extreme for something so harmless, how could he possibly handle what was next? A dripping faucet in the attached toilet room stole her focus. She got up and turned it off, then came back to admire herself in all the vanity mirrors. It was a relief to find that she still had it. Maybe she didn't have it in the way she'd had it at eighteen, but she looked good.

"Who was that guy?" Drake blurted. "In the movie."

Ellie sat down again. Drake was jealous of the landlord she'd had a total of three interactions with—a landlord who was ill-equipped in more ways than one. She'd lived in a truly awful apartment her freshman year of college. Her mom had eventually insisted she move to the campus dorms where she could be around less ominous influences.

"He was the landlord," Ellie said. "He was there to fix the dishwasher."

"So, he fixed the dishwasher, and then—"

"Oh, no. He didn't fix it. Terrible landlord."

Drake winced. The thought of an appliance remaining broken

that could be easily fixed was too much for him to handle. "Why that guy?" he asked. It was hard to believe the "why" part was up for debate. The landlord was cut straight from an early 2000s teen movie with gym-rat muscles and an unfortunate puka-shell necklace. "That thing you were doing on the bed looked like a health hazard."

"I used to love health hazards." Ellie glanced up to see the two of them there on the chaise. There were so many mirrors, and in all of them, his judgment flashed back at her. Not everyone was as lucky as Drake—meeting a perfect person with their own store and a whimsical cat named Pasta. *Pasta.* Ellie had repeated the name in her head since she'd heard it. "She came with the name when I adopted her," Melinda had said in the memory. Drake used the same line the night when he first described Nancy. Was that a coincidence, or was he nodding to something from his past?

The door of the ladies' lounge swung open. Natalie cleared her throat to make herself known as she moved through the sitting area and ducked into a stall. Once Ellie heard the lock slide closed, she motioned Drake toward the door. The two of them scooted out of the room and back to the stairwell that ran up to the main lobby.

"Why are you freaking out?" Ellie asked at the bottom of the stairs.

"This guy must have meant something to you."

"Hilarious," she said, without humor.

"Well, if he didn't mean something, then why are we seeing it?"

Drake had a point. Ellie had wondered the same thing herself. She'd almost mourned that the cinema skipped over so many childhood and teenage memories she assumed would be in the cut. Already, it had jumped to her as a young adult. What was it trying to tell them?

And then, she remembered the robbery. They had left the auditorium before the robbery played out. Ellie shared how in the moments that followed their escapade, someone walked into the apartment and stole her broken television set. After hearing the noise, the landlord went into the living room in his underwear, holding a hanger—the only sharp object in the bedroom—to find that both the robber and the television were gone. "It was scary at the time, but in retrospect, it's really funny," Ellie said. She felt herself starting to laugh, just as she had when she'd told Jen the story a few hangouts into their friendship. They had laughed so hard, in fact, that the students in the dorm below them started to bang on the ceiling.

"I don't get why that's funny," Drake said.

"Because the television was broken," Ellie explained. "It's funny because of the bad luck for the robber. Of all the things they could have taken. Sort of a tragicomedy."

"You were robbed, Ellie. You didn't lock your doors?" Drake had flipped the switch from jealousy to concern. She rolled her eyes.

"No, I didn't lock the doors. Nobody locked the doors back then."

"Back . . . That's not true." Drake climbed up and down the stairs, collecting his thoughts with each one. "You were being irresponsible."

Ellie followed him halfway up. She had earned her chance to point fingers. "Speaking of relationships," she said, "what happens next with the two of you?"

Drake stopped moving. "What?"

"Melinda," Ellie said. "How far does this go? She's been in two memories now. I mean, I never even saw you as the mascot. I didn't see your college years. I've barely seen your parents. Melinda is the main plotline. She must be pretty important, right?"

"I don't want to . . ." His mood shifted at the mention of Melinda. Ellie had caught him on a tightrope. It was her turn to feel sick. "Look, Ellie, you were right."

"What was I right about?"

"The rules. We should stick to the rules."

"Got it. So, we're going to stick to the rules when it's convenient for you."

"It's not like that."

"That's what it sounds like."

Natalie bounded back up the stairs and pretended to have her blinders on, which made her presence much more apparent. Her signature gold suit was hard to miss.

"Hey, I didn't mean to judge you," Drake said. He stepped down to face Ellie in a silent compromise, his hands soft on her arms. "I was worried. I was worried about you, okay? Worried about the guy you chose, worried about the locks." He was calming down. "I wanted to protect you in that moment, and I couldn't."

Ellie still wanted to fight. It was her turn to sink her teeth in and dissect Drake's life. He felt it was acceptable to critique her experiences but wouldn't even give her answers about his own.

"Let's get out of here," Drake said. "Can we just go? Leave this behind like we're supposed to? I'm sorry I got weird."

Ellie nodded, but she wasn't agreeing, exactly. Her mind was already elsewhere. She was making plans to do research when they got home. She needed to see what had silenced him and made him change his tune—why he was acting so strangely. When Drake went to bed later that night, what she was looking for was so easy to pull up.

Soon, the address to My Mother's Shop appeared on her glowing laptop screen.

16

Ellie wasn't technically lying when she told Drake her plans for the day. She mentioned she would overstay her welcome at a coffee shop, which was true. The only thing she failed to admit was the large detour she planned on taking before that coffee.

Drake slid over a paper box of blueberry scones he'd picked up that morning. The scones were an apology for the conflict the night before, and also, for having to work on a Sunday. Ellie tried to hide her relief when he broke this news. She had stumbled into a day without supervision. Now that Drake was busy, she could take a long morning drive to the shop on Main Street with no questions asked and still make it home in time for dinner.

Ellie and Drake had always avoided Main Street during their visits to see his parents. For Thanksgiving last year, they had stayed the weekend in Drake's childhood bedroom, which was slowly being overtaken by secondhand fitness equipment. Ellie had asked him to give her a tour of the town. Drake sequestered them inside instead. "It's just a couple of blocks," he told her, flipping on the Macy's Day Parade. "I don't think you'd love it," he insisted as a large-scale Sonic the Hedgehog flirted with Miss Piggy.

But almost a year later, when Ellie pulled up to the place they'd so often avoided, she realized Drake was wrong. Right away, Main Street made her feel like a figurine in a Christmas village. Cheerful red and white awnings were cozied together above windows showcasing toys, hardware, and trinkets. Train tracks cut through the center of town, headed by a tiny brick station.

As Ellie parked, a grown man in a newsboy hat boarded his bicycle, balanced a glass bottle of milk in the rattan basket, and cruised down the middle of the street. Bad things didn't happen here, she could tell. Neighbors returned the sugar they borrowed from each other. People had picnics. Bedtimes were kept promises.

A bell sounded as Ellie entered My Mother's Shop. The Persian rug was gone, leaving the dark hardwood floors exposed. All the home treasures had disappeared; the store was now filled with dresses. A cotillion of creamy pastels dangled from copper racks around each wall and along the front window, leaving plenty of breathing room for a shopper to begin their textured odyssey.

"Welcome in," a voice sang from the front counter. Melinda popped up behind it. A silver tray of beads and trim was balanced on her arm.

Ellie startled. Though she had expected to see Melinda, it was as if she had materialized from a movie character into a real person. Ellie searched for something to say. During her morning drive, she'd listened to a podcast about the history of marbles. Her time would've been better spent coming up with an excuse for her visit. Instead, she grasped for the simplest thing to say. "I was just walking by."

"Well, I'm glad you stopped walking."

When Melinda looked up at Ellie, her eyes narrowed in a quizzical expression that couldn't be recognition. Could it? Drake wasn't one to post on social media; he was usually eager to ditch his phone after a day of endless calls and emails unless there was something pressing on his plate. Still, a quick search would've revealed photos of Ellie and Drake at various events if Melinda was the type to google him.

Her comfortable air implied otherwise. Normally, Ellie wasn't the google-an-ex-type person, either. But after seeing his memories, she wanted to experience, in person, who Drake had fallen for before her. This wasn't a situation that often presented itself in nature unless there was an awkward run-in at a restaurant, or worse, the person stayed friends with their ex, leaving their new partner to force a smile over miniature golf on a dystopian double date.

Time had been gentle on Melinda. She reminded Ellie of an art teacher, the sort of ingenue made more alluring by the paint splotches on her wrists—or in her case, square silver glasses, a messy top bun with rebellious loose strands, and thread wound through her delicate fingers. The light-blue dress she wore must have been plucked from one of the racks. Her feet were bare despite the chill outside, her toenails left unpainted.

"You're even more beautiful in person," Ellie said to herself.

"Sorry?"

Ellie searched for a quick response. What was she doing here? What was her plan, even? To make sure Melinda wasn't secretly hung up on Drake? "I mean, the dresses," she said. "They're even more beautiful in person." Melinda squared off some champagne-hued velvet under the needle of a sewing machine. "I've seen some photos online." This admission directly contradicted Ellie's "just walking by" bit, but Melinda didn't seem to notice. "I didn't realize you made them."

Melinda swatted the credit away with her hand. "Oh, no. Trust me, I don't. I just buy used dresses that were special to begin with and give them a bow." The needle cranked through the velvet with precision. "Or a belt. Or some beads."

Ellie couldn't help but relate. "That sounds a lot like what I do," she said, with immediate regret. She needed to change the subject again. "I bet if you stay here long enough, the dresses start to talk to you."

"Funny you say that. They do," Melinda agreed. She blew some of the hair off her face in a big gust.

A staircase behind her desk blocked off by a small red rope started to groan under the weight of footsteps. "Ah," the man said as he pulled a latch to open the barrier and entered the shop. "Customer," he mouthed to Melinda. He hadn't meant to be discreet. The look he gave Ellie was an invitation to their secret club.

"Don't make it seem like we don't get customers," Melinda told him.

"I did not say that."

"Even though it's the truth."

"Write-offs. Gimme." He extended his hand out to Melinda. She stuck a pile of papers on his palm. The shrinking space between their bodies defied the boundaries of colleagues. As if to confirm what Ellie suspected, the man kissed Melinda's cheek.

Ellie was fascinated by Melinda's current paramour. She loved to figure out what drew people together, the way a string of lovers got grouped into a category. *Bad Boys. Eco-Warriors. Librarians.* Was it fair, she wondered, to date the same kind of person over and over again? Were people re-creating something that had once been comfortable, or were they collecting pieces of the person they were meant to be with so they would one day recognize it when they found that person?

Ellie wasn't sure. Drake hadn't been her usual type.

But he sure was Melinda's.

She did a double take. The current boyfriend was older, sure, but his wholesome grin, shaggy dark hair, and goofy T-shirt made him look exactly like Drake. The two men even moved the same way: in big strides, with a bounce to their step—although Older Drake walked with better posture, Ellie observed. *Older Drake* wasn't an appropriate thing to call him. Surely, he had a name.

"Jamie," Older Drake said. He stuck his hand out for her to shake.

"Ellie," Ellie offered, accepting the gesture. Melinda slid her fingers around Jamie's arm to casually claim him, which is when

Ellie realized she had missed a telling piece of jewelry. Jamie wasn't the boyfriend at all. A classic bezel-set diamond ring glittered on Melinda's hand. "You're married!" Ellie nearly shouted in relief. Then, to match her unwarranted enthusiasm, "Congratulations!"

"She's stuck with me," Jamie said. He turned to go back up the stairs with his papers in hand, humming something that could only come from a person in a rare state of happiness.

"Ellie," Melinda repeated. "I'll let you look around. Have fun."

Ellie should've left. She had her answers about Melinda—and her *husband*. Bringing up Drake seemed silly at best and invasive at worst. But Ellie wasn't ready to leave. For a moment, the current company slid away. Ellie ran her fingers over the dresses in a commune she couldn't have had looking at them online: buttery silk and darling tulle were right within her reach. Near the back of the room, a dress pulled her closer.

Silver beading laddered up the back of the silk gown. A flowing skirt spilled onto the ground in a soft waterfall, and the neckline fell in an organic drape that plunged low. The best part, though, was the shade of the fabric, a deep crimson that would highlight her hair. This was a dress that would tell people she was different from other brides. It was an exclamation mark. It was a magnet.

"Good taste," Melinda said, following her eyeline. Ellie tried to imagine what Melinda would've worn on her own wedding day. Were Melinda and Jamie content with living in a place where the people knew each other too well and everything probably took too long? Did they like those qualities, or did they daydream about Paris? "Try it on, try it on," Melinda insisted.

"Oh, I'm just looking." Ellie knew she absolutely could not find her wedding dress here, of all places.

"This isn't a shop where you come to look," Melinda said. "You come here to experience something."

Yet again, Melinda had spoken her language.

Behind the safety of a heavy violet curtain, Ellie stepped into the dress. The fabric hugged her hips, smoothing itself against all the right places on her curves as she draped the elegant straps over her shoulders and straightened her posture. The front hem was tapered shorter, which she hadn't noticed on the rack; it lifted so the crystal heels she'd already bought would always look like they were making an entrance. This silhouette had been made for her, she believed, crafted with her measurements and mischief in mind.

But surely, buying a wedding dress from Drake's ex was some kind of bad omen. The dress would heckle them from inside the closet. Eventually, after years of wedded bliss, Drake would demand to know where the dress had come from because it had always felt familiar. Ellie would resent that familiarity, that he would still be able to feel Melinda's presence in the room.

"Let's see it!" Melinda called out. Her voice was right on the other side of the curtain.

Ellie stepped out of the changing room and turned her back to Melinda, who finished pulling up the zipper. "I loved it on the hanger, but wow," she said. "It came to life on you." Together, they moved to a full-length mirror near the cash register. Ellie took herself in, admiring the legacy of this dress and all the contenders that sighed behind her, waiting to be wooed. "We can do any alterations you want, but it already fits really well."

"I don't know," Ellie said, even though she very much did know.

Melinda's eyes had landed on something. It was Ellie's ring. She reached out and pulled her hand toward the light streaming through the window to get a better look. "It's . . . gorgeous on you," she said, taking a long time with the stone, as if seeing the ring put something into perspective for her. "He's lucky." Melinda dropped her hand and slid some black heels onto Ellie's feet. "And I love the story behind it."

"The ring?"

"The dress," Melinda told her. "It belonged to a stage actress." She shortened the back straps a little without Ellie's asking. "Apparently, she wore it the night she was about to give up acting. A producer spotted her in a horse-drawn carriage, hunted her down, and the next day, she had an offer to act in a production of *Harvey*."

"I'll take it," Ellie said, outside of herself. Drake had wanted her to be more involved in the wedding. Ellie could make the argument that buying a dress was very much a form of involvement.

As Melinda rang the dress up, Ellie was trying to ignore something she'd pieced together in her time there. The store wasn't doing well. Melinda brought this up directly as she pulled out a gray dress bag and tucked the hanger through the slot. The right people had never found her. Recently, she'd gone from selling dresses and antiques to specializing in dresses, but having a focus didn't help, either. "No one from the city wants to drive an hour and a half to a dress shop their mom told them about."

"Well, don't worry," Ellie said. "I found this one myself. My mom isn't in my life much." Guilt immediately wrapped itself around her. Melinda's mom wasn't around at all, and it had been insensitive to phrase it that way. Just the night before, she had seen Melinda talk about her grief. Ellie had witnessed parts of this woman's life that weren't meant to be shared with everyone. Especially her. "I just mean, we're not close," she clarified.

Melinda fiddled with the register, then looked up at her in a direct plea. "Tell me, Ellie. How do I find more women like you?"

No, Ellie reminded herself. She couldn't.

But maybe—probably not, but maybe—Drake would want her to help someone he'd once cared about.

She willed Melinda to wrap things up faster, making it her personal mission to exit the store without saying what she was thinking. Finally, the dress was walked out from behind the counter and placed in her arms. She was seconds from the door.

"Oops," Melinda said, grabbing a lavender-hued scroll of paper from the front desk. "I almost let you leave without your note! These things keep falling off the hangers." She motioned for Ellie to open her palm and dropped the paper into her hand like a rare treasure.

"What is this?" Ellie asked.

"My mom had this special tradition," Melinda revealed, settling right into intimacy so naturally. "Everything she sold came with a note. When someone brought a piece in, she'd ask them to write a few words for the new owner. It was always thoughtful, always on this purple paper. Now, I hunt down the dresses in here myself most of the time, which means I write most of the notes. They're just simple little things."

Ellie attempted an easygoing "awesome," even though the inside of her mouth had turned into sandpaper. She had found this exact style of note, written on lavender paper, inside the music box Drake had given her—the one that was now perched on a shelf in their living room. *Find someone who makes you dance*, the note had read.

Melinda had danced with Drake at the school dance and in her shop.

Drake had shopped for Ellie in Melinda's store.

The choice would've made sense if he was on great terms with her. But he never mentioned Melinda before the cinema, and when she made an appearance, he pretended she was no one special. He changed the subject. He got cagey.

Drake was hiding more than she had realized. The purple note held a match to Ellie's curiosity. Still, it was too late—and too odd—to bring up Drake now, out of the blue. She would need more time with Melinda to learn her side of things.

Find something you're obsessed with, Nolan had said. Maybe this was the story she needed.

"What you mentioned earlier," Ellie started, "about finding women like me. I can help you with that."

"Really?" Melinda asked.

"Yeah." Ellie did her humble elevator pitch about work. She called her book a coffee-table book. She referred to the show as a documentary. "So anyway, I'd love to interview you and learn all about the store. No rush. Whenever you have time."

"How about now?" Melinda said, tugging out a leather armchair like she'd been prepared for this chance encounter.

Ellie was still far from home, but Drake would be gone all afternoon.

"Great," Ellie said, succumbing to the armchair. She reached for the notebook she kept in her bag and began to scribble down every word of Melinda's story as it spilled out.

17

All of the awe that tended to sweep Ellie away upon her discovery of a magical place was back. Since visiting My Mother's Shop, she was losing track of time again, positioned for hours above a noisy keyboard in her office. Melinda had spouted off so many tidbits about the town that inspired her, like the trees being named after local do-gooders, and how she believed her dresses had personalities. Ellie tried to imagine the distinct voice of each one. What would a mermaid dress whisper? *Ahoy, ye wayward sailors.* No. *Let me be your muse.* That was it.

Ellie added that line to the story draft she'd been working on, attached the document to an email chain with Nolan, and hit send. She was so wrapped up in the accomplishment of writing something new, in record time, that she jumped at the sound of Drake's voice.

"Whatcha doin' there?"

Ellie's spine straightened. He was right behind her. Surely, he must have seen her screen. Now was the appropriate time to surrender with her hands in the air. "I've been writing about your ex," she would have to admit. "The one who I drove out to the suburbs to meet without telling you. After seeing her in your memory."

But when Ellie turned to face the music, Drake was sporting a cheesy grin. "I'm taking you out tonight," he said and pulled her off her chair.

"Out where?"

Drake spun her into him, landing a move from the one swing class they'd been dragged to by Jen and Marc. "Not The Garlic Bread Place. Somewhere spicy."

Sal's Cantina was a time capsule. Nothing inside its walls ever changed. Layers of Christmas lights draped from the ceiling, and glow-in-the-dark cutouts of Día de Los Muertos skeletons grimaced on the walls. The photo booth where Ellie used to pose with her dates of years past still sat at the back of the dining room. All those black-and-white strips had been lost to time, except for the one on Ellie and Drake's refrigerator from their first official date.

"Back to our booth," Drake said as they slid into the bruised brown enclave. He always said this when they went to Sal's: "Our place. Our booth." Ellie didn't bother to tell him that Sal's couldn't be their place because it was her place with everyone else.

As soon as the chip basket hit the table, Drake shoved a handful of the salty bites into his mouth, barely stopping to chew. Ellie knew why he was stress eating; things between them were a little uncomfortable after the most recent movie. They had spent the last few days being absurdly polite to each other, folding their small talk into something soft and presentable. Verbal origami.

"Isn't it . . ." Drake rummaged around the chip bowl. Ellie flagged down the waitress for margaritas. "Isn't it mind-blowing to think that each of these chips was a tortilla?" He held one of them up for reference. "Maybe not one chip per tortilla, but I'm sure the chip-to-tortilla ratio would baffle us. I've probably eaten like a hundred tortillas already."

A familiar band started to play in the back of the restaurant, a band Ellie had heard on so many previous dates. She swore the players were focused on her, that their eyes were criticizing her for coming here on repeat. Ellie lost track of the lyrics. Each line joined into a damning chorus of *You've Done This Before*. When the song finished, Drake went up and threw a five in the tip jar.

"That was a good one," he said. "I loved it." He clapped until his hands must have hurt. Ellie found it irresistible when Drake was so genuine and, in that moment, oblivious to the fact that two booths had turned to study his thunderous burst of applause.

After the song, the waitress came by and scribbled down their orders. Their menus were folded. Fajitas were on the way. Drake reached for the chip basket again, but Ellie pulled it back in her direction. "Do you want to talk about it?" she asked him. "The reason you already flew through a whole basket?"

"I mean, maybe," Drake said. The margaritas landed quickly. He spun his glass around before picking it up. "I guess I feel like things have been distant between us the last few days. Am I breaking the rules by saying that?" Drake took a too-large sip.

"I think it's fine," Ellie told him, grabbing the glass to slow him down.

"Our conversations since the last ticket feel like we're—"

"Two strangers on a cruise trapped at the same dinner table against their will?"

"Right." He nodded. "Well, first I wanted to clear the air and say—you don't need to worry about Melinda. I mean, bottom line, we weren't right for each other. Really." Ellie took a sip of her margarita at the mention of Melinda. The same Melinda he had zero clue she had just met in person. Drake *was* breaking the rules, but she was happy he was being more forward. She decided to let it slide. "And what I was trying to say—I'll keep it vague—but I was trying to tell you that . . . It's hard to see the person you love in that . . . *situation*. I didn't mean to judge you. I was being a real boy about it."

"You are a boy," Ellie said, quoting the crying girl from his second memory. They were setting the rules on fire tonight, weren't they? Drake started to laugh. His laugh, and how easy it was, took her back to their first date at this same booth.

At the beginning, Drake had been good at dating but assumed he was bad at it. He didn't care about having slick moves. In the part of the relationship when most people were likely to Frankenstein versions of themselves together, Drake had been honest. He talked about getting overwhelmed when breakfast restaurants gave him too many bread choices and how he was afraid of space because it was so vast. He also insisted they pose in the photo booth. When they did, he set his hands on his legs and told her he was emulating the Lincoln Memorial.

"The photo booth," Ellie remembered out loud. "Can we go back to the photo booth?"

Moments later, the curtain clinked open. Ellie and Drake stepped inside the carpeted walls, squared themselves off toward the camera, and tapped the red button to begin the shoot.

Drake started with jazz hands, Ellie with an air-kiss.

"You're so schmaltzy," he told her.

Snap.

Drake switched to the thinker. Ellie fanned her hands over her eyes.

"You look like a poster boy for a department store portrait studio," Ellie said.

Snap.

Drake gave her a little nudge. Ellie retaliated. He tickled her. She squealed, delighted he'd brought her there tonight. Romantic gestures really were his opus. A part of Drake was still the boy doling out roses and chocolates. These days, his offerings were going to a more receptive audience.

Snap.

Drake sat on the small bench behind them and pulled Ellie onto his lap. "Why don't we give them a show?" he said. She could taste the salt on his lips.

"There aren't any photos left," she said.

He pulled her closer. "Even better."

After dinner, they walked past a familiar street corner. Drake guided Ellie beneath the pale blue sign for LOVE YOU A LATTE. It was the exact spot where he'd kissed her at the end of their first date. Ellie had felt like the high-rise building nearby was cheering them on, all those illuminated windows chanting, "You've got this!" After the kiss, Drake drove her home and walked her to her door.

But this time, Drake didn't wait to kiss her in front of the coffee shop, and he didn't stop kissing her when he walked her to her door. Their door. He pressed Ellie against it, her hair already tangled in his hands as the key slid in, then against the railing and onto the stairs. Her tights peeled down and off each foot, her lips still warm with tequila on his neck.

And then, as they bumped their way up the stairs, flung the door to the bedroom open, and climbed on the bed, something unfortunate happened.

Another person popped into her head.

Melinda.

Ellie swore Melinda's eyes blinked right in front of her. She was stunning, wasn't she? It was the ease of Melinda's beauty that was unsettling, Ellie decided. The ease that magazines and movies so often attempted to portray. *I simply wake up this way*, the beauty proclaimed. *I scoff in the face of makeup and skincare. Life is so good.* Did Drake ever miss her rosy outlook? As he'd mentioned earlier, it was hard to see him with someone else. On-screen, he was having a true romance. Ellie's memories, meanwhile, played out like violent B-roll footage from the film *True Romance*.

Then, something that had been at the back of Ellie's mind demanded her focus. It was startling how wrong she'd been about herself. Before the first movie, Ellie had thought she was above jealousy. She'd held her head high and perhaps even judged other people for feeling such a human thing. The past was the past, she believed, and nothing Drake had experienced before her could change what they had.

But Ellie had been wrong. What she could easily handle was a *story* about the past—a skewed retelling with certain details left behind, where genre and tone shifted. Engaging with Melinda in person had only made things worse, Ellie decided as Drake went to light a candle. The visit had brought Melinda even more into their present. She needed to pull the story she'd already written and leave Melinda to the past. Nolan had the draft, but nothing was in print. Besides, there was no guarantee he would even like it. She would call it off before Drake ever found out.

"Ellie?" Drake said. He was beside her again. "Hey. Where are you right now?"

"I'm with you," Ellie told him, getting up to close the door and shutting the rest of the world out with a single click.

18

Ellie hated to break bad news over the phone. Any lull in the conversation made her wonder if the other person was processing what had been said, or if they'd dropped their phone in the toilet. Since she didn't want to wade through that ambiguity with Melinda, she suggested they meet up for drinks.

"I'm actually seeing a friend in the city this afternoon," Melinda said on the other end of the line. "Is tonight good?"

"Tonight is great," Ellie told her, even though it was terrible. She collided with her desk as she slid around her home office, forcing her glass mushroom lamp to wobble. Nancy tucked her wet nose under the door and sniffed at the chaos. Ellie would need an excuse to go out. Thursdays were their Thai food and monster movie night. She and Drake tended to get into character, smashing the plastic cartons of noodles with their fists and raising their utensils high above their heads like they were ready to fight.

"Are you headlining a pop tour or something?" Drake asked when Ellie came down the stairs later. She'd spent an embarrassing amount of time trying to pick the right outfit and had landed on a funky silver jumpsuit she'd never worn.

"I'm getting a drink." Ellie's hair was having a tantrum. She pushed it away from her face and hoped it appeared dramatic.

"What, do you have a big date?"

Ellie angled herself away from him when she used Jen as her alibi. "She keeps wanting to party with mocktails now that she's pregnant."

Sometimes, it amazed her how easy it could be to lie.

Inside Strange Alchemy, the smell of craft spirits kissed her. The bar was one part mixology, one part sultry cavern, with a dash of Jim Henson whimsy. At the back of the room, a bartender slid a cocktail menu Ellie's way while pouring a sky-high gin fizz.

"Ellie?" Melinda called. The sight of her, otherworldly in a green silk dress, made Ellie question her jumpsuit. Melinda's carefree air was now overtaken by a polite glamour. The look felt like the aftermath of a high school movie makeover where the lead actress was always beautiful: glasses off, hair down, *now she's got it*! If Drake saw both of them for the first time tonight, who would he have spoken to?

Ellie was overthinking things again. Where was the confidence that was her superpower? "Well, come on," Melinda was saying as she reached for a hug. Ellie wasn't usually a hugger. "I found us a booth."

Melinda took her time ordering a rose gimlet. She asked the waiter an encyclopedic number of questions about the drink with a kind, slow affection, as if to underline that she was still a small-town girl, despite the dress. Ellie got the Dragon's Lair. It was her favorite drink on the menu. The cocktail came with a yellow Szechuan flower rim that caused invisible lightning bolts to strike the inside of her mouth.

"I'm glad we're doing this," Melinda said. She seemed energized to be out with a potential new friend. Ellie regretted not getting this over with on the phone. "And I'm grateful you're doing the story."

"You don't have to be grateful. It's a story, not a kidney."

"Can I be honest?" Melinda asked. Ellie offered a quick nod. "I thought this would be awkward at first."

"Oh, yeah," Ellie said, before she realized she didn't know what Melinda meant. Ellie assumed she was referring to how nerve-wracking it is to be out with a new friend, so she said, "Don't worry, I save all my celebrity impressions for the second outing."

Melinda chuckled. "No, I meant . . . because of Drake."

Ellie froze. She searched for the right move to make, but she wasn't sure what game they were playing yet. Melinda had looked her up. She'd claimed to be a writer who could help her store, and what—Melinda wouldn't do a quick search to make sure that was true? The room was closing in on them; the perimeter pushed itself so close that the velvet paintings hanging on the walls were about to rub up against her bare arms. Ellie expected, knew, that she was about to be called out.

"I recognized . . ." Melinda started. "Well, mostly, I recognized you from Beth's photos," she admitted, which Ellie was not expecting. Surely there was another Beth, a communal Beth, a Beth who wasn't Drake's mom. There had to be a *Beth* who she'd met at some cocktail party who somehow kept a trove of Ellie's photographs strewn around her apartment. Oh, *that* Beth. Stalker Beth.

But she only knew one Beth. And if anything, Ellie was the stalker here.

"We bake together sometimes," Melinda said. "We've stayed close." Ellie was ready to spit fire. The Beth who was about to be her mother-in-law had "stayed close" with Melinda? The horror grew as she imagined Melinda attending casual gatherings at the Nielsons' condo, Melinda spooning some kind of deliciously complicated casserole on each plate. "Anyway, I know why you didn't tell me."

"You do?" Ellie asked, curious to be enlightened about her own antics.

"Drake would want this whole thing to seem random," Melinda explained. "Gosh, it's typical Drake, isn't it?" She rested her head on her hand. "I mean, he *would* send you to help me stay open and make it seem anonymous. You know how he is." The you-know sneered at Ellie. She did know. She didn't need Melinda to tell her about her fiancé. "But I'm not good at secrets. And I also figured that's why you called me here."

The drinks landed, along with some chips. Ellie took a big gulp of her Dragon's Lair and started to cough.

"Are you okay?" Melinda asked.

"Oh, I'm fine." Ellie pointed to her glass. "My drink has a spicy rim. It's a festive kind of affliction." Melinda shook her hair down her back and took the smallest sip of her gimlet, like she was at a tea party. A memory came back into play again: Drake and Melinda on the hardwood floor, sipping hot beverages from chipped mugs, all starry-eyed. "Anyway, you got me," Ellie said. She wasn't sure why she was about to go along with Melinda's version of the truth. If, and more likely when, Drake found out about all this, she'd be digging herself deeper. "Drake did want it to seem anonymous." Now that Ellie was in the hole, why not keep going? "Speaking of," she said, "he's been fairly shy about the whole thing. What happened between you two, anyway?"

Melinda pushed back a little in her seat. "He didn't tell you?"

"I mean, he did, yeah." Ellie chewed on some of the chips. She was doing a bad cover-up job. "I'd just like to hear it from your perspective."

"Ellie," Melinda said. "Look, I'm all about honesty. But it seems like this is a conversation for you two." Ellie could see Melinda piecing together their relationship in her mind. She had decided something was wrong with it, Ellie suspected. She and Jamie probably sat around the table assigning colors to their feelings, or whatever it was that show-off communicators did when left to their own devices.

Melinda's judgment made Ellie want to play her own power

card—the *I'm calling the story off* card—but the events that would follow unfolded in her head. Melinda would reach out to Drake, heartbroken, and detail Ellie's transgressions. Drake would sympathize. He might even go to the shop to comfort her. Maybe he would bend over to pet Pasta the cat and a wave of nostalgia would take over. Ellie was spinning in circles, all the more reason she should've untangled herself right then. But she couldn't; she was stuck in a trap she'd built herself.

The plan had changed. Ellie would keep the story. She needed to show Melinda that she was the one in control of this narrative.

The waiter arrived to check on them, and Ellie turned up the charm. "Drake and I will talk," she said casually. "But, back to business. Now that we got *why* I asked you here out of the way, tell me more about Jamie," she said, crossing her fingers under her chin. "I'm almost done with my new draft, and I'd love to add some detail there."

Ellie replayed the exchange with Melinda in her mind as she drove home. She now knew more about her fiancé's ex than was healthy, through no fault of Drake's. It was always going to bother her that Melinda and Beth were friends. What else would she discover if she kept this investigation up?

As Ellie pulled into the driveway, she debated calling the story off for the second time that day, but her thought spiral was broken by the chirp of a text. It was from Nolan. He'd already read the draft she sent him and sent a frenzied paragraph-long response using too many emojis. He wanted to meet for breakfast to talk. Was she free tomorrow?

Tomorrow was eager. Nolan was excited about something.

Ellie's biggest mistake in all of this, she realized, was not telling Drake first. He would be furious when he found out she'd gone behind his back. She vowed that she would sit him down and tell him the truth that night, but when she got home, he immediately hopped up to microwave a buffet's worth of leftover Thai food for her.

"Is it too late for a movie?" Drake asked.

"Sure," Ellie said. "I mean, no. It's not too late."

"It's your turn to pick," he told her, setting their food down, along with a small snack plate for Nancy so she wouldn't feel left out. "Any genre. We don't need to be monster-exclusive tonight."

Ellie chose a French film. Drake disliked the foreign films she loved. When she had put on *Amélie* for him one time, he insisted the subtitles were too fast and couldn't follow the plot. Knowing he would fall asleep in minutes, she pressed Play on a movie musical called *The Umbrellas of Cherbourg*.

"Just what this night needs," Drake said next to her on the couch, stealing a bite of the food he had heated up. "A musical about a struggling umbrella shop."

Ellie nearly choked on her noodles. "Have you seen this before?"

"No," Drake insisted. "Not my thing. Hey, how was Jen?"

"Why?"

"Because you were just out with her."

"Yeah, sorry," Ellie said. "I'm kind of tired."

"Are you hiding something from me?" He went for another bite.

"No." She was jumpy.

"I'm kidding." Drake laughed. He pulled her closer into him until they were one snuggly human.

Halfway into the movie, Ellie took a breath and pressed pause. "Actually, Drake, there is something I wanted to tell you—"

His snore landed next to her on the couch. He was already asleep. Ellie tossed a blanket over their legs and set her head on his shoulder.

The news, she decided, could wait a little longer.

19

The restaurants Nolan picked felt the same to Ellie. There were always fresh-cut flowers, pressed white linens, and brown sugar cubes tucked inside decorative dishes fit for royalty. The hostess led Ellie toward a small, round table next to a trickling fountain. Ellie was too preoccupied to enjoy these luxuries—even the ornate menu descriptions, which leaned into words like *foraged*. Instead, she waded through what Melinda had said over drinks: "You know how he is."

The table rattled. Nolan had landed, frazzled in a navy suit that likely cost a fortune.

"First off, I want to give the air a spritz and say, I'm sorry for our last meeting," he told her after they ordered. Two juices and local biscuits with marmalade were set down for each of them. They hadn't asked for either of these things. "I shouldn't have said that your work was *okay*. Artists go through phases. It's a part of *the process*."

Ellie spread some marmalade onto a biscuit. The first warm bite crumbled apart in her mouth. "Thanks," she said. "But you were right."

Nolan tugged at the sleeves of his shirt. "This new stuff . . . the piece about the dress shop. It's compelling. You found something you're obsessed with."

Ellie wiped the marmalade off her mouth. "I'm not obsessed with Melinda."

"Who?"

"The . . . owner." Ellie took another bite of the biscuit. Nolan wasn't eating his. He slid it over her way. "The owner of the dress shop."

"Right. Well, whatever you did, it worked. This was the best thing you've written since Finn's."

Warmth coursed through Ellie in response to a compliment. She'd missed those.

"Your timing was perfect. You sent me the draft. Then, you were fresh on my mind when a friend brought up a new project over lunch yesterday. It's a little different, this thing. Something that could be great for you, honestly."

There was a holiday home show, he explained over his egg whites with foraged herb salad. The producer was casting a host in advance for next year's winter season. Finding the right person and having time to build chemistry around them was important. Normally, casting would turn to the morning-show hosts, followed by people from interior-design shows or reality stars, but this project called for someone more avant-garde. "Turns out, you're very avant-garde, in a network television way."

Hosting a holiday show on its own wouldn't have interested Ellie, but the show's premise intrigued her. Old houses were going to get revived, Nolan explained as she wolfed down her chocolate crepes with organic berry mélange. "Revived and decorated in lights." For free, or the cost of playing along, a home that would normally be turned over or flipped got to stay with its rightful owner. "The same bones in better form." It wasn't a guarantee that they would choose Ellie, but the producers had trouble finding a host to fit the bill. They were eager for her to come in for a meeting.

"I don't know," Ellie said. "My last show was a disaster."

"The last show wasn't your fault. You were great! What wasn't great was the screenwriter they hired right out of college." Nolan pushed his plate away. "Look, Ellie. The thing about this gig is that, if we get it—which I believe we will—we can easily land another book. You'll pick up lots of fans. Then, we go where the wind takes us."

Ellie had to admit there was something enticing about being on television during the holidays. "I'm afraid," she told him. She was surprised to say that out loud. "Of failing yet again."

Nolan softened. "Look around the room," he instructed. Ellie did. "Everyone in here is afraid."

"Not you."

He moved closer and pushed the small vase of greenery between them out of the way. "Sure I am. I'm scared that if I don't dress this way—and eat at places like this—people won't take me seriously. He pulled the corner of his shirt up to display where some red fruit punch had left its mark. "Or if they see the juice stain on my sleeve. We're all a little messy."

"Wow, Nolan." His candor was refreshing. "Thanks."

He shrugged and brushed the bread off his hands. "I guess I'm softening as a dad. And also, I really want you to go for this. Because you're good. You're a perfect fit. And, I do like money."

Money. Ellie had barely considered the money. The thought of having a network television budget to do what she loved was alluring. How many homes could she save—and people could she help—with a big crew on her team?

It was a dream job, the kind of thing Ellie couldn't have even imagined existing. And yet, she couldn't shake the reason she was in consideration: Melinda. The story about Melinda was the reason for the call, the reason for this breakfast. Drake's past had made Ellie relevant in the present. After being in a creative rut for such a long time, she wasn't about to throw away this newfound relevance.

By the time Nolan snatched the bill and ordered a pastry to go, Ellie agreed to put her name into the hat. On the walk to the car, she texted Drake. She reminded herself that it was good news she had to share, albeit with a challenging layer.

Want to get dinner out tonight?

Three typing dots appeared, then:

It's another late, annoying day. Rain check for tomorrow? Before our midnight movie.

"Did you just thank the maps lady?" Ellie asked on their way to dinner the next night. The GPS had told Drake to make a right turn, and he'd responded back to her. He was impossibly polite, even when bantering with inanimate objects.

"Gertie?" he said. "Yeah. Of course, I thanked her."

"I need to share something," Ellie said, eager to get everything out and off her chest. Her guilt had grown larger over the last day; the lunch with Nolan had made Melinda's story even more of a reality. "Some *things*, actually." Ellie's eyes moved back to the map on the phone. Drake had plugged in an address she recognized. It was a street she knew well.

"Sure," he said. "Tell away."

Finn's. Drake was taking her to Finn's. She couldn't ruin their special place with her confession. They had only gone to Finn's once since they'd met. Ellie insisted they shouldn't visit too often; things tended to lose their luster when they were overdone. But Drake seemed to think tonight deserved a stop, and she agreed. It had been a tough week. They needed this lift, this mood boost. Ellie stuffed her guilt in her mental junk closet and moved on.

"The thing I wanted to tell you," she said, dancing her hand up his arm, "is that I could really use an old-fashioned."

"Well then," Drake said. "You're just in luck."

Finn's was busy that night.

Sam was still behind the bar. Ellie knew from checking in

every now and then that his uncle had promoted him to manager. Copies of her book with the Finn's story inside were stacked on top of the liquor shelves. There were a few newer touches, too—lights behind the bottles, some more modern vinyl selections, and a food menu of small bites. Sam stopped midpour as Ellie and Drake moved toward their meeting spot.

"It's been a while, bar saver," he said.

"Didn't technically save it," Ellie reminded him. "Just wrote about it."

"Yeah, okay, sure." He finished the drink he'd been making and started to pour an old-fashioned without asking. "Sometimes, people ask to buy those books, but I won't let them out of my sight. They're my good-luck charm." After passing over Ellie's drink, he finally acknowledged Drake. "Hey, man. You want a beer?"

"You know what?" Drake said. "I'll take an old-fashioned, too."

Ellie lowered herself onto the same stool as that first night. Drake went to the bathroom, which left her alone with Sam for a moment. She glanced behind her to make sure Drake was out of earshot, then tapped her hands on the bar to get his attention.

"Psst," she asked. "Can you do me a favor?"

A few minutes later, Drake shuffled onto the stool next to her. "Hey, again," he said. "This is really taking me back. I was sitting here." He brushed the bar. "You were there. And I was like, hey, whatcha working on?" Drake pretended to lean over her shoulder to check out a notebook.

Ellie smirked. "And I was like, oh yeah, there's this big vampire project."

"No, I said the vampire thing," Drake clarified. "I said something like, you're becoming a vampire?"

"And I said, yes, I'm a Vampire in Progress. A VIP. And you," Ellie pointed to him, "you seem like you'd go to a lot of restaurant birthday parties? Am I right?"

Drake grabbed her hand. "You know what I was thinking?"

"I don't remember this part."

"Back then, I mean," Drake said. "I thought you were the most interesting woman in the world."

Ellie mocked disbelief. "You thought I was the Dos Equis man?"

"Right. Spitting image. What about you? What did you think when you saw me?" Drake spun his stool to the side to show off his profile.

"I thought," Ellie said. "Okay, well at first I thought you were cute."

"I'll take cute."

"But you know what I love about you now?"

Sam dropped off their drinks, and they placed an order for a few small plates. Drake took a sip. "Rocket fuel," he said. "*Delicious* rocket fuel."

Ellie's first sip went down easily. "I love how you snack when you're stressed, so I immediately know if there's something wrong," she said. "I love how you care about other people so deeply that you even care about the feelings of the maps lady. I love how I catch you smiling at me when I'm not looking. I love how stupidly earnest you are. And speaking of earnest, I love your optimism. I love that you're everything I'm not, and that we have almost nothing in common except for having the exact same sense of humor."

Drake touched her arm to pause her. "All along, I thought you were Sally Albright. But here you are, doing the Harry Burns speech."

Ellie melted a little. "I love how you act like the side-of-a-truck guy sometimes, but you're really a Nora-Ephron-Mariah-Carey guy."

"What's a side-of-the-truck guy?"

"You know. The guy on the side of the truck in an advertisement. *We do tough law. We want to buy your house. We crush cans with our fists.*" Drake laughed. "I know I teased you the first time we sat here about only going to the same three places. But, now I know why."

"Which is?"

"You don't give up on people or things that you care about." Ellie took another sip. "You never make me guess if you're going to show up. You tell me how you feel. You surprise and delight me. And I'm not good at any of those things, but you make me want to be better."

"You're unusually feely tonight."

"What can I say," Ellie told him. They needed this, a good moment. The calm before the storm. "Maybe Finn's makes me nostalgic."

"I love you, Ellie."

"I love you, Drake. But wait. There's more to what I want to say . . . Umm—" She motioned to Sam from across the bar. He nodded back at her. "I Will Always Love You" started to blare. It was too loud for the space and immediately shut down all conversations. "Sorry everybody," Sam shouted, adjusting the levels back to something more reasonable. "Carry on."

"This is my favorite song," Drake said, acknowledging Ellie's gesture.

"I know."

"This means a lot—"

"I know."

They listened to the song play out. It was late enough for inhibitions to be lowered, and about halfway through it, the few remaining patrons started to sing. Though they'd only had one drink themselves, it was impossible not to join in. Drake started first, right around the chorus. Ellie was his backup singer. In a move she hadn't predicted, Sam hopped up on the bar and used a bottle of bitters as a microphone as he reached for a high note.

Their food came and the conversation kept buzzing. Eventually, Ellie noticed the time: It was 11:40 already. They needed the check. Fast.

Energized from Finn's, Drake chatted nonstop in the car. He asked how her meeting with Nolan went earlier. Ellie kept it general since the good news she had to share was now tied to Melinda. She wanted to stay wrapped in the laughter, the breezy conversation, and the warm glow of the bar for a little longer.

But as the car neared the cinema, Ellie's dread made itself known. The memory she had brought them there to watch had to be so close. She'd convinced herself she could handle it. Enough time had passed since that night, she'd repeated in her head. Now, just the thought of the movie and its horrors was enough to make her jaw clench.

I think something awful is coming was on the tip of her tongue.

"Drake," Ellie said. She grabbed his arm as he parked the car at the bottom of the alley. "Do we have to go in tonight?"

He laughed in disbelief. "What do you mean?" he asked. "All this time, you've been begging me to go here."

"I know," she said. "It's just that . . . there's something you don't know about me yet. Something that's been . . ." They weren't even in the cinema yet, and she could already feel herself tearing up. "Something that has felt impossible to talk about."

"Okay," Drake nodded. He left the car on and turned up the heat a little, as if to say: continue, time is of no limit. But the time did have a limit. It was 11:53. How had she avoided the topic for this long? They needed to get inside. If they didn't, she would miss the exact reason she'd brought them there.

"We've got to go," Ellie said.

"We could go to Mae's instead," Drake suggested. "Grab an ice cream and call it a night?"

It was 11:54.

"Let's start walking," Ellie insisted. Reason kicked in. "We can't be late."

"All right," Drake said, resigned. He opened her door and softly pushed her forward through the alley's entrance and up the cobblestones. "Whatever it is, Ellie, I'm here for you."

With a brisk walk, they made it just in time. They sat, the lights lowered, and the hot dog Charleston dance began. Then, Ellie's body froze as a title appeared on the pitch-black screen.

TICKET FIVE: *RIDE*

The party buzzed with college kids.

Nothing in the living room made sense together. A Jimi Hendrix tie-dye tapestry was faced off with modern IKEA wall art. Nirvana and Rihanna mingled on a confusing playlist, and a rowdy game of beer pong was juxtaposed by the placid nature documentary on television. Ellie watched a school of yellow fish thread through a vibrant coral reef while her date traded conspiracy theories with his friends. Would he even notice if she left?

He didn't notice.

Ellie climbed the beige stairs up to the home's second level, each step soft under her feet. At the top, the door to a sky-blue bedroom was open. She poked her head in. The walls were plastered with photos of a blonde girl and her friends. Something about her carefree smile was reminiscent of a missing person poster. Behind her, on the bedside table, was what she'd been looking for: a coveted, freeing, landline. She picked it up and dialed.

"You have to come get me," Ellie said, lowering herself to sit on the bed. Her hand brushed against some weathered books as she flipped the bedside lamp on. A copy of *The Great Gatsby* was particularly dog-eared. "I'm on a bad date," she admitted. "Yeah, he *is* cute, but he's also one of those government-faked-the-moon-landing types." Ellie twirled the phone cord around her wrist. "Because my phone is dead," she explained. "No, I didn't bring a charger to a party. Come and get me." She paused, then switched tactics. "I'll buy you fries."

Twenty minutes later, Ben was perched inside his car at the end of the driveway. Ellie flung the passenger door open. Gone was his last decade of anarchy. In was an air of academia: neat-trimmed hair, a forest-green cable knit sweater, and based on his cupholders, an espresso habit. But as his arms stretched toward the wheel, an artifact of Ben's rebellion surfaced. There it was—the tattoo he sat for on his twentieth birthday—*The Shining* twins, but really, the two of them.

A whistling teakettle backed by spacey synths greeted Ellie as she hopped inside the car. "What's this music?" she asked.

"It's plant music, sis," Ben said. His face was gentle, almost serene.

"Plant music?"

"Yeah," he told her. His bright olive eyes, which Ellie shared, glowed in the seat next to her. "This is an album that helps plants reach their potential." Ben turned his arms into the limbs of a *Monstera*. He swatted her head as he peeled the car from the curb. Ellie pictured a group of plants swaying inside the party instead of confused college students. Plants with beer cans. Plants with hookah habits or inferiority complexes. At the end of the song, the music clicked to a stop. "Rewind," Ben insisted, rolling his finger around in the air.

"Rewind it?"

"It's a tape, sis."

Ellie relaxed a little. Her brother hadn't changed all that much;

the tape was proof he still frequented vintage stores and estate sales. Ben also probably flirted with the shop girl about some offbeat hobby of hers, like growing turmeric. Static filled the space between them as the tape rewound, then snapped back to the beginning.

Ellie hit Play and the music dragged her deep into the hazy part of her brain. The alcohol and car's speed transformed the road outside into streaks. Her eyes were closing. She couldn't fall asleep this early, not yet. Spending time with Ben was a rare luxury these days. They would sit on the floor of his apartment and split the day-old noodles in his fridge, gossiping about their dates, their part-time jobs, their trivial encounters. It always felt so good to come back together, like they were still kids and life didn't have any big stakes yet.

Her eyes opened again as the car pulled up to the illuminated square menu outside their favorite fast-food place. Ben ordered large fries through the speaker. "With extra ketchup," he said, leaning out the window. "And extra napkins," he added, glancing at Ellie in camaraderie. "We're messy like that."

Ellie searched the radio for something that would keep her awake. The announcer on the local station teased a contest coming up. Listeners could reveal a personal secret about themselves and win tickets to see Interpol.

"Speaking of secrets," Ben said after they ordered, "why don't you spill yours?" They slid up to the window. Ellie set crumpled cash in Ben's hand. He arranged the fries between them in the cup holder and squeezed a few ketchup packets over the steaming golden rectangles.

"You want my secrets?" Ellie asked. She grabbed two fries. "Do you have Interpol tickets?"

"Seriously, Ellie," Ben said. After they paid, they pulled back onto the dark street. "I want to know what you've been thinking about lately. We talk about the trivial stuff, but I think it's time for you to make a plan. What you're going to do with your life after college. Where you're going to live. How you're going to avoid parties that require fleeing."

"My plan," Ellie said, "is to eat my weight in fries."

"Well, instead of that, I think you should write." Ben pulled one of her fries away. "You're good at it."

"Writer, schmiter," she said. Ben's timing for a serious conversation was terrible. Ellie was half-drunk, half-falling asleep, and he was hitting her with lofty questions. Her annoyance kicked in. "Why are you asking me this now, Ben?"

He sighed. "Because we should talk about these things before I leave."

The word *leave* reached out and struck her. They were supposed to be acting like it wouldn't, inevitably, happen. Ben wouldn't head off to med school. Ellie wouldn't have to take a flight, albeit a short one, to see him. He barely seemed to mourn this distance. They'd been attached at the hip since she was born. When he'd gone off to college, it was only an hour from home, and she'd soon followed him there. Where would Ellie even fit in once he began his new life?

"I don't get why you're suddenly telling me what to do," she retaliated. "You've gone kind of cliché lately. Now you're running off to become one of them?"

"What's your beef with med school, man?" Ben asked, more curious than upset. They turned onto the freeway.

"No beef," Ellie said, despite a clear beef. "I think it sounds boring."

He nodded a little. "Well, I think it sounds nice."

"Nice?"

"Nice." Ben rolled his sleeves up a little more and crunched down on another fry. "Yeah. Helping people. I mean, look, I'm not squeamish. I'm good at memorizing things. I want to listen to people, sis. Save them. Give them another chance."

Ellie sighed. They had usually been on the same page about everything: life was about fun, and excitement, and mischief. While Ellie had flailed around at college and continued to change majors, her brother had found a new purpose. His passion fired up her attitude. "Well, I'm sure they throw great parties, those doctors in training," she pouted. "You'll all get to drinking and start practicing your sutures—"

"I'm not going there for the parties, Ellie. I'm going to be studying. I'm going to be *busy*—"

"If you're going to be so busy, I guess I won't visit you."

"Don't get all drama school on me. You know that's not what I meant."

"It's fine," she insisted. "You're going to be busy. I won't visit you."

The radio announcer brought up the contest again. *Spill. Your. Secrets.* Ellie sighed and turned the volume down. "I don't think I ever told you, but . . . I went on a date with this guy," she admitted.

"With the radio DJ?"

"DJ makes it sound fancy," Ellie said. "It's college radio. I think five people are listening." Ben skipped the exit that went to campus and moved toward the one leading to his apartment. He must have intuited that Ellie would want to stay there instead of the dorms, a choice that meant he wasn't holding her tantrum against her. "Anyway, this *DJ* had amazing taste in music, but an exhaustive number of food allergies."

Ben chuckled. "Oh, yeah?"

"It took an hour to order at dinner."

Ben gave a single "ha." Ellie smiled.

She often swore they were the same person, but it was their differences that made him better. Ellie liked to sink her talons into a good grudge. Ben was quick to forgive, especially when it came to her. "I'm sorry I said all that," she told him. "I think it's beautiful you want to help people."

Ben gave her a skeptical eye. "Beautiful, eh? You really think so?"

"I do," she said.

They got off the freeway, onto a smaller highway, and eventually slowed for a stoplight in a more residential area. As the circle overhead flashed red, an embarrassing thing happened. Tears streamed down Ellie's face. "I'm being a jerk because I'm crushed that you're leaving," she admitted. "You're my favorite person, Ben. I say that without irony. I look up to you so much. And I'm a jerk because I can't stand that I'm not going to have you to *Spill My Secrets* to anymore. And I'm crying because I do think it's beautiful you want to help people. And also, because—green light."

"Green light?" Ben asked. He was lost in the middle of her words. This level of confessional was rare for Ellie, even though they were close.

"The light's green," Ellie said. Ben didn't move. "Go!"

Here was her saving grace: something as simple as a green light. She had been about to say something humiliating. The light had helped her reel it back in. *Go!* She'd said instead.

The car flew into the intersection on her command. *Go!* Ben's eyes were transfixed on her, his expression so sympathetic, wanting to help.

Go! she'd said. And he'd listened.

Only, Ben hadn't looked away from her face.

And Ellie hadn't looked both ways.

Lights filled the inside of the car to Ellie's right, growing brighter until they became blinding. What was that look on Ben's face? *Surprise.* Was it surprise? As if saying, "Why *go?*" Why—he must have wanted to know—had she really seen a green light? Metal collided deep in her ears, followed by the punch of an airbag to her chest. The smell of thick chemicals was everywhere, dust deep inside her lungs.

The car began to spin off the road. It wasn't a real car that could respond this way, was it? So flimsy. It was a toy car on a track, a car moved by a troubled child—by Ellie herself, maybe. Eventually the car stopped. The windshield was busted. Every part of her chest felt bruised, and bits of sharp glass strung in her hair.

"Oh my god." Ellie reached out for Ben's arm. "We're so lucky," she said, straining to catch her breath. "That could've been bad. Really bad. But we're okay. We're okay!" She believed this because Ben was always okay. Despite his adventures and escapades, he narrowly dodged the worst side of things.

Only this time, Ellie realized, he hadn't.

Ben's airbag had malfunctioned, turning his body into a rag doll over the steering wheel. There was blood on the dashboard. Blood on the sides of his green sweater, like a terrible, sticky belt. Blood pooled out and around on the gray seat of the car. The dinosaur key chain dangled from the rearview mirror.

Ellie searched Ben's face for help. He would know what to do. He always knew what to do. Helping people—people in emergencies like this—was about to be his specialty. Did she soak up the blood? Did she sit him up straight? Did she get him out of the car?

Air. She needed air.

"Call," Ben said. His voice was quiet.

Call for help. Of course, she should call for help. Ellie fumbled for the phone in her pocket. The screen was black and very dead.

She hadn't charged her phone. If she had just . . .

Next, Ben's pocket. She checked his jeans, tapped the seat beside him—

His blood, on her trembling palms.

"Compartment," he was saying.

"Compartment. Compartment?" Ellie repeated. Time ticking

away, energy draining, precious seconds lost. Finally, Ellie figured it out. She clicked the compartment between them open. His phone was in her hand. It was charged. She punched in 9-1-1.

What's your emergency? a warped voice asked. It was coming through a tin can.

Ellie undid her seat belt to get a better look at Ben. Her bones hurt. "Uh, there's been an accident. My brother was driving."

Where are you? the tin can asked.

"I don't, I don't know where, I don't know where we—"

Can you give me some landmarks—

The exit name came to mind. Ben liked to growl when he said it. *Grrrr-over.* "Grover exit," she said. "On . . ." What was the highway called? Ellie couldn't tell. Any sort of sign was out of sight.

We're on the way, said the tin can, which became not a voice on the phone, but a drill bit inside her head. Ellie could feel the voice on her teeth as it asked a series of follow-up questions. *Talk to your brother,* her teeth vibrated.

"Ben, please."

"Okay, Ellie," Ben said.

Keep talking. We're going to be there soon.

"Yes, you're okay," Ellie said. "You're going to be fine."

"It's okay," he repeated.

The heaviness of *it's* sank in. Ben wasn't okay, he meant. *It's okay.* As if to say, a life without him would be okay for Ellie. She would move on. She had their mom and dad. She would make friends that felt like family. She would meet someone and start a family and tell her kids about their wild, wonderful uncle. Those stories, the framed photos on the walls, the smell of him she might catch as she rounded a corner during the holidays, would be enough. A lifetime of feeble attempts to connect stretched out before her like a lonely, wavering road.

"Don't forget me," Ben said, his voice getting smaller.

"Ben, of course, I won't forget you. I could never forget—I promise I could never forget you. But, hey. You're not going anywhere."

A horrible irony settled in as Ellie said the thing she couldn't at the green light. It was even truer now, even more relevant, and so easy to put to words. "I can't do this without you," she begged.

Ben didn't respond.

A little later, Ellie and Ben were drowned in a sea of lights and the hot red sound of sirens. A man pulled her from the car. There was a scratched-up blanket, a ride to the hospital, a dreamless sleep. Or maybe the whole night was a dream, a terrible, vivid dream.

Ellie was in the hospital where Ben was born. It was a hospital so illustrious that Sandra and William Marshall had driven an hour to have a child there. William had filmed Sandra, wound up in pain, as they walked to the delivery room. Sandra grunted for a few minutes, then her baby came out in "the world's shortest labor."

Later that afternoon, her dad brought Ben to the window, according to Marshall family lore. "Look there. At the world," he whispered. It was a view of the parking garage. The idea of the world was enough, though. There were so many possibilities waiting for him, possibilities that had been better than what they'd had.

A new generation. A fresh start.

Now, Ellie was three floors up.

Inside the room with her was a swarm of doctors, specialists, and questions she couldn't answer. The room smelled like Jell-O. She started to feel like she'd crawled inside the mold and was wobbling with humans around her, speaking a foreign language. Then, something clicked. Ben's name. They were saying Ben's name. Her dad was next to her. He asked the doctors to leave them alone for a while. Ellie shivered under the crisp, white sheets.

William leaned toward her but didn't take her hand. He broke the news so simply; confusion must have marked her face because he could tell she didn't understand. His voice was mundane. The moment itself was heartbreakingly mundane: the gasping of an IV bag draining fluids into her. Talk-show hosts who droned on in the background about travel destinations. *Cancun. Belize.* Where was the moving overture? Where were the tears? Why hadn't her dad turned the television off?

Ben had died, she learned, right there at the hospital. Her dad sat with her for a few minutes after he explained it again. He told her she was in the car with him, near the Grover exit. The other driver ran a red light. So far, it seemed like the other driver wasn't drunk. It was just "one of those things."

One of those things.

Ellie's dad left the room. Her mom was somewhere down the hall. Ellie could hear her crying, she thought, or maybe it was somebody else. How many families were grieving in this space, at this precise moment? Losses wrapped around them like bad wallpaper. Grief pushed down on her chest and made it hard to stay in her body, but there was a tinge of something else there, too.

Guilt.

Ellie forced her eyes shut and tried to remember the accident. Sober driver. Red light. Grover. Sober driver. Red light. Grover. Grover, Ellie, and Ben—Ben who was such a good driver, wasn't he? The best driver. Responsible. Wild in his whims, but never when it came to safety.

Which only pointed to one thing.

Sitting in the theater, Ellie realized there was a reason her mind had blocked out what happened. Her body was trying to protect her.

She was, as she'd always feared, to blame.

20

The prickle that formed in Ellie's chest was like the tail end of a firework; hot to touch, fleeting, an ending. On-screen, the movie blurred, and Drake's memory started to play, but Ellie was already standing, flinging the auditorium doors open, and moving down the curved stairwell through the pulsing red lobby. The prickle became pressure. Doom swirled above her head, but Ellie wasn't going to give in to it. No, if she could get out of there fast enough, away from the theater, maybe she could outrun the memory.

Cold air stung her cheeks as she pulled on the heavy brass handles and burst out into the night. Ellie wrapped her coat tight around herself and started the descent down all the slick cobblestones. If only she could press rewind. Had her strategy of forgetting been so bad? Clarity was overrated. And at least, before that night's showing, she didn't have to live with the truth.

She had gone to the cinema hoping it would prove her fears wrong.

Instead, it had proven them exactly right.

Ellie felt herself pulled in by a big black coil. Mae's Famous Scoops was on her periphery, but the world around her wasn't real. She had the sense that if she reached out and touched anything—an iron bench or a wooden store sign—they would evaporate. Ellie was wound farther into the coil. The only comfort came from the glow of the theater growing dimmer and dimmer behind her.

"Ellie. Slow down." Drake's voice.

Drake.

He'd never see her quite the same way again, would he?

"Ellie?" His hands brought her shoulders to a stop. "I think you wore the wrong shoes for a chase sequence." His humor was an attempt to speak her language. When tough things happened, Ellie leaned on levity. But right then, she didn't want to make light of things. She started to move again toward an unknown destination. The idea of *away* grew shinier in her mind. "Can, can you slow down?"

Ellie couldn't slow down. She only wished her feet would move faster. Her heels got in the way as she darted toward the bottom of the alley, leaped through the open doorway, and returned to the street lined with whimsical storefronts. A beeping sounded in her ears. Drake's truck was being unlocked. He ran ahead to grab the passenger door for her, sending out smoke signals with his breath.

"I can't—" Ellie told him. She didn't finish the thought, but Drake seemed to read between the lines. Ellie could not, under any circumstance, get inside a car after what they had just seen. Drake flicked his watch forward to check the time. He opened the trunk to rustle around for something and returned with a fleece blanket, which he draped around her like a cloak.

"What are you doing?" she asked.

"It's late," he said, rubbing the soft material over her shoulders. "And cold."

"So?"

His hands found his pockets. "So, everything around here is closed."

"So—"

"So now you're the queen of the blankets." Ellie's fingers started to thaw. Drake's thumb brushed her face and rubbed off some of her tears. "I'm here," he said. "Whenever you're ready to talk."

"The rules," she reminded him.

"I think this is a good moment to press pause on those."

Ellie knew she was closed off when it came to sharing her inner world. People before Drake had hinted at this. Lucas, one of her boyfriends in her twenties, had described her as a castle. She was beautiful, he'd told her, but out of reach, full of mysterious hallways and secrets. His assessment was right, she worried.

Yet, Drake had just seen it all. She feared he'd love her less after learning the truth. But no, he was standing on the castle drawbridge, waiting to be invited in.

Where should she start? Ellie's mind strained to hold on to every detail about Ben. It was important, she recognized this time, to preserve the nuances of her brother. Because she had promised she wouldn't forget him, and she had been failing at that.

The moment he died, an hourglass had flipped. The harder Ellie gripped onto the fragments of him, the faster the grains of sand slid to the bottom of the glass. Memories of events together were first to fade—holidays, birthdays, bits of conversation. Next, she lost the sound of his voice. Lately, Ellie was losing the way Ben looked. Giving away his things was one of her biggest regrets. She'd thought she couldn't handle the weight of them, but they were pieces of him. Now, she studied the same photographs over and over again, confined to a flattened version of him.

Until a few weeks ago.

Ellie had come to the cinema wanting to fill in the gaps of her memory, but she'd found something better: her brother, alive. There he was again, on a big screen. There was his cheeky smile, his Hollywood charisma, his lightning-sharp wit, the bounce in his confident gait. There was her brother in the driver's seat right next to her, eating french fries, listening to obscure music, giving her advice. Advice she desperately needed. Why had she resisted his guidance?

And now, she'd lived through losing him for a second time and felt the full burden of it.

Green light. *Go!*

Drake was pulling the blanket away from her face to get a better look. "Ellie?"

The Case of the Girl in the Car Accident.

"It's all my fault," she said finally.

"Oh, hey. That's not true, Ellie." Drake moved closer. "It wasn't your fault what happened. At all. It was a green light. You told him it was a green light . . . Anyone would've done that. The other driver is the one who ran it—"

"If I hadn't been making such a scene," Ellie said. "If I hadn't taken up all his attention, he would still be here. You would meet him and know him. You would love him, Drake."

"My heart is breaking for you." Drake was tearing up now, too. His arms hugged her blanketed form, and she planted her head on his chest. "I had no idea you were there that night. I mean, when you told me about the accident, I should've put that together. Asked more questions. Or . . . I don't know. I'm so sorry, Ellie." Drake's arms wrapped tighter around her.

Ellie's weight gave into him. Sharing her grief was new; now she didn't have to do the work of carrying her past by herself. Drake was proving he could handle the elements, the cold, all of her pain. So she sobbed in the empty street while Drake held her.

She described the weight of missing Ben. She shared the way the loss had pulled her family apart, slowly and painfully. And Drake didn't move. He didn't even flinch. He stood on the sidewalk with her, in the dark, and took in every word.

21

Ellie's renewed grief warped her sense of time. She could check out for hours, then experience seconds of remembering that felt like days. Sometimes, there were rare, blissful moments when things were normal, and she could rely on clocks again before everything came crashing back down.

Ellie barely noticed that a week had slipped by until Drake brought up the next ticket on the following Saturday afternoon. He thought they shouldn't go back to the cinema; they could skip a visit at least, couldn't they? Ever since they'd talked last week, the rules were still officially on pause. Ellie was quick to agree with his suggestion. Revisiting the place where she'd watched her brother die, again—and where she would soon see the ugliness that ensued with her family in the aftermath—wasn't high on her list.

"In that case," Drake said, "let's take a walk." He pulled her arms up and over her head. "I don't think I've seen you move from the couch once this week." The assumption wasn't quite true. Ellie had moved from the couch while Drake worked, typing away at a new draft of her piece on My Mother's Shop, which he still didn't know about. She needed to tell him, but there wasn't enough space inside of her to start that conversation; her mind and heart had reached their capacity for what they could handle. When Drake wasn't home, she threw herself into her work to ignore the pain, a familiar way of coping.

"All right. Let's get out," Ellie agreed. There was no use fighting the suggestion. Besides, Drake had been so kind to her that week—glued to her side, missing afternoons at work. The least she could do was give in to his support. As they put their coats on, Nancy's feet clicked toward them on the wood floor. Her eyes pleaded to join them. "We could all use some fresh air," Ellie said, snapping the leash on Nancy's collar.

Excitement for the holidays was blossoming outside. New lights dotted windowsills, and inflatable reindeer covered lawns draped in fresh snow. As they moved down the slick driveway to the sidewalk, Drake's gloved hand squeezed hers. "Checking in," he said. "How are you doing?"

She had been trying to figure that out herself. Not well was putting it too simply. "I feel like I'm riding circles around my own guilt," Ellie admitted. "I'm on some kind of cursed unicycle."

"Yeah, that's what I thought," he said. "And . . ." They passed an older couple out for a walk. Ellie smiled at them, surrendering to how disheveled she looked. She loved their neighborhood; it was calm, but it didn't lack movement. "I don't want you to feel that way," Drake told her. "I mean, you have a right to feel how you feel, but . . . it really wasn't your fault."

On a factual level, Ellie knew she was being hard on herself. The accident wasn't entirely her fault. After all, she hadn't run a red light. "I can't shake the guilt from all the tiny decisions that led to what happened," she said. "Decisions that I made. I mean, if I hadn't called him for a ride. If we hadn't stopped for fries. If I had charged my phone and hadn't wasted precious time looking for his. If I hadn't said 'Go' . . ."

Drake nodded. "Analyzing all the little things that could've happened differently isn't scientific, you know? Like, it assumes we can control the future, and we can't. This is hard for me to admit, as someone who loves planning for every error or possible outcome that could go wrong. But that's not how life works."

The sky was overcast, which gave all the houses a grayish tint, even though they were different hues. The last week was the first time Ellie had let Drake, or anyone, in about the accident. She'd always wondered why she struggled to share herself with others. Now she knew: the moment she started to peel herself open, her brother had died. As the years passed, this single experience had solidified into a lifelong belief. Being vulnerable was dangerous.

"It feels good to let you in," Ellie said. "I'm sorry I didn't tell you everything sooner. Of what I remembered, at least."

"Hey, don't worry about that." Drake pulled her hat over her ears. "It makes sense not to want to revisit the worst night of your life. Honestly, I'm surprised you wanted to go to the cinema at all, knowing that might play."

"About that," she started. "I took us there *to* see that night. I had to see it. I couldn't remember anything, so I spent all these years worrying. Imagining awful details. Feeling that maybe I was to blame. I needed to know for sure."

"You didn't remember anything?"

"Not much. Just bits and pieces," Ellie told him. "So I had to find out what happened."

"Are you relieved you saw it?" Drake asked.

"Not at all," she said. "But, in a way, yes. It was time for me to face it." The sidewalk moved down a slight slope. Ellie tightened her grip on Nancy's leash. Beyond all the familiar homes, the city's tall buildings poked out in the distance. A cloud hovered above the skyline, creating the illusion that the many floating floors extended into space. The limitlessness of it made Ellie uneasy, as if reality itself was bending. She needed a distraction, some levity, anything to make the grief hide out for a second.

Before she could express this, Drake moved down the sidewalk, bent to pack some snow together, and threw a snowball her way. Ellie cracked a smile as the white crumbles fell down her coat, then knelt to the ground to make one of her own. After her snowball smacked onto Drake's black puffy coat, he raced toward her in an act of comedic revenge, grabbed Nancy's leash, and picked Ellie up, moving them farther down the sidewalk and eventually setting her on some snow-covered grass. She reached her arms out to make a snow angel. Drake tumbled onto the ground beside her. Nancy wrapped them closer together with her leash.

"I think we're in somebody's yard," Ellie said.

"It's probably okay." Drake's face was concealed behind his hood. "They're never home. We could stay here all day. Throw a bash. Winter barbecue—"

"Drake. I need to tell you something."

He pushed some hair out of her face. "Let's wait until we're home and cozy?"

Ellie steeled herself. She had to get it out. He'd made her laugh, which gave her exactly enough relief to voice the second elephant in the room. "Drake, I've met Melinda," she confessed.

Confusion took over his face. "What?"

"I drove to her shop after watching you there together. I had to see it. I don't know why. I told myself I wouldn't be jealous. But it rattled me how happy she made you. I worried, what if I can't make you that happy? And when I was there, Melinda and I started talking. The shop was struggling. I needed a story. So, I agreed to write about it." Ellie searched Drake for a reaction. He looked concerned, she thought.

"But then, you and I had this incredible night at Sal's, and I realized I should call the story off. I told you I went out with Jen. I lied. I went to meet Melinda. Then before I could break the news, Nolan put me up for this job. An amazing job. And he only thought of me because of the Melinda story. Anyway, it's a home show like the ones you watch, but it's completely within my wheelhouse. And so, I kept writing about Melinda behind your back. I wanted the story to make me relevant to the producers. I really need a win right now. If I don't get one, I'm worried I'll fade away and so will all the places I love. I'm sorry, Drake."

He was parsing through the confession, she sensed, spending a second processing each individual piece. Finally, he looked right up at her. "Seriously?" he asked.

"Yes." Ellie sighed. She felt infinitely lighter with the secret off her chest. She was ready to handle the consequences. "Seriously."

Drake moved up onto his elbow. "I . . . What did you two even talk about?"

"Not you," Ellie assured him. "Well, other than her thinking that you set this whole thing up, which she does, by the way. Mostly about the store and your town. Nothing too personal."

Drake paused and assessed the facts. He turned himself to look out at the skyline. The clouds had lifted a bit, giving the buildings the right sense of scale again. "Okay," he decided with a nod.

"Okay," Ellie repeated. She couldn't believe it was that simple. Once again, they were in a situation where telling Drake the truth would've made much more sense than the challenging maze she'd put herself through. She wished she'd raised this conversation days ago. "Just, okay?"

"Yeah. Okay."

"I mean . . . Are you sure? You don't want to hash this out more? I can go all in on a hash—"

"Well, it's weird. Right?" Drake asked. "It's weird to keep massive secrets like this from each other."

"I know," Ellie said. "It *is* weird. Look, if you ask me not to release my story about her shop, I'll listen."

Drake nodded. "I know that. I don't want that, though."

Nancy pulled them tighter as she tried to inch her way toward a tree trunk. Drake put his arm around Ellie.

"I'm sorry, too," he said.

"Why?"

"I'm sorry I made you doubt if I was happy with you. Things with us are so good that I still question how this can be real. I'm not exactly lucky with other things. How did I possibly get this lucky with you? I need you to know that there's nothing for you to worry about with Melinda. It was this young love. That's it."

Ellie wanted to believe him, but she couldn't quite let go of the memories. "That day she brought you to the shop just seemed perfect. Like, this total movie moment."

"Yeah. You're right. It was a movie moment." Drake nodded. "But you have to think about all the things the cinema didn't play. I mean, when I was leaving the shop that night, I tripped and crash-landed on my face. My palms were all scuffed up. I wouldn't go back in the store because I didn't want to embarrass myself, so I went home a mess. It's like what Natalie said at the beginning. The cinema has only been showing us moments worthy of a big screen."

The crunching of boots came behind them, followed by the face of an upside-down girl in earmuffs. The owners were, in fact, home, it seemed. Ellie and Drake sat up.

"Sorry, sorry. We were just having a rest," Drake apologized. The girl seemed more curious than bothered.

"Nice place you have," Ellie told her before they started the return walk to their own home. As they did, Drake brought the conversation back around to the holiday home show. He wanted to know everything about it. This was big, he kept saying. Plus, she was going to have so many "Oh My God" moments.

"What's an 'Oh My God' moment?" Ellie asked. They took their time walking. Holiday lights tucked around windowsills were slowly starting to hum with life.

"You know, when the owners walk around the house at the end and their eyes get wide and they say 'Oh my god!' They look kind of possessed, but like, with joy? Those are my favorite parts of those shows."

"Yeah, well, let's not get too far ahead of ourselves . . . I don't know if I'm going to get it for sure."

Drake stopped walking for a second to make a point. "You will," he said.

"How do you know?"

He placed both hands on the side of his head like a TV psychic. "Because I'm the guy watching all those shows. And there's no one who makes me say 'Oh my god' quite like you."

When they got home, Nancy bounded inside. The space had loosened; the living room felt less like a trap and more like a quiet refuge. They lit a fire and played poker on the floor, using their old Halloween candy to place bets. Neither of them were good at it, but that wasn't the point.

Time made more sense again, at least for the night.

22

The following Friday, Drake suggested they sit out the cinema a second time. "In fact, I don't think we should go back," he said, sitting next to her at the kitchen table and nibbling on some leftovers. Ellie weighed what would remain for them to see on her side of the story. Family feuds. One-night stands. Being impulsive through her twenties until she landed right here. Drake was the best thing that happened to her since Ben died. Maybe it was better to stay in the present than relive the rest of it.

"Okay," she agreed. "Fine by me. I saw what I went there for."

"Good." Drake nodded. "I have my mom's Early Christmas Dinner thing tomorrow night, anyway." He put his arm around her. "I was thinking I could head out there, leave early, and come home with armfuls of leftovers."

Ellie was familiar with Early Christmas Dinner. The superfluous event was a chance for the Nielsons to gather and officially kick the holiday off before it happened. To mark the occasion, Beth regaled everyone with the three holiday carols she could play on the keyboard, and Drake banged away on a triangle instrument he'd been given as a child. The evening wasn't a replacement for Christmas, merely an opening act.

Last year, she would've loved to have skipped it. But now, Ellie didn't want to be alone. Sitting in the quiet house with only her thoughts sounded too unbearable.

"I'll go with you," she said.

"You really don't have to do that," Drake insisted. "You've had a rough couple of weeks. I know it's not your thing. You can come to real Christmas."

"No," she pushed. "I want to come."

"It's okay if you—"

"I'm coming to dinner, Drake," she said. "With bells on."

To make good on her promise, Ellie found a dress with literal bells on the sleeves for Early Christmas Dinner. When Robert opened the door in his holiday sweatpants, she realized she'd overdressed. The three of them jingled their way through hugs and hellos. The kitchen's small dinner table was set up with festive paper plates and a homemade reindeer centerpiece featuring buttons for eyes. Before Ellie and Drake sat down, the table started to tilt as it always did. The silverware came dangerously close to hitting the floor.

"Oh boy, here we go," Robert said. "Table on the run."

"Do we need to have another talk about replacing the table?" Drake asked.

"No," his dad insisted. "No. We're not replacing the table."

"Why not?" Drake argued. "It's broken. It's always been broken."

"Kids!" Beth shouted from the hall, her hands in the air. "Oh good, we're fixing the table, how fun!"

"This isn't fun, Mom," Drake said. He bent to start repairing the leg. Ellie chuckled, charmed by the routine.

"How about when you get that table all squared away, you make the front door jealous?" Beth suggested with a pat on Drake's back. The front door hadn't been closing properly for a week, she explained, which was likely the reason for the chill inside.

While Drake went to work on the door, Beth pulled Ellie down the hall toward his room for her design expertise. They were slowly turning Drake's room into a home gym, Beth explained, even though Ellie already knew this from their last several visits. His bed was still in its place, but it was now accompanied by more rogue exercise equipment than Ellie remembered. At the center of the room was a tiny trampoline most appropriate for a cat.

"I don't know a lot about decorating gyms," Ellie said. This was an understatement.

Beth ignored her comment. "I need something to liven it up in here." She gestured toward a blank white wall.

Ellie wanted to be helpful. "Maybe you could do a simple mural?" she suggested. "You know, a word that inspires you, or—"

Beth smiled and snapped her fingers. "Ooh, babies!" she said. "I have some framed Anne Geddes babies in Drake's closet. Do you think that might work?"

Ellie swallowed the laughter that was trying to escape. "Yeah," she said. "Nothing says *home gym* like Anne Geddes." It came out with more bite than she meant, but Beth didn't seem to notice. She was already sorting through the closet with determination. A large cardboard box was right in her way, bulging from the sides. As soon as Beth bent to grab it, Ellie darted over to help. It was terrifically heavy; her shoulders retaliated as she picked up one side. There must have been stones in there, Ellie thought. Mallets. Dozens of nesting dolls. "What's in this thing?" she asked.

"Oh, it's the photo albums I made of Drake over the years," Beth said with a proud smile. "I used to love scrapbooking."

Ellie eyed the box once it was situated at the center of the room. She tapped on the lid. "Do you mind if I have a look?"

"Of course not," Beth told her. She continued digging through the closet, calling out to Ellie from behind the door, "There are some great memories in there."

Ellie wiggled free the tape on the lid of the box and pulled the first album out. Closest to the top was a scrapbook labeled

DRAKE TWENTIES. The cover was decorated with too much fanfare and big cutout letters. Ellie got comfortable on the bed. A certain sadness came over her as she flipped through the pages. They weren't going back to the cinema. These pictures were the closest she would get to seeing Drake at this life phase.

Here he was holding a giant plastic fish inside an apartment she didn't recognize. Then, a little older, at work. Drake looked so proud to be building homes in his neighborhood. Homes that would last. It was a pride Ellie had never seen in his current role. How could she help him get back there?

"It's relaxing, kind of," Beth was saying.

"Huh?" Ellie asked, mesmerized.

"Scrapbooking. It's good to do something with your hands. That's what they say."

"Right."

And then, when Ellie least expected it, even though she should've expected it, there was Melinda. There were pages of Melinda, actually. The album had been mislabeled. It should have been called THE MELINDA ALBUM. Drake had just told her there was nothing to worry about; that it was some young, nonserious romance. Yet right before her, Ellie watched years of their relationship expand before her eyes.

Drake and Melinda were happy, so very happy, in each photo. They were camping in the woods. They were posed around their small town. They were sharing a ham with Beth over a holiday dinner, so casually, as if Melinda were always at that table. The photos gave away more than the memories Ellie had seen. She closed the book about a third of the way to the end. She couldn't handle any more of it.

"I know that maybe I shouldn't ask this, but . . . what happened between Drake and Mel—"

The oven timer sounded in the distance before she could finish her question. Beth gave up her search, and Ellie followed her into the kitchen. A ham flew out of the oven—a ham just like the one she'd seen Melinda posed with in the photographs. "What were you saying back there, hon?" Beth asked.

"Nothing," Ellie said. "It smells delicious." She hated ham.

Beth set a hand on Ellie's shoulder. "Only my very favorite people get a ham," she told her. Then, the front door clicked shut. Drake was done with his repair work.

"Say goodbye to the gust," he said, and shot Ellie a wink.

Sitting through dinner was miserable, even though Drake gave her the floor to talk about her show with a captive audience. Beth had a million questions about the potential job as the second-most avid viewer of home renovation programming. They passed around an ambrosia salad Beth had forgotten about in the refrigerator. Drake raised questions about the definition of what classified a *salad*, a topic Ellie would've normally been eager to explore. When his mom pulled the keyboard from the spare closet to regale them with Christmas carols after dinner, Drake asked her to dance.

Ellie refused to get up.

He grabbed her hand and made a cute plea for her to join him. He was being kind, she knew, trying to include her. On any other night, the gesture would've gone far. But Ellie wasn't in the mood. The photo album had tipped things over the edge. During her loneliest years, Drake had lived a full life with Melinda. There was nothing to worry about, he kept insisting, but their relationship had spanned at least two of his ten movies—and now, it took over his photo albums, too. The youthful happiness that Drake had with Melinda made Ellie's body physically ache.

Drake must have sensed her sadness; he pulled her into the hallway to ask if everything was all right as his dad rattled a tambourine and his mom sang "Rudolph the Red-Nosed Reindeer."

"I don't want to talk about it," she told him, moving back into the living room. What was there to say? Ellie wondered how to convey her feelings as the lyrics took on a menacing tone. Her mind spiraled away from her.

Drake was the one who suggested they stop going to the cinema. How convenient, she thought.

Ellie needed to get him back there. He wasn't telling her the whole story with Melinda—she felt certain of this—and she had to see how it all played out. If they left the condo soon, there would still be time to lure Drake to the sixth screening. There was one thing she needed to reinforce first, though: the rules. Ellie had no desire to talk about what would play next. The way she treated her parents. Her temporary affairs.

Maybe the part with the cowboy, even.

"I'm going to go warm up the car," Ellie said when the three-act version of "Rudolph" reached its lackluster conclusion. The suggestion was a cue for Drake to leave with her. His parents took forever with goodbyes, and she had been ready to head out hours ago. "Thanks for having us, Beth," Ellie said, darting out the door. When she turned around, he was still inside.

Her anger curdled as she moved toward the car. It was only photos she'd seen. She was overreacting. Why was she so obsessed with Melinda? Until recently, Ellie had been confident in herself, confident in them. It wasn't like she was afraid of Drake running off with Melinda. She was with Jamie now. She wasn't, in any tangible way, a threat.

But more than anything, Ellie wanted to know that Drake chose her. Drake was it for her, the person who felt like family. Yet Melinda had been so much more of a *fit* for him on paper that it was hard to get past. Drake's parents must have loved her. She spoke their language, ate their ham, and would probably even pull a tiny bell out of her purse to accompany the carols. Also, unlike Ellie, Melinda didn't wear a decade of grief on her sleeve.

There it was again, that easygoingness that had tormented Ellie the night of the dinner at Sal's.

Life with Melinda was carefree, the photos reinforced.

Life with Ellie would never be easy.

Maybe she'd tried to play it off that way at first with Drake. Maybe she'd tricked him into thinking this life, their marriage, would be straightforward. But the cinema forced them to acknowledge the truth. The scenes exposed her cracks, her flaws, her deep wounds. She possessed a depth of pain that Drake would probably never have had to experience with Melinda.

Could Drake handle a life with more ups and downs, more challenges, more complications? Most of all, did he want to?

Ellie needed answers.

Act Two

DRAKE

23

Drake could pinpoint the moment Ellie's mood had changed earlier that night. He was in the middle of fixing the door when she walked out of his bedroom-turned-home-gym with a dark cloud over her head. It was normal for her to be a little distant, given what she'd been through recently, he reminded himself. Besides, Early Christmas Dinner wasn't really her thing. On the drive home from last year's festivities, she'd suggested Drake go on his own next time. She could handle Christmas, New Year's, the usual stuff—but did people really need to gather for an *extra* version of those holidays?

But despite giving Ellie an easy out, she had insisted on joining him. Drake didn't want to leave her home alone, either. He had always known Ben's absence this time of year must be hard. Now, he could feel that absence himself. What were the holidays without someone to crawl out the window with or carry out a prank with? Drake couldn't fill that void for her, but he could try to soften its edges. So, to channel Ben, he'd told some jokes. He'd encouraged Ellie to sing and dance when the keyboard made its appearance. He also teed her up to own the spotlight.

Still, Ellie had fled the condo with a stiff escape. "I'm going to go warm up the car," she'd blurted as soon as his mom sang the last words to "Rudolph the Red-Nosed Reindeer." Drake was standing in the living room with his parents, halfway through the long goodbye it would take to get out the door. Twenty minutes was the average exit time to leave the Nielson home. After the goodbyes were given, other topics surfaced until they had to redo the routine all over again.

"Hey, ah, Mom?" Drake said while his dad put some food away. He picked up a blanket on the couch and started to fold it. "Thanks for having us tonight."

"And?" Beth asked with a hand gesture that implied she knew there was more on his mind.

"And . . ." Drake wasn't sure he should mention how distant Ellie had been, but he wanted to know if his mom had picked up on anything he missed. Beth may have even caused the mood. She could be overly informal, a quality that didn't always sit well with Ellie. "What did you and Ellie talk about?" he asked. "When I was doing the door."

Drake watched his mom replay the night in her mind. "Uh, boxes," she said, taking a seat on the couch. "Home gyms. You."

"What about me?"

Beth fiddled with the holiday earrings tucked behind her soft, gray hair. His cousin, Sarah, had hot glued the pom poms on them in her childhood. Sarah was nearly thirty, and the earrings were still a yearly statement. How Drake had become so sentimental wasn't a mystery to him. "Not you, exactly," Beth said. "Ellie helped me move a box from the closet. Then she went through one of your old albums—"

"Which album?" Drake asked. In lieu of making home videos, his mom had scrapbooked every moment of his life. Drake was already embarrassed about what Ellie might have seen, even though he didn't know what it was.

"It should still be in there, hon. Is everything okay?"

Fixing the door had been a mistake. He should've known better than to leave Ellie alone inside his childhood condo, searching for clues and Easter eggs. If he shared his concerns with his mom, he'd never leave. He'd end up telling the whole story—about the cinema and their challenges—over the table, which was probably already broken again. "Everything's fine," he said.

The photo album Ellie must have flipped through was on his bed. DRAKE TWENTIES the cover read. He sat, and his fingers pried open the pages. There was a photo of him at his friend Steve's apartment. A few on his first construction sites. One was taken inside of Melinda's apartment. Had Ellie visited Melinda's place? Would she have recognized this photo?

Drake's fingers flew faster.

He was with Melinda at a park. Melinda at a lakefront beach. Melinda at Nathan's Diner. Melinda, everywhere.

Ellie knew he had been with Melinda. He didn't think she would be surprised by this. But then, he flipped to the final spread at the back of the book and saw exactly what had upset her. His heart sped to dangerous levels. Here was the start of her bad mood. Of course, it was. Ellie had stumbled onto this section on her own without any heads-up or explanation for it. And what she'd found was much worse than he could've imagined.

The photos revealed everything Drake hadn't told her yet.

Ellie was in the driver's seat when Drake got outside. Her breath fogged up the windshield. She was probably furious. "Look," Drake said as he opened the passenger door. "I know what you saw up there. I didn't mean to hide anything from you." Ellie turned his way. Her eyes were curious. "And I feel so bad." Drake ran his hands through his hair. "I should've explained everything at the beginning. I didn't know how." He waited for Ellie to let him have it. Somehow, the silence was worse.

He had to admit that the photo looked bad without context. But it wasn't the explosive secret Ellie probably thought it was. Drake wished she could experience everything as it had happened, right there at his side, before reaching a verdict. And then, he remembered, she still could.

It was 10:03. It was also Saturday night.

If they didn't stop on the drive back to the city, they could make it to the sixth screening. Drake had been the one to suggest not going back, but he thought it might help smooth things over. The cinema could fill in more detail than a photo ever would. Ellie had once argued this herself. "We need to catch the movie," he said.

"You said we shouldn't do that, Drake—"

"I know I said that, but . . . I want—no, need—for you to know everything about me. The whole story. We should see this thing through."

Eventually, Ellie nodded and threw the car in reverse. "Well, if you really want to," she agreed, with a bite, "I guess we better get driving." Just like that, they were back on the road, back on schedule. Drake was going to show her the truth. This would fix everything. "But, Drake," Ellie said, and he could already feel a part of her closing off to him again.

"What?"

"I think it's best to bring the rules back."

Drake was oddly comforted by this suggestion. He needed the rules more than she did. The rules would keep them from fighting until they reached the end of the screenings. "Okay," he said. "Back to the rules it is."

Ellie and Drake had cut their timing close with every visit to the cinema. This night was no exception. At 11:55, they landed at the window for their usual exchange with the ticket boy. Inside the lobby, Natalie wanted to know if something was wrong. "Maybe a problem with the picture?" She had noticed they left halfway through last time and missed a week, too.

"Yes," Ellie said. "There was definitely something wrong—"

"The picture was fine," Drake assured her. Natalie didn't necessarily know the content of the movies. He saw no reason to involve her.

"Okay." Natalie nodded. "Well, let me know if you want me to screen something else tonight. I've got a few movies in rotation that I love. Like, *Jaws 2*. Ever seen *Jaws 2*? It's so much more suspenseful than the original."

"I think we're good," Drake said. He guided Ellie back toward the stairs leading to the balcony section where they liked to sit. "But thank you. Thanks." Once Natalie was out of earshot, he let out a chuckle. "That's a pretty unpopular opinion," he said. "*Jaws 2*? I mean, it's fine, but the first one is a classic. It's probably a top five movie for me."

Drake reached to pull the door open for Ellie when they reached the balcony level, and she stepped inside the auditorium. He continued to ramble as they found their seats. He was waiting to be called out. Where was the explosion? Where was the confrontation about why he'd concealed something so important from her? How little Ellie was talking put him even more on edge.

As always, the lights went down, the hot dog cartoon played, and a new title appeared.

TICKET SIX: *HAPPINESS*

Ellie had told Drake about the city apartment where she lived after college. They were seeing that apartment now, which meant Ben had probably died around two years earlier. Her place was on the second level, sandwiched between a loud walker and a fledgling tenor, as she'd described. But the call from the doorman to announce a guest gave something away that Ellie hadn't brought up: her parents must have paid her rent. The building was more luxurious than her odd jobs would've afforded.

The visitor was Sandra. When Ellie opened the door, they stood in silence for a moment, each searching for the right thing to say and coming up empty. Then, Ellie did something surprising. She wrapped her mom in a hug. Sandra stiffened at the warmth of the gesture but eventually gave in. The goodwill melted away when her mom noticed Ellie's crop top and a belly button piercing, which may have been news to her. "Is all of this the right look, Ellie?" she asked. "For a birthday?"

Ellie rolled her eyes and grabbed a jacket on the way out. "I don't think he's going to mind much," she said and closed the door too hard behind them.

The Marshalls were going to the cemetery. William blurted out the destination as soon as their seat belts clicked. His declaration was forced; he seemed set on tearing a bandage off, even though everyone knew what was underneath it. Ellie and Sandra ignored him, perhaps hoping they could enjoy the illusion of driving anywhere else for a little longer.

The cemetery upheld this pretense. What followed beyond the curved red-brick entrance could have been mistaken for a college campus or a park. Sun streamed through the windows as the car glided along a freshly paved road. The dying grass outside was flecked by trees clinging to their last foliage.

"Where did you put the flowers?" Sandra asked as they slid into a parking space.

"What flowers?" William killed the engine.

"Ben's flowers." She set down her lipstick and snapped her mirror closed. "I left you a message."

"Didn't get a message." William shrugged.

Sandra shook her head in annoyance. "So, there aren't any flowers, then."

"I guess not."

"And how do you think that will look?"

"It's going to look like someone forgot flowers."

"It will look like we forgot *him*, Will."

Ellie glanced up from her phone in the backseat. She was thinner than the last memory—too thin. Despite the tough exterior she'd worked hard on, Ellie flinched easily, and her body tightened in reaction to the tension unfolding in front of her. "What's going on up there?" she asked. Sandra crossed her arms over her chest.

"I say we tell her," William said. He leaned his seat back to get comfortable for whatever reveal was about to happen.

"You know this isn't the right moment," Sandra insisted.

"Tell me what?" Ellie asked.

"Well, when would be a better moment?" William wanted to know. He ignored Ellie's question. "She's always busy. I've tried calling." He turned to look at her in the backseat. This must have been the newer, free-spirited version of her dad. Ellie had mentioned how he had switched from a person who cowered behind her mom to a fan of radical honesty immediately after the accident.

"Please wait, Will."

"Can somebody fill me in?"

"We're getting divorced," her dad announced.

Sandra winced like an insect stung her.

"Are you . . . You're serious?" Ellie gripped the door handle, ready to run away from it all. "You're telling me that you're getting divorced. At the cemetery. On Ben's birthday."

"I've tried to call," William told her. "We've tried to set up dinners. I offered to swing by your place."

"No. You don't get to put this on me." Ellie looked between her parents. "It's you, Dad, isn't it? This was your idea."

"Why would you say that?"

"Because," she told him. "Because Mom's not saying a word. And because you've always talked about living somewhere far away as this big aspiration of yours. So, why don't you just do it, huh? Go off the grid? You have my permission." Ellie brushed her hands clean. She paused and waited for her dad to fight her.

Or, to fight *for* her, Drake considered. Neither parent moved to comfort Ellie.

"Let's not get cruel. We're here for Ben," William reminded them. "And it's his birthday. So, let's go pay our respects."

Ellie pushed back in her seat. "I think I'll stay here."

"You're going to see your brother, Ellie," Sandra insisted.

"What are you so afraid of, Mom? That a stranger will notice I'm not there?"

"We need to show up for him."

"Show up for Ben?" Ellie asked. "Ben is gone. Mom, you care so much about what people think. Do you want to know what I think about you? I think you're terrified of people seeing that you're broken." The target switched over to William's back. "And, Dad, don't worry, I won't miss you when you leave. You're barely around now."

"You're being hysterical, Ellie," Sandra said softly.

"She's ticked off," William observed. "She's ticked we're getting divorced. We hear you on that, Ellie."

Ellie gave a concerning laugh. "You don't hear me, Dad. Neither of you ever ask what I need. What's going on in my life. You lost the kid you liked better, and you can't stand to face the one you're left with."

"That's not—" William started.

"But thanks for the news." Ellie nodded, preparing to sink her teeth in. "You two were never right for each other. Maybe you'd have been happier if you were never together. And speaking of bad past decisions, maybe you should've thought a little harder about becoming parents."

She could say awful things when she was hurt. They were all hurting, weren't they? Her parents couldn't step up because they were grieving. Ellie's grief pushed them further away. It clicked for Drake why the Marshalls didn't talk much, so many years later. They each seemed to share the quick ability to judge and inability to bend. They would need someone, or something, to bring them back together.

In the seat next to him, Drake heard Ellie whisper something.

"Jerk," she was saying. "Jerk. Jerk."

"Who?" Drake asked.

"Me," Ellie said, her eyes glued to the screen. "I was a jerk," she said. "I don't remember being a jerk this day. I just remember getting that news and being furious. How I assumed the divorce was my fault, too."

The movie kept playing. Drake talked right over it. On-screen, William got out of the car, and Sandra walked behind him. Ellie stayed put. "You're not being a jerk here," Drake said. "Come on. You were young." He motioned to the movie. "It was a rough time to give you that news. Of course, you would have a reaction." The familiar blur and switch of the memories happened. Drake held his breath and hoped the cinema would be on his side tonight.

"I pushed my dad away," Ellie said. "Shoved him, more like. Maybe I'm the reason he moved. I'm probably the reason my mom and I barely talk. And I didn't . . . I didn't even visit Ben that day. I still haven't. Can you believe that?"

Drake set Ellie's head on his shoulder.

Shortly after, Melinda's face took over the screen.

On their first real date, Drake and Melinda huddled up inside their town's only Thai restaurant. Melinda ordered drunken noodles. She made a joke about not getting the noodles too drunk. "I'll have the same," Drake added, and then they were alone again.

"You look . . . great tonight, by the way," he told her. His hands fidgeted on his lap under the table. He wasn't hiding his nerves well.

"Thanks. So do you." Melinda tugged on the pink-and-white

gingham fabric that reminded Drake of a chessboard. "This dress was in bad shape when I picked it up from the thrift store," she said. "But I added some sleeves and cleaned her all up. Now she's like new."

The waitress dropped off some free spring rolls. Melinda reached out to grab one. "Nice of them to bring these," she said, dunking the top into a fragrant peanut sauce. "They must know they've got a customer for life in me."

Her words unsettled Drake; they reminded him that he hadn't thought through the logistics of them being together. Sure, their town was a nice place to visit on holidays, but unlike Melinda, he didn't want to stay there. Since living at home after college, he'd felt stuck, held back, limited in every way. Drake dreamed of big-city skylines. He wanted to be surrounded by one-of-a-kind homes and people. Everything was the same here. The same as what he'd always known. "A customer for life, huh?" Drake tried to ask casually.

"Oh, yeah," Melinda said. "Why go anywhere else when you've found a good thing?"

Drake wanted to take Melinda somewhere more grown-up for a second date. He'd picked up an extra shift at Peat's Hardware to make sure he could cover the bill at Lake Lounge. Out the window, boats glided over the surface of a small, dark marina. The restaurant was romantic at first glance, but as he took in the expensive wine list and stiff white tablecloths, he feared he'd made a mistake.

"I'm sorry if this place is a little stuffy," Drake said. They had just learned from the waiter that their dinner did *not* come with a free appetizer or even free bread. His stomach protested.

"This place is nice," Melinda told him. The corners of her lips turned into a smile. "Although, it would make things more interesting if you kissed me." She set the menu up in front of them, and Drake kissed her then. His heart was beating so fast that it became a cartoon heart he worried she might see. It jutted right there out of his sweater, like he was an illustrated animal responding to the swell of keys and strings.

The third date was more intimate. Melinda had invited Drake to her home, which was an apartment above the shop. He jumped a little as she slammed a knife into a wooden cutting board, chopping up ingredients for homemade sushi. She was tired of going to restaurants, she told him, especially ones that didn't come with bread. Bread was a staple of the human experience. If it wasn't provided freely, the restaurant wasn't for them. Drake watched her float around the balmy tiled kitchen as she rolled salmon and avocado into sticky rice.

"This dinner was a mistake," she said after trying a bite. The sushi looked irritated, but Drake told her it was delicious. She served it on her table lined with two taper candles tucked inside antique gold mice.

This apartment always felt like an attic to him; the lines of the roof moved into an A-frame shape, and patterned rugs rested on floors that were nearly covered by the bed in the center of the room. "Never compromise on a bed," Melinda had insisted when she gave him a quick tour. "Get your shoe budget under control and buy yourself a nice bed."

Drake woke up in her nice bed that week and the following one. When they weren't in bed, they sat at the terrible tiny couch that faced her wood-burning fireplace. Melinda met Drake's parents at the Edison building and stayed for dominoes. They went to Nathan's Diner for grilled cheese sandwiches and ate candy that hurt their teeth from the gumball machine. They shared lime kisses inside Drake's parked car.

Eventually, an invitation broke their small-town routine. Melinda asked Drake if he wanted to join her at a friend's baby shower in the city. The friend had a modest, but airy, apartment with a second bedroom where her baby would sleep. She mentioned an Italian restaurant that she and her husband frequented in the area. Drake suggested they stop by on the way home. Their menus arrived, and before the waitress could give them time to think their choice over, Melinda asked if the meal came with bread.

"Of course, it does," the waitress said. "Although, I do have to recommend you order the garlic bread, too. It's kind of what we're known for."

"Makes sense," they agreed in unison.

"I'm really happy, Drake," Melinda told him. How long had it been since they started dating. A month? Two?

"About the double bread?" Drake asked.

"With you," she said. "I'm really happy with you."

"I love you, Melinda."

The statement was true at the time. Drake did love her. Drake loved her in that insatiable, first-love way—the kind that resulted in late-night talks on the phone about nothing in the hours they weren't together, winding the cord around his wrist as he heard her voice. He had loved her since that night at the school dance, he believed. It was an easy love, though, a love without challenge or growth. A love of sameness, much like the town itself. But at the time, at that moment, it was just love, and it was the only romantic kind Drake had known.

"I love you, too," she said.

The bread arrived. They kissed, and the red lights cast over them from a blinking sign in the window that spelled out the name of the restaurant: THE GARLIC BREAD PLACE.

24

The house had been quiet since Saturday's screening. Too quiet, Drake felt. For the last three mornings, Ellie's office door was already closed when he got up. He couldn't blame her for throwing herself into her work. It was probably a nice distraction from everything. Right after seeing Ben's death, she'd watched Melinda and Drake fall in love.

And he'd declared that love for the first time at The Garlic Bread Place.

Drake hadn't been trying to repeat his own history by bringing Ellie there. His excuse was much more innocent: The Garlic Bread Place seemed like the kind of under-the-radar restaurant she would love. He had wanted to impress her with amazing food. Drake had tried to explain his rationale as they left the cinema that night, but Ellie darted outside, and the rules forced his silence. She was left with a story that lacked context.

This morning, something was different. The door to Ellie's office was open, and her desk chair was empty. She wasn't downstairs, either. In the kitchen, a couple sheets of paper waited for him on the table. They were still hot from the printer. Drake sucked in a deep breath. He knew, based on the title alone, what he was about to read.

The Place Where the Dresses Talk

My Mother's Shop isn't a shop. A shop suggests a choice. Inside a shop, you pick out a little round pair of gold-rimmed spectacles that perch on the bridge of your nose and make you feel studious. Out to dinner that night, you lean forward into the conversation with the air of an Ivy undergrad. Your gaze in the mirror lingers a second too long. You look good. There it is, staring you in the face. Your choice.

At My Mother's Shop, you don't get a choice. The dresses choose you. They're polite about it, sure. Each dress is spaced ten inches apart on beautiful copper racks that line the edges of the room like ballet bars. Fabrics are shaded in Painted Lady row home hues: cream, dusty rose, violet. The swirl of tulle and lace brings to mind hundreds of blushing girls posed for a cotillion. When the front door swings open and a breeze inspires them, the girls start to dance.

Ellie made Melinda's idea of a dress shop sound like a romantic endeavor. Really, it had been a strategic business decision. Drake had turned over late one night to find Melinda reading a book called *Small Business: An Art Form.* "Specificity is key," the first chapter said. Also, "have a niche." Despite becoming a known presence in the community, her mother had struggled to find regular customers for her antique shop. Was there a way to focus on one thing? Melinda had wondered out loud.

She'd spent the next few weeks writing down niche ideas on a yellow-lined pad. Then, when one of their former teachers brought in her old wedding dress and asked if she would want to sell it, Melinda wrote down a new niche and underlined it: <u>Previously loved dresses</u>.

Drake scanned the next section.

There are wedding dresses and party dresses, tea dresses and Sunday-afternoon dresses. There are "this old things?" and picnic-in-the-park dresses. None of them try to hide that they've lived. When a garment comes in—usually by way of the shop owner, Melinda, herself—it is revived by hand with love. Melinda waits for a whisper to tell her what to change and where to embellish. Then, she writes a note for the next wearer based on what that whisper tells her.

It's a written game of telephone, if you will.

On the front counter of My Mother's Shop, a candle burns that's worth a visit in itself. Cinnamon and sage bubble inside a handsome cauldron.

Melinda was still burning those candles. Drake had started the long lineage. Liquid Gold, they were called. The wax was poured inside fancy jelly jars. He'd bought the first Liquid Gold from Clara's, their town's only gift shop. Clara herself had helped him pick out a gift for Melinda. "This one," she'd said, tapping her spindly finger on the top of the lid. "She'll love it."

Apparently, Melinda did love it, or maybe Jamie had the same great idea.

The scent has a melody that washes over you as you wander the racks and stop to admire the handwritten lavender notes tucked inside each dress.

"Your wish comes true at midnight" the first one says. Reading the words etched in calligraphy, one can summon an author with tousled blonde curls, the presence of a grandfather clock ticking its way through a wicked, late night, and a Louisa May Alcott book hinged on the edge of an antique desk. The note, fittingly, is paired with a traditional white bridal gown. Pearls hug a sweetheart neckline that begs to be worn by someone who believes in romance, the kind of love that ran through meadows and pledged itself to someone in an oath.

A cheekier dress with a seafoam beaded bodice tells the wearer to find the best man at the wedding. It knows its audience.

A plum silk dress with a plunging neckline and soft flutter sleeves kindly requests: Meet me in a reverie.

Pause, now.

Zoom out for a second.

Imagine you're standing in the textbook definition of an idyllic small town. A towering old-fashioned clock tower tells the wrong time, making everybody a few minutes late to their appointments. That kind of thing is okay here. The streets of this traditional block are theme-park clean, and the trees that line those pristine streets are named for the folks who live there. One of them, a spruce called Mayor Steve, is dedicated to a man who ran for mayor years ago and just missed the mark. They named a tree after him to smooth over any friction.

If Ellie had found the tree assigned to Drake for his ambitious community service efforts, she didn't mention it.

When you see people at the grocery store and ask about their families, you care about those answers. You feel the reward of buying an incredible scented candle at the one gift shop in town, knowing you're truly supporting local businesses because you saw for yourself the way that the owner, Clara, was able to expand into a bigger storefront.

Zoom back in.

The dress shop is nestled right in the heart of all that.

The door jingles as you enter. It gets stuck when it's halfway open. Jamie, Melinda's husband, might run over to give it a pull like it hurt your feelings. On my first visit to My Mother's Shop, Jamie disappears into the attic apartment above us. Then, Melinda explains the truth about the surroundings. She is fascinated by giving previously loved things a second chance. She believes that old items passed to a new owner are a reminder that we should appreciate the imperfect versions of ourselves. The dresses represent all the lives we've lived. Even though we're different than we used to be, evolving is safe in this space. Sacred, even.

"Go explore now." Melinda waves from behind the counter. Jamie returns to her side. They drink peppermint tea with honey sticks, each reading their respective hardcover books behind the desk. When Jamie laughs at a line, Melinda turns to smile at him like she's the luckiest.

Drake didn't love reading about Jamie. He wasn't jealous, but did anyone want to read about their ex and the person they ended up with?

Beyond that laugh, though, and the crinkled books turning to a new page, the store is silent. It's designed that way. Because if you listen closely, the girls will start to chatter.

"Lift up my train on the stairs, won't you?"
"Take me out to a garden, I want to see the roses."
"Somebody, buy me a pony."
"I. Want. To. Tango!"
"Let me be your muse."

And then, you'll hear the voice that's meant for you to chime in, a little louder than the rest. It might be a voice you didn't know you needed to hear. She offers you a piece of advice. The whole thing feels monumental, so much bigger than shopping, than a dress.

"You picked well," Melinda tells me, returning us to the

illusion of choice. I've learned better in my time here. She rings up my dress and places it into the safety of a dark travel bag with a silver zipper on it. "By the way, I wrote the note on that one myself."

The dress I'm buying tells me this: When things get hard, think of the very first time you met them. The very first time.

So, I close my eyes. I grin. I do.

Drake set the story down. When he looked up, Ellie had come through the back door. Nancy's leash was still in her hand. "Well," she said eagerly, sipping a latte from the coffee shop she never went to before ten. "What do you think?"

"I love it," Drake said. There were details about his town he would've tweaked for accuracy, but it was well written. "It's well written."

Ellie slid into the chair across from him and unbuckled Nancy from her restraint, leaving her to tuck her nose into all corners of the kitchen. "Okay," she said. "Good. What else?"

Drake wasn't sure what Ellie expected. He worried there was a trap here, a catch, some hidden statement she was waiting for him to make about Melinda. "I think," he said, patting her coat, which resembled the Stay Puft Marshmallow Man, "I think you really captured the town . . ." Tread carefully, he reminded himself. "The store," Drake told her. "And the town."

Drake could feel Ellie struggling on the other side of the table. This was the first work she was proud of in a while, a story people were going to read and enjoy. It was also a story that would tie Ellie's and Melinda's names together. He felt for her. Yes, she'd looked up Melinda and tracked her down, but she hadn't known where this would all lead.

"Did you find my tree?" Drake asked her. "When you were walking around Main Street?"

"I . . . no!" Ellie said. She perked up. "They named a tree after you?"

"Yeah. It was for community service. Really, I just ran around fixing a lot of things. People would come by Melinda's shop to find me whenever something broke."

"Wow, Drake," Ellie said. Her expression started to sour. He should've known better than to mention the shop. "It seems like there's so much I still don't know about you."

25

Since reading Ellie's story, Drake kept returning to one thing: the photos. Their details became more menacing with time. Why had Ellie not brought them up yet? He reminded himself, for the third time that week, that this was how she handled conflict. Her big moments were stored out of reach until they exploded.

Drake feared the explosion would happen soon.

As Ellie and Drake parked that Saturday night for the seventh showing at the cinema, paid for the tickets, and found their seats, Drake hoped it would show the end of his love story with Melinda. He was ready to see it all come crashing down. But the title that appeared after the dancing hot dogs warned him there was more romance in store.

TICKET SEVEN: *TOGETHER*

The movie's structure was different that night, Drake noticed right away. They weren't seeing a single memory. Instead, they watched a montage of younger Ellie's romantic escapades with a string of eccentric characters:

The dry cleaner heartthrob.

The park guy.

The professor who played Professor Harold Hill in *The Music Man*.

The opera guy.

The silver fox with a front-tooth gap who sang while he made burrata.

The girl with the—Drake sputtered a cough—girl with the paint-stained overalls and Joni Mitchell collection.

The photographer with a bunker-style loft.

The dancer into dark wave.

The taxidermist-motorcycle man.

The Orwell-quoting line cook.

And so on.

Drake sighed. The sequence overwhelmed him. He considered ducking out of the theater, but that had led to an argument last time. So, Drake stared at his feet while the show continued, glancing up every now and then in morbid curiosity. It was humiliating—not what Ellie was doing, exactly, but the act of having to watch it back with her. How was she so calm in the seat next to him? The liaisons progressed:

At the dry cleaners.

In a park.

In the dressing room for a production of *The Music Man*.

In the empty reception hall of an opera house.

Over the kitchen counter.

Inside a pair of paint-stained overalls.

In front of a camera.

On a worn-out leather recliner.

Watched by hundreds of carefully placed dead animals.

In the parking lot of a restaurant.

And so on.

Drake squirmed. It was just sex, he reminded himself. So, Ellie had a life before him—a vibrant and experimental life. Who was he to judge her for it? He channeled his calm side until the movie took a new turn and focused on the *endings* of these encounters. Ellie was always the one who left. At first, she told lies to untether herself, but then seemed to realize disappearing was simpler. She was ruthless.

She darted out the door before the burrata was ready.

She crawled out the window while Joni was *Blue*.

And snuck down the fire escape of the photographer's loft.

She changed her walking route to avoid the dancer.

She left the taxidermist on read.

She ignored the doorbell when the line cook placed dinner on her doorstep.

And after all of that, the memory slowed down. Ellie met someone new.

The guy with the rooftop-level loft had the right things to say and the right suits. His name was Lucas. Lucas also had a specific glass for everything. Wines got the correct swirl, morning espresso came in bright stacked cups, and he knew what kind of liquor to put in a Nick and Nora glass. But along with being slick, he was sweet. In the mornings, Lucas left sticky notes by Ellie's bed with sayings that made him think of her. He talked about his family often. On her birthday, he rented out a roller rink and invited Ellie's friends. He held her hand as they wound their way through neon lights to slow jams, bumping shoulders with other twentysomethings already nostalgic for their youth.

Drake couldn't help but compare himself to the person he was seeing on the screen. The similarities were easy to stack up. Lucas was Drake, but successful. Drake, but smoother around the edges. If there were an ideal person for Ellie to build a relationship with from her past—anyone to end the casual string of cameos—it should've been this guy. But the morning after the roller party, after he'd told her he loved her, Ellie snuck out his door while he showered.

"It's over," she told Jen later over scrambled eggs at brunch. "With Lucas, I mean."

Jen hesitated. "But he's perfect for you."

"Meh." The waitress topped their mimosa glasses.

"Lucas is the guy everyone wants," Jen told her. "He's so *thoughtful*."

"Or boring."

Jen grabbed Ellie's arm. "What kind of person rents a roller rink for their girlfriend?"

"Girlfriend?" Ellie threw her hands up in protest. "No. No."

"Okay," Jen said. "Well, if it's not Lucas, then who?"

"I'm not sure." Ellie shook herself out. Her smile reminded Drake of a pharmaceutical ad. Ditching Lucas brought about the same feelings as leaving those pesky seasonal pollen allergies behind. "Maybe I'm meant to be free. On my own." She crunched down on the edge of her English muffin. "Men get to do that. I want life to be exciting. I want to get somebody's number as I walk out the door right now. I want to fall in love with my work."

The check came. Jen tried to grab it, but Ellie reached it first. "I've got this," she said. "Just promise me something. If I ever become some boring married person, please come over and shake me by the shoulders."

As usual, the memory started to blur.

Drake felt Ellie nudge him as the movie prepared to switch protagonists. She was asking if he was okay. Nothing is wrong here, she seemed to insist. But Drake had learned something different. It was so easy for Ellie to lie, to leave, to skip out on a good thing, and the person she was with was always the last to know. Would Ellie wake up one day and believe that she had made a mistake with him?

Did she even want to be married?

"I'm okay," he swallowed. "I just—"

Suddenly, Melinda got in the way of everything all over again.

Melinda had the world's worst couch; it was more like a chair for one person. Drake's half of the couch-chair creaked as he settled in and started up the movie. Melinda didn't have a television, so he'd carried over a grainy spare, plus a dusty DVD player from his parents' storage closet. And then Drake, in the audience, remembered where this memory was headed.

Oh. *No.*

The Umbrellas of Cherbourg was the entertainment for the night. It was the same movie musical he had watched recently with Ellie. Melinda was pitched forward in the seat next to Drake, her eyes glued to the screen.

"I saw the cutest kid at the hardware store today," he mentioned a few minutes into the film. Melinda pressed pause and her body stiffened as she set the remote down between them. "Anyway, this kid came in and asked for gardening shears. Well, they were for his mom." Drake was mostly working construction jobs at this point, but he still picked up the occasional shift at Peat's Hardware. "I thought," he said. "I don't know, it's weird, but this kid kind of looked like me?"

"That's sweet," Melinda said.

Drake wasn't sure why he brought up the kid. Since leaving Peat's that afternoon, he kept thinking about him. When he turned to the passenger seat to grab his mom's groceries, he pictured the kid sitting there instead of the lemons. When he pulled up to Melinda's shop, he felt a little hand in his, too. It was new, the presence of wanting another, smaller person around. He liked it.

Melinda pressed Play on the movie. She reached for one of the French macarons she'd set on the coffee table and took a bite before hitting Pause again. "Drake," she told him, turning her focus in his direction. "You know I don't want kids. Right?"

The television had frozen on the lead actress inside of the film's titular umbrella shop. Drake tried to remember if he'd ever seen a store that specialized in umbrellas. Maybe Melinda should add that to her growing list of niche ideas she was keeping, he thought. The Umbrellas of Main Street. So what if the shop in the movie wasn't doing well? It was fiction.

"I didn't say I *wanted* kids," Drake insisted, even though that's exactly what he'd been thinking. Voicing the truth when Melinda didn't want them was too big of a risk. It opened the possibility of conflict. An ending, even. Then, "Why . . ." He cleared his throat. "Why don't you?"

Melinda tried to face him. There wasn't enough space on the couch. The two of them shifted apart a little to look at each other. "I just don't," she said. "I'm loving how simple things are right now."

Drake thought her words over. They were vague, weren't they? He knew she'd had a tough childhood and lost her mom not long ago. Maybe time would give her a new perspective. Maybe he could change her mind.

"You're not going to change my mind," she insisted before he said it.

"No," Drake told her. "Of course not."

"If that's going to be a make-or-break for you, we should talk about—"

"It's not. You're everything I need."

Melinda put her feet up on his lap and pressed Play. Drake, in his memory of this conversation, hadn't noticed the way she watched him instead of the movie. She was sleuthing. Analyzing. Trying to figure out what he might not be telling her.

"Hey, are there really shops that exclusively sell umbrellas?" he asked.

"Shh," Melinda said, finally easing back into the plot.

"I bet that's a thing in Seattle—"

"Shh," she warned again, handing him a cookie to quiet him.

· · · · · · · · · ·

The screen turned black. The lights rose.

Drake stood first. He knew Ellie wouldn't be happy with that night's screening. He'd lied about having seen the French musical because what was the point of telling her he had watched it with Melinda? But between The Garlic Bread Place and the movie, it could seem like he was repeating his last relationship all over again.

Ellie got up quietly. Her half of the movie wasn't great, either.

Drake couldn't help but wonder about her past relationships. She'd left so many people before things could develop. Had she ever been in something serious before him? *Could* she be in something serious? The night at the taco drive-thru, she'd mentioned that Drake was her first love. A quote came to mind from her piece called "Yellow Dress." "A first love is about finding yourself. A second love is about sharing the self you found with someone new."

Which person was Drake in this equation?

He thought back to one of the plaques inside the lost and found he'd seen. *Love Affair*, one of Ellie's items had been called. Drake couldn't remember what it was, though. He needed an excuse to look again. So when Ellie wasn't paying attention, he reached for the excuse Ellie had used the night they returned to the cinema with Jen and Marc. He set his scarf on the seat and left it behind.

The bokeh of soft lights, dusting of snow, and cheery music on the radio must have brightened Ellie's mood because she seemed okay in the car. Drake did his best to let the night's memories slip away. When she suggested they put on a movie back at home, he agreed.

"What do you want to watch?" Drake asked.

"Oh, why don't you pick?" Ellie suggested. Her tone was

playful, but the remote hit his lap with a hard thud. "I wouldn't want to choose something you've already seen."

It was understandable she'd be hurt by his omission, even if it was small. Drake tried to turn things around.

"Well, it's two days till Christmas," he said. "How about a holiday movie? One where some guy who works at a tree farm falls for a city girl, and she learns the magic of the season?"

"Sure, Drake." Ellie nodded. "There's nothing quite like watching a small-town romance, is there?"

Drake ignored the comment.

Later, as the movie played, Drake couldn't focus on the plot as a girl who volunteered at the petting zoo fell in love with an animal whisperer. How many little moments, Drake wondered, had he repeated in their relationship without realizing it?

And why the hell was he doing that?

26

Christmas Eve was supposed to be cheerful, but Drake woke up claustrophobic in his own house. As he moved about his morning, he felt Ellie's former lovers cast their critical eyes on him. The dry cleaner heartthrob scolded him for not hanging up his delicates sooner. The line cook insulted his amateur scrambled eggs. Lucas, the last boyfriend, called him out for using the wrong glassware.

"Happy almost-Christmas," Ellie said, holding her coffee mug close. Her soft skin brushed Drake's face when her chin found his shoulder. "What should we get up to this morning?" she asked. Her playful mood surprised him; she had ignored Drake since the great *Umbrellas* debacle until now.

"I have to do a few walkthroughs and snap some photos of the new cabinets," Drake told her. "I just got a last-minute call this morning." He hoped his reflection in the kitchen window didn't give away his lie. Last night his boss, George, had asked if anyone would volunteer. The chance to get some fresh air—and space from Ellie—had been too hard to pass up. Drake needed to shake off the complicated story he'd woven in his head. The story went something like this: Ellie wouldn't be able to commit to him. She would leave him behind in the sea of ghosts that now haunted their old house. The story wasn't true or fair, but that didn't make it go away.

"Oh," Ellie huffed. She stepped back. "You're working. Today?"

Drake turned to her and leaned against the kitchen counter. He needed to be kind. He didn't want Ellie to shut down again. "I'll be home tonight," he said and pulled the belt on her plush robe toward him. "We'll figure out something fun. A big dinner. Pajama party."

"Okay," Ellie finally agreed. "Fun," she repeated like a threat. Her feet moved in hard steps out of the room, leaving him to drink his coffee alone.

When Drake reached the entrance of Wakeford Heights, he immediately regretted volunteering to work. The community was everything he hated in one place, from the smell of manufactured vanilla in the prospective buyer's office to the home exteriors that were hard to tell apart. Drake once asked the developer why it was called Wakeford Heights. He was told that Wakeford sounded energetic but not alarming. Maybe his assessment was unfair. Some people loved communities like this.

But for Drake, Wakeford Heights was a daily reminder of his own failure.

By now, he was supposed to have his own business building homes that were passed through generations. Instead, he was pushing paper on homes where most people would live, he guessed, for about two years before they moved on.

The only silver lining about Wakeford Heights was that it made him appreciate his home with Ellie. He couldn't help comparing the Finch, a three-bedroom unit that was first on his list to check out, to their Queen Anne. Sure, their place was somewhere between fixed and falling to shit. But unlike the fake marble countertops and cheap fixtures found here, it was built to last. For as much as Drake teased Ellie about her need to buy everything used, it meant something to live in a house with a history. He almost pitied the thirtysomething couple he saw banging on the door to the buyer's office as he passed it. They were so eager to check out a modest, two-bedroom Cardinal on a holiday.

The woman in the couple wore a baby in a carrier and was supported by her husband's arm. Drake caught the guy's profile as he leaned forward to peek inside the door. Then, his features filled in. Drake nearly slipped on the sidewalk. There, in a winter scarf and hat, was one of the cameos from Ellie's last memory.

It was the park guy.

"Hey," Drake shouted at them. He had no plan of what to say next.

You're the one who had sex with my soon-to-be-wife in a public park. A public park of all places, who does that? Maybe you're a voyeur. Maybe you're here for all the dumb windows. The wife would cover the baby's ears. *Just think about all those geese you messed up for life.*

The park guy turned toward Drake. When the sun caught his face, his features became clearer. On closer inspection, he wasn't the park guy at all. He wasn't even Ellie's type.

Now the cinema was making him hallucinate.

"Sorry," Drake said. "I thought you were someone . . ." He scratched his head and tried to figure out a save. "You look like someone."

"I get that a lot," the guy said.

"He does get that a lot," his wife agreed with a knowing chuckle. The baby cooed.

"Anyway, I wanted to let you know that the office is closed," Drake offered.

"Yeah, too bad," the guy said, rubbing his hands together. "We were driving out to my parents' and saw this spot. Gorgeous homes."

Drake's mistake was pathetic. It was a sign that he needed to let the past go. To leave those other guys behind and drive back to their beautiful, not-bird-themed, home. So Drake did that after a quick check on a Starling unit, picking up Chinese food along the way. When he walked in, though, the house was empty. It was after his shower, change into sweats, and unanswered text message that he heard the doorbell.

Ellie was always forgetting her house key. Drake swung the door open, expecting to find her there. Instead, Sandra stood on the snow-dusted porch. She held a wrapped gift box and small bakery tray against her cashmere sweater dress.

"Drake," Sandra said. She was formal with his name.

Drake tried to cut through the chill. "Sandra," he greeted her. "Hey. Hi."

"Ellie told me no gifts." She looked at the box as if yearning for whatever was inside of it. "But I've wanted her to have this. I've been meaning to drop it off for a while, and . . ." Her words, which were usually an effortless display of rehearsed charm, stalled. "Oh, and cookies. There are cookies here for both of you."

"That's really nice." Drake reached in to relieve Sandra of the gift and the tray, setting them both on the shelf by the door. With his hands free, he went in for a hug. There was slight resistance from Sandra's end; he worried the gesture was too familiar. Drake pulled away and waved her inside the house. "Come in, come in," he said. "Ellie should be home soon."

He wasn't sure why he told her that. There were no signs of Ellie at the house, no half-filled mugs or stray blankets. It was wishful thinking, he decided.

Nancy bounded toward their visitor as she stepped inside the entryway. Sandra pulled her hand away as sloppy, wet kisses landed on it. Nancy set a paw on her shoe, as if asking her to stay, and Sandra sidestepped the advance without looking down.

Then, Sandra made a face Drake recognized. It was the same face Ellie made as she analyzed a new place and pulled it apart in her mind. He could feel Sandra's critical gaze as she tallied the unrepaired holes, old moldings, and Ellie's antique collections on their living room shelves, which her mom would probably describe as *creative* or *eclectic*.

Drake couldn't blame Sandra for being curious. It was her first time in their new house. His own parents had been there the week they moved in and brought a six-pack of beer for a toast. Ellie later had joked that the beer toast was tacky, which rubbed Drake the wrong way. Now he wondered if she was hurt because it was another milestone not shared with her own parents.

"Do you want to stay?" Drake asked. He motioned to the food containers somewhere behind him. "For dinner. It's just takeout, but . . ."

Sandra seemed to consider the invitation. Drake should've known better. It was an innocent offer, but would Ellie see it that way? "No, no, but thank you," she decided. "I can't eat things like that anymore." Drake wasn't sure what the *like that* meant, but he nodded in agreement. Drake was looking at Sandra with fresh eyes after watching the memory with Ben. He sensed her chilly exterior covered up what hurt her.

Would Sandra spend the holidays alone? Had Ellie even given her mom gifts from them? He wasn't sure. Ellie also hadn't gone to Sandra's for a holiday dinner this year, as she usually did. Sandra and Ellie had grown even farther apart since the mess of the engagement party.

"We would love to have you over soon," Drake suggested. "Umm, for dinner. A home-cooked dinner? I mean, neither of us cook, but we can figure something out."

"I will look forward to that." Sandra straightened herself out. She pointed to the box on the shelf. "Tell Ellie . . . When she opens it . . . That she shouldn't have been alone." She paused and rubbed her throat like it hurt. "And let her know that I went back that day."

Before Drake could ask what she meant, Sandra slipped out the door.

Ellie had narrowly missed her mom by about ten minutes. She came home with her arms full of various cookies and cider. "You're here!" she said. "Good, good. I hated that you were away on a holiday. I was losing it. So, I got cookies." She waved the plastic bag in the air.

"Love it," Drake told her with a kiss on the cheek. "Although, the cookie fairy has already visited us." He picked up the tray of beautifully iced snowflakes that Sandra had brought them.

"Oh!" Ellie said. "You got cookies, too!"

"They're from . . ." Drake paused. When he'd tried to bring up her mom since their engagement party, the mood had soured, hadn't it? He didn't want to ruin their night by explaining her visit. It could wait. "Me," he said. "The cookies are from me. I got Chinese food, too."

"Well, the more cookies, the better."

They set the spread on the coffee table, piled two plates high, and read their fortunes out loud on the couch.

"'A secret will soon be revealed,'" Ellie said. The message seemed ominous to Drake. Maybe it was because Sandra's wrapped box still sat near the front door. Ellie hadn't noticed it yet. He made a mental note to put it in the closet the next time she was upstairs. "Anything you want to tell me?"

Drake snatched the fortune cookie away from her. "I would like to tell you that I call dibs on this."

"Good," she said. "You can have that one. I'm going to eat *all* of these life-changing cookies you picked up." She ate her fourth cookie in a row. "Where did you get these, anyway?"

Ellie was in good spirits on Christmas morning and later that night for Actual Christmas Dinner with Drake's parents. She lit up the conversation and complimented their food. She even asked Beth for hair advice, although that was the last thing Ellie needed. These attempts meant something to Drake. But when they got home later, some of the cheer drained away. Between their weekly cinema visits and all the wedding planning, there hadn't been time to decorate the house. Two sad presents waited for them on the bare living room floor.

Drake suggested they open the boxes. They could do that, at least, couldn't they?

"A sweater," Ellie said, holding her unwrapped gift up in front of her. Drake had spent hours at a vintage store trying to find something she'd like. He wasn't sure where to start—what was classified as cool and what fell into the ugly camp. He'd landed on a new sweater from the mall that looked like an old sweater. "Thanks," she told him, tucking it back inside its box.

Ellie hated the sweater.

A better partner would've known what to get her. Lucas wouldn't have been caught dead with a mall sweater gift. He'd rented her a roller rink. And still, she'd walked away from him.

Ellie passed Drake his present. This year, she'd bought him something new, too. It was a men's bath set. Ellie, the queen of nostalgia, had bought Drake a brand-new men's bath set straight from department store shelves in a scent called Deep Pine. The choice was so unlike her that Drake couldn't help but be hurt. She normally put effort into picking gifts, despite her resistance to holiday fanfare.

On their first Christmas together at Ellie's apartment, their gifts had been much more intentional. Ellie had given him a relic of a toolkit that was supposedly plucked from a Hollywood movie set. Drake had bought Ellie a new record player. Her old one was dying and had started to make the singers sound like distortions of themselves. But Ellie was resistant to throwing away the current player—Dorothy III. This was how Drake had learned that Ellie's belongings had names and came in a series, like a child's goldfish. He had found this so endearing at the time.

Two years later, he was annoyed to be listening to Etta James on Dorothy III when Dorothy IV was right there in the closet. Maybe it was the soulless gift that was getting to him. What was she trying to say with it?

"Thanks for this," Drake said, clumsily taking the bottles out of the plastic container and smelling them. "Smells amazing."

"And thank you," Ellie told him, patting the box. "The sweater looks . . . cozy."

Drake still wasn't sure what to do with Sandra's gift in the closet. If she were to send Ellie a text about it, he'd have no excuse. The last thing he could handle was another misunderstanding. "There's one more thing," Drake said. Ellie started to get excited. "It's not from me," he told her to temper expectations, then retrieved the perfectly wrapped box and placed it in front of her. Ellie stared at it.

"What is this?"

"It's . . . I don't know what it is," Drake admitted. "It's from your mom." He said the word *mom* lightly, as if she might miss it.

"My mom," Ellie repeated. "My mom was here?"

Drake nodded. "She stopped by yesterday. Just for a minute."

"And you didn't tell me?"

"I wanted to," Drake said. "But you walked in so happy. I didn't want to ruin those cookies for you."

He shouldn't have brought up the cookies.

"Anyway, she said something when she dropped it off. She said that you shouldn't have been alone that day. And that—"

"I don't want to hear it," Ellie blurted. "You were right not to tell me." She stared at the gift for a moment, then put it back in the closet where he had pulled it from and shut the door. "I'm tired," she told him, even though she was an eternal night owl. "I'll open it another time."

They washed up and tucked into bed. The glow of Ellie's phone illuminated the dark room, despite her suggestion of sleep. There were so many things left unsaid, so many invisible boxes of memories that had been unwrapped but not yet put away.

27

"What is it you're missing?" Natalie asked the following Saturday night as she led them over to the glass lost and found case for the second time.

When Drake intentionally left his scarf behind, he had been wondering the same thing. What was he missing from Ellie's story? Last week, he'd watched her fly through dozens of quick-lived flings. Seeing her lack of commitment play out had shaken him. What if their relationship was a science experiment to test if Ellie could handle something real? He knew this fear wasn't fair or warranted. He also knew the movies would give him more information in time. But Drake's curiosity was insatiable, and he couldn't wait another week to see what memory might be tied to the plaque labeled *Love Affair*.

His eyes darted around in a desperate search. On the bottom shelf, an object that had once seemed innocent took his breath away. *Witness to Ellie's Accident*, the plaque read. The object was devastating having learned its story, the cheap dinosaur toy from Ben's rearview mirror so small and vulnerable inside the glass case.

A white Stetson cowboy hat was one spot over from the dinosaur. *Cowboy Love Affair*, the plaque read. *Cowboy* love affair? Drake pictured Ellie on the back of a horse, wild wheat waving, a small wooden cabin on the horizon. He saw her in a white dress, petting a goat, sitting by a crackling fire. He turned to look at her behind him. Technically, they were inside the cinema walls. He could ask the question on his mind.

But Drake wasn't prepared to talk about what sat at the far corner of the bottom shelf from his own life, so close to the item in question.

"I'm glad they have your scarf," Ellie said, breaking him from the visuals that were best left in a country music video. Natalie handed the scarf over, and Ellie pulled them toward the staircase on the right that led to the balcony level with a quick "thanks" thrown behind her. Halfway up the stairs, Ellie paused and looked out. "I want to know that . . . I think I overreacted," she told him.

Drake stopped at her side. "Overreacted about what?"

Ellie hesitated. "I mean, since we're inside cinema doors, I guess I can say it. Seeing that you'd watched the same movie with Melinda got to me. I think it was because we had just seen The Garlic Bread Place. You told her you loved her there."

"I know." Drake sighed.

"But look, it's just a few similarities," Ellie decided. "I get how it could be a coincidence. In a long relationship, things might get repeated, right? I was mad about it until I remembered Sal's Cantina."

"Sal's?"

"I took you there on our first date," Ellie said. "You called it our spot. I let you. But I wrote about Sal's a few years before we met, and I took . . ." She made a tally on her fingers, then gave up. "I took a lot of dates there."

"Oh." Drake gained a better understanding of her jealousy. All along, he'd thought Sal's was their place. Their photo booth moment. How many people had Ellie shared that moment with before him?

"Anyway, I get how that could happen," she said. "The restaurant. The movie. Just . . . don't go repeating yourself again. Okay?" There was some humor in her voice, although she was a little serious, too, he could tell.

Inside the auditorium, they chose a row where they had never sat before, near the front of the balcony. Drake tensed, waiting for some kind of cowboy on a white horse to whisk Ellie away. The lights lowered. Drake tried to push the cowboy out of his mind.

After the cartoon, a new title flashed against the screen.

TICKET EIGHT: *I WILL ALWAYS LOVE YOU*

Tonight's movie took them to a vintage shop.

Drake recognized the shop right away. In the years since Ben had brought Ellie there on her birthday, organizational changes had been made, and someone had added bright signs to help customers navigate the racks. WESTERN WEAR one of them read. COWGIRL said another, which seemed to be the more adventurous version of WESTERN WEAR. He wondered if this was where the cowboy entered the story. But GRAPHIC TEES was the rack Ellie sifted through before she headed to the front counter.

"Can I help you?" the salesgirl asked. She was dressed like Wednesday Addams, only with two blonde pigtails stuck against her shoulders.

"Hi," Ellie said. She was a little older here than in the last memory, and her hair was chin-length now. The cut made her features look larger, or maybe it was just the raw emotion on her face. Grief still, and something else. Loneliness, maybe. "Do you, umm, take donations?"

"Sure," the girl said. "But there's a Buffalo Exchange down the street."

Ellie recoiled. "No. I don't want a *Buffalo Exchange*."

"They pay at Buffalo Exchange." The girl dropped her head in apology. "Here, it's—well—we pay almost nothing."

"Well, it's not about the money."

"Oh. Well, then why don't you keep your stuff? You never know when extra clothes will come in handy for a costume party—"

"Because," Ellie snapped. "I don't have the room for it." She sighed. "Anyway, it's all in the car."

Ben's clothes filled the space inside of Ellie's trunk. Most of the items had been bagged up, but a few were still loose, as if thrown in at the last possible second: button-down shirts and distressed graphic tees. Blue jeans, black jeans, and a questionable pair of white overalls. Drake wondered if this meant Ellie had sorted through Ben's closet by herself. It would've been a terrible task to push on a kid, even a twentysomething kid. And was Ellie, who coveted old things, really about to give up her brother's treasures?

Ellie shifted in the seat next to him; Drake sensed she was far away, digging until she hit her deepest layer of regret. As younger Ellie threw the loose clothing items into one of the bags, the significance of the memory clicked together. Drake had known that Ben was the reason Ellie loved old places. What he hadn't quite understood was her logic for choosing the heirlooms that piled on their shelves. Ellie's vintage hunting extended beyond the practical need of furniture or the aesthetic one of art. She picked up personal items, too—abandoned trophies or the occasional family photo tucked inside a souvenir frame.

Watching this moment, her behavior made sense. Ellie had given the last pieces of Ben's life away to a stranger. Since she could never get his things back, she collected the aftermath of other peoples' lives and relationships. She treated these items with care and love—the same way she hoped someone out there was watching over Ben's things.

Drake heard himself sniffle. He hadn't felt himself tearing up and hoped the light from the projector wouldn't give him away. Embarrassment rolled through him. This was her pain, her grief. He needed to be the strong one. It was the thought of Ellie going through Ben's clothes, scraping the dirt off his sneakers, hoping for the last time that he would come back and fill them—

Drake sniffled louder the second time.

Ellie pulled his arm tighter around her. Her face surprised him. Was she relieved? Maybe this is how it was meant to be—that Drake was meant to share in this pain, to wade around in it with her so it was less lonely.

"These are all the things," Ellie told the salesgirl. "What I want donated. Wait . . ." She held her hand up. There was one more item in the front seat. It had earned a special place in the car, a special goodbye. Her hands found the studded leather jacket Ben had worn the night they went to the abandoned mansion. Ellie hugged it to her chest, then passed it over to the girl while trying to not look too hard at it. "This, too," she said.

"I'll get a cart," the girl told her. Moments later, Ellie's trunk slammed, and the physical contents of Ben's life wobbled from the car and into the shop.

When the salesgirl handed over a few measly singles, Ellie quietly pleaded, "Please make sure this stuff finds a good home." She set a hand on the salesgirl's shoulder. "Please."

Drake could guess the plot of the next memory. He also knew that Ellie was going to lose her mind. But in his defense, it was only a song. "You take the John Mayer, I'll take the Whitney Houston" wasn't something people negotiated during a breakup. Besides, Drake loved the song before he'd even met Melinda.

Based on the hissing sound Ellie was making, though, that detail wouldn't matter. She leaned so far toward the screen that he imagined her head might spin and get stuck in the wrong direction, like a scene from *Death Becomes Her*.

On-screen, Melinda rolled the car windows down and Drake turned up the stereo. They were belting along to Whitney Houston; both of them were terrible singers. Melinda punched her fists into the air as the song transcended into a new octave. There was a naive twinkle in Drake's eyes. They weren't singing. They were serenading each other with the lyrics of "I Will Always Love You." This was it, the moment in the movie when the audience realizes the leads are supposed to make it.

Only, Drake had shared this same movie moment with Ellie a few weeks ago at Finn's.

What was she thinking as she moved around in her seat? Why did he keep repeating moments he had experienced with Melinda all over again? Here he'd thought he was building something that would last through unique gestures, everything tailored to their life together. All along, he'd been on rinse-and-repeat mode, relying on song suggestions or restaurant ideas that were no more original than the homes in Wakeford Heights.

He'd first brought up the Whitney Houston song on an early date with Ellie. Drake asked Ellie's favorite song, and she mentioned "Built to Roam" by a singer named Shakey Graves.

"Okay. What do you like about it?" Drake wanted to know.

Ellie pursed her lips. "It's a modern song, but it makes me feel like I'm in high school, about to sneak out a window," she said. "And, I love his voice. It's got scrapes in it. What about you?"

"'I Will Always Love You' is my favorite," Drake admitted. He rattled off the next part quickly, so it didn't seem like he was making a declaration that would've scared her. "By Whitney Houston."

"You mean Dolly Parton." Ellie set her head on her hand, so sly.

"Yeah." Drake nodded. "Okay, right. But the Whitney Houston version."

"The Whitney Houston *cover*."

"Whitney . . ." He laughed in disbelief. "You call that a *cover*?"

Had they been at a vodka bar that night? No, it was a gin bar. The bar specialized in gin and had all-pink walls. Drake had never heard of a gin bar. He didn't even like gin. It tasted like soap to him. He downed the tiny glass of soap cocktail. Ellie asked something about why that song was special as she spun around a seashell-shaped chair. What did he say?

What he said was that Whitney had the best voice ever.

No, it wasn't that. He said the song was catchy as all heck.

No. Drake said something like, the song had a lot of great memories attached to it that he never wanted to lose. Why the hell did he admit that? Hopefully Ellie had forgotten that part.

In the memory on the screen, the song finally ended. Melinda pulled the car into her spot directly in front of her store. They were home again. Her apartment was Drake's home, even though he didn't technically live there. She didn't need a reserved parking spot because that spot was her spot, and everyone knew better than to park there. Melinda was the entire town's sweetheart.

"You coming up?"

"You know it," Drake said.

She turned off the car. Drake hopped out and opened her door for her. Once they were inside the empty shop, he swept her in his arms and carried her up the stairs that made too much noise. It was dark inside the attic apartment. Pasta slinked her way across the floor, brushing Drake's leg as he moved Melinda toward the bed. When he set her down, she lit one of the many candles he'd given her on the bedside table with a matchbook from their first date. His hands were in her hair, on her dress, pulling on its cold zipper. She kicked the fabric away and the dress fell onto the floor, like a mouth open in disbelief. Were they about to do this for an audience?

Yes, they were. Is that what Drake looked like getting things started? He hadn't known himself to make those sounds. Maybe, hopefully, he didn't always make those sounds. Why was he seeing this night, and why was he here, in the audience, analyzing himself? How could he possibly stay seated as his pants came off and he kissed the softest place on Melinda's neck behind her ear? Did he look the same way with Ellie? He wanted to leave, but he was too miserable to move. They stayed there and punished themselves until the lights turned on again.

Ellie locked eyes with the ground as they walked down the stairs and back into the lobby.

"I've always loved Whitney Houston, you know," Drake told her. She was a few steps ahead of him. "Before that particular night. And lately, I love her even more. After that moment we had at Finn's—"

"It's a Dolly Parton song," Ellie said. It wasn't a repeat comment. She was letting him know she remembered everything he'd admitted on that date where he mentioned it was his favorite song.

Drake played dumb. "What?"

"Drake." Ellie gritted her teeth. They had just pushed the lobby's doors open and were hit with a wall of cold. "Damn it, Drake. You keep saying it's a Whitney Houston song. It's a Dolly Parton song. Dolly Parton, she wrote this song. She never gets the credit for it. And just because Whitney Houston is also a powerhouse doesn't mean that we should run around not crediting the writers. Okay? Writers are doing important things. Writers deserve to have their work remembered."

"Okay," he said, even though they weren't talking about Whitney Houston and Dolly Parton. They were talking about Melinda and Ellie, of course, but Drake wasn't sure who was who, and he wasn't about to ask.

The timing of the movie was terrible—it made the tension that had been developing between them worse. They couldn't start the next year, the year they were getting married, on this note. So he would go home and plan something for tomorrow night. He would beg on hands and knees for a last-minute dinner reservation if needed. This called for a grand gesture, and there was no better time for beginnings than New Year's Eve.

28

There were two hours until midnight.

Drake had found the perfect place for dinner. According to the internet, an heiress had met her demise in the banquet room of the steakhouse and spent her afterlife waiting for a dance partner. Their booth with a white tablecloth and wraparound stained glass windows could've belonged to a ship on the edge of the Atlantic.

But despite the old-school setting Ellie would usually love, she seemed distracted. She stared off into space as Drake explained that he wanted to get home for the ball drop. There was something about the tradition of watching it on TV that made him feel hopeful about the year ahead. Ellie's phone rang while he was still midsentence. She picked it up, right there at the table. For a person who wanted to live in the past, Ellie was glued to modern technology. Drake's hand dove toward a basket of warm breadsticks.

"Hey," Ellie said. "No. Now is fine." Drake could hear Nolan's voice on the other end of the phone. It was a really inconvenient time to call. It would've been nice, Drake thought, if he had considered waiting until after the holidays.

"What do you mean, they're not sure?" Ellie asked. Diners poked their heads up as they ate. Ellie needed to lower her voice. Three tables down, the waitress sang "Happy Birthday to You" to a table of white-haired women. They looked like a secret club or a sorority. How lucky to have a birthday on New Year's Eve, Drake thought. He swore one of the ladies gestured for Ellie to keep it down, but maybe she was just pushing the candle smoke away from her face. "You said I was a *perfect* fit," Ellie snapped. "I have hosting experience, and . . . I mean, the show wasn't all *that* bad, was it?"

The show, Drake had always felt, was that bad. He was no expert in the arts, but Ellie had seemed physically uncomfortable on camera. She did a confusing thing with her eyebrows where she raised them too high on her head, so she always looked like she'd walked in on someone evading their taxes. The magnetism and cleverness Drake knew her for had been muddled down, which made her come off as pretentious, even to him.

"Well, who is she?" Ellie asked. She reached for a breadstick and snapped it in half.

"Maybe you want to step outside for a minute?" Drake asked. The suggestion had sounded a little rude, so he played it off as helpful. "I mean, because it's kind of loud in here."

"Hold on," Ellie said as she pressed the mute button. Wisps of her hair fell out of her high bun. She didn't bother to fix it. "It's Nolan," she said. "They're considering somebody else for the show."

"Well, maybe . . . that's okay?" Drake offered. He'd meant that it would be okay either way. They didn't need the money; Ellie had achieved a good amount of success, and maybe she would find something that was a better fit. His message hadn't come through, though. Daggers lit up in Ellie's eyes. "I mean, maybe they're seeing someone else as, like, a formality," he backpedaled.

Ellie unmuted her call. She wanted to know what the *other* girl was like. Before Nolan could answer, she hung up and occupied herself with the leather-bound menu. Her mouth made cryptic sounds as she scanned the salad section, a tsk here and there, like a cheeky snake.

"This is really unfair," Ellie pouted. "Nolan made it seem like I had it." She gave Drake a look that commanded him to do something. He wasn't sure what that was. He was amazed from the beginning that Ellie was convinced she would land this. It took a certain amount of audacity to assume that a role she had no experience in—hosting home renovations—would be hers. If anything, Drake had more experience in that arena. He wasn't going to point that out.

"I'm really sorry, Ellie," he said. She had been through so much recently. He needed to lift her up.

A little later, their waitress, Charlotte, stopped by the table. "Have we figured out what we're having?" she wanted to know. The old-timey places Ellie frequented were always using *we*, as if the waitress planned to sit down and ask them to pass the asparagus. Ellie said she needed another few minutes to look, even though Drake knew she would order the salmon and an espresso martini. Eventually, she did.

It was almost eleven by the time the food came out. They weren't getting home for the ball drop. In the lounge behind them, a singer started into a jazz standard. She was striking, in her thirties or early forties, wearing a silver dress that grazed the floor.

"I'm sorry," Ellie said, probably noticing the look on his face as she took her first bite. "I just . . . I really want this job. Not because I want to be on television. Or home shows. As cheesy as it sounds, I think I would be good at this. I mean, these shows usually tear everything down and make it all new, you know? But I wouldn't do that. I would give people new appreciation for the things they already love. Make their spaces really work for them."

Drake softened. He hadn't heard her talk about the show in that way before. How she felt about this job was how *he* felt about his job. At least, the job he hoped to have one day.

"Thank you for bringing me here," Ellie said, reaching for

Drake's hands. "I love it. Martinis. Ghosts with good rhythm. Totally my thing." Drake smiled. He felt bad for doubting her earlier.

Ellie finished her drink, so Drake flagged Charlotte to get another one. "Uh, no," Ellie said. "We're going to go home. For the ball drop. Or, actually . . ." She grabbed Drake's wrist and looked at the time on his watch, then moved her head around the room, searching for something. "We'll take the check and move to the bar," she told Charlotte. "I saw a TV over there."

At the bar, there weren't any stools left, so Ellie and Drake huddled with the rest of the crowd around the TV. As eleven thirty rolled toward midnight, the singer, on break, put two party hats on their heads and handed Drake a kazoo. Drake wrapped his arms around Ellie's waist, and the countdown began.

Ten! Nine!

"I've never liked New Year's much," Ellie said.

Eight! Seven!

"It's gonna be a good year," Drake told her. "I don't know if you know this, but I'm getting married this year."

Six!

"You don't say?"

Five!

"Thanks for doing this," Drake said. "The ball drop. I thought you weren't listening earlier."

Four!

"I'm always listening, Drake. The holidays are just hard for me. But you know what? This year, I'm excited for midnight, too."

Three!

"You are?"

Two!

"Yeah. You make me want to celebrate things. And I love that about you."

One!

Someone shot Silly String out of a can. Cheers whooped across the bar, and people bumped into Ellie and Drake as they kissed, but it didn't stop them. Another year together, the year of their wedding, was set in motion.

29

Drake's plan for a fresh start was working. Some of the tension from the last movie had been washed away by the holidays; it was like a storm had dropped in and swept up the debris. They kept their conversations light. They finalized flowers for the wedding. They burned a roll of premade cookie dough, then scraped the seared edges off the pan while inventing real-life mysteries for Nancy to solve. *The Case of the Scorched Chocolate.*

But under the surface of the calm was a knowing that Drake couldn't ignore. There were still two movies left to watch. Ellie would see the worst of it, of him, soon.

And when they sat down for the ninth movie that night, Drake learned that the worst was moments away.

TICKET NINE: *HEARTBREAK*

Drake glanced at Ellie in the seat next to him and gave her a nod of encouragement. *This is all going to be okay*, the nod was trying to convince her. *I promise that what you saw in the photo album will make sense.* But before he could get any of that out, the memory started to play.

Ellie was inside of a grief group. A circle of fold-out chairs was arranged at the heart of the depressing space; it must have been a school on summer break or community center. Vague inspirational posters plastered the walls. *You've Got This. The Only Way Out Is Through.*

Drake hated that she was there alone. But then, she wasn't.

"I tried therapy, but it was too stuffy," Ellie told the man in the white Stetson. Dark circles underlined his stoic eyes, and a tattoo of a crow perched on a black fence decorated his forearm. The man had about ten years on Ellie and the kind of smile that might inspire her to make bad decisions.

Cowboy Love Affair, Drake remembered from the plaque.

"Anyway, that's how I ended up here," Ellie said. The cowboy nodded. He told Ellie about his late wife before he shared his name. "I'm Hudson," he said a few minutes later, reaching for a glazed cruller inside a cardboard box. "Give me a doughnut, and I'll play nice anywhere."

Neither of them spoke much in the meeting. When a woman went on a tangent about the printer at her office, which was somehow related to her grief story, Hudson squeezed Ellie's leg. Her eyes noted his touch; Ellie was drawn to him more than to the string of casual boyfriends they'd seen in the other movies. When Hudson and Ellie walked out together after the meeting, she toyed with his brim. "What's with the hat?" she teased.

"I'm still trying to figure out who I am without her," Hudson admitted.

"So, now you wear hats?"

"Yeah. I'm trying a hat thing. Don't knock it." Hudson spun toward Ellie and tipped the hat. Then, he opened his passenger door to give her a ride. While they rode to Ellie's apartment, he mentioned a cabin his parents didn't use anymore. "It's a short-enough drive to get glued to an audiobook—then—bam, you've arrived." He went there to be away from everything. "I cook shit, blare the Lacrimosa movement, weep. It's super healthy. I call it Grief Mountain." Hudson made the motion of gliding up a mountain with his hand.

"Sounds depressing," Ellie said. "I think that would be good for my writing. Although I tend to hate cabins. And bugs."

Hudson leaned closer to her. "Think of it as a small lodge. What do you write about?"

"Complicated people and things," Ellie told him without hesitation. "Tragedy." Hudson straightened in his seat. "Not really. But I am interested in things on the brink of death."

"That's not dark at all." He nudged her. "So . . . do you want to join me at Grief Mountain sometime, or what?"

Grief Mountain was rustic. Hudson's parents had left their mark everywhere, from WELCOME TO THE LAKE! signs to a statue of a proud bear holding a bass it presumably caught. Family photos clung to the wood-paneled walls of the living room, surrounding a flickering fire and suede couch.

While Hudson plated the complicated stir fry he'd "thrown together," he shared more about his wife, Vanessa. They'd met at her friend's bachelorette party where he had worked as the private chef. He and Vanessa chatted in the kitchen, then snuck a bottle of champagne out by the pool later that night. The bride was "so very pissed off" by the distraction.

"I can't imagine what it's like," Ellie said. "Losing your first love."

Hudson shook his head as he tasted the food. "My first love was Jade Needer." He got up and ducked his head inside a few cabinets, then turned back to Ellie. "Speaking of needer. This food *needs* . . . something."

"What a name."

"Yeah," he agreed, returning to the table with a jar of chili oil. "Yeah. But she inevitably broke my heart. So, I dated a lot. Et cetera." Hudson made a hand gesture meant to explain away a series of life decisions. Then he drizzled some oil onto Ellie's plate, even though she was midbite. "When I met Vanessa, I was ready. I was older. I had lived. I knew *this is the person for me.*"

He sighed. "I like to think that a first love is finding yourself in someone else. And a second love," he said, looking right at Ellie, "well, the second love is just sharing the self you found with somebody new. The real self, of course."

"So, you felt more like yourself when you were with Vanessa than with Jade?"

"Yeah," he told. "Yeah. Like . . . Okay, I used to think too much when I was younger, right? But Vanessa and I—we left that bachelorette party when it was over and drove off into the sunrise together. We stopped at this hole-in-the-wall burger place on the way home. I don't think it had a name. The menu was, like, written on scratch paper. We ate one burger off the same plate. Fought over the fries. You learn a lot about a person that way," he said.

"Which way?" Ellie asked, hovering off her chair.

Hudson set his fork down. "Doing something intimate right off the bat."

They kissed. It happened so suddenly that it was hard to tell who started it. Ellie dragged Hudson forward by the neck of his weathered black shirt. He stripped off the shirt she was wearing, mesmerized by each button. Then they fought their way to the couch, hell-bent on tearing each other apart.

A couple of nights later, Ellie found the dress in the cabin's spare bedroom.

She was rummaging around the closet to look for cupcake pans. There, behind all the coats and sweaters, Ellie spotted it—a pale Easter yellow with gold flowers running along the neck. Abandoned. Lonely, she seemed to think. Ellie's pajamas dropped to the floor. She stepped inside the dress and pulled the zipper up right as Hudson moved behind her.

"Take it off," he demanded, planting his hand on her shoulders. Ellie mistook Hudson's tone and spun to kiss him. He jerked away from her. Why was she wearing his wife's dress?

Ellie struggled to explain, as she did take it off, that she felt objects that were left behind deserved to be used. She'd done the same thing when she was younger. She tried to give things that reminded her of her brother away or push them to the back of a closet. But you could revive someone through their things and stories, she argued in her defense. She hung the dress back up, slammed the closet doors closed, and sat next to Hudson in the dark bedroom. Neither of them bothered to turn the lights on.

"What are we doing here, man?" Hudson asked.

"I don't know," Ellie said. "I like you. A lot. I haven't been tempted once to sneak out your window, which is unusual for me—"

"I don't think this is good for us, Ellie." He hung his weight over his knees. "Good for me. You and me—this thing—feels like, the world's most dysfunctional bereavement group."

That night, after Ellie packed her things, Hudson drove her down Grief Mountain, parked outside of her apartment, and gave her a light kiss. When Ellie's hand reached for the car door, he stopped it. "Two things," he said.

"All right." She was icy. Rejected.

"I lied about the hat." Hudson was wearing it again. He took it off and dusted the crown with his hand. "Vanessa gave this to me. It was meant to be a joke. Because I was so far off from being a cowboy. But, umm. Hey, why don't you take it? Something to remember me by." He placed it onto Ellie's head.

"I couldn't," she said.

"I insist. It looks good on you. I think it makes me sad."

Ellie offered a reluctant nod.

"One more thing." He bit the edge of his fingernail. "The hat is kind of a gesture for what I'm going to say next. You told me that you write about these fascinating, tragic situations. And I've got this sense . . . I'm asking you not to write about anything I've shared the last few days. Please don't drag all that up for me." His eyes begged. "Please, Ellie."

"Even if I did, it's not like anyone would read it."

"Ellie?" He turned her chin toward him. "I can trust you. I can trust you, can't I?"

"Yeah," she said. "Of course, you can."

"Good. I'm glad. Really." He brushed his hands off over his lap to mark something important had been cleared. "Okay, well good night."

Ellie left him there and scurried up the stairs of her apartment. Without even taking the hat off, she sat down and started to write. It was a story about the importance of bringing back old things, she would tell people later, the one that began with a lonely dress tucked in a closet. It was the first story in her book, the one where she quoted Hudson. The one that dragged up ghosts.

The one that made her famous.

Ellie's lie made Drake sick. She should've understood Hudson's grief and respected it, considering her own. She spoke the lie so easily, without a care in the world about what the ramifications would be for him.

"Drake?" Ellie asked in the seat next to him. He was too upset to face her. He stayed focused on the movie, watching her younger counterpart type away, happily. Smug, almost.

Then, before he could dig deeper into what happened, the scene blurred and switched over.

The memory started in the high school hallway, as he'd remembered. With his mom's silk blindfold shielding Melinda's eyes, Drake steered her down the rose-petal aisle, past the dusty orange lockers, to eventually face the circle of candles surrounding the ring box. "Are you kidnapping me?" Melinda asked.

"Not a kidnapping. I promise." Drake moved to grab the small music box in the middle of all the candles and landed at her feet. He cleared his throat, announcing Melinda could remove the blindfold and face the banner he'd strung from the ceiling. A question was suspended in the same space where streamers from school dances once decorated the halls.

WILL YOU MARRY ME?

Drake waited for her response. It was hard to gauge her reaction. Melinda's hand went to her mouth, and a big breath filled her chest. She was surprised, but it wasn't clear whether it was a good or bad surprise. Drake's knee started to hurt; the hard floor pressed back on him as he willed an answer out of her. *Yes*, he thought. How difficult was it to say yes? They were so close to a life together above her shop. He had never wanted to stay in town, but with Melinda, it would be all right. Life would be good.

"I can't do this, Drake," Melinda said as she stared at the ring inside the box.

"What do you mean, you can't?" His face felt hot.

"It isn't working," Melinda said. Then, her back was to him, and she was moving away. Was she leaving? No, she was sitting—right on the floor against one of the lockers and patting a space next to her. Drake accepted it. They weren't far from where they once had talked at the entrance to the dance. He swore he could hear the thud of the heavy bass knocking on the gym walls, that he could smell the perfume that lined her wrists that night.

Melinda's thumb ran over the splinter Drake had gotten that morning. Hours ago, they had joined the limbs of a wooden side table together, then climbed back in bed. He made eggs and English muffins. When had this feeling started for her, this feeling of an ending? Even as he parked the car outside the school, they had spoken about taking a vacation. Melinda wanted to go to Italy. They would rent Vespas. They would eat offensive amounts of pasta.

"Since when is it not working?" Drake struggled to get out. "Five minutes ago, everything was fine."

"Five minutes ago, we were just kids," she said.

"What do you mean?" He set down the music box at his side.

"I think that—you and me—we're stuck in the past," she told him. "In this idea of what *was*. We live like we're in high school still. You're even proposing at our high school, Drake. But we're adults now. You haven't taken a single step forward in your career since we've been together. And I haven't pushed you to do that, either."

"That's not true," Drake said, even though it was true.

"Look, I want to stay in this town forever. These people, my store . . . It's my future. And you, Drake, this isn't for you. You love big gestures and tall buildings and places with possibility. You fight it, but you do love those things. And I love slow mornings where we sit reading in bed and everything is simple."

"I could work on homes in the city," Drake insisted. "Spend some time there. Then drive right back here—"

"It's not just about your career." She wrapped her arms around her knees. Melinda had a way of getting comfortable wherever she was, even in the middle of a breakup on a cold floor. "Everything is so easy with us. We don't push each other. Challenge each other. We're so agreeable that I'm afraid if we got married, one or both of us would wilt." Melinda noticed the word *wilt* had particularly crushed him. She pressed on. "I don't even know if I want to be married. I mean, I love your company, but—I'm independent and . . . also, I'm not going to change my mind about kids. I couldn't live with myself if I pressured you into a different life than the one you want."

Melinda rested her head on his shoulder. Then, things got embarrassing.

"I love you," Drake pleaded. "Please, just think about this. Please. Just . . . Please." Melinda covered his lips with her finger.

The begging carried on for several brutal minutes. They were meant to be together. Drake didn't care what his life brought, so long as they were together. Dreams, who needed them? She was his dream. He threw the word *destiny* around until it got grimy. Tears were shed, the picture someone would point at to define an ugly cry.

Eventually, Melinda helped him blow the candles out, which was somehow more devastating than doing it on his own. Before that, though, she flipped the lid of the music box back open and spun the key several times. Soft piano poured out from it, and a ballet dancer spun at the center with her arms extended over her head. The song stopped and started again, stopped and started.

Melinda held her hand out and asked Drake to dance. After a few rounds of the music, she set her head on his chest. She smelled like millions of flowers distilled into two spritzes from the pink glass globe bottle he'd watched her use so many mornings.

"You're going to find that person," Melinda said.

Drake pulled away. Even if he did find someone else, he was always going to love her. "I will love you forever," he repeated. His own word—forever—wagged a finger at him. A diamond was forever. He wished he'd gone with the stupid diamond.

Instead, he'd chosen a sapphire.

The exact sapphire that was now on Ellie's hand.

When the lights went up, she was twisting it around her finger.

"You proposed to her," she seethed. "You proposed with *my ring*."

"I know." Drake swallowed. It was unusual to sit in the auditorium with all the lights on; they usually left right away. There was safety in the darkness. Everything suddenly felt much more severe.

"I thought if you saw it all play out, it would make it better," he said. "But look, the memory didn't happen how I remembered it, Ellie. Not at all." Drake was rambling; he could barely punctuate his sentences. "The breakup was more mutual than what we saw. Sure, I proposed, but I remember being okay after she turned me down, you know? I remember feeling like not getting married was right. I don't know what the hell just happened. Maybe I forgot the details because they were hard for me. Almost like how you forgot—"

She shook her head to stop him. "Don't even think about making that comparison. Just don't."

Drake nodded. He was searching for common ground, but he'd taken a misstep. Ellie's hand trembled on her lap. He reached for it. "That night you found that photo at my mom's place—those few photos at the end of the album . . . I wanted you to understand the full story. That's the only reason I suggested we come back here. But I'm afraid I made everything so much worse."

"What photos, Drake?" Ellie asked.

His stomach turned. Something was wrong. Her question should've come with a tone of accusation. At least a knowing smirk. But Ellie was genuinely curious. He'd assumed that she was holding the secret above his head like an invisible lever she was waiting to pull. But what if she'd never flipped to the back of the album? What if she'd never seen what he did—a few photographs of him in the jewelry store picking out Ellie's sapphire ring years before they'd met. For someone else.

Ellie's forehead creased in confusion as she waited for an answer, which confirmed what Drake had pieced together. She hadn't known about the proposal, or the ring, until right now. And Drake had dragged her there to watch every miserable detail magnify before her eyes.

Ellie wouldn't look at Drake as they drove home. They drifted through the streets, passing all the familiar neighborhood landmarks in silence. There was the house that put out too many inflatables for the holidays, the one with the bright red mailbox, the one with the neighbor who always called them by the wrong names.

But even in this world of sameness, everything was different.

Ellie hadn't known about the proposal until tonight. Now she had seen it happen with the same ring on her finger and the same music box that was on their shelf. The memory was much worse than he'd remembered. He had been so stupid. If they had only talked, she could've learned the truth without having to live it. Instead, Drake had forced her to watch him declare his undying love for Melinda.

"I'll love you forever," he'd repeated over and over.

Those same words he used when he proposed to Ellie.

The car slid into the driveway. Drake opened Ellie's door for her. He held the front door open, too, which he'd fixed the squeak on last week, but she still hadn't noticed. Ellie needed space, he figured. The whole thing would blow over. He sat on the couch while she threw the keys onto the shelf over their shoes and stomped into the kitchen. Drake could hear the spoon clinking inside the expensive canned food the vet gave them for Nancy's upset stomach, then the sound of her aggressively eating the food from the bowl.

He waited and waited for Ellie to emerge from the kitchen, but she didn't. The house was too quiet; he put on one of her crooner records to make it feel more lived in. When Drake swung the kitchen door open, he found her sitting at the table they never used, her eyes wide and possessed, like a still image from one of their Thursday-night monster movie marathons. Ellie looked like she had "*seen* things."

Cautiously, he slid out a chair, sat across from her, and cleared his throat. "We should talk about all of this, Ellie," he said. "Where do you want to start?"

30

Ellie set her hand on the table, forcing Drake to address the ring. "Let's start here," she said. She was right to be mad about the ring. Drake still hadn't thought of an excuse she would find acceptable. To say he felt attached to it in the store—and later believed it was meant for her—wouldn't be easy to digest, even if it were true.

"I'm . . . I'm so sorry, Ellie. I know how this all must look—"

"Well, let me summarize it for you. It looks like you used my ring"—she wiggled her fingers—"to get engaged to someone else."

"I wasn't engaged," Drake insisted. He cleared his throat and slouched his shoulders. "I'm sorry," he repeated. "But to be engaged, the other person has to say yes. It's a two-way thing."

Ellie scooted her chair out. He was going for cute or sarcastic, but neither was landing. Ellie got to be the cute, sarcastic one. "But you would've been engaged," she said. "How could you not tell me that?"

The loud ticking of their wall clock took Drake's focus. Ellie had hung up a nineteenth-century Vienna Regulator that never displayed the correct time. Their conversation was either happening five minutes early or five minutes late. "I thought you knew," Drake explained. "That night at my parents' place? I thought you saw photos of the ring in that album. I figured that's why you weren't yourself." Drake reached out for her. Ellie pulled her arms to her sides. "But I should've told you everything way before that. At the beginning. I just didn't know how you'd take it."

Ellie shot up to stand. She hovered over him on the other side of the table. "No. No, don't make it sound like I can't handle difficult conversations. You didn't tell me about the proposal because it was too hard *for you*. Because you're such a good person, Drake. You're so, *selfless,* you know?" She smirked as she bent forward and pinched his cheek. There was that sarcasm part.

Drake's mouth dried out. Ellie couldn't even hear his side of things. The meanness in her tone lifted him by the shirt collar and threw him into a fight. "You know what I can't believe?" he said, pushing himself up to her level. "That you wrote about that guy's late wife. And not even accurately, by the way."

Ellie moved to the darkest corner of the room. Ironically, this was the place where the sunlight came in strongest during the day. Nancy would sit there and sunbathe, tethered to the floor. It was supposed to be a happy pocket. "There are . . . creative licenses you're not considering," she huffed. "As an artist, you can't get all caught up in other people's feelings—"

"You started your career on a lie, Ellie," Drake summarized, to underline his point. He walked toward her. She flinched. "And now, I can't help but be nervous that you're going to start our marriage on a lie, too."

"And what lie is that?" Ellie turned to him.

"I don't even know," Drake said. "You didn't tell me about going to see Melinda for *so* long. You didn't take the time to explain to anyone in your long string of boyfriends why you were leaving them—"

"Are we back to this?" Ellie snapped. "Your utter woe and bitterness over my sleeping with other people before we even met?"

The clock got louder. Tick. Tick. Tick. Stupid clock.

"I'm not jealous," he said. "I'm upset about the way you left them."

Tick. Tick. Tick.

"Like how she left you?"

TICK. TICK. TICK.

"No!" Drake insisted. He slammed his palm against the refrigerator. He could hear the bottles shifting inside, ketchup on the run. "Melinda and I, that's not the same. It's not. None of those people you dated even got a goodbye. You ran out their door or snuck down their fire escape before you had to face anything real." Ellie wove behind him and sat back down. He joined her on the other side of the table. The table was keeping them safe, Drake felt. "You've built this career around connecting to the past, but a part of me thinks you're just afraid of connecting with people in the present."

"My career . . . You hate that I'm successful, right?" Ellie asked. "You never went after what you wanted to do, and here I am, rubbing that in your face."

He could feel her disdain. Ellie hated that Drake's choices didn't *align* with her *lifestyle*, despite that lifestyle beginning with a long history of family money. "You know it must be really nice," he said, leaning forward. "To start what you wanted to do with all that cushy support."

"Cushy support," Ellie repeated. "From the parents who barely spoke to me after my brother died."

"Your mom just threw a party for us," Drake said. "Your dad had us over for Thanksgiving. And you sat there and picked apart every little thing wrong with his house and with him. Just like you do with my family."

"You're right." Ellie nodded. "I don't fit in with your wonderful family and all of their unnecessary second holiday celebrations. But you know who does? Melinda. I bet they wish that ring was on her finger."

"Come . . . Oh, come on," Drake said. "That's so far from the truth. The truth is so far away from you right now. It's out in

Boise." He pointed in the general direction of Boise behind him. Suddenly, the wall clock chimed to announce a new hour. Drake jumped. Ellie let out a shriek.

"Holy shit," he said.

"God dammit."

"That thing really got me." Drake felt himself start to calm as they shook off their nerves. "Look," he told her. "Let's slow down. I love who you are now, Ellie."

"Right." Ellie nodded. "And what if I miss who I was then?" She started to shake. Something was wrong. Tears wet her mascara. "I mean, I used to go out and *live*. I would listen to records on strangers' beds, meet weirdos at house parties, people you should never meet in real life. I once met a man named Gilligan. Gilligan. And he'd never heard of the show. You can't make this up. And I think those are the kinds of moments that made me write well. That made me myself. Only now, they're drying up."

"Because of me," Drake pieced together. "That's what you're saying. Right?"

Headlights flooded the windows and car doors slammed outside. There were smiling voices. Laughing voices. They paused and waited to continue.

"That's not what I said," Ellie insisted.

"It is, though," Drake told her. "Everything has to be so *interesting* with you. You can't sit still and be comfortable. You can't buy a new rug or a new sweater or make anything easy on yourself because easy is *boring*, and God forbid anything be boring, even for a second. It's reckless, Ellie. Truly."

"Well then," Ellie said, "what do you love so much about me, Drake?"

"Oh, come on. Don't do that. You know what I mean."

"No. I really don't."

"Okay. Well, I love that you're passionate and artistic, and we have so much fun together, and you appreciate old things—"

"Huh. That sounds familiar." Her face turned red. " 'I'll love you forever,' " she recited. "I'll love you forever?" Ellie stood and pushed the door to the living room open. Drake followed behind her. The record he'd put on earlier was skipping as they circled the coffee table like animals in a chase. It was tough to tell who had the advantage. Finally, the skipping stopped, but the music sounded like it was playing underwater because it was on Dorothy III. Nancy had ducked behind the couch to hide.

"I said the same thing to you," Drake told her. He stopped moving and held his hands up. "That I'd love you forever. And I meant it."

"Right. Thanks for making that point for me." Ellie stopped straight across from him. "You said *the same things to both of us*. You used the same ring, played me the same songs, took me to the same restaurants, watched the same movies, gave me the same sappy proposal. You love me because I remind you of her, Drake." Ellie marched over to him. "You can't even be original with who you love."

"That's not true."

"It is, though. You have decades of memories. The cinema could play any of them. And the only thing it ever seems to play is you with Melinda. She is the storyline that haunts you the most. Ben, and the aftermath, is mine."

Drake paused. He knew Ellie was right, in a way. Only, he didn't still love Melinda. Why were those memories the only ones that came up? This realization had been bothering him for weeks. "I want nothing more than to marry you," Drake told her. "Tell me you still want to marry me?" He made it sound like a question, but really, he was groveling again. Groveling for her to stay, to tell him this wasn't going to end in another failed proposal. A part of Drake always imagined Ellie would leave. He was trying to stop her from proving him right, but it came out all wrong. "Tell me, Ellie. Say you want to marry me."

Ellie ignored his plea. She turned to look up at the wooden wall shelves. Her hands passed the antique ship they had been gifted on the night of their engagement party, beyond the framed collection of matchbooks, and then she had a firm grip on something. Her fingers curled around the music box Drake hadn't intended to give to her so long ago. She set it down on the coffee table so it couldn't be ignored. "She's always been in the room with us," she said. "Right from the beginning. Hasn't she?"

Every part of Ellie was pulling away from him. Her footsteps were loud against the stairs. Drake waited in the living room as her bag unzipped, followed by the sound of items making a crash landing inside of it. A few minutes later, she came out of their bedroom with her packed bag.

It wasn't the duffel bag she used for overnights. It was a much bigger bag.

Halfway down the stairs, Drake begged her not to do the thing she always did. He wasn't sure how to walk back from this.

"I'm going to Jen and Marc's," Ellie said. "I need space."

Drake wanted her to stay so he could convince her that, yes, he had loved Melinda, but his love for Ellie was different. It was real. If she stayed, she would brush her hands through his hair. They would talk it out. They would wake up the next morning and have breakfast together. They'd break the spell they'd put on the now-cursed kitchen table, and also, the now-cursed coffee table. "I'm sorry," Ellie would say. "I love you, Drake. Pass the milk?" Drake would pass the milk. He would hear her laugh again. Not the laugh that she laughed for other people, but the one that was just for him.

But that's not what happened.

Drake followed Ellie outside to the driveway. The car beeped as it unlocked, and the ignition gave in to her demands. She lingered for a moment, probably to call Jen, and then he was alone.

31

Drake almost fell off the couch the next morning. The sound of the doorbell, and Nancy's mission to destroy its ringer, had jolted him awake. Sleeping there had saved him from facing Ellie's empty side of the bed, but it didn't come without consequences. Pain flew down his back when he stood. He was too old to be sleeping on couches.

A brown cardboard box waited on the front porch. Their neighbor, Rich, had left a note on it: "think I got your delivery yesterday?" Drake carried the box inside and let it fall to the living room floor with a thud. Lifting it was a struggle. What would the guys he worked with say if they saw him like this? He could've carried hundreds of similar boxes a few years ago.

Ellie Marshall and Drake Nielson, the label said.

The cardboard scratched his hands as he tore the top open. Nancy set her head between her paws and burrowed into the rug, bracing herself for impact. Drake didn't have to reach far to find the green cards inside.

The Save the Dates were one of Ellie's few contributions to planning their wedding. He'd practically begged her to pick them out. "Choose the color," Drake had said as they circled the stationery shop. "Please?" Ellie paused in the green section. The lady who worked at the store buzzed over and told them that green was a good choice. Green meant money and success.

"And they say you can't buy happiness," Ellie smirked. Drake wanted to leave the card color to her, he reiterated. If she left it up to him, he probably would've picked red.

"Red. Really?" Ellie thumbed through some mint-hued sample cards. "Drake. Red is an omen."

"That's what I'm saying. I'm not thinking of this in, like, a philosophical way."

They settled on the mint color. The name was cute, mint chip, which is what won Ellie over. The hard part, she decided, was going to be finding the right visual for the front of the cards.

The right visual was now staring up at Drake. There they were again, posed in front of a white limousine. A fabric rose dangled from Ellie's mouth. They were drunk and happy and in Vegas. As he studied it more, though, the photo found an edge. Ellie had chosen to feature the wedding that never was on their Save the Date cards. Was their marriage all some big joke to her?

Drake checked his phone. She still hadn't called or texted, so he distracted himself by watching home renovation shows. The banter and beautiful reveals he usually found satisfying were spoiled on him. There was something on the coffee table that stole his attention—the object that Ellie had pulled from their high shelf and left there for him to face.

The music box.

Drake picked the box up for the first time since they moved. A purple paper was sticking out of the bottom compartment. He recognized it right away; it was one of the notes Melinda wrote to the new owner of whatever treasure she had sold. He hadn't read *this* note before because the box was never his, technically speaking. But last night, it had entered their world in a new way. Whatever was inside of the scroll now seemed personal.

Drake opened the cold silver compartment on the bottom, yanked the paper out, and read what it said to Nancy. "Find someone who makes you dance."

Nancy sneezed.

Find someone who makes you dance?

The advice Melinda had written didn't add up. She penned this note for an anonymous buyer, not knowing it was *him*. Right before she had broken Drake's heart, Melinda doled out advice based on their relationship. The person who made her dance had to be him, didn't it? This note was proof that something had changed for her so suddenly in those weeks before the proposal. She woke up one day, decided he wasn't for her, and said goodbye so easily.

After last night, Drake feared the same thing was happening again.

A wave of red peaked over him—a dark, deep red that took him by surprise. He didn't let himself get angry often. If he did, it was in a controlled setting. The Wakeford Heights units were a safe place to smash a hammer against something while looking productive. But now, it all came pouring out. The music box represented the way the past kept repeating itself, the cycles he couldn't break. His fight with Ellie. His breakup with Melinda. His failure all around.

Drake set the box back down on the shelf. The top lid flipped open, and he turned the key to punish himself. Slowly, classical music filled the room. The same song that had played when he danced with Melinda mocked him.

It felt like a soundtrack to endings.

In a wave of anger, Drake shoved the box to the ground. Tiny parts shattered at his feet, a beach of gold and silver bits and white limbs.

He was out of control. Waiting around for Ellie and ruminating would only lead to more bad decisions. So he got in the car, without a destination, and started to drive.

Drake only realized he was headed to his parents' house when he was halfway there. He knew his mom would sit him down and offer some good advice. "Fighting's normal, hon. That's when you know it's real," she'd insist, even though Drake couldn't remember the last time he'd seen his parents fight.

But as he neared the condo, Drake kept driving. Then, he surprised himself. He was turning onto Main Street, right in the direction of the shop-filled downtown. Avoiding this area had become Drake's party trick; he'd mapped another route for his mom's errands that bypassed Main Street by taking three extra right turns. He even managed to steer Ellie away for a while by telling her, "It's not very charming." This street, he knew, was the poster child for charm.

And now, he was sliding into a space right in front of Melinda's shop.

He'd come here, for what, some kind of delayed closure? For finally facing the music? His hands gripped the steering wheel. Did the music need to be faced? Backing out was the best choice, but by the time he made that call, a loud knock landed on his passenger window. He glanced up, anticipating Melinda. Instead, he found Jamie, waving and motioning for him to roll the window down. Two coffees wobbled inside the carrier balanced on his arm.

"Hey, man," Jamie said as the cold air poured in. "You in town for the party?"

"Party?" Drake asked. It was early in the day for a party, but that's how things went around there. The entire town was on a self-imposed curfew. Stores closed at four, dinner happened around five, and people were tucked into bed by nine.

"Melinda's having an event for the customers later," Jamie explained. "You should come!"

"I'm just driving through," Drake insisted. He spotted the sign on the door at Smithe's for an all-day pancake special and used it as an excuse. "My mom wanted late-afternoon pancakes."

Jamie raised a skeptical eyebrow. "Smithe's only does the all-day pancake special on Mondays now." Drake pointed in the direction of the sign in protest. "You can't trust the signs around here," Jamie said.

"What kind of place does a Monday pancake special?"

"Smithe's does," Jamie emphasized with a goofy grin. "What are you doing right now?" he asked. "Let's grab coffee. Get to know each other better."

Drake had met Jamie a few times at town functions. That was enough for him.

"You're holding coffee," Drake reminded him. "Two coffees."

Jamie ducked his head into the open window. "Oh, this? This is an appetizer, my man."

For years, the sign at Nathan's Diner had read Nahan's, but the spinning parking lot emblem had recently acquired a new *t*. The diner sat on the outskirts of town, in a place where people still cared about the safety of their family, but a little less about jagged sidewalks. As soon as the diner's door opened, they were cocooned in the smell of maple syrup and butter. Jamie threw a few coins into the gumball machine by the entrance. He squatted to watch a purple gumball roll out of the winding tube and spit out from a small silver flap. "I never get over this place," he said, before popping the gum in his mouth. The host stand was empty, but a waitress came over and guided them to a booth where it seemed Jamie always sat, a booth Drake instantly recognized.

It was his booth with Melinda.

Drake retraced his steps and tried to figure out how he'd ended up in this particular booth with Melinda's husband. Something about being back in his hometown made him too polite. Jamie seemed like a nice-enough guy, but the only thing they shared, other than their looks, was being with Melinda. He tried to think of some excuse to leave, but came up short.

The waitress handed them two menus as they settled in. "Thanks, Cindy," Jamie said, then rattled off a series of questions at her that exuded familiarity. Was Cindy's furnace fixed yet? How was her birthday? Drake wasn't some kind of human census for the town, but it was unusual he'd never met Cindy. Maybe he'd just forgotten her.

"I'm glad we're doing this, man," Jamie said after he put in an order of pancakes for himself and the coffee was poured. He got up and grabbed the local paper from a nearby table, sat back down, and fanned it open. His finger searched for something in the pages until he located an illustrated ad in the back section for My Mother's Shop. "Snazzy," he said, tapping it. He looked up to Drake for a reaction.

"Yeah," Drake agreed. "Super snazzy."

Jamie must have detected some of Drake's unease, because he brought up the pancakes again. He hoped Beth didn't mind the pancakes at Nathan's instead.

"No," Drake told him. "Nathan's pancakes are fine."

Jamie leaned forward. "Good. Good." He closed the paper. "Although I'm thinking Beth Nielson would know better than to believe Smithe's Dairy would still be running their weekend pancake deal. Especially with all the bits your mom has going with Marla Smithe."

"Bits?" Drake asked. "What bits?"

"Oh, you know. They moo at each other when Beth walks in the door, for one. Because, *Dairy*."

"They . . . they moo at each other?" Drake had never known his mom to moo.

Jamie brushed this revelation aside. "You're not here for the party," he reiterated. "And I'm getting the sense you're not here for the pancakes. So, what brought you to town today, bud?"

Panic set in. Drake didn't want to admit that he was on his way to see Melinda, but the truth was obvious. "I was driving to my mom's," he started. "For advice, I guess. I wanted some advice, and then . . ." Drake made the motion of heading past the condo with his arms. "I went to the shop instead."

"Ah." Jamie nodded. "So, you need advice. From someone who's not your mom."

"I don't know . . . maybe," Drake admitted. That was why he had gone there, he realized. He had wanted advice from someone who knew what he was like in a relationship. And the best person for that would be, of course, Melinda.

"Well, Melinda's busy with the whole party thing, but why don't you try me?" Jamie suggested.

Drake hesitated. It was hard to believe he was this calm talking to Melinda's husband. Was he calm? He wiped his forehead. He wasn't sweating. Jamie was easy to talk to, and Drake feared he might be having a good time. "Well," he started. Some of the story slipped out. Then, a lot of it. Drake was spilling his guts about Ellie, minus the magical theater. He even admitted to repeating things he'd done with Melinda all over again in their relationship. Now, Ellie was repeating what Melinda had done to him. "She's going to call off the wedding. I'm sure of it."

"Slow down," Jamie said, holding a hand up. "How do you know that?"

Drake explained that Ellie had a habit of locking people out. Leaving without saying goodbye. Jumping ship.

"You seem pretty focused on the past," Jamie pointed out. "And who you both were with other people. Which isn't all that relevant now. Frankly, it sounds pretty unhelpful."

Drake nodded. He took a sip of his coffee. "I guess I'm thinking about the past because I'm hoping it'll show me what's going to happen with Ellie. Maybe even explain why she wants to be with *me*."

"Why?" Jamie asked. "You seem like a great guy. Very good-looking." Jamie pointed between the two of them. "Yes, I've noted the resemblance. So why do you question that?"

"Because she's amazing," Drake said. "She's confident and adventurous. She's talented. She's *passionate*. She, she pours herself into things without thinking about why she shouldn't and goes for what she wants."

"And you're not those things?" Jamie clarified. "Passionate? You don't go for what you want?"

"Not really," Drake said. "I'm not great at taking risks. New endeavors. That kind of thing." It was uncomfortable to admit this truth out loud, especially to someone he'd met only a few times.

"Well," Jamie said, placing his hands on the table. "I think you need to trust Ellie when she says she wants to be with you, man. And I think, for your own sake, you need to go after what you want in life."

"Just like that?" Drake asked.

"Just like that."

When the food arrived, Jamie loaded his pancakes up with butter and syrup. They talked about the town and its traditions as they ate. When they were finishing up, Jamie signaled for Cindy to come back. "We'll take an order of pancakes to go," he told her. "This is Beth Nielson's son, by the way."

"Oh, I love Beth!" Cindy said. "Get that coffee in my belly!" she shouted, pointing at Drake before she walked away. Jamie laughed at a punchline that Drake didn't understand.

"What was that?"

"Another one of your mom's bits," Jamie explained. Seeing Jamie's comfort in the place where he grew up and ease with Cindy made Drake realize something about the booth. He had thought this was *his* booth with Melinda, but it wasn't. Restaurant booths, and the people in them, were always evolving. Drake wasn't meant to sit there forever, and Melinda had made new memories there with Jamie. Now, it was *their* booth—a place where the two of them talked about their friends, the store, and philosophies on life.

"Well," Jamie said once the check was wrapped up, "you

ready? I've got to get back to the party. You know how Melinda is with setting things up."

Drake nodded. He recalled the gathering she'd once thrown on his birthday. Thirty minutes before their guests arrived, the kitchen had sounded like a full brass band was clattering around. "Yeah," he said eventually with a chuckle. "I do know, actually."

Drake's dad was out for a walk when he arrived with the pancakes. His mom, delighted over the unexpected drop-in, started asking too many questions about why he was there. A show starring two sisters who renovated tiny homes was on television. Beth was such a creature of habit that Drake had correctly predicted the exact outfit she'd be wearing when he walked in: navy sweatpants and her white sweater embroidered with London's Big Ben.

As he often did when he arrived there, Drake fixed the leg on the kitchen table that always gave out. Then his mom sat in one of the dining chairs and opened the Styrofoam food container, pouring the syrup on top of the pancakes and taking a big bite. "They're good," she said. "Not like Smithe's, but good." The credits for the show started rolling. Drake already knew the show they liked about beach apartments would play next.

Beth spilled a little syrup on her sweater and wiped it with a napkin.

For some reason, Drake was fixated on that London sweater tonight. He was pretty sure he'd never asked his mom about it. It was an odd choice because it looked like something she would pick up on vacation, but Beth had never been to London. "Why London?" he asked.

"Hmm?" Beth paused midbite and glanced down at her own sweater again. "Oh this," she said. "I bought it over at Clara's a few years ago. She had it out on the display table next to all those candles."

"But why?" Drake asked.

Beth chewed and shrugged. "What do you mean, why? Because your dad and I have wanted to go to London our whole lives. I saw that sweater and thought, that's nice. It's like going to London."

She smiled. Her smile made Drake sad. He shook his head to indicate that he didn't agree. "But it's not at all like going to London," he said, stealing a bite of her food. "It's more like . . . You bought a travel sweater from a store you can walk to from your home. Why wouldn't you just go to London?"

Beth took a few more bites of pancake. "What's all this about?" she asked.

"I want to know why you never went."

His mom proceeded to list a series of small, but inconvenient, events that could potentially take place if they traveled internationally. She mentioned some kind of ticket fraud. They could get food poisoning and be far from her doctors. There were loads of scams there; she'd seen a special about London scams on television. "Plus, why leave this place when it has everything we need?"

"Because . . ." Drake started. He felt his eyes water a little bit. Something clicked together in his mind. A part of him understood Ellie more, her resistance to the mundane, her desire to push him toward what was special in life. "Somewhere out there could be a great thing," he said, paraphrasing what she had told him when they first met. "The best thing ever might be a place you haven't gone to yet. And by staying here, you're missing it."

Drake's phone beeped. *Ellie.* Ellie was texting him. He rummaged around to find his phone. Only the message wasn't from her. It was Marc. *Baby's coming soon*, it read. *Head over when you can.* Ellie and Drake were on call since their friends' parents hadn't flown in yet. Drake showed Beth what the text said, gave her a kiss on the cheek, and flew out the door to drive to the hospital as fast as he could.

It wasn't just about the London sweater, Drake realized in his car.

His parents' life was a series of comfortable decisions. It was safer to stay in the familiar than to risk something new, they had taught him, on repeat. Flying to London could come with food poisoning and travel scams. Taking any kind of risk was to be avoided.

There it was: the lesson he had been taught growing up. Taking risks led to pain.

When Drake was young, he'd taken risks anyway. He bought every girl in class a Valentine's gift. But Drake stayed in the safe zone after that day, hadn't he? He volunteered to become the school mascot instead of going out for the basketball team. He worked for someone else instead of starting his own business. He didn't tell Melinda that he *really* wanted kids because it would disappoint her. And then, when Drake finally put himself on the line again with a proposal, it came back to bite him.

So Drake returned to a life of familiarity. He changed jobs to something even safer. He ate at the same three restaurants. And when he met Ellie, he re-created all the special parts of his last relationship without even realizing it. He'd regurgitated lines Melinda once loved, brought up things she'd laughed at, and repeated moments she found charming. He gave Ellie the same ring.

None of it was fair. Ellie and Melinda weren't the same person.

Ellie nudged him in ways Melinda never had. What did he want? Where was he going next? What new place could they try that night? Didn't he want to visit a magical movie theater that would reveal things they needed to see about themselves?

She had her flaws. He was still irritated by how brash she could be. But Drake loved Ellie, fiercely and passionately. Marrying her was a risk, he knew—an exciting, beautiful risk he couldn't wait to take.

Maybe the cinema had been trying to tell him this.

There was a memory they'd only seen the first few minutes of—the one that started playing the night of Ben's death, before Ellie left the theater. Drake and his dad went on a long ride out into the woods for a camping trip. Only the first moments of the drive made the screen, but Drake remembered everything that followed. After they set up the tent, his dad gave him the jean jacket he still wore. They didn't camp much, so Robert insisted they not leave the area. But in the middle of the night, Drake couldn't sleep. He hiked out for a few minutes on his own to a small lake they had passed earlier in the day. The moon and the stars were reflected in the water. Then, a shooting star. Drake was in awe that he'd seen something so serene. He thought about waking up his dad to join him, but knew he wouldn't come. He was sad that his dad was missing out on something this special.

Drake turned onto Main Street again; it was the fastest route to the highway. The party at My Mother's Shop was just beginning. He could see Melinda inside. She was helping a woman pick out a light pink dress. It was a party that, without Ellie, wouldn't have existed. Her article had come out the week before, and people were already vying to get inside. Ellie, he realized, despite her love of the vintage, the decaying, the almost-broken, wasn't a collector of old things at all. She saw the new possibility in them. And in him.

Melinda must have noticed his car had slowed outside because she looked up and waved through the window. Drake smiled and waved back. Then, she was interrupted by something. Jamie was passing out appetizers on a plate and stopped to give her one. He kissed her. They looked happy there, in this life, and Drake got the sense they were exactly where they were supposed to be.

He was headed that way, too.

32

It seemed like the whole world was at the hospital that night. Drake parked near the farthest edge of the visitors' lot and jogged through a labyrinth of minivans to reach the entrance. Automatic doors whooshed open to greet him. Everything smelled too clean inside; lemon and mint were working hard to cover up secrets.

"Baby. We're having a baby," he told the receptionist. The running, coupled with an aversion to medical buildings, had taken Drake's breath away. "I mean, my friends are having a baby. I'm not. That would be a wild ride, wouldn't it?" Drake waited to be directed somewhere, but the receptionist was too busy adjusting pens inside a cup. "Where do I go?"

Past a gift shop, Drake was greeted by a cardboard stork. The chairs in the waiting area were as uncomfortable as they looked. A gap-toothed kid grinned up at him from the front cover of a parenting magazine: *5 Ideas to Make Your Toddler Smile This Fall*. Drake flipped through the pages and got lost in an article about creative uses for raisins until someone took the seat next to him.

Ellie. There she was.

"Hey," Drake said, trying to sound casual. Ellie wore a lacy black cocktail dress that didn't belong in a hospital. She looked ready to blow on a pair of dice for an oil tycoon. Was this just what she had packed in a hurry, or had she been out with someone? Drake stopped that thought in its tracks. He tried to calm himself down before he responded, pretending to be invested in the syndicated comedy show playing on the small television set above their heads.

Finally, he spoke. "I'm so happy to see you."

"Me too," Ellie said. He could feel her waiting to see if he was going to ambush her in some way. And if this were a different night—say, last night—he would've called out what she was wearing. The dress was all the proof he needed to know that she hadn't been at Jen and Marc's. Instead, he waited for her to fill in the gaps.

"I stayed at a hotel," Ellie admitted.

"Room service?"

"Oh yeah," she told him. They seemed to have both cooled down in their time apart, but the tension was still there. Ellie shrugged. "Once I headed to Jen's, I realized that it wasn't fair to show up on the front step of my super-pregnant friend. There's enough on their plate right now."

"Understatement of the year," Drake agreed.

Another couple walked behind them. The husband assessed a vending machine that needed to be restocked. Drake pictured Ellie at a hotel with dark lighting. Lighting made a big difference when it came to hotels. If the lighting were dark, she might've called one of her ex-boyfriends and insisted she'd made a mistake back then.

He sounded bizarre, even in his own head.

An ad about a lotion for back pain with a ten-syllable name teed up a commercial break.

"I'm really—"

"I'm sorry," Ellie told him, before he could say more.

"I'm sorry, too."

"I shouldn't have left," she said. "I was so mad at you about what happened, but I realized that I proved your fears right."

Drake turned toward her a little more. "I shouldn't have freaked out," he admitted. "I mean, I don't love some things you did, but . . . It's not fair to be mad about what happened in the past."

She gave a little nod of acknowledgment. "Thank you."

"You can be nasty in a fight."

"I'm self-aware enough to know that." Ellie nodded.

"And I can be—"

"Presumptuous."

"Exactly."

The hospital probably wasn't the time and place to get into things. Still, Drake was relieved to have started the conversation. He didn't even care that the couple getting snacks was possibly trying to eavesdrop. They were never going to see them again.

Before he could say more, a nurse interrupted them.

"Are you Jen and Marc's friends?" she asked. Ellie nodded. "They're ready for you."

Ellie and Drake followed the nurse into a hallway plastered with stickers and construction paper signs. It alarmed Drake that a place responsible for life-or-death matters was decorated the same way as an elementary school.

"This is it," the nurse announced in front of a large room with a view of the parking lot. The room was unexceptional, except for the baby crying in Jen's arms. Drake had seen a lot of babies at parties and potlucks. This particular baby moved him to the point of losing his balance. She was tiny and scrunchy with a little pink hat on her head. Marc waved them in from the edge of the bed with a sweet, exhausted look on his face.

"Here she is." Jen beamed. "Our Lola."

Lola could barely open her eyes. Drake feared he was going to be asked to hold the baby. He might break her. Could Drake be responsible for a human that small? He was clumsy. Dinner plates feared him. He was an actual ball of nerves. Not Ellie, though.

Lola was cradled in her arms right away, and Ellie smiled at her in a vow of aunthood, of slight rule-breaking, of loving her fully.

Ellie softened when her eyes met his. The next part of the conversation they needed to have happened without words. Drake could see that Ellie was capable of committing to people that she loved, he conveyed to her in silence, over the beeping IV drip. And Ellie loved Drake like she hadn't loved any of those other people, she seemed to tell him. She wasn't going to leave.

And Drake wasn't going to let her go.

They stayed at the hospital late. Jen originally asked for them to "pop in for five minutes," but once Ellie and Drake appeared, she wanted them to share in the excitement. Marc put on the original *Vacation* movie where the Griswold family goes to Walley World. "This movie's pure cheese," he said. "But, you know what, it's about *family*." Halfway through the movie, when the leather couch that Marc was using as his bed became too cramped for the three of them, Ellie suggested a trip to the gift shop.

"I think an award would be the most fitting thing," Drake told her, faced with a row of depressing cards.

"I agree," Ellie said. "This is definitely an award situation."

They swirled around the aisles, beyond the flowers, then vetoed a section of stale Gummi Bears. The store was having a sale on balloons; there was a steep discount for purchases of twenty or more. Drake and Ellie marveled over the logistics of carrying that many balloons into a hospital room.

"Should we just go with chocolate?" Drake asked.

With five types of chocolate in hand, they returned to the hospital room. The lights were still on, but Jen was asleep. Lola was cradled in Marc's arms. Ellie flicked the switch and made a quiet promise to call in the morning, setting the candy stash on Jen's bedside table. Ellie and Drake walked out together, and she pushed the elevator button.

"It's weird to be here," Ellie said. "In a hospital, I mean." Drake nodded. In all the commotion, he hadn't considered how the memory of the loud beeping monitors and harsh lights might affect her. The elevator hummed as it went down. He took her hand. "It's nice to be here for something good, though."

"That is one cute baby," Drake said.

"I think," Ellie whispered, looking up at him, "I want that."

"Chocolate money?"

"No." The elevator doors split open in front of the empty cafeteria. Neither of them moved to step out. "You know what I meant."

Drake did know what she meant. Ellie's face as she cradled Lola already told the whole story. She did, in fact, want kids. Still, he'd learned in recent weeks—and conversations—not to assume things Ellie hadn't told him herself. "Are you saying you want kids?" As he waited for her answer, the elevator doors snapped shut. They had missed their chance to exit and were headed back toward the third floor.

"Whoa," Ellie said. "Let's not get all plural yet, okay?"

"Deal."

The elevator paused on the third floor. A woman holding a large stuffed bear entered, along with an absurd number of balloons. The balloons took over the space, forcing them to physically duck under a canopy of pink in every shade. They fought to withhold their laughter as the elevator headed toward the hospital's ground floor. The doors flew open and closed as the woman tried to make an exit without much luck. Drake reached out to help her, but some balloon stragglers kept getting in the way. Ellie stepped back with bated breath, waiting for one to pop.

As soon as the woman finally got the handle on all her balloons and left, Ellie lost control of her laughter. There was the laugh Drake loved so much. She snorted through her nose and bent at the waist to gain composure. She was messy, and honest, and beautiful. Drake wanted decades of this. He couldn't wait to see what they would become. But in order to get there, they needed to finish facing, and accepting, who they used to be.

"Well," Drake said, grabbing the elevator doors before they could close again, "you ready to go home?"

"Yes," Ellie said, then hesitated. "Under one condition."

"What's that?" Drake asked.

She set an arm on his back to ease his concern. "We need to set the rules on fire."

Act Three
TOGETHER

33

Drake and Ellie lucked out; Nancy had not eaten the aftermath of the music box mess on the floor. Ellie spotted the remnants after they changed into their pajamas. The dancer had taken the brunt of the fall; she was without an arm and a leg, putting her in a tipsy fifth position.

"What do you mean, you broke it?" Ellie asked when Drake explained what happened. She held the tiny toy arm under the light. The edges were sharp on her fingers.

"I sort of threw it." Drake shuffled around the rug to make sure he picked up all the other elements of the crime scene. "Not sort of. I definitely threw it."

"Well, okay." Ellie nodded. "That adds up." She flipped the broken box on its back to assess the damage. The edge of a familiar lavender paper was still sticking out of the small slot in the bottom. "Ah-*ha*," Ellie said. She thumbed it out, unrolled it on the table, and read the message that Melinda must have written for the next owner. "Find someone who makes you dance."

Ellie remembered those words. She had read them on her first visit to Drake's old apartment. As he gave her a tour, she noticed everything he owned had a function; even his wall art let the viewer know they were near a big city. The music box was so out of place that it had grabbed her attention. Ellie picked it up, lifted the lid, and twisted the music key. The dancer began to spin. How could Drake have known she'd had one just like it when she was a kid? It was the perfect gift. At least, it had seemed like the perfect gift before she knew its backstory.

"It was kind of a weird gift," Ellie called out. "Why did you give this to me?"

"I didn't," Drake clarified.

Ellie pointed a finger into his chest. "Yes, you did!"

Drake pulled the accusing finger off him. Ellie was wrong. He never gave her the box; she had *found* it. Ellie had arrived early that night and caught him in the middle of trying to stash anything off-putting out of sight. He'd managed to grab his embarrassing childhood heirlooms, but he'd missed the most important thing to hide. "I had the box out because I was going to get rid of it," he explained. "But you found it first. I agreed it was a gift because you decided it was one."

Ellie nodded. Everything about that night made more sense—how Drake had avoided eye contact and left the room before she read the purple paper to him. "There are so many things that could've been solved if we'd talked to each other," she said, leaning back onto her elbows. Drake shot up off the floor with new determination.

"Speaking of talking," he said. "I liked your idea to burn the cinema rules."

Ellie hadn't meant a literal fire. But minutes later, she found herself following Drake outside and watching him stack wood in the backyard fire pit. The blaze smoldered and twisted into the dark sky. Drake dropped the paper with the rules on it above the red waves, and they crinkled to ash. The cold air made Ellie's shoulders shiver, despite the pyrotechnics. As she jogged in place a little, she started to speak.

"In honor of burning the rules," Ellie said. She looked at Drake for reassurance. He nodded for her to keep going. "The worst part of watching your memories was, I could really see you with Melinda." Drake heaved another log on the fire. "I know she's with Jamie, but I could see you happy together. Even now." Ellie's words struggled to come out. It was like she was tugging on a zipper that kept getting mired in fabric. Eventually, though, the zipper budged. "I wondered if she would've been better for you. You had so much in common—"

"Too much," Drake blurted. "We had too much in common. With you, there's friction. I think I need that friction, or I'd never grow. But sometimes, I get this sense . . . I'm afraid you think I'm boring. I mean, I'm no cowboy."

"How did we get to cowboys, partner?" Ellie was dodging that she'd been called out. She knew what Drake meant; Hudson had drawn her in more than anyone she had dated back then. While Ellie had been busy thinking about how similar she and Melinda were, Drake had been weighing how *different* he was from what he believed her type to be.

"That guy was so complicated and artsy," Drake said. "I'm nothing like the cowboy. I'm more like that Lucas guy with the loft. Only Lucas with a less expendable income. Lucas, without glassware."

Ellie didn't care about glassware, but she couldn't get this out before Drake continued his thought.

"You told Jen you didn't want to end up with someone like him," Drake explained. "So, I'm sitting there thinking, *that's me. She doesn't want to end up with me.* And when I saw the cowboy, I kept coming back to that quote in 'Yellow Dress.' Your first love prepares you for your second love, which is the real love. It scares me that I'm your first love, Ellie. What if I'm the one you leave?"

Ellie nodded. "I get that fear," she said. "I think mine was the opposite. Like, what if I'm just a replacement for the person you can't let go of?"

Drake wrapped his arm around her waist. He'd thought he

was the only one with that nagging worry of being abandoned, but Ellie had felt it, too. Drake had been so lost in his private world that he hadn't done enough to show her there was never a competition. Melinda was only a chapter in the story that led to him ending up with Ellie. "You're not a replacement," he said. "Not at all. But I get why you would think that, seeing as I repeated pretty much everything in our relationship."

"Yes." Ellie nodded. "Thank you."

Drake shared the breakthrough he had on his trip home. He was afraid of risks because his parents were afraid of risks. He repeated parts of his old relationship because those elements were comfortable and familiar. But in doing that, he'd failed to help them build something new together. They hadn't gotten a true fresh start.

"I've been afraid of risks, too," Ellie admitted. "Loving someone *is* scary for me. I don't want to have to say goodbye to a person I love again. You're the only person who has been worth that risk."

They both fell silent. A dog next door howled over the wood fence, the moon beaming bright overhead. The conversation was freeing. And the rules, they both realized without acknowledging it, had turned to ash. The rest came tumbling out quickly.

"I shouldn't have lied to Hudson."

"I should've told you where that ring came from."

"I shouldn't have bought my wedding dress at her store. God, that was dumb."

"You bought your . . . I shouldn't have assumed you saw the ring in those photos. Or brought you back to the cinema—"

"I shouldn't have forced you there to begin with, Drake."

"You didn't *force* me."

"Well, I gave you a push in that direction." Ellie hesitated, about to surface a thought that surprised her. "For someone who insisted we go there, I'm not sure it was the best thing. I mean, what if the details of the past are supposed to stay fuzzy for a reason? Maybe we should trust each other to share what's important from our history and let everything else fall away."

Drake considered this. "Maybe," he decided eventually. "But I think it's good we went."

"It is?"

"Yeah," he said. "I know you mentioned that the cinema shows what haunts us. But I think it shows us what we need to see to move forward. And I want to move forward with you, Ellie. I want to move so far forward that we reach places most people never find—whether it's a magical cinema or a precipice overlooking the ocean, or—"

"The precipice part sounds a little edgy for you."

"I guess you're changing me."

Ellie nodded. "You should know that I wasn't alone at the hotel, Drake."

He resisted the strong urge to press on the statement.

"I got all dressed up earlier before I went to the hospital. I went to the lounge. And you were there. What I mean is, I sat—really sat—with the piece I wrote about Finn's, the piece that's actually about you. I hadn't read it in a while. Sure, I wrote about the bar, but the reason people love that piece is that it evoked the feeling of new beginnings. Every word was charged with this excitement. And I kept thinking how you make my work better. And you make me better," she said. "We just need to open up to each other more. I know that now. So let's keep talking."

"Okay," Drake agreed, putting the fire out. "We can keep talking. But can we do it inside? It's freezing out here."

Back in the house, a fog had lifted; everything was more comfortable than it had been earlier that night. They made tea, lit the indoor fireplace, and took both sides of the couch next to Nancy.

"Do you ever think . . ." Ellie started. The cadence of her words slowed and softened. "Do you think that maybe the most significant moments in life aren't cinematic at all?"

Drake knew what she meant. The best things in their life together weren't sweeping, symphonic moments. The comfortable, quiet memories were the ones worth reliving. Watching a fire. Eating takeout. Lying on the couch where they were right then.

He loved their world.

Then, a loud sound interrupted his thoughts. Near the front door, Nancy was pulling a box apart with her teeth. "Nancy!" Ellie clapped without getting up. Nancy made no move to come over. Ellie got up to remove her from the box and peeked at what was inside.

"Are these . . ."

"Hundreds of Save the Dates," Drake told her. "Yes."

Ellie reached to try to pull the box away from Nancy, but it was too heavy to move. "I can't lift the box," she said. "Maybe we have too many people? I don't know if I like this many people."

Drake agreed. Ellie had pointed out the same thing he felt when he first opened the box and saw the stacks of stationery staring back at him.

"What if," Ellie posed, "we scrap this plan and rent out a tiny old hotel instead?"

"I'm in," Drake told her, even though he had a hunch the idea came from wanting to save another old place. Ellie never stopped fighting for what she loved. "We can get married anywhere you like. But I would prefer somewhere not haunted."

The next morning, the music box was back on the shelf where it belonged. The outside was patched, and the doll's arm and leg had been reattached with two ribbon casts.

"I sort of thought you'd want to get rid of this," Drake said when Ellie came behind him with a coffee.

To be fair, Ellie had seriously considered getting rid of the box. But as she sat with it last night after Drake went to sleep, she acknowledged that she was in no shape to discard something with a past. Instead, she fixed the dancer's injuries and twirled her inside the box, rediscovering the simple beauty of being able to make her dance. As she did, Ellie returned to the lavender note for the last time.

Find someone who makes you dance.

The words were never about Drake and Melinda, she knew then. They belonged to the dancer in the box. The ambiguous *someone* was whoever was lucky enough to spin the key. In this case, Ellie.

Lately, they had been reading into the subtext of every little thing. Even innocent ones.

Drake sat behind her on the couch and cleared his throat. When she turned, he patted the space next to him. "There's one more thing I need to tell you," he said.

Ellie accepted the spot. "What's that?" she asked.

Drake took a sip of his coffee. "We need to finally address what happened that night with Ben. It's time, Ellie. You need to stop beating yourself up about it."

"Yeah. Well, that's a nice idea."

"I think that what you need is . . . I think you need to give yourself permission to move on. You don't have to forget Ben, but it's time to start loosening your grip. Letting go."

"I have zero clue how to do that," Ellie told him.

"Well, I've been thinking about it, and I have an idea," Drake said. "If you trust me."

34

The cemetery's entrance was bleaker than Ellie remembered. New snow covered the red bricks, and grass hibernated under an endless white landscape accentuated by the dramatic blue sky. The tires caught a patch of ice as Drake steered them into a parking space. He hadn't told her where they were going, but she'd had a gut feeling this was it.

"Is this okay with you?" he asked. "Coming here."

"Yeah," Ellie said. "I mean, I would've preferred brunch, but—"

"We could visit another time. If you're not ready."

"No." Ellie turned the music down a little. "I want to do this." She could feel herself stalling. "I mean, *want* is a strong word." The actual headstone was what she dreaded most. In her mind, she'd always pictured a fake version, like something from the Halloween store. Facing Ben's name etched in stone, lodged in the frozen earth, would make it all real. Still, as hard as it would be to see, hadn't she learned that not knowing was worse? She had already confronted the worst night of her life at the cinema. She'd survived it. "I'm ready," Ellie said.

Drake opened her car door for her, then headed to the trunk. The wind was strong; Ellie could hear different tones in it. Behind her, the trunk whooshed open. Snow glued itself to her black tights as she followed the path Drake's shoes forged. When she reached his side, he concealed whatever he had taken out of the trunk under his coat and offered up his left arm for support.

"I brought something for Ben," he said. "It's not flowers."

Ellie rested her head against him as they walked into the distance. She was clueless about the actual location of the grave, but Drake's footsteps were purposeful. Two people waited at the edge of the cemetery far from the main road. Ellie's fingers clenched as they came into view. She stopped walking.

"You invited my dad?" she asked. Naomi waved in the distance. "And Naomi. *Naomi.* What is this, Drake? An intervention? A séance?"

"We can still turn around." His grip was firm on her shoulders. "But I know you can handle this, Ellie. It's time." She tried to worm her way out of his grasp. He pulled her closer. "I'm here with you." Drake's words were soft. "We can do this together."

A new voice caused them both to turn back toward the car: "Sorry I'm late!" Sandra wore a floor-length black coat that looked surreal dragging along the winter landscape. Her dyed blonde hair was held back by a sheepskin hat, and as usual, her makeup was pristine. "Ellie," she said. "How are you? Did you like the gift?"

Ellie sighed. It was so like her mom to bring up a gift at the most inopportune time. "Yes, Mom," she said, though she still hadn't opened it. "I loved it."

"You did?" Sandra pulled Ellie close and whispered right in her ear. "It's time you had it," she said.

After the five of them said their hellos and exchanged hugs, they huddled around the headstone together.

BEN MARSHALL
1985–2007
A LOVING SON AND KIND BROTHER.
YOU'LL STAY IN OUR HEARTS.

Drake thought the whole thing was going well so far. It had been easier than he expected to get her parents there. Calling them individually and admitting that he thought Ellie needed this closure was enough. Despite her constant monologue about how they didn't care, they'd shown up on time, without judgment.

William suggested they take turns addressing Ben. Since no one else piped in to start, Drake broke the ice. "Hey, Ben," he said, taking a step closer to the headstone. Ellie's family turned their attention to him. "It's great to finally meet you."

Drake started to regret his bravery. He was the only one who hadn't met Ben. He probably shouldn't have volunteered to go first. "I, uh, didn't know you, but it's been incredible to learn more about you lately. I think that so many things I love about Ellie are hijinks she picked up from you." *Hijinks*, meaning rule-breaking, might have been the wrong thing to say with her parents present. Drake glanced between William and Sandra.

Neither of them seemed offended, and William used Drake's hesitation as his cue to take over. "You know, I say that I'm out there, in the woods, building this life I love. And that's true." The squeeze he gave Naomi's hand was so slight that Drake almost missed it. "But I think the truth is also, it was too hard to keep going on like everything was fine when . . ." William nodded. Naomi patted his shoulders. "When you were gone," he said, then looked right at Ellie. "But I'm sorry I haven't been here for you."

The wind howled. Sandra cleared her throat to speak. "I was going to bring flowers," she said. "Then, I thought, you don't need flowers. I realized the flowers have always been for me. I want it to seem like I'm holding it together. But what you really need, is us to be here for you. To remember you."

Sandra pulled her hat down on her head. Ellie inched closer to her mom, and she started to speak. "Hey, Ben. It's good to see you. I'm sorry I haven't visited before. Avoiding. That's what I do best. Not grief." Ellie paused. Across the huddle, her dad motioned for her to keep going. "Listen, I'm so sorry for what happened that night. For someone who loves the past, I've tried really hard to push my own away. But the truth is, I could never push you away. You are the inspiration for my life's work, Ben. Because I save places that are special. Places that are beautiful and quirky and wonderful. Places that remind me of you. Places that deserve a second chance. Because I couldn't save you."

William moved over to put his arm around Ellie.

"I've spent the last years punishing myself for what happened. I could've called faster. I could've not asked you for a ride at all. I could've not pointed out that the light was green . . ." Ellie was stumbling. She paused to find clarity. "But I think maybe I also feel this way because if I'm to blame, then there's something to point to. It's somehow, in this super messed-up way, easier than thinking that the world just takes the people we love from us in an unexpected moment. Eating french fries or listening to cheesy college radio. This thought that people I love could be gone at any moment is so terrifying that it makes me hide away."

This time, Ellie's mom moved closer.

"Because I miss you so much." Her voice was shaking.

"You've got this, Ellie," Drake said.

"But I think, what I need, Ben, are other people," she was louder now. "I need to stop believing that losing you is all mine. Losing you is all of ours. And I love you. We love you. We love you so much, Ben."

Ellie broke down. She felt her head in her dad's hands and her mom's nails running up and down her back. Naomi and Drake moved in, too. The tears fell fast. Sandra made humming sounds, not to quiet but to soothe, and Ellie cried harder at the revelation that her mother could—on rare occasions—nurture her.

Sandra broke off from the group first. She touched the stone with her hand, then bent down to get a better look. "It's not exactly right, is it?" she admitted, cutting through the tears. "The epitaph. I wrote it in the middle of everything, but I'm worried it doesn't suit him."

"Maybe it's a little plain," William agreed.

"I'm pretty sure it's a Phil Collins song," Ellie said, trying to pull herself together.

"Not exactly," Drake added. "But close."

Ellie spread her hands out, as if quoting something. "How about, Ben Marshall: Mischievous brother and kindhearted troublemaker."

"A loving, goofy, stretcher of truths," William piped in.

"A wonderful son and window–escape artist," Sandra added, and gave Ellie a knowing look. "Oh, don't act surprised, Ellie. I saw everything."

For some reason, all of them found this terrifically funny.

They told stories about Ben until the sun began to set. Ellie explained that, on one of their many nights escaping through the window, they drove three hours to stand on the state lines. Ben made them do all kinds of tricks with the goal of breaking a world record: the most cartwheels on a state line or most pretzels eaten on a state line. Sandra brought up a year when Ellie and Ben turned the guest bedroom into a haunted house for Halloween without telling her, and she'd walked in to find it covered in cobwebs and Victorian dolls.

When the sky stretched into different shades of orange, Drake brought out what he'd grabbed from the back of the trunk. It was a black tape player like the one Ben had brought to the abandoned mansion. He set it in Ellie's hands.

"What is this?" Ellie asked.

"Maybe . . . Maybe this will help you stay connected to Ben." He pulled her close. "I mean I know he's not *here*, here. But after all those years of trying to forget, maybe it's time to remember."

"Drake," she said, beginning to tear up again. "Thank you for doing this."

"It's nothing."

"It's everything. I mean, how can I thank you for bringing—"

"Easy," he told her. "Just press Play."

Ellie pressed her thumb down. David Bowie's opening to "Oh! You Pretty Things" came through the speakers. The music moved its way into the cracks of the earth around Ben's grave, floated above their heads, and spread out and around to mingle with the ghosts. It was the same song that played so many years ago on the night when Ellie learned a powerful lesson.

Visiting people, and places, could keep them from being forgotten.

35

On the morning of what would be their last movie, the cinema was far from Ellie's mind. Instead, all she could think about was the exhilarating call she'd just received.

Despite her usual resistance to Christmas—and the fact that it was now January—she wanted their house to feel festive when she told Drake what she'd learned that morning. What better way to deliver good news than under the soft lighting of an ornament-clad tree? So, while most responsible people tucked their lights and garlands back into the trenches of the garage, Ellie pulled their box labeled CHRISTMAS! out and shopped for a few finishing touches on clearance.

The cinnamon broom caught on their door as she dragged it inside; the slightly stale scent of the holidays clung to its dry branches. A fire blazed beneath the television set, and Bing Crosby joined her as she wrapped two boxes for Drake. Once the bows were on, Ellie turned their living room into a wonderland. She placed a committee of Nutcrackers on the mantel next to curious, sparkly reindeer. Green and red candles illuminated the hard surfaces, and 1950s-style ornaments dangled from a tree relieved to be out of its box. The final touch was the Christmas village, which Ellie arranged over a blanket of cotton snow on the coffee table. Happy and exhausted, she sank into the couch and waited for Drake to come home.

· · · · · · · · · ·

Drake couldn't contain himself at the sight of Ellie's efforts. He had started the day annoyed that he had to go to work on a Saturday and had come home to Christmas again—their first *real* Christmas in this house. Ellie scurried off to the kitchen and came back with hot cider.

"What is all this?" he asked.

"Well," Ellie started, "I figured, what could be more in the Nielson spirit than a third Christmas event?" She reached toward a small box under the tree and handed it to Drake.

"You shouldn't have," he said.

"Technically, that gift is kind of for me," Ellie explained. Drake handed the box over. She pushed it back his way. "I mean, you should open it still. But, well, it'll make sense."

Drake tore into the paper and pulled the lid off the small box. Inside, Ellie had folded a message into a paper square. He jumped up when he read what was on it. "You got the show," he said.

Ellie nodded. The producers wanted to audition another lead with a connection to the director, she said. Eventually, they came back to her as their top choice. In the year ahead, a supporting cast and crew would be hired based on their chemistry with Ellie. Visiting Ben yesterday, Ellie believed now, had made space for something new. "It was silly to wrap that in a box," she said. "But I wanted to celebrate, and I didn't know how—"

"You got the show!" Drake nearly shouted this time. He set the box next to the Christmas village. "Which means I'm marrying a two-time television star, an author—"

Ellie filled in the last part before he could. "And a detective."

"The Case of the Girl at the Bar." Drake picked Ellie up and spun her around the room. "I want to know everything. I mean, what did they say? When do you start? What do you wear?" He set her down. Before he could ask more questions, she handed over a second box. This one was much bigger.

"One more thing," she said. Drake started to tear it open. Nancy had a sixth sense for fallen paper. Within seconds, she was at their feet, circling as Drake finished unwrapping and rolled the paper into a ball for her to fetch.

Inside this box's lid was a red toy train. It was just like the one he had as a kid. Ellie must have remembered it from the photo she pulled out of their MEMORIES box and tacked to their wall. "This is . . ."

"For around the tree," Ellie told him. "You want to set it up?"

"Is that even a question?"

Within minutes, the train cars whirred their way around the tree, circling in search of the North Pole. Nancy paced a bit to follow its path before settling down. Ellie and Drake rested on their stomachs to peer inside the tiny windows.

"I'm glad we got a Christmas redo," Ellie said.

"I feel bad I don't have another gift for you," Drake told her. "I mean, the sweater was dumb—"

"Not dumb. It's pretty."

"I wanted to find something cool and old, but I couldn't, so . . . I found something new that looked old."

"And I got you that silly bath set," Ellie said. "It reminded me of this cologne you put on the night we met. I thought it would be romantic. It wasn't."

"I didn't know that's why you got it. That's really thoughtful."

It was serene lying there and reliving the holidays. At the beginning of the screenings, Drake figured the cinema would show them more memories like this one. The toy train. His chapter as a school mascot. Family vacations to national parks. "I was surprised we didn't see more holidays and childhood memories,"

Drake admitted. "But it hasn't been all bad. Has it? Seeing the past."

Ellie shook her head. "No," she agreed. "It hasn't been *all* bad." The cinema had forced them to reflect on who they had been before. For so long, she had been trying to shut those parts of her life away. It hadn't worked. Finding the courage to address them, honestly, was the only thing that had.

A moment later, Ellie got up and walked back to the thing she'd been avoiding inside the closet. Her mom's gift was still there, exactly where she had left it on Christmas. Wordlessly, she sat back down next to Drake and began to rip it open. She had told her mom years ago that they shouldn't do presents anymore. Ellie liked to buy thoughtful gifts when she found them—not commercial gifts in service of some holiday. Still, over the years her mom had persisted in giving her too-small, expensive dresses or perfumes that evoked the insides of country clubs.

But this year, her mom had gone in a very different direction.

Ellie hugged the studded leather jacket to her chest.

She'd last seen it in her twenties, but she swore it still smelled like him. She pulled her arms through the sleeves and ran over to the closest mirror near the front door. She'd thought it was gone forever when she dropped it off at the thrift store. It felt so right to wear Ben's jacket. His favorite jacket.

"How did she . . ." Ellie started.

"When she dropped off the gift, she said you shouldn't have done that alone," Drake told her. "And that she went back for it. I didn't know what it meant at the time. I started to tell you that when you went to open it but didn't get it all out."

Ellie looked up at him. She noticed that Drake was starting to tear up. It felt good to face their past together; to wear it proudly.

"Do you think . . ." he started.

"Should we . . ."

They hadn't discussed if they should go back to the cinema

yet. Now they were tiptoeing toward the same idea. Ellie checked the time. It was a Saturday night. It was also, conveniently, 11:03. They had both assumed they wouldn't watch the final movie after their big fight, but they'd never firmly decided.

"We could still make it," Drake told her. "We could be a little early, even."

"With time to finally try the popcorn."

Minutes later, Ellie and Drake were in the car headed downtown. Staying cocooned in the warmth of their festive home would've been easier, but they understood why they couldn't. The cinema had made them more honest, hadn't it? And it was only fair for them to go into their wedding knowing the full truth about everything.

Ellie chewed on her lip. Drake pretended to pay attention to the radio. But they were both lost in their own worry.

Because they each had a final secret, and they suspected it would play that night.

36

Ellie and Drake returned to the alley, walked back through the curtain of fog, and stepped under the glowing marquee for the last time. *The Story of You*, it read, as it had every other visit. Inside the lobby, though, Drake broke their usual routine. "Let's see what those hot dogs are dancing about," he suggested as he traded his last remaining cash for a large bag of the popcorn. The ticket boy dumped some of the dried-out kernels into a red paper bag without acknowledging them and handed it over.

"It's inedible," Ellie decided after the first bite.

Drake scooped a handful into his mouth. "It's fine," he sputtered with a cough. "If you can get past the tar aftertaste."

They took their time as they moved up the stairs to the balcony, each admiring the cinema with new eyes. Their lives had been gutted since they found this place. Soon, the past would be back on the timeline where it belonged. Life would be normal again. Coming here had been a constant source of juxtaposition: of laughter and hurt, nostalgia and guilt. And they knew the last memory would be no different. Excitement and dread walked hand in hand beside them as they prepared to enter the movie.

Ellie and Drake both sensed what would play. Seeing their own meet cute felt inevitable; it was where the story had always been heading. How thrilling would it be to finally relive the sparks of that first conversation at Finn's? But with that thrill came something they had left unsaid about that night. There was a hidden layer to their beginning that they hadn't discussed yet, and it made them stall halfway up the stairs to buy more time before facing it.

Drake dove his hand back in the popcorn. He was eager to stress eat and disappointed by the results. And, as he had decided back at the house, they both needed to know what the cinema pieced together for this one, final movie. They had been more honest with each other in these last weeks than their entire time together. He didn't want to keep any more secrets.

"Whatever happens in there, we'll be fine," Drake said, searching Ellie's face for reassurance. "Right?"

Ellie hesitated. She had never told Drake what happened right after they met at Finn's. She'd convinced herself that the choices she made before—and immediately after—their meeting would tarnish an otherwise perfect encounter. "You know, we could still turn around," she said. As soon as the words were out, she knew they couldn't do that. Ellie wasn't pushing the past away anymore. "But let's not. We've got this."

"I think you should know . . ." Drake started pulling her back up the stairs again. "I have an idea of what this last movie is going to be—"

"Same," Ellie admitted.

"And it might not paint me in the best light. We're not talking a villainous light here, but . . . Not the best light."

"Same," Ellie repeated. "For me, fluorescent light, at best." Their baby steps had led them to the balcony-level door of the auditorium. The only thing left to do was to go through it. Ellie straightened her posture and pushed the sculpted handle open, relieved to find the comforting presence of Drake right behind her.

"New rule," he whispered as they sank into their seats. "Whatever happens in the cinema, *doesn't* stay in the cinema."

"Deal," Ellie agreed softly.

Then the lights lowered, the hot dogs danced, and their fingers laced together as the title surfaced on the screen.

TICKET TEN: *MEET-CUTE*

Ellie remembered this part well; there was a man in her bed. She'd met him a few nights earlier at her book reading, where he'd bought three copies of *The Compendium of Forgotten Things* for her to sign. He wanted a congratulations message to his aunt in the first copy, a dedication to a girl who was "strictly a friend, but don't write that," in the second, and "your phone number," in the third. Ellie gave in to all three requests. As a result, he was in her room, leaning against the headboard with a cup of coffee and an air of rebellion.

"Big plans today?" He stretched his arms overhead with an exaggerated yawn.

"I've got to get writing." Ellie hoped he would pick up the hint. He'd made the coffee himself, so it wasn't likely. Her escape routine was easier at another person's house. Instead, she hopped out of bed, tossed on her jeans, and slid the balcony door open. A few resident birds battled it out for fallen cereal on the patio.

"Swing by the bar where I work tonight?" Hints, begone. He had followed her outside.

"I don't know if I can," Ellie told him. She pulled away from his kiss on her neck. The act was too intimate for daylight and balcony neighbors. He didn't seem to notice that she was willing him to leave. Instead, the man sat at the tiled table she'd picked up during an event called Vintage Crawl a few weeks earlier. People like Ellie gathered and roamed through a series of bars and thrift stores. By the end of the night, she'd inherited this table, a 1960s rain lamp, and a raging hangover.

"Come on," he baited. "I want you to see the bar before it closes. It's a neighborhood place. Low lights. Jazz records. Might be your thing."

His words were espresso to her ears. *Before it closes.*

"It's closing, huh?"

"Yeah. It's a classic story of not being able to make ends meet. Customers want trendy places now. Fake speakeasies. Pop-ups."

Ellie pursed her lips. Not on her watch. "Maybe I could make an appearance." She had already decided to go. "What's it called?"

"Finn's," he offered, with a sense of pride. "It's Finn's Bar."

"You've got a date," Ellie told Sam.

Drake recognized Sam as the bartender from Finn's right away. He also knew that Ellie was exactly Sam's type, thanks to all those nights he had spent watching him twirl bottles and finesse eight counts. Before Drake could process this twist, he was faced with his own half of the story. Tonight, instead of the fuzzy blurring that usually separated their memories, the moments joined together smoothly.

There was Drake at Finn's, sitting across the table from Melinda.

He searched for Ellie's expression in the seat next to him and held her hand tightly in case she decided to take off. This screening would be different, he reminded himself. They burned the rules. They could talk it through when they left.

"It's good to see you, Drake," Melinda said. Her right hand held out a cold beer for him, the left, an old-fashioned for her.

"Oh, we're drinking whiskey now?" Drake asked.

"I am," she said. Melinda scooted her chair toward him and took a little sip. "The girl at the bar recommended it. Just your type." She pushed the beer over to him.

"The drink?"

"No, *her.*"

Drake followed Melinda's eyeline and caught Ellie in the middle of a laugh. Sam must have told a joke. "Her?" He brushed the comment off because it made him uncomfortable to talk about another woman, or even the possibility of such a thing, with the history they shared. "She's got nothing on you," Drake told Melinda. He wanted to put her at ease. "Thanks for driving all the way out here. I could've come your way."

"You're worth it," she told him. "Besides, it's fun to see one of your spots."

"More like, *spot*," Drake said. "I'm uh, glad you asked me to hang out. I was kind of surprised," he admitted. "In a good way."

She nodded. "Well, it's about time we act like friends—"

"I still love you," Drake blurted. Terror set in. Why the hell had he done that? He hadn't meant to say it then. Not yet, anyway. The confession sat at the center of the table like a conversational fruit cake. Was it even true anymore?

"Whoa," Melinda said, setting her drink down. "It's been a long time. A really long time. I thought you wanted to be friends."

"You said we should hang out. Like a *date*." Drake danced his finger over the tea light, getting it dangerously close to the leaping flame.

"I used the phrase *hang out* because it isn't a *date*."

Drake blushed in his seat. He was ruined. He'd thought the proposal was the most humiliating scene from his life. But no, he decided right then, this confession was so far out of left field that it stole the trophy. He worried that Sam had overheard the whole thing and was laughing at him. Sam was an excruciating caliber of cool. Sam would never faceplant like this. "I thought . . . I shouldn't have said 'I love you,'" Drake admitted. "Shit. I just said it again. I wasn't repeating the 'I love you' then, I was summarizing what happened, and . . . Sorry. I'm sorry."

Melinda pushed her loose hair out of her face; it was messy, like she'd come from running errands. All signs indicated that this wasn't a date. He should've paid more attention. "Look, Drake.

You're incredible. And you're going to find someone great," she said.

Their eyes connected.

Drake shook his head. "If I do, I'll be pretending she's you."

The statement forced Melinda out of her chair. "I should probably go." She wove past the marble tables toward the bar's door, and Drake trailed a few steps behind. Then, she spun to face him right before stepping outside. She'd forgotten something, it seemed. Her hand reached for something inside her bag, and then she was handing him the familiar sapphire ring.

"I wanted you to keep it," he said, making no move to grab the box.

"We both know this is meant for someone else," she told him. "And when you find her, she's going to love it. Okay?" Melinda didn't wait for his reaction. A second later she was gone. Drake followed her right out the door.

Sam must have had the best view of it all: Melinda leaving him out there alone on the street—and then, the beginning—Drake's eyes moving back toward the bar to look at Ellie, and really taking her in this time without distraction. Her face was set right above the window logo he loved, one hand holding her chin and the other jotting something inside a notebook. She was effervescent. Each of her features was a magnet drawing him closer. He'd lied to Melinda, or maybe he hadn't looked hard enough earlier.

The girl at the bar was mesmerizing.

Drake opened the door and moved back through the space with new purpose, settled onto the stool next to Ellie, and said he was sorry to interrupt. Then, everything played out how they both remembered, but this time they saw details they'd missed.

Sam's face was overtaken by the sting of rejection when Ellie and Drake left together.

Ellie called Sam about an hour after Drake dropped her off

to apologize. Did he want to come over that night—no strings attached—and just have fun? Sam showed up at her door with the smell of lemon zest on his hands and spirits on his clothes. Almost immediately, those clothes came off.

Drake called Melinda on the cold walk home and told her he was sorry he wasn't clear about his intentions for the night. He stopped and waited for the streetlight to fully change and admitted it was true that he still loved her. He was pretty sure he was always going to love her. But he was going to try—to do his very best—to start something new. He promised her that. Someday, maybe, they could hang out as friends. "And hey, thanks for pointing out that girl, by the way," he said.

Then, the movie cut.

Ellie and Drake stayed in the audience for a moment. Both were expecting *The End*, but it never came. The lights went up. Wordlessly, they waited for the other person to move.

Ellie was the first to stand, and Drake followed behind her. They walked through the lobby under thousands of crystals on the great chandelier and passed the ticket boy forever preparing popcorn. Natalie waved goodbye from behind the snack counter, like she was on a parade float.

In silence, they descended the alley. Each step felt heavy. When they tried to talk, the words went missing. Drake turned to Ellie in front of Mae's Famous Scoops and held her in place by the shoulders.

"Stay here a second," he said, racing back to the top of the alley alone and leaving her to wonder what he was doing.

Drake wasn't sure if he'd even be able to enter the lobby without a ticket. Luckily, the doors swung right open, but the ticket boy was there to stop him when he stepped inside. "You can't go in the auditorium," he said. "You don't have any tickets left."

"I know." Drake nodded. "I'm not here to watch a movie."

He rested his weight on his knees, out of breath. He'd been running more than usual lately. "I'm looking for the lost and found."

"You lost something?" Natalie asked. She'd surfaced in the middle of the lobby, as if from thin air.

"Uh, yeah." Drake turned to face her, a little disoriented. "I mean, no."

"So, you do or don't need the lost and found?"

"I do need it. Uh-huh."

As soon as he asked for it, the glass counter appeared again at the front of the lobby. Natalie guided him over to it. The previously blank wall now held posters for movies that weren't memories. The two of them had been replaced by sequels to popular hits.

Drake had been so preoccupied with *their* movies that he'd never asked about one of Natalie's quirks he'd noticed. "What's with you and sequels, anyway?" he asked. "*Grease 2? Jaws 2? Miss Congeniality, Armed and Fabulous?*"

Natalie flashed a smile meant to signal he finally asked the right question. She leaned over the glass display counter that showcased their lost items—from the green plastic dinosaur key chain to the blindfold from his proposal on the bottom shelf. On their previous stops to the lost and found, Drake had done everything in his power to keep Ellie from reading the plaque on *Drake's Failed Proposal*. "Let me tell you something," she said in a hushed voice. "I'm a sucker for sequels."

"Why?"

"Because, Drake," Natalie confided, "I love second chances."

Drake nodded. He wasn't sure if she was being flip or trying to impart words of wisdom. But Drake didn't have time to parse her meaning; he'd come for the preserved red rose on the top shelf: a relic from *Drake's Valentine's Day Fiasco*.

"I'll take the rose," Drake said, tapping against the glass. "The rose, please."

Natalie ducked down and emerged with the ancient red flower. "Nice choice." She set it on the glass counter between them.

"Thanks," he told her, resting it in the palm of his hand.

"I hope you liked the movies," she said, locking the case with a small silver key. "Whether you did or you didn't, don't come back."

Drake nodded. "I won't need to." As his spare hand moved to open the cinema's doors, he paused. "By the way," he said, addressing both Natalie and the ticket boy, "the popcorn here is terrible." The ticket boy poured butter sauce on his newest batch. "No offense, man."

Natalie winked, and then Drake slipped out the door.

Running downhill was easier. The sound of his footsteps on the alley's cobblestones made Ellie look his way. He remembered the first time she'd turned to him in the bar. It was like all the parts of his life had been moving and changing shape, and that exact moment had somehow snapped them into place. Once Drake reached her again, he steadied himself and tried to channel confidence. "Turns out, my mom was right," he said.

"What do you mean?" Ellie asked.

Drake put both hands on her shoulders, still holding the rose in the right one. "A long time ago, she told me I was going to find that person who wanted to be my Valentine—and when I did, not to let her go. But look, I think I took the not-letting-go part too far." He paused to gather his thoughts. "I tried to hide everything about myself that you might not like because I was afraid of losing you. But now, you've seen all my baggage. You know I'm not perfect. I hope you still love me, knowing everything. Because despite buying a lot of these roses, you are the only valentine I want."

Drake held the rose out to her.

As Ellie took it, she noticed a feeling similar to what she'd experienced on that first night together. There was a charge running through her that made her feet lighter on the ground. Here it was again—the intoxicating rush of a new beginning.

The sky rumbled above them. A storm was coming. Tonight, Drake hadn't brought an umbrella. Within seconds, a rare winter rain crashed over their heads.

Ellie slid the rose under her leather jacket to keep it safe. Drake's strong hands found her back, more confident than usual. He was going to pull her to safety, she figured, but then, he took her by surprise. Drake had *dipped* her. He wiped the rain out of her eyes with his thumbs and moved in for a kiss. It was a kiss that would've warranted applause if there were an audience.

Ellie was still hurting from everything she saw, and she also felt guilty herself, but it would be okay. They could still save this.

Drake straightened himself out and reached his hand toward Ellie. She grabbed it.

"I'm sorry I called Sam that night," she told him. "I only did it because I wanted to be with you. I thought if I invited you in, I'd mess everything up. I didn't want for us to become a one-night thing. And I'm really good at self-sabotage, as you've probably noticed."

"I'm sorry, too," Drake said. "I liked you a lot. So much, Ellie. But we'd just met. I wondered if it was too good to be true. I also felt like if I mentioned why I was there that night, it would have changed the way you saw everything."

"Yeah," Ellie said. "I definitely didn't love all that. It was excruciating to watch. But now, I understand that . . . Melinda isn't actually in our way. I mean, if you think about it, she set us up."

"I wouldn't give her that much credit. I guess I should be thanking Sam, too. If he hadn't told you to come to Finn's that night—"

"You and I never would've met."

"Geez, Sam," Drake said. "He's been so nice to me. That guy should hate my guts."

"Hardly," Ellie told him. "The story of how we met saved the bar he loves. I think that's a part of why he invited me there that night."

Ellie turned to look back at the theater. She wanted to remember the way it had come to them by magic. Even though she couldn't technically write about it, she could save every detail in her mind's eye. She hoped to memorialize it in some way. Despite everything, it had brought them closer together.

"Okay," Drake said. "So, now that we've finished watching our lives, what do we possibly do with our night?"

Ellie yawned. "You know, I'm pretty tired."

"You want to go home?"

"I do, yeah," she said.

"Okay," he agreed. "Home is good. Home it is."

So they drove home and flung open the door to the place where they lived together—a house where their life would happen. It was a house where they would fall deeper in love and have kids. They would watch as those kids grew bigger, learned to drive, and moved out. Even as life started to move faster, they would return to this place to reminisce about that past and the things they were looking forward to together.

But for now, as the sun rose, they set the future aside and lived in their firsts a little longer—their first date, their first kiss, and the first time they watched a Thursday-night monster movie at Drake's apartment.

"I love you, Ellie," Drake said, admiring the view outside and inside.

"I love you, Drake," she told him. And then they both fell asleep on the couch, Nancy at their feet, a life together on the horizon.

When summer came, Ellie and Drake were the stars of a film again, but this time, it was different. They chose this spotlight. Curled under the quilt Ellie's grandma made, with Nancy at their side and a delicious bowl of stovetop popcorn balanced between their knees, they pressed Play and watched.

The boutique hotel had almost closed before Ellie found it, not long after their last night at the cinema. "It looks like a cake," she'd said when she spotted the taffy-pink facade. "A cake you'd never want to eat." Flower beds lined the windows, scaling up to a glowing sign that painted the hotel's name in the sky: The Bernadette.

It had been named, Ellie heard on her first visit, after a rival hotelier who became the owner's sweetheart. Guests filtered through The Bernadette's revolving door into the rose-colored world. The now-defunct art deco elevator was set up as the altar. Marc adjusted his lift man costume from behind the podium, waiting to pronounce them husband and wife.

Drake's parents sat with Sandra in the front row. Naomi, oblivious to her fashion faux-pas of wearing a long white dress, scooted in next to them as guests milled about waiting for the bride and groom. Each of the guests settled into their seats with help from Jen and Lola. Eager to assign himself a task, Nolan handed out the programs. Ben was there, too, by way of the photos Jen arranged next to the guest book. "No *headshots*," Ellie had told her. Instead, Jen featured shots of the siblings in their wild Halloween costumes, one of the proms where Ben paired his tux with sneakers, and the Polaroid of Ben and Ellie at the run-down historical society house from so long ago.

Drake teared up when Ellie appeared at the start of the makeshift aisle on her dad's arm. Ellie looked ethereal in the dress she'd bought at Melinda's shop; her crystal-embellished heels that peeked out from the bottom of the dress; and a cranberry lipstick that stoked the fire of her hair, which was piled high in an updo.

During the vows, Drake confessed that there wasn't another person he'd want to discuss weird facts with over breakfast, and that he loved how she made him more brave and adventurous.

Ellie narrated a part of her story about Finn's from a leather notebook. Their guests laughed at the punchlines in their vows. Marc's chuckle was louder than the rest.

The camera did a close-up on their dramatic first married kiss inside the elevator, where thousands of introductions had once happened within its opening and closing doors. After watching other people dance at a small ballroom reception and cutting their cake, Ellie and Drake skipped down the seashell-patterned carpet of the twelfth floor and rounded the corner into their suite, the lens blurring on their wave goodbye as the door clicked shut.

The television screen turned black. Ellie and Drake each took a pause to process the film until Nancy hopped down and broke the spell.

"Now, that was my kind of movie," Drake said. He tossed the remote off to the side. "Hey, have you seen this lead actress in anything else? I hate to tell you this, but she's my hall pass."

"Yeah, the lead actor is really something, too," Ellie teased, putting her fuzzy socks up on the ottoman.

Drake gave her a playful nudge. "Want to watch it again?"

"No," Ellie said. She tossed a handful of popcorn in her mouth. "I think I've watched enough memories now."

"What do you want to do then?"

Ellie wrapped the blanket tighter around them, then reached to pet Nancy, who had curled up at her feet on the floor. "I want to just be here," she said. "To be right here, in this moment with you."

SECRET SCENE

Stephanie was obsessed with Ellie's book the moment she spotted it. She plucked a hardcover copy off the Staff Picks table at All Novel Things, toted it up a perilous spiral staircase to the cookbook section, and sank into the persimmon armchair pushed against the window. Stephanie sat there so often that the shop workers called it her chair. Reading at home came with challenges. Lucas would interrupt her, midsentence, to ask what they should watch—as if she would want to trade whatever imaginative world she was wrapped up in for a syndicated crime show.

The spine made a beautiful creak when she opened its glossy cover.

As a high school English teacher, the classics were supposed to be her go-tos, but Stephanie was looking for something different. She wanted to devour stories about rodeo clowns in love or espresso bars that stayed open late to teach their beloved customers calligraphy. Ellie's writing brought back her own past like a subtle fragrance. Her book carried notes of the time before Stephanie was a teacher, before she struggled to keep track of what was happening with denim, before she spent all her extra money on crafts she never finished.

A time before Lucas, even.

Stephanie brought the book home with her, along with an extra copy for Lucas's birthday gift. His copy remained unopened, but the pages of Stephanie's were dog-eared. Every time she read it, new discoveries and questions surfaced about her own life. How could she reconcile who she used to be with the current version of herself? Would Lucas understand who Stephanie was in the past? Would he have loved her back then?

She set those questions aside for years. The two of them fell deeper into their routines. She stopped going to the bookstore so often.

Then, everything shifted on the crisp fall night of her friend Katie's birthday happy hour. After two rounds of house red and one depressing birthday cantata, Stephanie wandered past her favorite bookstore on the way to the car. A poster in the window caught her eye. *The Compendium of Magical Places*, it teased. Ellie had written a new book, and her laminated headshot was marked with a reading date. Serendipitously, it was *that* night's date. Stephanie checked the time. The event was just beginning. All of her friends had gone home to the kids and responsibilities waiting for them. Not Stephanie. Not tonight.

"Hi," Stephanie greeted Ellie after the reading. She had waited in line for thirty minutes to get her book signed. A waterfall of red hair tumbled around Ellie's shoulders; she wore a creamy button-down shirt with a studded leather jacket thrown over it. Ellie looked the same in person as she had on the adorable holiday home renovation series. *Holiday Home, with Ellie and Drake*, it was called. Over a twinkly soundtrack, Ellie encouraged people to share heartfelt stories about their homes, while her husband, Drake, rebuilt them to better fit their daily lives. Ellie and Drake would walk each homeowner to the door, pull a bright red blindfold off their eyes together, and reveal the remodeled house draped in over-the-top Christmas lights.

For such a simple concept, the show was irresistible. Lucas had rolled his eyes during an episode when Ellie announced her pregnancy at the family condo they renovated for Drake's parents. He could be so cynical.

"Hey." Ellie motioned to Stephanie at the signing. Her bump was bigger now than on the show. "It's . . ." She pointed at Stephanie as if they'd met before and waited for her to fill in her name. Stephanie gave herself permission to think she was special, that maybe she'd earned a different introduction than the other readers.

"Stephanie."

"Stephanie," Ellie said. "I'm Ellie. Marshall. I wrote that thing you're holding." Her crimson lips parted, poised to make an observation, then hesitated. "If you like it, tell everyone you know." She leaned forward and lowered her voice to a whisper. "If not, it's great for stopping doors or murdering bugs."

"I'm sure I'll love it," Stephanie gushed. Her eagerness embarrassed her.

Ellie tapped her pen on the edge of the table. "What should I write in this thing?"

Stephanie shrugged. She hadn't considered the inscription. "Write something honest?" she asked.

Ellie weighed the request for a second. Then she nodded, beginning to jot a note down on the blank page that hugged the front cover.

"We love your home show, by the way," Stephanie mentioned to make conversation. "You and Drake are amazing together. Not that we're not—Lucas and I—but . . ." Ellie finished what she was writing, closed the book, and met her eyes with a sly smile. Had Stephanie gotten too personal? She overtalked when she was nervous. What she was trying to say was that the chemistry between Ellie and her husband was unmissable on-screen. She wanted to know how they kept that spark alive after years together. "All I meant was that you're the opposite of a boring married couple," she said. "I'm curious how you keep things feeling . . . fresh."

Ellie slid the book over across the table. "Drake and I weren't always this way, if I'm being honest," she admitted. "I mean, we were right for each other, but we still had to work on ourselves before we got married." Stephanie nodded. "First, we looked at our past. We shared where we had been and what was holding us back. And then we worked to build the life we wanted together. But to do that, we had to make space for the parts of ourselves we had been ignoring or hiding—the dark parts, the grief, the creativity. All of it."

Ellie had barely looked up to acknowledge the rest of the line forming behind Stephanie. She had the uncanny ability to make the rest of the world fall away. Still, Stephanie realized she'd stood there long enough and took the book back in her arms. "Thank you," she said. "For this, the advice, everything. And congrats on the baby, by the way."

"Oh, thanks," Ellie said. "We're excited. I miss wine. Just don't ask me about ginger chews." Stephanie wasn't sure what that meant, but she nodded and started to walk off. The next person in line stepped up. Still, moments later, Ellie called her back over. "Stephanie," she said. Stephanie turned around. "Feel free to skip around my book. In fact, I think you should start with the piece about Mae's Famous Scoops."

A few nights later, Stephanie and Lucas ran out of ice cream. Lucas offered to head to the store, but Stephanie had a better idea. "Let's go out and get some," she suggested. "I learned about this place the other night. It's in the city."

At Mae's Famous Scoops, they ordered sundaes. Lucas led them to a pink booth with its own jukebox. The table shook a little when Stephanie threw her purse down.

"What do you have in there, exactly?" Lucas pointed to her bag.

Stephanie grabbed the book and set it between them. "Do you remember Ellie?" she asked. "Ellie Marshall, I mean."

Lucas took a sloppy bite of his sundae. Vanilla drizzled down his chin. "Ellie?" he asked, reaching for a napkin.

"The author. The author of that book I got you for your birthday a couple years back? And the host of that holiday show we watched? She wrote another book." Stephanie navigated the pages. "I actually found this ice cream place right . . . here." As they ate, she tapped the spread on Mae's Famous Scoops and recounted the book signing. Lucas's face soured when Stephanie described asking Ellie to write her a note inside the front cover. "'Please don't forget me,'" Stephanie read from Ellie's messy scrawl. "'Love, Ellie.'"

Lucas grabbed the book from her and slid it his way to read the inscription for himself.

"What is it?" Stephanie asked.

"Nothing." He was clearly bothered by something. "Brain freeze," he lied and pushed the glass dish away. "Look, it's really late." Lucas nodded toward a girl in a red-striped uniform with Shirley Temple ringlets. She was hanging a CLOSED sign up in the window. "I think that's our signal—"

"I want to keep walking," Stephanie insisted as they slid out of the booth. This decisiveness wasn't like her. She was the easygoing one in the relationship. Something about the book, though, was guiding her back to the past, back toward the more adventurous parts of herself.

She wanted to revisit the girl who once drank a handsome Irishman under the table, who donned black head to toe and performed at college poetry slams, who briefly dated an athlete now too famous to be believed. Ellie had been right about the alley. For some reason, being here made the past feel right within her reach.

"I never would've known it on first glance," Ellie wrote in her piece about Mae's, "but something about walking the silent alley that night illuminated parts of myself that slipped away—parts of myself I needed to see. Some might call it magic."

Those words were convincing enough for Stephanie. So, she closed the mint-green book, tucked it back inside her bag, and continued the walk, with Lucas dragging his feet behind her.

"Nothing's going to be open this late, you know," he called out.

Still, Stephanie pressed forward. They strode over the quaint cobblestones, beyond all the empty storefronts Ellie had mentioned, and paused in front of something she hadn't. To Stephanie's delight, Lucas was wrong. Something *was* open. Warm lights glittered at the top of the midnight-black alley, an invitation to keep going.

"What is that?" Lucas asked. He stopped walking.

"I'm not sure," Stephanie said, squinting ahead. "It looks like some kind of theater?" She took a few steps toward the glow, then extended her hand out behind her for Lucas to accept. A few moments later, he did. "Let's find out."

FIN

ACKNOWLEDGMENTS

This is a book about memories, so if you'll indulge me, I'd like to share a few people I'll never forget.

Amy Tannenbaum is not only the best agent, but the best agent for me. She resonates with the same philosophical questions, is brilliant at navigating this industry, and fills in story gaps that I can't yet see myself. I look forward to the moments I get to chat with her on the phone. Amy, thank you for finding me on the slush pile and becoming the biggest champion of this book.

Speaking of Amy, Jane Rotrosen Agency is a bibliophile's dream: think, walls lined with bestsellers housed inside a Manhattan brownstone you'd never want to leave. Thank you to Allison Hufford and Celine Yarde for making subsidiary rights a breeze, to Logan Harper and Casey Conniff for offering valuable insights on multiple drafts of this book, and to all the others at JRA who have supported me.

I adore the authors Atria Books publishes and am grateful to be one of them. Every pass with my editor, Laura Brown, brought the characters to life and cracked open the themes I hoped to express. Laura, thank you for sharing my vintage sensibilities, always having the perfect reference point, and welcoming me so warmly to the Atria team. Natalie Argentina, Laura's assistant, streamlined every step of this process, kept things on track, and answered the million-and-five questions I sent her way.

Gena Lanzi, I feel like I've been nodding my head since I first met you. I love your passion for books and your vision of where to take this one. Thank you for your enthusiasm and understanding of how to get *The Second Chance Cinema* into the right hands.

Libby McGuire, Dayna Johnson, Dana Trocker, Morgan Pager—I so appreciate you being early champions for the book! Shelly Perron, your copyediting and attention to detail are just amazing.

To Kate Byrne, my editor at HQ—thank you for giving my book a wonderful home across the pond. I'm incredibly grateful for your support.

Berni Vann, my film and television agent at CAA, has been a powerful and passionate advocate for this book. She has already put me in rooms with people I never thought I'd meet and set up conversations I never thought I'd have. Berni, you're the best. Thank you to Jamie Stockton at CAA, who has looked over potential deals with a careful eye, and Emily Calomino, who has scheduled so many video calls without batting an eye.

Jana Casale, your inspiring Zoom workshop and feedback on the earliest pages of this book helped me shape the story and build momentum. I'm very grateful.

To the creative folks I've been blessed to call my friends in Denver, Los Angeles, Chicago, and beyond—I'm blown away by your support. Valentina Valentini, thank you for brainstorming this story with me for weeks on end at the beach in Santa Monica and winding through Laurel Canyon. Dena Stewart, I'm not sure I would've written this if we hadn't done The Artist's Way together. To my oldest friend, Samantha Meeker, thank you for inspiring many of the cultural references in this book and its sense of mischief (apologies to the World's Biggest Applebee's in Times Square for the cutlery we stole in 2006).

My family has offered cheerleading, babysitting, and love at every step of my writing and editing process. Thank you to each of you, especially my father, J.R., who fostered so much of my creativity and curiosity about the world. He can charm any stranger, light up any room.

Okay, I can hear them playing the music that tells me to get off the stage.

Thank you to my husband, Chris, for being my first reader, for your brainstorming prowess, and for encouraging me at every step of this adventure. I'm grateful you hovered over my shoulder (in hopes of nudging my procrastination) while I sent that query letter to Amy. Maeve, being your mom has made me braver, sillier, and kinder. Like Ellie, I can be nostalgic—but you make me excited to look ahead at the beautiful discoveries that will be on your path. Mae's Famous Scoops is just for you.

Finally, to the reader who picked this story up and spent time in a magical world with me, thank you for coming along on this ride. I hope this book lives on a cozy little place on your shelf, and I wish you all the good memories in the world.

ABOUT THE AUTHOR

THEA WEISS is a copywriter and screenwriter who previously contributed to the *Twilight* franchise. She lives in Denver with her husband, daughter, and dachshund—and loves going to the movies when she's not writing. *The Second Chance Cinema* is her first novel. Find out more at writtenbythea.com or follow her on Instagram @writtenbythea.

ATRIA BOOKS, an imprint of Simon & Schuster, fosters an open environment where ideas flourish, bestselling authors soar to new heights, and tomorrow's finest voices are discovered and nurtured. Since its launch in 2002, Atria has published hundreds of bestsellers and extraordinary books, which would not have been possible without the invaluable support and expertise of its team and publishing partners. Thank you to the Atria Books colleagues who collaborated on *The Second Chance Cinema*, as well as to the hundreds of professionals in the Simon & Schuster advertising, audio, communications, design, ebook, finance, human resources, legal, marketing, operations, production, sales, supply chain, subsidiary rights, and warehouse departments who help Atria bring great books to light.

EDITORIAL
Laura Brown
Natalie Argentina

JACKET DESIGN
Amanda Hudson
James Iacobelli

MARKETING
Dayna Johnson

MANAGING EDITORIAL
Paige Lytle
Shelby Pumphrey
Lacee Burr
Sofia Echeverry

PRODUCTION
Katie Rizzo
Vanessa Silverio
Shelly Perron
Esther Paradelo
Hannah Lustyik

PUBLICITY
Gena Lanzi

PUBLISHING OFFICE
Suzanne Donahue
Abby Velasco

SUBSIDIARY RIGHTS
Nicole Bond
Sara Bowne
Rebecca Justiniano